STARSHINE

AURORA RISING: BOOK ONE

CW00552175

G. S. JENNSEN

HYPERNOVA
PUBLISHING
2014

STARSHINE

Copyright © 2014 by G. S. Jennsen.

Cover design by Josef Bartoň
Cover typography by G. S. Jennsen

Hypernova Publishing
P.O. Box 2214
Parker, Colorado 80134
www.hypernovapublishing.com

Publisher's Note: This is a work of fiction. Names, characters, places, and incidents are a product of the author's imagination. Locales and public names are sometimes used for atmospheric purposes. Any resemblance to actual people, living or dead, or to businesses, companies, events, institutions, or locales is completely coincidental.

The Hypernova Publishing name, colophon and logo are trademarks of Hypernova Publishing.

Ordering Information:
Hypernova Publishing books may be purchased for educational, business or sales promotional use. For details, contact the "Special Markets Department" at the address above.

Starshine / G. S. Jennsen.—2nd ed.

LCCN 2014935734
ISBN 978-0-9960141-0-6

For Andy
without whom this would have forever remained
only a whisper in my dreams

ACKNOWLEDGEMENTS

I am very thankful for the support and encouragement of a great many people: Linda, Sunny, Claire, Jeff, Cheryl, Jim, Bill, Antonela, Ezri, Sarah, Lakatos, Rita, Brialyn and Monica, to name but a few.

A special thanks for editorial assistance, ideas, opinions and critiques to Sandy, Jules, Anne, Carole and Aleksander.

Above all, thank you to my husband (best friend, business partner, co-conspirator, soulmate), for all of the above and so much more.

AURORA RHAPSODY

is

AURORA RISING
STARSHINE
VERTIGO
TRANSCENDENCE

AURORA RENEGADES
SIDESPACE
DISSONANCE
ABYSM

AURORA RESONANT
RELATIVITY
RUBICON (2017)
REQUIEM (2017/18)

SHORT STORIES
RESTLESS, VOL. I • *RESTLESS, VOL. II*
APOGEE • *SOLATIUM* • *VENATORIS*
RE/GENESIS

Learn more and see a Timeline of the Aurora Rhapsody *universe at:*
gsjennsen.com/aurora-rhapsody

COLONIZED MILKY WAY

COLONIZED WORLDS

•••••• SENECAN FEDERATION TERRITORY
○ INDEPENDENT WORLDS

WORLDS VISITED IN
STARSHINE:

EARTH ALLIANCE	SENECAN FEDERATION	INDEPENDENTS
EARTH	SENECA	ATLANTIS
ARCADIA	KRYSK	COSENTI
DESNA	PALLUDA	GAIAE
DEUCALI		NEW BABEL
ERISEN	--------------	PANDORA
ORELLAN	METIS NEBULA	ROMANE
SCYTHIA		

MILKY WAY GALAXY

(View Online at http://www.gsjennsen.com/map)

DRAMATIS PERSONAE

MAIN CHARACTERS

Alexis 'Alex' Solovy
Starship pilot, scout and space explorer; daughter of Miriam and David Solovy.
Faction: *Earth Alliance*

Caleb Marano
Special Operations intelligence agent, Senecan Federation Division of Intelligence.
Faction: *Senecan Federation*

Miriam Solovy (Admiral)
EASC Operations Director;
mother of Alex Solovy,
widow of David Solovy.
Faction: *Earth Alliance*

Michael Volosk
Special Operations Director,
Senecan Federation Division of
Intelligence.
Faction: *Senecan Federation*

Richard Navick (Colonel)
EASC Naval Intelligence Liaison;
family friend of the Solovys.
Faction: *Earth Alliance*

Graham Delavasi
Director, Senecan Federation
Division of Intelligence.
Faction: *Senecan Federation*

Kennedy Rossi
Director of Design/Prototyping,
IS Design; friend of Alex Solovy.
Faction: *Earth Alliance*

Jaron Nythal
Assistant Director, Senecan
Federation Division of Trade.
Faction: *Senecan Federation*

Liam O'Connell (General)
Earth Alliance Southwestern
Regional Military Commander.
Faction: *Earth Alliance*

Noah Terrage
Tech dealer and smuggler on
Pandora; associate of Caleb Marano.
Faction: *Independent*

Marcus Aguirre
Earth Alliance Attorney General.
Faction: *Earth Alliance*

Mia Requelme
Entrepreneur/businesswoman on
Romane.
Faction: *Independent*

Olivia Montegreu
Head of Zelones criminal cartel.
Faction: *Independent*

(View Online at http://www.gsjennsen.com/characters-starshine)

OTHER CHARACTERS
(ALPHABETICAL ORDER)

Aaron LaRose
Director, EA Astronomical and
Space Science Dept.
Faction: *Earth Alliance*

Aristide Vranas
Chairman, SF Government.
Faction: *Senecan Federation*

Charles 'Charlie' Blalock
Ship mechanic for Alex Solovy.
Faction: *Earth Alliance*

Charles Gagnon
Majority Leader, EA Assembly.
Faction: *Earth Alliance*

Christopher 'Chris' Candela
Attaché, SF Trade Division.
Faction: *Senecan Federation*

Christopher Rychen (Admiral)
EA NE Regional Military Cmmdr.
Faction: *Earth Alliance*

Claire Zabroi
Hacker; friend of Alex Solovy and
Kennedy Rossi.
Faction: *Earth Alliance*

David Solovy (Commander)
Father of Alex Solovy;
spouse of Miriam Solovy;
Captain, *EAS Stalwart.* Deceased.
Faction: *Earth Alliance*

Donel Fergusson (Major)
Special Forces platoon leader;
Captain, *SFS Aegea.*
Faction: *Senecan Federation*

Eleni Gianno (Field Marshal)
Head of SF Military Council and SF
Armed Forces.
Faction: *Senecan Federation*

Ella Delaur
Resident of Pandora; friend of
Noah Terrage.
Faction: *Independent*

Ethan Tollis
Musician; occasional lover of
Alex Solovy.
Faction: *Earth Alliance*

Gabriel 'Gabe' Daniels
CEO of solar power satellite firm;
friend of Kennedy Rossi.
Faction: *Earth Alliance*

Hideyo Mori
EA Defense Minister.
Faction: *Earth Alliance*

Ilario Ferre
Head of Ferre criminal cartel.
Faction: *Senecan Federation*

Isabela Marano
Biochemistry professor;
sister of Caleb Marano.
Faction: *Senecan Federation*

Jules Hervé (Brigadier)
Director, EASC Special Projects.
Faction: *Earth Alliance*

Kian Lange (Major)
Director, EASC Security Bureau.
Faction: *Earth Alliance*

Laure Ferre
Lieutenant, Ferre criminal cartel;
Ilario's cousin.
Faction: *Senecan Federation*

Luis Barrera
Speaker, EA Assembly.
Faction: *Earth Alliance*

Malcolm Jenner (Lt. Colonel)
Captain, *EAS Juno*;
former lover of Alex Solovy.
Faction: *Earth Alliance*

Mangele Santiagar
EA Minister of Trade.
Faction: *Earth Alliance*

Marlee Marano
Isabela's daughter; Caleb's niece.
Faction: *Senecan Federation*

Matei Uttara
Independent agent.
Faction: *Independent*

Meno
Artificial owned by Mia Requelme.
Faction: *Independent*

Morgan Lekkas (Commander)
3rd Squadron, 3rd Wing,
SF Southern Fleet.
Faction: *Senecan Federation*

Omero Kouris
Director, SF Trade Division.
Faction: *Senecan Federation*

Patrick Foster (General)
EA NW Regional Military Cmmdr.
Faction: *Earth Alliance*

Peter Karolyn
EA Minister of Extra-Solar
Development.
Faction: *Earth Alliance*

Price Alamatto (General)
EASC Board Chairman.
Faction: *Earth Alliance*

Samuel Padova
Special Ops, SF Intelligence;
mentor of Caleb Marano.
Deceased.
Faction: *Senecan Federation*

Seraphina LaCasse
Resident of Gaiae.
Faction: *Independent*

Steven Brennon
EA Prime Minister.
Faction: *Earth Alliance*

Thad Yue
Mercenary in employ of Olivia
Montegreu.
Faction: *Independent*

Thomas Harnal
Resident of Palluda.
Faction: *Senecan Federation*

Tony Gesson
Enforcer for Zelones cartel.
Faction: *Independent*

William 'Will' Sutton
CEO, W. C. Sutton Construction;
spouse of Richard Navick.
Faction: *Earth Alliance*

CONTENTS

STARSHINE

PROLOGUE

T he end of the world began with a library query.

    ...or perhaps it was the space probe. The alien was being vexingly reticent on the matter, the man thought as he straightened his dinner jacket in the mirror.

"She is hardly the first person to express an interest in that region of space. Why are you so worried about her when the others didn't concern you?"

The others did concern us, but they were deflected with little difficulty. This woman, however, has exhibited a notable talent for discovering what others cannot. As such, we would prefer she never look.

The man smoothed out a crease in one of the sleeves then fastened the antique pearl cufflinks, an heirloom passed down to him from a grandfather that never was. "Do you want me to have her killed?"

Not unless alternative methods are unsuccessful. Her death could cause the opposite effect of drawing further unwanted attention.

The man nodded cursorily and stepped out of the washroom, crossing his spacious office to the windows lining the far wall. "Very well. I'll work to ensure she's distracted from this pursuit. What about the Senecans?"

They are a more troublesome problem as they have already discovered an anomaly exists. They will send others to investigate.

From the top floor of the Earth Alliance Headquarters building the man could see guests beginning to arrive in the gardens below. Another ten minutes and it would be appropriate for him to join them. He frowned, brushing a piece of lint off his lapel before he turned from the windows to face where the alien might have stood, were he actually here. "You know there's little I can do about them for the moment."

You needn't concern yourself with the matter. Other resources are at our disposal.

"I'm sure. And remember, you only need stall them for a short while. Soon *everyone* will be distracted, and humanity will be focused inward for quite some time."

Go forward with your plan. We hope you accomplish your objectives. Nonetheless, events are converging rapidly and they are not all within your control. Escalation may be unavoidable.

The man pulsed his wife to let her know he would meet her in the lobby shortly. "At least give me the opportunity to alter our course before you act. It won't be long now."

Certainly. Know, however, that the precipice is upon you; it may already have been crossed.

Preparations have begun.

PART I:

DOMINOES

*"There are two kinds of light –
the glow that illuminates, and the glare that obscures."*

— James Thurber

1

" **A** lex, I'm ready when you are."
"One more second...okay, Charlie, go ahead." The muffled response came from within the hull.

The young mechanic wove the crystalline fiber of a conduit into the power control grid. It took only seconds. He squinted into the magnification overlay to confirm the contact points. "All set."

"Here goes nothing."

Colonel Richard Navick watched from the entry of the hangar bay as a shimmer passed over the smooth, midnight black exterior of the ship.

Even marred by the docking clamps, the *Siyane* was sleek and graceful, with sweeping curves that converged on acute edges. Technical instruments and sensors were tucked discreetly under the wing-like midsection while the sLume drive was an elusive shadow beneath the tapered tail. The elegant lines disguised its size. Fully forty-two meters from bow to stern, it was enormous—at least for a personal scout ship.

He cleared his throat to announce his presence and stepped into the bay. "Alex, are you in there somewhere?"

A head dropped out of the belly of the ship. It was upside down and encircled by the orbiting screens of a holographic interface. "Richard, is that you?"

"Guilty as charged."

A pair of long legs appeared next as she swung out of the exposed engineering well and dropped a meter to land nimbly on the floor of the bay. The interface winked out of existence.

He was struck—as he always was after he hadn't seen her for some time—by how much she looked like her father. Tall and slender, with high, distinctive cheekbones and bright silver-gray eyes, she cut almost as dramatic a figure as David Solovy once had. In fact, the sole feature of note she had inherited from her mother was the thick, dark mane of hair. Whereas David's had been dusky blond, hers was the color of fine aged Bordeaux.

It was also currently twisted up in a messy knot, flyaway strands escaping to soften her features. She wiped streaks of a viscous gel off her hands and onto snug black workpants as she jogged over.

When she reached him she embraced him in a quick hug born of years of familiarity. "It's been too long, Richard."

"If you would stay in this sector for longer than a week at a time, I might actually get to see you once in a while."

Her eyes rolled a little as she settled onto her back leg. "Ah, no can do, I'm afraid. All the fun's out there." A corner of her mouth quirked up in a tease of a grin. He believed her.

"So I hear. All the money too, apparently." He canted his head toward the gleaming hull.

Her face instantly lit up; it often did when she was talking about her ship. "I just painted on a new f-graphene alloy lattice. It will reduce drag by another twelve percent, which will mean faster travel using less fuel."

"Nice...." The reduction from pico- to femto-scale alloys had only become commercially available nine months earlier; he shuddered to think of the credits she must have forked over for the new lattice. "We should have the budget to roll those out to the fleet in a decade or so."

She shrugged as if to say 'your loss' and met his gaze. For most people it would have been an uncomfortable experience. "So is this a social call? As glad as I am to see you—and I really am—I'm kind of in the middle of installing a stealth system upgrade. We could maybe have dinner this evening if you'd like?"

He mentally braced himself for the reaction he knew would be coming. "You caught me. It's not entirely a social call. Your mother wants you to come by the office if you have any free time this afternoon."

Her pupils constricted, the tiny flash of an ocular implant a hint she was checking her comms. They quickly focused back on him, bearing more than a little less warmth. "I don't have a message from her."

"I know. She thought the likelihood of you responding would increase considerably if I came in person."

An eyebrow arched. "She have you running her errands for her now? Isn't that a bit below your pay grade?"

"No. I *volunteered*, because I wanted to see you."

She smiled with what he recognized as kindness, but it was transitory to her glance over her shoulder at the ship that dominated the hanger. "Well, sorry, but I can't. I have to run diagnostics on the new dampener field and recalibrate the power system ratios. Assuming everything tests out okay, then I have to secure the fiber line to the hull and shield it."

His gaze flitted pointedly to the young man swinging in a harness near the stern of the ship. "Can't your mechanic do some of those things for you?"

At her deepening frown his brow creased in beseechment. "Please? For me? It'll only take an hour or two, and it..." he knew saying it would make her mother happy would be counterproductive "...will make my life rather easier."

Her eyes narrowed; her arms stiffened against her chest to complete the impression of staunch resoluteness. But this was not the first time he had faced down her defiant glare. He relaxed his posture, softened his expression and met her scowl with a pleasant smile.

After several seconds she exhaled to striking effect, all the tension leaving her body with the exaggerated breath. For just a moment she reminded him of the impish little girl she had once been.

"*Fine.* For you. I'm going to regret it, though."

 ✦

Alex stared out the window of the skycar while they cruised above Puget Sound before veering northwest over the Strait toward Vancouver Island. The unbroken line of skyscrapers to the right shone in the late morning sun from horizon to horizon, all polished silvers and whites flecked by deep green where the scrupulously maintained trees and numerous parks peeked through.

It was and had always been a beautiful view...but she was being a poor companion. She gave up steeling herself for what was sure to be the latest in a long line of unpleasant visits with her mother and shifted from the window to look at Richard.

Her parents' oldest and closest friend, she had known him for as long as she could recall, which was to say about thirty-five years. He was one of the very few people who had consistently accepted her for who and what she was—didn't want *more* from her, didn't helpfully suggest what her life *should* be like, didn't *tsk* disapprovingly at even her most unorthodox activities.

"So what's new with you? Work okay? How's Will doing?"

He relaxed in his seat and let the car auto-navigate the crowded airlanes. "Will is good, but busy. He's been on Shi Shen for the last month overseeing the construction of the new Suiren headquarters and finally got home day before yesterday. I'll tell him you said hello."

The muscles in his jaw clenched briefly, which was generally the extent of his outward signals of displeasure. "Work is rather tense, what with the Trade Summit coming up."

She gave him a blank look. "What is a Trade Summit and why is it coming up? Help me out here...."

"Right, you don't spend much time obsessing about the oh-so-fascinating machinations of galactic politics. The Trade Minister and his entourage will be attending a conference with the Senecan Trade Director—at a carefully selected neutral location naturally, on Atlantis." He sighed, his gaze drifting upward to grimace at the heavens. "It's ostensibly an olive branch intended to thaw relations with the Federation a bit, but I'm afraid in reality it's going to be little more than a media circus."

"And your people will be spying on the Senecan delegation, hacking their data streams every chance they get while fending off the same from their agents." Her teasing smirk served to emphasize the point.

His mouth worked to suppress a grin but mostly failed. "I can neither confirm nor deny any such suppositions on the grounds it would violate Earth Alliance security."

"*Of course....*" The car dropped through a thin layer of mist which hadn't yet burned off and skimmed above the choppy waves as the sprawling Earth Alliance Strategic Command complex came into view.

Stretching for three square kilometers across the southernmost tip of the Island, a network of midrise buildings, plazas and hangars fanned out from the towering structure that constituted the headquarters for what were, as a group, the most powerful men and women in the settled Milky Way. For better or worse, this included the EASC Director of Operations.

She could feel her expression tightening with every meter of their descent onto the open platform jutting out a third of the way up the headquarters building. "So how *is* the Admiral these days? As cheery as ever?"

He shook his head wryly, killed the engine and climbed out of the car. "She's the same as usual, busily supervising the entire organization while breaking in yet another new secretary."

"Lovely." She matched his stride to the glass-floored lift, not bothering to grasp the rail as it whisked them up a quarter kilometer to the command staff offices which comprised the top ten floors. After they had cleared the security scanners and were inside, she turned to him.

Though her mood was already darkening beneath the shadow of the looming encounter, she forced herself to smile with genuine warmth. "You better get on out of here before I start blaming you for ruining my day, especially when it *was* good to see you."

He laughed and patted her on the shoulder then headed toward his office down the opposite hall. "Try not to be too much of a stranger, okay?"

She waved him off as she crossed the overly bright atrium and stepped through the wide doorway into the EASC Operations suite.

The man behind the desk glanced up as she approached. After a blink his eyes widened precipitously. "You're *her*, aren't you? Ms—I mean Captain—Solovy. Ma'am."

She draped an arm on the high counter. "It's not a military title. 'Ms.' is fine. Would you please let my mother know I have answered her summons and eagerly await being granted the favor of an audience?"

The man—a 2nd Lieutenant according to the bars on his uniform—stared at her in horror, brow furrowing and unfurrowing in mounting panic. "Um, do you want me to say that, specifically, ma'am? I'm not certain the Admiral will—"

"Just tell her that her daughter is here."

"Absolutely. Right away."

She wandered over to inspect the newest addition to the artwork decorating the lobby. This secretary was unlikely to last any longer than the last one had. Even the most hardened soldier wilted in the face of her mother's disapproving glare.

She was pondering how many credits the military must have wasted on the spectacularly bad hack Picasso rip-off when the secretary informed her she could go in now. She walked in the large but spartan office to observe without surprise that nothing about it had changed in the near year since she had last visited.

Admiral Miriam Solovy didn't immediately turn her attention from the display panel in her hand. Her hair was drawn back in a severe bun; her uniform was crisp, its buttons spit-polished. When her gaze did rise to acknowledge Alex's presence, a tight, thin facsimile of a smile passed across her face for the minimum time required. "You look a wreck."

Ah, as kind and doting as always. She shrugged. "I was working."

"I see. Would you like some tea?"

"Water's fine," which she proceeded to go to the cabinet and get herself.

"How are you, dear?"

Alex took a long sip from the marbled glass tumbler and leaned in deliberate casualness beside the teak bookcase filled with antique texts on military and political history. "Fine. Busy. You?"

The tiny vein in her mother's left temple pulsed. She traded the screen for a teacup. "As well as can be expected. The Fionava Province has been a nuisance of late. I would share the details with you, but of course the parking attendant has a higher security clearance than you do."

The tenor with which the statement was delivered seemed to imply it was somehow a failing on her part. "Alas."

Miriam took a slow, measured sip of her tea then stared pensively into the dainty cup, as though it would magically supply her a suitable topic for small talk. "I ran into Malcolm at the Cascades Memorial Charity Auction last week. And met his new wife."

She needed a wiser teacup. Alex raised a studiously unimpressed eyebrow. "I'm sure she was lovely."

"Not so lovely as you, I must say, but attractive enough. He asked about you."

Her eyes flickered over to the window...*shit*. She bit back a cringe at the display of weakness, not wanting to compound the error. "And what did you tell him?"

"The truth—that you're still gallivanting around the galaxy, raking in millions and pouring it all back into that damnable ship of yours." She paused, undoubtedly for dramatic effect. "I do believe he looked a little morose at the notion."

Alex groaned and plopped down in the hard, purposefully uncomfortable chair opposite the desk. She pulled one knee up to hug against her chest. "I'm going to give you the benefit of the doubt and assume you didn't ask me here in order to throw failed love affairs in my face. It's a long list and I haven't the time. What do you want?"

Miriam placed the teacup on the hutch behind her and sat as well, rigid-straight spine not touching the back of the comparably luxurious chair. "I can't simply want to spend time with my only child?"

"You can—but you don't."

Her mother's shoulders squared with military precision, an indication she wouldn't argue the point. "Very well. I asked you here to share a wonderful opportunity for you. The Minister for Extra-Solar Development contacted me yesterday. He finds himself with a vacancy in his department. Apparently the Director of Deep Space Exploration is resigning to 'pursue other endeavors,' and the Minister would like to offer the post to you."

A flashing pinpoint of light in the corner of Alex's eVi signaled the delivery of the diagnostics she had set to run before departing the hangar. Her right pupil constricted to start the results scrolling on her whisper. "Prestigious position."

If her mother noticed the somewhat unfocused nature of her gaze, she hid it well. "It's not nepotism. While you lack oversight experience, you're otherwise more than qualified."

"More qualified than the parking attendant at least." The whisper blurred out of focus and auto-paused as she directed a sharpened gaze toward the woman on the other side of the desk. Her mother couldn't seem to decide whether to scowl or laugh; the result was an uncommonly animated expression. "But what exactly of everything you know about me says 'government desk job'?"

"It's not a desk job. You'll need to travel to evaluate new discoveries several times a year, I'm quite sure."

"Several times a *ye*—" her nose scrunched up in disdain "—you know what, never mind."

"So you'll consider it then."

The whisper snapped back into focus…she frowned at the percentages displayed. A blink and a small aural materialized, and the diagnostics data began flowing in greater precision and detail twelve centimeters beyond her right eye. "No."

Her mother's jaw clacked shut at the response. Or because of the aural. Possibly both. "I didn't say accept it unconditionally, merely consider it."

Damn, there must be a power leak somewhere along the fiber. She pulsed Charlie to send the bot in to inspect the line. The dampener had to be a minimum of twenty-eight percent more effective or it wasn't worth the diamond picocrystals which generated it. Her last find had almost been snaked out from under her because Terrence Macolly, too much of a lazy ass to do his own work, had tracked her emission signature and followed her into the asteroid ring orbiting Delta Lacertae. She didn't intend to risk a repeat intrusion. "No."

"Alexis—"

Her mouth twitched, though her focus didn't shift from the data this time. "You know I hate it when you call me that."

"I have every right to call you by your birth name. I am the one who gave it to you after all."

Alex spared a brief, withering glance. Her mother's eyes were averted downward, ostensibly studying the patterns of foam in her tea, perchance for more lousy ideas. When she spoke again, her tone was softer and no longer quite the voice of The Admiral.

"Your father was the first one to call you 'Alex.'"

She shut off the aural in frustration. "Don't you think I *know* that?"

"Yes, well." Miriam's chin notched upward. "I think you should reconsider the Minister's offer. It is a position of some prominence and will provide a measure of stability you could benefit from."

She snorted. "I realize you're used to dictating people's lives to them around here, but you *don't* get to make my decisions for me. You haven't for a long, long time."

Miriam nodded with measured grace, appearing to acknowledge for the moment, Alex had the upper hand. "Perhaps it was…inconsiderate of me to insist you come here."

"To order Richard to deliver your summons and drag me before you, you mean?"

She raised a hand in mild protest. "Richard wanted the chance to see you. I hope you don't blame him for any unpleasantness."

"Oh, I don't. I blame you."

To her credit, her mother was nearly impossible to provoke. If anything, her expression softened in response to the barb. "I'm not trying to tell you how to live your life. But I worry about you, out there all alone in deep space. That ship of yours is too powerful for one person to handle."

Yet even in her attempt at kindness or at least civility, she managed to choose the exact wrong thing to say.

Deep down, Alex knew it probably wasn't intentional. But there was too much—too many hateful words and spiteful reactions to them, too much water under a broken bridge—and she had no desire to grasp at a tenuous thread only to have it fray and dissolve like all the others.

"The past eight years would beg to differ with you. With all due respect, you have no idea just how much I can handle." She stood abruptly. "Is there anything else?"

"No. Not when you won't listen to reason."

She didn't rise to the bait. She simply wanted to be gone. "If you'd like, I will send a graciously worded response to the Minister thanking him for the honor of considering me but regretfully declining due to other obligations."

"That won't be necessary. I'll inform him."

"Suit yourself." She pivoted and headed for the door.

"Alexis?"

She paused mid-stride—an inborn response to a mother's plea—but didn't look back.

"At least be careful out there."

A tight nod and she was gone.

It was well past twenty-three hundred when Alex got home. The bot had found two micro-imperfections in the fiber which had to be rewoven. Then the diagnostics had to be run again, the ware remodded, and the power system ratios recalibrated *again* before she closed the ship up for the night. Securing the line to the hull and shielding it would have to wait until the morning.

She opened a bottle of Swiss cabernet and left it to breathe while she ran through the shower, then combed out her hair and slipped on a silk robe to wear back downstairs.

A glass of the cabernet in hand, she stepped out onto the balcony. The glittering night lights of the city spread out beneath her, the light reflecting off the full moon mirrored in the Sound beyond.

She didn't pour all her profits into her ship. The loft eighty stories above downtown had cost more than a few credits; the custom tech installed in it nearly as much again. Though she was only here maybe three months out of a given year, she wasn't above enjoying at least a few of the finer things her income now afforded her.

As the glass touched her lips her thoughts drifted to Malcolm. She hadn't done so in some time, but after the mention of him today quite a few memories had crept to the forefront of her mind. Most of them were good...she had loved him, after all.

But according to him she loved her ship more, and that was something he couldn't accept. And since he was mostly right, she hadn't fought him when he left.

She had missed him for a while, missed his warm smile and tender yet expert touch. But she had also welcomed the absence of the invisible leash which had tugged her back to Earth more often than she liked, which had whispered of duties to another and required explanations and justifications for every excursion. And eventually even the good memories had faded into the background, replaced by the thrill of new endeavors.

Her thoughts continued to linger on the past as she walked inside and her gaze fell to the far wall of the open room that constituted the entirety of the loft, save for the kitchen and the elevated sleeping area overlooking the main floor.

It was decorated in visuals she had captured in her travels across the galaxy. They included a supernova in bright, perpetual explosion, a comet on a flyby of a crescent moon, the slow pulse of a ghostly blue and lavender nebula and the gamma flare of a neutron star.

Those and others framed the centerpiece of the wall: a panoramic side-on image of the Milky Way, taken far from the light pollution of any suns or haze of any nebulae. Trillions of stars shone and sparkled to converge on the brilliance of the galactic core.

Malcolm hadn't been exactly right. Yes, she loved her ship more than she had loved him. But what she loved even more was what it gave her: freedom, and the key to the marvels of space. It gave her the stars, and she doubted she could ever love anything or anyone more than she loved the stars.

Speaking of...she refilled her glass and settled onto the couch. She sent a passcode to the control interface and the opposite wall dissolved into a three-dimensional holo of the nearest quadrant of the galaxy. A slight wave of her hand and it zoomed into the Metis Nebula and its environs.

Near to but definitively outside Federation-controlled territory and on the outer edge of explored space, it would take her five days to reach the periphery—far less time than most, but still a trek. It was an allegedly uninteresting, ordinary plerion wrapped in an ancient, gas-heavy supernova remnant which had stubbornly refused to dissipate into the interstellar medium.

But she had made a small fortune by seeing what others did not. The 'experts' had said the Lacertae asteroid ring was nothing but dead rocks until she had found the ultra-rare heavy metals in the cores of the largest ones. Now Astral Materials was using it to develop frames for space stations they claimed would be strong enough to withstand a Type Ia supernova shockwave.

The golden-blue glow of Metis had caught her attention several excursions ago and had danced and thrummed at the edge of her consciousness ever since. Now flush with the considerable proceeds of the Lacertae find and the resultant ship upgrades, she figured she could afford to indulge a hunch for a month or so.

Her eyes widened deliberately, pupils dilated and ocular implant flashing as she simultaneously reviewed the data she had pulled in her library query of the scientific archives—which was appallingly sparse—scrolling up her eVi, the rotating full-spectrum image of the Nebula, and her own data flowing alongside it.

"Well, you lovely, mysterious Metis...what secrets do you have to show me?"

2

*T*he kinetic blade slid into the man's throat like a knife through butter. Caleb held him securely from behind as the blood began to flow and the man jerked and spasmed.

He generally preferred clean, painless deaths. But he wanted to watch this man die, and die slowly.

When the man had lost all motor function, Caleb dumped him onto the desk and flipped him over. Eyes wide with fear, confusion and outrage met his. The man's lips contorted in a caricature of speech, though no words came out.

He had a good idea of the intended utterance. Why. It was a question easily answered. Vengeance.

"Justice."

As the pool of blood spread across the desk and formed waterfalls to the floor below, the eyes belonging to the leader of the Humans Against Artificials terrorist organization glazed over. The last spark of life within them dimmed, then went out.

One down.

⋏

Caleb Marano stepped out of the spaceport into the cyan-tinged glow of a late afternoon sun reflecting off the polished marble tiles of the plaza. The chill breeze caressing his skin felt like a welcome home. Cavare was always cool and often cold; Krysk had been a veritable oven by comparison.

He descended the first set of stairs and angled toward the corner to get clear of the bustling thoroughfare, then relaxed beside the ledge to wait for his companions.

Isabela exited the spaceport a moment later. She held a bag in one arm and a fidgeting bundle of arms, legs and long, dark curls in the other. She looked disturbingly 'momish' as she struggled to brush out Marlee's tangled hair—but he could remember when she had *been* that little girl with long, dark curls...and it wasn't so long ago.

With a groan she gave up the futile endeavor and allowed her daughter to escape her grasp and make a beeline for Caleb.

He crouched to meet Marlee at eye level. She plowed into him with almost enough force to knock him over backwards. He would've laughed but for the forlorn look in her pale turquoise eyes.

"Do you have to go away now, Uncle Caleb?"

He tousled her curls into further disarray. "Yeah, I'm afraid I have to go back to work. But it sure was great spending my vacation with you. I learned a *lot.*"

She wore her best serious face as she nodded sagely. "You had a lot to learn."

He grinned and leaned in to whisper to his co-conspirator. "You remember what all we talked about, right?"

Her eyes were wide and honest. "Uh-huh."

"Good. Want one more ride before I go?"

Her head bobbed up and down with gusto, instantly that of a carefree child again.

"Okay." He scooped her up in his arms and stood, made certain he had a solid grasp of her tiny waist, and began to spin around with accelerating speed. Her arms and legs dangled free to swing through the air while she cackled in delight.

After another few spins he slowed—he had learned her limits during the last few weeks—letting her limbs fall against him before he came to a stop. He gave her a final squeeze and gently set her to the ground as her mother reached them.

Isabela wore a half-amused, half-exhausted expression as Marlee started running in dizzy circles around her legs. "Sorry about the hold up. They let us back on the transport and we found Mr. Freckles under the seat." She patted her bag in confirmation of the stuffed animal's now secure location. "Are you sure you don't want to have a quick dinner with us?"

He responded with a dubious smirk. "You can be polite if you like, but the truth is you are sick to death of me and counting the minutes until you are at last rid of me."

"Well, *yes.* But I never know when I'll get to see you again...." The twinkle faded from her eyes, replaced by something darker and heavier.

She knew he didn't work for a shuttle manufacturing company, and he knew that she knew. But they never, *ever*, talked about it. Partly for her safety and his, but partly because he preferred to continue being in her mind the strong, stalwart older brother with the easygoing demeanor and wicked sense of humor, without introducing any moral grayness to the relationship dynamic.

Because he never wanted her to look at him with caution, disillusionment…or worst of all, fear.

He merely nodded in response. "I'll come visit again soon. Promise."

She reached down to pause the cyclone at her legs. "I'll hold you to it. I'm going to take Marlee to see Mom, then we'll head back home."

He leaned over the struggling cyclone to embrace her. "Thank you for the extended hospitality. I'm glad I was able to spend so much time with you."

"Anytime, I mean it," she whispered in his ear. "Stay safe."

He kept his shrug mild as he stepped away. "Of course." Not likely.

Two insistent and tearful hugs from Marlee later, they parted ways. He watched them disappear into the throng of travelers, then headed in the direction of the parking complex.

ℛ

Caleb stepped in the adjoining lavatory and washed the blood off his hands and forearms. Then he returned to the office, reached under the corner of the desk and triggered the 'Alert' panic signal—the one he had never allowed the dead man to reach. There was a surveillance cam hidden in the ceiling, and he looked up at it and smiled. He had a number of smiles in his repertoire; this was not one of the more pleasant ones.

The commotion began as he exited the building. He quickened his stride to his bike, jumped on and fired the engine. Three men bolted out the door, two Daemons and a TSG swinging in his direction.

It wouldn't do to get shot. A flick of his thumb and the bike burst out of the parking slot. He laid it down as laser fire sliced barely a meter overhead, his leg hovering centimeters above the ground while he slid around the corner and onto the cross-street.

He heard them giving chase almost immediately. So late in the night the street and air traffic was sparse, which was one reason he had begun the op when he did. It reduced the chances of his pursuers taking out innocent bystanders—and gave them a clearer line of sight to him. He wanted to make certain they knew where he was going before he left them behind.

Their surface vehicles didn't stand a chance of matching his speed and it would look suspicious if he slowed...but as anticipated, they had grabbed a skycar. He kept an eye on it via the rearcam, making sure it succeeded in following him through two major direction shifts.

Satisfied, he kicked the bike into its actual highest gear and accelerated right then left, fishtailing around two street corners in rapid succession. He activated the concealment shield. It didn't render him or the bike invisible, but it did make them blend into the surroundings and virtually impossible to track from the air at night.

Then he sped toward the Bahia Mar spaceport. After all, he did need to get there ahead of them.

Tiny flecks of light sparkled in the night-darkened waters of the Fuori River as Caleb pulled in the small surface lot. It was nearly empty, as most people took the levtrams to the entertainment district and had no need of parking.

Once the engine had purred into silence he swung a leg off the bike and glanced up. A smile ghosted across his face at the dozens of meteors streaking against the silhouette of the giant moon which dominated Seneca's sky.

He noted the time. He had a few minutes to enjoy a little stargazing, though the conditions were far from ideal here in the heart of downtown. An exanet query confirmed the meteor shower continued for eleven days. Maybe he'd have a chance to get up to the mountains before it ended.

Committed to this plan, he secured the bike in its slot. A last glance at the sky and he crossed the street and took the wide steps to the riverwalk park.

The atmosphere on the broad promenade hovered at the optimal balance between deserted and overrun by masses of people. As it was a weekend night the balance wouldn't hold for long, but for the moment it pulsed with energy while still allowing plenty of room to move about and claim your own personal space. He noted with interest the outdoor bar to the right, complete with live synth band and raised danced platform. *Not yet. Business first.*

He slipped among the milling patrons until he reached a section of railing at the edge of the promenade to the southeast of the bar. Here the crowd had thinned to a few meandering couples and the music thrummed softly in the background.

The light from the skyscrapers now drowned out the light from the meteors, but he couldn't argue with the view.

A thoroughly modern city to the core, humans having initially set foot on its soil less than a century ago, Cavare glittered and shone like a sculpture newly unveiled. The reflected halo of the moon shimmered in the tranquil water as the river rippled along the wall beneath him, winding itself through the heart of the city on its way to Lake Fuori. Far to his left he could see the gleam of the first arch which marked the dramatic entrance to the lake and the luxuries it held.

It was an inspiring yet comforting view, and one he had spent close to forty years watching develop, mature and grow increasingly more lustrous. He contented himself with enjoying it while he waited for his appointment to arrive.

The message had come in the middle of dinner at his favorite Chinasian restaurant. He hadn't even had the chance to go home yet; the entirety of the belongings he had traveled with were stowed in the rear compartment of his bike. But in truth there wasn't much of consequence waiting for him at the apartment, for it was home in only the most technical sense of the word.

Never have anything you can't walk away from. A gem of advice imparted by a friend and mentor early on in his career, and something he had found remarkably easy to adopt.

ℛ

He stowed the bike in a nearby stall he had rented in yet another assumed name and hurried to Bay F-18. He made a brief pass through the ship to make sure the contact points on the charges were solid, then sat in the pilot's chair, kicked his feet up on the dash and crossed his hands behind his head to wait.

They were hackers as much as terrorists. It wouldn't take them long to break the encryption to the bay. The encryption on the ship's airlock was stronger—for they would expect it to be—but not so difficult they couldn't crack it.

Planting enough charges at the headquarters to take it out would have involved significant risk of discovery and ultimate failure. But here, he controlled every step and every action.

The hangar bay door burst open. Three...six...eight initially. He sincerely hoped more showed up before they got into the ship.

His wish was granted when three minutes later seven additional members of the group rushed in. The surface pursuit, he imagined. The initial arrivals were still hacking the ship lock. He gave them another two minutes.

With a last gaze around he pulled his feet off the dash and stood. He headed through the primary compartment and below to the mid-level, opened the hatch to the engineering well, and positioned himself in the shadowy corner near the stairs.

They wouldn't all come in at once, lest they end up shooting each other in the confusion. Three, maybe four to start, plus two to guard the airlock. They would fan out to run him to ground quickly.

The first man descended the stairs. As his left foot hit the deck Caleb grabbed him from behind and with a fierce wrench snapped his neck. He made a point to throw the body against the stairwell so the loud clang echoed throughout the ship.

Two down.

ℛ

Caleb looked over his shoulder to see Michael Volosk striding down the steps toward him. Right on time. Everything about the man's outward demeanor projected an image of consummate professionalism, from the simple but perfectly tailored suit to the close-cropped hair to the purposeful stride.

He extended his hand in greeting as the Director of Special Operations for the Senecan Federation Division of Intelligence approached. A mouthful worthy of the highest conceit of government; but to everyone who worked there, it was simply "Division."

Volosk grasped his hand in a firm shake and took up a position along the rail beside him. "Thanks for agreeing to meet me here. I have a syncrosse rec league game down the street in twenty minutes, and if I miss another game they'll kick me off the team." He wore a slight grimace intended to hint at the many responsibilities a high-level covert intelligence official was required to juggle…then presumably realized the impression it actually conveyed, because he shifted to a shrug. "It's the only opportunity I have to blow off steam."

Caleb smiled with studied, casual charm. "It's not a problem. I just got in anyway. And if the surroundings happen to discourage prying eyes, well, I appreciate the value of discretion."

Volosk didn't bother to deny the additional reason for the choice of meeting location. "It wouldn't hurt if your coworkers didn't know you were back on the clock yet—and that's one reason I chose you. Your reputation is impressive."

He chuckled lightly and ran a hand through disheveled hair made wild by the wind. "Perhaps I'm not discrete enough, then."

"Rest assured, it's on a need-to-know basis. I realize we haven't had many opportunities to work together yet, but Samuel always spoke of you in the highest terms."

He schooled his expression to mask the emotions the statement provoked. "I'm humbled, sir. He was a good man."

"He was." Volosk's shoulders straightened with his posture—a signal he was moving right on to business, as though it didn't *matter* how good a man Samuel had been. "What do you know about the Metis Nebula?"

Caleb's brow creased in surprise. Whatever he had been expecting, this wasn't it. *Okay. Sure.*

"Well, mostly that we don't know much about it. It's outside Federation space, but we've tried to investigate it a few times—purely scientific research of course. We know there's a pulsar at the center of it, but scans return a fuzzy mess across the spectrum. Probes sent in find nothing but ionized gases and space dust. Scientists have written it off as unworthy of further study. Why?"

"You're very well informed, Agent Marano. Do a lot of scientific reading in your spare time?"

"Something like that."

"I'm sure. The information I'm sending you is Level IV Classified. Fewer than a dozen people inside and out of the government are aware of it."

He scanned the data file. In the background the synth band shifted to a slow, rhythmic number threaded by a deep, throbbing bass line. "That's...odd."

"Quite. The Astrophysics Institute sent in a state of the art, prototype deep space probe—the most sensitive one ever built, we believe. Honestly, it was solely for testing purposes. The researchers thought Metis' flat profile offered a favorable arena to run the probe through its paces. Instead it picked up what you see there.

"Obviously we need to get a handle on what this is. It came to my desk because it may represent a hostile threat. We've put a hold on any scientific expeditions until we find out the nature of the anomaly. If it *is* hostile, the sooner we know the better we can prepare. If on the other hand it's an opportunity—perhaps a new type of exploitable energy resource—we want to bring it under our purview before the Alliance or any of the independent corporate interests learn of it."

Caleb frowned at his companion. "I understand. But to be frank, my missions are usually a bit more...physical in nature? More direct at least, and typically involving a tangible target."

"I'm aware of that. But your experience makes you one of the few people in Division both qualified to investigate this matter and carrying a security clearance high enough to allow you to do so."

It wasn't an inaccurate statement. And if he were honest with himself, it *would* probably be best if he went a little while without getting more blood on his hands.

R

He slid open the hidden compartment in the wall and climbed into the narrow passage, pushed the access closed using his foot and crawled along the sloped tunnel. When he got to the end he activated his personal concealment shield—which did very nearly make him invisible—and with a deft twist released the small hatch.

He rolled as he hit the ground to mask the sound. The lighting in the bay was purposefully dim, and he landed deep in the shadow of the hull.

As expected, there was a ring of men guarding the exterior of the ship. He waited for the closest man to turn his back, then slipped out and moved to the corner of the bay to settle behind the storage crates he had arranged to have delivered earlier in the day.

He was rewarded by the arrival at that moment of an additional six—no, seven—pursuers. A significant majority of the active members were now inside the hangar bay. Good enough.

They moved to join their brethren encircling the ship—and he sent the signal.

The walls roiled and bucked from the force of the explosion. White-hot heat blasted through his shield. The shockwave sent him to his knees even as the floor shuddered beneath him. Pieces of shrapnel speared into the wall above him and to his right. A large section of the hull shot out the open side of the bay and crashed to the street below.

One glance at the utter wreckage of his former ship confirmed they were all dead. He climbed to his feet and crossed to the door, dodging the flaming debris and burnt, dismembered limbs. The emergency responders could be heard approaching seconds after he disappeared down the corridor.

He didn't de-cloak until he reached the bike. He calmly fired it up, cruised out of the stall, and accelerated toward the exit.

Mission fucking accomplished.

ℛ

Caleb nodded in acceptance. "I'll need a new ship. My last one was, um, blown up."

"My understanding is that's because you blew it up." The expression on the Director's face resembled mild sardonic amusement.

He bit his lower lip in feigned chagrin, revealing what he judged to be the appropriate touch of humility. "Technically speaking."

Volosk sent another data file his way. "Regardless, it's been taken care of. Here's the file number and all the standard information, including the hangar bay of your new ship."

He ignored the mild barb and examined this data with greater scrutiny, but it appeared everything had in fact been taken care of. "Got it. This all looks fine."

"Good…there's one more thing. It's no secret with Samuel gone there's a leadership vacuum in the strategic arm of Special Operations. He believed you were quite capable of taking on a larger role. Based on your record—a few isolated excesses aside—and what I know of you, I'm inclined to agree. So while you're out there in the void, I'd encourage you to give some thought to what you truly want from this job. We can talk further when you return."

Caleb made sure his expression displayed only genuine appreciation, carefully hiding any ambivalence or disquiet. "Thank you for the vote of confidence, sir. I'll do that."

"Glad to hear it. Now if you'll excuse me, I have to go get my ass kicked by ten other men and a cocky, VI-enhanced metal ball, after which I get to go back to the office and review the Trade Summit file for the seventeenth time this week."

He grimaced in sympathy. It was impossible to escape the growing media frenzy surrounding the conference, even with it over a week away.

Twenty-two years had passed since the end of the Crux War; it had been over and done with before he was old enough to fight. The cessation of hostilities after three years was officially called an 'armistice,' but Seneca and fourteen allied worlds had—by the only measure which mattered—won. They had their independence from the mighty Earth Alliance.

Now some politician somewhere had decided it was finally time for them to start playing nice with one another. He wished them luck, but.... "If it's all the same, I'd just as soon not be assigned to that one, sir. It's going to be a clusterfain of epic proportions."

Volosk exhaled with a weariness Caleb suspected was more real than contrived. "Don't worry, you're off the hook—wouldn't want to endanger your work by putting your face in front of so many dignitaries. *I*, however, won't get a decent night's sleep until the damn thing's finished."

Caleb sighed in commiseration, playing along with the superficial bonding moment. It seemed the higher-ups had decided he was worthy of being nurtured, at least enough to make certain he stayed in the fold. Bureaucrats. They had no clue how to manage people; if they did, they would realize he was the last person who needed *managing*.

"Well, I'm sorry I can't help you there, sir. But I will head out on this mission once I've pulled together what I need. It should be a few days at most."

Volosk nodded, transitioning smoothly to the closing portion of the meeting. "Please report in as soon as you discover anything relevant. We need to understand what we're dealing with, and quickly."

He responded with a practiced smile, one designed to convey reassurance and comfort. "Not to worry, I'll take care of it. It's what I do." He decided it was best to leave *when I'm not blowing up three million credit ships and two dozen terrorists with them* unsaid.

After all, he fully intended to *try* to return this ship in one piece.

$$\mathcal{R}$$

After Volosk had departed, Caleb remained by the river for a while. His outward demeanor was relaxed, save for the rapid tap of fingertips on the railing.

He had been on leave ever since the post-op debriefs for the previous assignment had wrapped up. Whether the vacation had been a reward or a punishment he wasn't entirely sure, despite Volosk's vague hint at a promotion. Nor did he particularly care. He had accomplished what he had set out to do, justice had been served— albeit with a spicy dash of vengeance—and the bad guys were all dead. But it appeared it was time to get back to work.

The serenity of the cool night breeze and river-cleansed air juxtaposed upon the pulsing thrum of the music and swelling buzz of the crowd made for an appropriate backdrop. Time to retune himself.

He had enjoyed spending time with Isabela and her family, especially getting to play the bad uncle and fill Marlee's head with rebellious and unruly ideas sure to drive her mother crazy for months. The little girl had spunk; it was his duty to encourage it.

It had been a welcome respite. But it wasn't his life.

He pushed off the railing and strolled down the promenade to the bar area. The throbbing of the bass vibrated pleasantly on his skin as he neared. He ordered a local ale and found a small standing table which had been abandoned in favor of the dance floor. He rested his elbows on it, sipped his beer and surveyed the crowd.

It was amusing, and occasionally heartbreaking, to see how people doggedly fumbled their way through encounters. All the cybernetics in the world couldn't replace real, human connection, which was likely why physical sex was still the most popular pastime in the galaxy, despite the easy availability of objectively better-than-real *passione illusoire*. Humans were social animals, and craved—

"What are you drinking?"

He glanced at the woman who had sidled up next to him. Long, razor-straight white-blond hair framed a face sculpted to perfection beyond what genetic engineering alone could achieve. A white iridescent slip minimally covered deep golden skin. Silver glyphs wound along both arms and up the sides of her neck to disappear beneath the hairline.

He smiled coolly. "I'm fine, thanks."

She dropped a hand on the table and posed herself against it. "Yes, you are. Would you like to dance?"

He suppressed a laugh at the heavy-handed come-on. "Thank you, but…" a corner of his mouth curled up "…you're not really my type."

Her eyes shone with polished confidence. She believed she was in control. How *cute*.

"I can be any type you want me to be." The glyphs glowed briefly as her hair morphed to black, her makeup softened and her skin tone paled.

So that's what the glyphs were for. A waste of credits born of a desperate need to be wanted. He gave the woman a shrug and shook his head. "No thanks."

She scowled in frustration; it marred the perfect features into ugliness. "Why not? What the hell *is* your type?"

He took a last sip of his beer and dropped the empty bottle on the table. "Real."

He walked away without looking back.

3

ERISEN

Twelve screens hovered in a grid pattern above Kennedy Rossi's desk.

She regarded them with a critical eye. Her head tilted to the left, then the right, on the off chance the shift in angle might reveal a new perspective. After further consideration she backed up to lean against the window. The distance allowed her to better analyze the overall effect. At least in theory.

The desk was made of nearly transparent polycrystalline alumina glass. It displayed any information transmitted to it—in her case typically ship architectures and schematics—with micro-scale accuracy and detail. It also happened to act as a rather beautiful complement to the bright, elegant décor of the office.

This project wasn't so far along as to require the desk's particular capabilities, however. Not yet. The presentation contained in the hovering screens focused on the big picture. Its purpose was to weave a story the less technically minded (she was being charitable) directors might understand and, more importantly, believe in enough to invest significant funds in the project.

She gazed out the window. Large, feathery snowflakes danced in the air yet again. Maybe she should go skiing this weekend....

Erisen was the closest habitable world to Earth and had been one of the first extra-solar settlements. In a nasty storm she occasionally questioned the 'habitable' part, but colonists had put the chilly environs to good use. Due to little orbital tilt there weren't seasons to speak of and while it did snow often, the low humidity resulted in a dry, champagne powder snow. Those features meant, in addition to creating a skier's paradise, quantum-scale and other manufacturing that required supercooled conditions could be made cheaply here without the need for orbital facilities.

The colony had wasted no time in crafting the advantages into an economic boon, building a manufacturing sector which was all too happy to supply materials for the rapid galactic expansion of the late 22nd century. More than a hundred fifty years later, Erisen was among the most prosperous Alliance worlds and a hub for electronics, orbitals and starship design and construction.

Which was why she was here, despite the reality that the social and cultural offerings still paled in comparison to those of home. But Earth was a mere three hours away, and it was easy enough to hop a transport when something interesting caught her fancy.

With an almost wistful sigh she turned away from the snowflakes and back to the presentation. A palm came up to rest beneath her chin.

As onboard CUs grew increasingly powerful and attained greater range, long-distance hacking of ship systems constituted a growing crime. The chart hovering to her left indicated the rate of increase in such attacks threatened to become exponential.

A heavily cyberized merc ship was able to hide in the shadow of a moon and remotely take control of a corporate, personal or possibly even military ship halfway across a stellar system. Mercs were then free to disable it for boarding and raiding, turn its weapons on its friends or send it crashing into the nearest planet.

The problem hadn't yet hit the radar of the general public, but it would do so soon enough. If she had her way, IS Design would be waiting in the wings to offer the finest in EM reverse-shielding to counter the threat—for the right price, obviously.

She had already drawn up rough schematics for how the shielding would integrate into standard ship infrastructure, determined the estimated power and material requirements and developed a lattice formulation to best improve its performance. Really, all she needed to do now was add some flowery words and a couple of charts projecting outrageous profit percentages, and she'd be ready to present to the board of directors.

She reached over and flipped the trend statistics and market analysis scr—

—a flashing light in her eVi signaled an incoming holocomm request. She stashed the screens and allowed the holo to take their place.

"Kennedy Rossi speaking. I'm seeing the back of a head and a knot of dark red...Alex?"

"It says so right there on your screen, Ken."

"Oh, I never check that. I prefer to be surprised."

Alex chuckled and finally looked up. She sat cross-legged in the middle of the engineering well of the *Siyane,* an open panel exposing the engineering core beside her. She blew a wisp of hair out of her face. "Sorry, final diagnostics check. I have a question."

"And I have an answer—or if I don't, I have an entertaining-yet-relevant anecdote."

"Uh-huh. Is it safe to tune the power outflow to the dampener field down fifteen percent or so, then run it through an mHEMT amp on the way? I don't want to blow up my ship."

"Hmm...give me a second and let me check the field test data." She flicked her index finger against the edge of the desk to display the product files and scrolled down a series of tables and charts, pausing a few times to study one. "Not quite, but you *can*—do you keep a silica-sapphire matrix filter on board?"

"Yep."

"Okay, if you run the conduit through it after the amp you should be fine. The dampener doesn't like power spikes." She picked up a diagram out of the files. "Here, I'll send you the schem flow. I'm sure the CEO won't mind if I toss around a bit of proprietary information."

"Terrific, thanks." Alex relaxed back on her hands while the file transmitted and loaded. "How's life on Erisen? Have the dinner parties lowered your IQ precipitously yet—or would it be the board-rooms? I can never tell which is worse."

She rolled her eyes with dramatic flair and flopped down in her chair. "*Dreadfully* boring. Yesterday I had to politely educate three visiting investors on how we would not be switching to the trendy new tungsten metamat for our starship hulls due to the fact it *melts* in warmer planetary atmospheres. They kept getting distracted ogling my legs and—well, I won't put you to sleep with the tiresome details of what followed.

"Although, I did meet a delicious eco-dev executive at a cocktail party later in the evening, so the day wasn't a complete loss. We're having dinner tomorrow night. I have high hopes." Her eyes sparkled with deliberate playfulness. "Speaking of tall, dark and handsome, have you listened to Ethan's newest music?"

"I have. It was surprisingly mellow. He's getting complacent in his wealth and fame."

"Angst and rage is for the young and poor, right? You know, you should totally stop by and see him for a quick lay before you hit space again."

Coaxing Alex to stop working for five minutes and, heaven forbid, engage in *fun* had been an ongoing project of hers since university, where inventing the most clever and efficient engineering designs had competed for attention with frat parties and beach bonfires.

Of course Alex had never wanted to go to the frat parties, preferring her men brooding and intellectual; the bonfires she had been only a little more amenable to. But Kennedy was nothing if not persistent, and she had on occasion relented, even if she had usually ended up fucking *with* the boys rather than actually fucking any of them.

Alex worried at her lower lip while she gave a stellar impression of scrupulously studying the incoming schem flow. "Ken, it's been eleven years. I am not going to 'stop by for a quick lay.'"

"You're forgetting that time you *did* stop by for a not-so-quick lay after Malcolm broke up with you. When was it, two years ago?"

"Two *and a half* years ago and I haven't forgotten. It doesn't count, because I was wasted...among other things."

She twirled a long lock of hair around a finger. "All weekend?"

Alex's eyes narrowed; it magnified the effect of the arched eyebrows above them. "*Soglasen—past' zakroi.*"

Kennedy laughed but raised her hands in mock surrender. "Okay, okay, I'll let it go—but my point still stands. I'm sure he'd be thrilled to indulge you again. He's always had a soft spot for you." She definitely saw a brief flash of amusement cross Alex's expression before she tamped it down.

"And *you've* always been entirely too nosy when it comes to my sex life. Now about the field's power requirements. You said it doesn't like spikes. Just how much fluctuation can it tolerate, really?"

SIYANE
EARTH, SEATTLE

Alex took a few steps back and let her gaze run over the length of the ship.

She had spent more than three hours the previous evening working the silica-sapphire matrix into the control grid and recalibrating the power outflow, then testing and retesting the entire system—but the results were worth it. While even extensive testing couldn't replicate real-space conditions, the sims averaged a 39.2% decrease in emission leakage with the new dampener field engaged.

Already an extremely quiet ship, presenting a sleek, subtle profile that shrugged off seeker pings like water down a sloped roof, her stealth level might now be unmatched. She wasn't invisible to sensors, not altogether. But she would be damn close.

A self-satisfied smile grew on her lips. Part of her mind ticked through the list in her head to ensure all was as it should be, any issues had been addressed and she was prepped to fly. The other part giggled silently in pleasure at the beautiful creature which hung before her. The new f-graphene alloy muted the reflective characteristics of the hull, giving the *Siyane* a dangerous, sinister appearance. That suited her just fine.

Her reverie was interrupted by Charlie coming around the rear of the hull to stand beside her.

"Everything checks out. I believe you knew it would, but thanks for letting me pretend to do a little work."

She grinned and elbowed him lightly in the side. He was right of course. She understood the intimate details of every subsystem far better than he did. But his *job* was making sure starships operated correctly; he had checklists for each subsystem and methodical processes to confirm their proper functioning. It was simply good practice for the ship to regularly undergo a thorough operational review—particularly after installing substantive upgrades, which she had most certainly done.

"A pleasure doing business with you, as always. No idea when I'll be back, but I'll let you know when I know."

"Yes, ma'am. Safe travels."

As soon as he had left she jogged up the extended ramp to the open airlock hatch and headed straight for the cockpit. She had earlier confirmed the food supply delivery and stored her clothes and personals below. Nothing left to do but leave.

She settled into the supple leather cockpit chair, and with a thought the HUD came to life. The Evanec screen displayed the formal communication with the spaceport's VI interface.

EACV-7A492X to Olympic Regional Spaceport Control: Departure sequence initiation requested Bay L-19

ORSC to EACV-7A492X: Departure sequence initiated Bay L-19

The docking platform whose clamps held the ship slid toward the interior of the spaceport. It then became a lift and rose to the roof along with dozens of other lifts in the stacked rings of the facility. All departures occurred above the ceiling of the skycar airlanes, for obvious reasons.

The platform locked into position on the rooftop deck. She idled the engine and waited for the clamps to disengage.

ORSC to EACV-7A492X: Departure clearance window 12 seconds bearing N 346.48° W

EACV-7A492X to ORSC: Departure clearance window accepted

The platform rotated to the indicated bearing and the clamps retracted. The *Siyane* hovered for 1.4 seconds before the pulse detonation engine engaged and she was flying over Whidbey Island. Eighteen seconds later she passed into the Strait of Georgia and beyond the purview of ORS Control.

Outside a spaceport's airspace and above two kilometers altitude, air traffic was managed by a CU under the guise of the Earth Low Atmosphere Traffic Control System. Its job in the main consisted of ensuring starships and planetary transports didn't crash into one another. It was a task uniquely suited for the raw processing power of a centralized synthetic construct, and the CU performed it flawlessly.

She veered west. The coast receded then disappeared from the stern visual screen and the Pacific Ocean stretched out beneath her. She far outpaced the sun, and like a clock winding in reverse dawn soon turned to night.

"Alex, would you like to fly her?"

The smile breaking across her face morphed to a frown at the midway point. The viewport revealed only the stars above and moonlight reflecting in the water below. They had left the San Pacifica

Regional Spaceport after breakfast, but this far out over the Pacific the sun had not yet risen. "But Dad, I can't see anything. It's too dark."

"You will, moya milaya. Come sit in my lap and I'll show you."

She scrambled out of the passenger seat and onto his thigh in a flash, fidgeting a bit to get situated. Though she was tall for her age, her feet didn't quite reach the floor; instead they danced an excited rhythm in the air.

"Are you ready?"

She absently tucked minimally brushed hair behind her ear and nodded. "I'm ready."

"Okay. I'm going to send you the access code for the ship's HUD. You won't be able to control it right away though. I want to walk you through what each of the screens mean first."

A tiny light in the corner of her vision signaled a new message. She zoomed it, and a question floated in the virtual space in front of her. 'Access ship flight displays?'

She both thought and exclaimed "Yes!" Her father chuckled softly at her ear.

The world lit up around her. A wall of semitransparent screens overlay the viewport. They painted a canvas of aeronautical splendor in radiant white light.

Airspeed. Altitude. Bearing. Pitch angle. Air temperature. Atmosphere pressure and air density. Radar. Engine load. Other readings whose purpose were a mystery. The screens' relative focus and opacity responded to every shift in her gaze, then to her intentional thoughts. Secure in her father's lap, she grinned in delight.

Her life would never be the same again.

At seven kilometers altitude she began maneuvering toward the Northeast 1 Pacific Atmosphere Corridor. Technically two corridors—one for arrivals and one for departures to avoid nasty collisions—it was one of twenty-two such passages located on the planet, spaced 4–5,000 thousand kilometers apart at 55° N, 0° and 55° S latitudes.

Nearly all starships possessed the drive energy, hull strength and shields necessary to pass through any planetary atmosphere having an escape velocity value within fifty percent greater or lesser than the habitable zone. The exceptions were dreadnoughts and capital ships, which were built and forever remained in space. But that didn't mean it was an especially fun or comfortable experience, and the wear and tear from frequent atmosphere traversals wreaked havoc on a ship's structure and mechanics.

The solution was the corridors: reverse shields which held back the majority of atmospheric phenomena from a cylindrical area. A series of rings made of a nickel alloy metamaterial absorber generated a plasma field between each ring to create the corridors.

On Earth the rings measured half a kilometer in diameter and stretched from an altitude of ten to two hundred sixty kilometers, well into the thermosphere. The details varied on other worlds, but every planet with a population in excess of about twenty thousand had at least one paired corridor.

It was midmorning back on the coast and traffic was brisk. She slowed and eased into the queue of vessels departing Earth.

For basic security or record-keeping purposes or perhaps merely to give a few bureaucrats something to do, a monitoring device recorded the serial number designation of every vessel to enter the corridor. If one was flagged for any of a variety of reasons—but most often due to a criminal warrant—a containment field captured it at the second ring, immobilizing it until the authorities arrived.

She'd seen it happen once or twice and found it an absurd annoyance. The system was ridiculously porous; if someone wanted to avoid capture, he or she simply wouldn't take the corridor (except for the brainless idiots who evidently did). But thankfully there appeared to be no brainless idiots in the vicinity this morning, and in minutes she was accelerating into the rings.

Without the buffeting forces of the atmosphere fighting against her, it was a brief four minute trip. A swipe of her hand brought up the engineering controls and she initiated the transition to the WM impulse engine. Then she curled her legs underneath her and surveyed the view.

Earth's outer atmosphere constituted a barely organized chaos of commercial and residential space stations, zero-g manufacturing facilities, satellites and military defense platforms. The cornucopia of structures sped along a dozen progressively larger concentric orbits. Up close, it made for an extraordinarily beautiful vista: sunbeams reflecting off gleaming, smooth metals streaked in the luminous glow of the lights within. A testament to the triumph of human ingenuity.

As her distance from Earth grew, however, it began to more closely resemble a swarm of ants feeding upon the discarded remnants of a meal, a dichotomy which had always amused her. The ship's acceleration increased as the engine reached full power, and the ants soon faded into the halo cast by the sun.

She stood up and stretched. It would be four hours before she reached the Mars-Jupiter Main Asteroid Belt and was 'allowed' to engage the sLume drive.

Originally named the Alcubierre Oscillating Bubble Superluminal Propulsion Drive when the first working prototype had been developed nearly two hundred years earlier, a clever marketing executive had quickly coined the far more consumer-friendly term 'sLume Drive.'

The mechanism which propelled her ship across the stars bore little similarity to the initial prototype. The ring which held open the warp bubble was now dynamically generated and consisted of exotic particles too small even en masse to be visible. The energy requirements were met in full by the He3 LEN fusion reactor thanks to the boost in negative mass provided as a byproduct of the impulse engine.

And while the first prototype had achieved a mere seventy times the speed of light, her drive was faster by a factor of thousands. Admittedly, it was a *very* high-end model.

The particles released by the bubble's termination were funneled into micro-singularities so as to not destroy everything in a 0.2 AU vicinity. Still, space traffic in the Earth-Lunar-Mars conjunction was quite heavy, as the region housed greater than fifteen percent of the galactic population. Though volumes of research indicated it was perfectly safe, Alliance bureaucrats insisted on concern over the idea of billions of micro-singularities being created every day in such a congested sector—some notion about destabilizing the space-time manifold.

So superluminal drive operation by private spacecraft was forbidden inside the Main Asteroid Belt; military vessels and commercial transports naturally got a pass. And she wasted half a day on 0.1% of her trip.

Her natural instinct would normally be to work up a case of righteous indignation at the blatant capitulation to fear rather than science, but she just couldn't muster the necessary outrage.

After all, she was home.

4

The members of the Earth Alliance Strategic Command Governing Board positioned themselves around the oval table. Five of them were present in the flesh, the four Regional Commanders via full-dimensional holo.

The table was a true antique, crafted for the Politburo Standing Committee headquarters in Zhongnanhai in the waning years of CCP rule. Constructed of natural Burmese Teak and lacquered in the ancient Chinese tradition, the finish now lay buried beneath multiple layers of AgInide secure conductive glass.

The table was, of course, impressively large—far larger than required for a mere nine occupants—but a more practical table would have been less *grand* and not befitting the importance of those who utilized it.

A late afternoon sun shone through the floor-to-ceiling windows lining the penthouse conference room. Shielding filtered the sunlight to reduce the glare without marring the view of the Pacific, seeing as the room had been placed on the western-facing side of the building specifically for its magnificent view.

General Price Alamatto waited until the door had closed behind the departing aides before turning back to the gathered Board members. "As I was saying prior to the interruption, with a minor readjustment to the Sol System construction budget we will have the funds to assemble an additional six high-orbit arrays and deploy them to the Fionava and Deucali Provinces."

Miriam Solovy leaned forward in her chair while keeping her shoulders firmly squared. It was an assertive posture she used often to persuasive effect. "And if we supply them to Fionava and Deucali, then New Cornwall and Messium will want them as well, and probably Karelia and Nyssus, too—all on account of a mythical threat from nonexistent aliens forever on the cusp of the frontier. And indulging them will *wipe out* the Sol System construction budget."

She shook her head in a terse but firm motion. "No. If those funds are truly available, better for us to use them to reinforce Earth's outer defense web with a redundant backup power grid and install the new longer-range emission signature sensors. Added redundancy will increase security and the sensors will give us significantly earlier warning should unwelcome visitors target Earth."

General Liam O'Connell cocked an overly bushy eyebrow in her direction. "Careful Admiral, lest someone insinuate you were advocating an 'Earth First' agenda."

O'Connell was the Southwestern Regional Commander, and seemed to believe overseeing the largest region in terms of kiloparsecs gave him the right to be an arrogant prick. He was incorrect, not that it stopped him.

She regarded him coolly. "I don't particularly care what *someone* insinuates about me, General. I am doing no such thing, save for the irrefutable fact that both the knowledge and capabilities of the Earth Alliance are concentrated here on Earth, and we should recognize this and act accordingly."

Alamatto cleared his throat from the head of the table. "You make a commendable and valid point, Admiral. Nevertheless, we must not appear to be Earth-centric in our decision-making. Earth has plenty enough resources on its own. We need to be cognizant of the reality that the colonies often lack our inherent means and require our protection."

A strong Earth *was* a strong Alliance; she'd never understand why more people didn't see this. She worked to protect the best interests of the entire Earth Alliance, colonies included.

Her glare was steel across the table. "Which protection we won't be able to provide if our defense web goes down and we come under attack."

O'Connell snorted from the safety of his holo. "Who do you think is going to attack Earth, Miriam? Seneca? They wouldn't dare. Raiders from New Babel, or maybe some nutcases from Pandora? Be realistic. Earth is by far the most fortified, heavily defended world in settled space. *No one* is coming for Earth."

Inwardly she sighed, though she was careful not to let it show. At this point the Board was in danger of becoming completely dominated by the Regional Commanders. Alamatto was too weak a leader to keep them in line and there wasn't another faction to counterbalance them. The other three Earth-based members were too beholden to competing political benefactors to act in concert with her *or* Alamatto.

She was fighting a losing battle and she knew it. But so long as she held a position of any power, she would not fold. She dropped her chin and gazed slightly up and sideways at O'Connell, one eyebrow arched; the impression created was of a master disappointed in the ignorance of the student.

"If I could predict the nature of the adversary, rest assured we would already be meeting the threat. You believe we've thought of everything. But the real danger is, as it has been since the dawn of history, the enemy we cannot predict. This is what I seek always to defend against."

Alamatto placed both palms on the table and pressed into it in an attempt to reassert control over the meeting. "You *both* raise valid concerns which we must weigh alongside other considerations."

He paused to grace the table with a smooth smile; the poised, confident yet nonthreatening countenance ranked as one of his strongest assets.

"In my view the defense web is sufficiently strong for the time being, but mine is not the only opinion which matters. Are there any further observations, or shall we vote on the initiative?"

DEUCALI
EARTH ALLIANCE SW REGIONAL MILITARY HEADQUARTERS

General Liam O'Connell barreled down the hall from the QEC room toward his office. His nods to the junior officers he passed, when they occurred at all, were curt. The base headquarters bustled with activity even on this most typical of days; nevertheless, the crowd unfailingly parted to let his tall, burly form pass unhindered.

The Board meeting had gone well he thought. Personally he wasn't all that worked up over the need for additional high-orbit defense arrays, but as a power play he must admit it was a shrewd maneuver.

Fionava seemed to be genuinely concerned by potential dangers from the frontiers of space beyond its borders. This world wasn't subject to those concerns to so great an extent, but he was more than happy to join their cause if it meant greater resources and increased influence would come his way.

Deucali was one of the largest 'Second Wave' colonies, and its population continued to grow. With each passing year it exercised greater control over the smaller settlements in the Province. The colony's star was on the ascension, no question about it. Without slowing he barked an order at a passing Lieutenant regarding the unfinished upgrades to the QEC room.

Alamatto was a weak-willed pussy. His entire career had been based on nothing more than the military establishment's respect for his father—but were he alive, the elder Alamatto would be mortified by his excuse for a son. Solovy could be a royal pain in the ass, but she was little more than a pencil pusher; if she had ever seen live combat it had been back in the Bronze Age. As for the remainder of the Board, they weren't worth wasting energy over.

At a crossway he abruptly stopped and pivoted to face the young man traversing the opposite hall. "Corporal, did your babysitter teach you to tuck your shirt in like that? Sharpen those creases before I lay eyes on you again, son."

"Y-yes, sir!"

He had turned and moved on before the Corporal managed to stutter out the reply.

Well, that wasn't *quite* true. The Northeastern Regional Commander, Rychen, was an obstacle waiting to happen. He oversaw the region closest to Senecan space, which alone made him a significant player. Granted, he also had won numerous medals in the Crux War, was respected by his peers and by all accounts was a shining beacon of honor and integrity. The man was without a doubt dangerous. But for the moment their interests were aligned, so Liam played nice.

He waved off a couple of officers trying to vie for his attention, strode into his office and closed the door behind him. In an earlier time it would have slammed, but doors didn't do such things anymore. A shame, really.

After a quick sip of water he shifted his focus to the series of flashing files on his desk overlay. He evaluated, assigned and dispatched them with brutal efficiency, pausing only to scowl at the status update on the construction of the new sim training complex. He personally preferred old-school live fire exercises—sim training produced weak-willed soldiers like Alamatto—but the decision came straight from the politicians. No actual action required, he sent it on its way.

His scowl vanished at the next item; in the privacy of his office, it morphed into a smug smile. The Annual Founding Day Parade was next week. The entire 1st Deucali Brigade would be out in their dress blues, proudly showing what it meant to be an Earth Alliance Marine. It never failed to bring a tear to his eye to march through the streets at the head of his men. Though the Public Relations Staff Commander was responsible for the preparations, he had taken an active oversight role. He scheduled a meeting for 0700 the next morning to review the state of readiness.

The voice of his secretary interrupted his train of thought. "Sir, Commander Bradlen has arrived for your meeting."

With a grimace he closed the various screens and straightened his jacket. "Send him in."

An upstart lad, Bradlen had risen quickly in the ranks due to an overabundance of competence. He returned the salute of the young Commander. "At ease."

"Yes, sir." Bradlen sat down across the desk and opened a series of screens between them. "I've uploaded the latest supply reports and inventories as well as the shipment schedule for the next three months."

He paused while O'Connell accessed the files. "As you can see, we'll receive a new shipment of test drones next week, along with the new ware for the existing high-orbit defense array. I heard a rumor we were getting another array soon, sir. Any chance it's true?"

Liam smiled thinly, the curl of his lips not otherwise impacting his expression. "I'm afraid that's classified for now."

"My mistake. Um, about the ware for the array...Earth says it's ready for deployment, but I assume you'll want it tested thoroughly first, sir?"

"You assume correctly, Commander."

"Understood. I'll arrange for it to be routed through Configuration/Testing before Implementation Services gets their hands on it." He cleared his throat and seemed to hesitate in uncertainty.

"Spit it out, son, I don't have all day here."

"Right. Sir, I feel I should draw your attention to a discrepancy in the inventories for our VI short-range missiles. There's a report on it in the files. The discrepancy occurred in the middle of the transition to the new inventory system, so it's probably just a glitch, but...."

Liam snorted in clear disgust. "Goddamn warenuts. Every time they push out something 'better' it only makes things worse."

"I...yes, sir. I can have Support run some diagnostics, see if they can find the problem—"

Liam shook his head in a manner which brooked no dissent. "Won't be necessary. I will take great pleasure in informing Logistics Command they need to fix their crocked ware."

"Of course, sir. If there's nothing else?"

He had begun pulling up other reports; his head jerked in the direction of the door. "Dismissed."

Once Bradlen departed, he dropped the illusion of activity. He sat silently as an epoch passed...then reopened the Inventory Discrepancy Report. Seconds ticked by while he simply stared at it, as though the authority of his glare might melt it away.

He didn't know why he was hesitating. The decision had already been made; the deed already done. In many ways the decision had been made twenty-four years ago when he stood over his mother's grave and made a vow, even if it had taken until two months ago for the opportunity for him to fulfill his vow to finally knock on his door.

He had expected the discrepancy to be discovered. In this hyper-cyberized, always-connected world they lived in, it would have been impossible to hide it—so he hadn't tried. Instead he'd made sure the materials vanished during the hectic, confused inventory system transition, thereby providing a ready explanation for their 'absence.'

Deucali Military HQ housed tens of thousands of armaments. Anyone who noticed a couple of dozen missiles unaccounted for would merely nod in agreement at how annoying the 'damn ware bugs' were and move on with their lives.

He swallowed hard, annoyed at the sudden dryness in his throat. No reason to become all emotional about it now. He had already sold his soul for a chance at vengeance, and there was no getting it back.

He deleted the report from the system.

5

Caleb idly toed the pilot's chair side to side while he stepped through the preflight checklist a final time, mentally verifying every component which was checked off deserved to be. He had one remaining item to acquire, but it wouldn't be on any official checklist.

Satisfied the systems were a go, the food stores stocked, the engines prepped and the weapons in working order, he killed the power and headed down the ramp. At the bottom he turned to give her one last glance-over.

He had to give Division credit; they didn't skimp on ships and hardware. One step removed from a fighter, the scout ship wasn't luxurious or roomy but she was lean and fast. The weapons tubes tucked into the lower hull so as not to increase drag. The custom EM sensors had been mounted beneath the nose the day before.

Yeah, she would do.

He slung his pack over his shoulder and headed out to the government spaceport's surface parking. Yet when he reached his bike, he hesitated.

Traffic whizzed along airlanes overhead in the evening sky and beside him on the streets. Rush hour appeared well underway, which meant he was going to have a bitch of a time getting across the city to Mom's house—which in turn meant he'd be late for his meeting.

The devil on his shoulder whispered in alluring, dulcet tones that he should skip the visit home and head straight for the bar. She was *fine*. And it wasn't like he'd be standing her up. Unless he showed up at the front door, she'd never know he'd passed through Cavare.

But she was alone. With Isabela on Krysk for the year doing a visiting professorship, she wasn't able to check on their mother nearly as often as usual. Mom might have had an accident, or forgotten to shop for groceries, or....

But Isabela went by a few days ago.

And won't be back again for a month.

He groaned aloud as a guilty conscience shoved the devil aside and reasserted its dominance. "Shit."

More than a little disgusted with himself, he swung a leg over the bike, revved the engine and floored it out of the parking lot. He swerved into a service alley. The least he could do was take a damn shortcut.

"Oh, Caleb darling, it's so nice of you to visit."

Yes, that's exactly what he was. *Nice.* He hugged her, trying not to stifle within the desperate embrace. "Hi, Mom. I don't have long, but I wanted to stop by and make sure you were okay."

"Yes, I'm just...." She ambled into the kitchen, wisps of dull brown hair falling out of a messy bun and to her shoulders. She pushed half-finished sketches off the table to the floor and gestured for him to sit. He complied, then watched her as she searched in the cabinets for tea to brew.

He remembered when she had been a vibrant, smart, funny woman. For the entirety of his childhood that woman had been his mother. Now she was merely...pathetic. He knew this—he'd known this for a long time—but coming face-to-face with the stark reality still sent him for a loop. Old memories never die.

"It's okay, Mom. I'm good. Come sit with me for a few minutes."

She paused in the middle of the room, her unfocused gaze wandering across the kitchen. It was as if she had completely forgotten where she was. Seconds ticked by. Finally she jerked, a fleeting, erratic jolt of movement before her bearing returned to its former listless, empty state. She gingerly sat down opposite him. "How's work, dear? Is the plant doing well?"

"Absolutely. We're rolling out a new line of six-person skycars, geared toward families. In fact, I'm headed off to Elathan tomorrow to oversee the ramp-up of the production line." After years of practice, the lies rolled off his tongue more easily than truth.

"How nice." She nodded. It was an uneven, haphazard motion. Her eyes didn't quite manage to meet his, which was just as well. "I've been talking to Federation Athletics about a design for their new regional office, so...we'll see, maybe...."

"That's *wonderful* to hear." It took all his considerable skill to inject a note of enthusiasm into his voice. Even so, he managed only the mildest cheer. She hadn't completed an architectural design in at least fifteen years. This one would be no different—and there would be no value in him pointing it out. "So, you're set then? You have everything you need?"

"Oh, yes." She gave him a vacant smile. "Glados and Meriva from the neighborhood association stop by once a week, we go out shopping and such." The smile faltered. "I thought I saw your father the other day while we were at the syn-org market…" three seconds passed until she blinked "…anyway, everything's fine. You go see to your shuttles and don't worry about your mother." She patted his hand to emphasize the point.

Harsh, frustrated words rushed forth; he choked them back in his throat. "Okay, Mom. I have to go, I have a meeting—about the plant. I'll try to stop by again when I can."

He prepped his most affectionate facsimile smile—but she had already drifted off, dreamily caressing the incomplete sketch of a low-orbital bio-friendly campus which had clung to the edge of the table.

He nodded to himself and stood, leaving the house without looking at the wall of visuals in the hallway displaying a couple in love and a happy family at play. He *definitely* didn't look at the largest visual, the one dominating the entryway. It portrayed a distinguished-looking man with close-cut black hair wearing a perfectly pressed suit, taken two months before his father had packed a bag, walked out the door and not come back.

As he cruised into the lot behind the *Crux Happy Nights Cantina*, Caleb decided he was exceedingly ready for a drink—so much so he didn't even cringe at the dreadful title. Granted, he didn't laugh either.

But the beer turned out to be quite cold and surprisingly crisp. He welcomed the assistance it provided in forcing away the darkness which never failed to haunt him after a visit home. Escaping the gloom was an acquired skill, and he had largely regained his form by the time Noah Terrage slid onto the stool next to him.

He flung long bangs out of his face and dropped his forearms on the chrome bar. "Caleb, friend, how's it hanging?"

The first rule of undercover work, spying and black ops in general—okay, probably the third or fourth or perhaps even fifth rule, but it certainly made the list—was anyone who made a point to call you 'friend,' wasn't.

Still, Noah was a good guy, and he felt inclined to give him a pass. Despite the rebellious attitude which came as an almost inevitable consequence of the man's upbringing, Caleb suspected an honorable soul resided somewhere beneath the bravado and shady deals and wild stunts. For one, it spoke in his favor that he had managed to overcome the fairly significant disability of being a 'vanity baby.'

Cloning remained legal on most worlds with the express consent of the cloned—new births only though; all attempts to grow a fully developed adult body from existing DNA had thus far proved horrifically disastrous. Clone clauses in wills were, while not common, growing in popularity for what might be understandable reasons. Vanity babies, however, were frowned upon in most circles and rarely worked out well for either party. Nonetheless, there always seemed to be another billionaire narcissist convinced he or she deserved one.

A clone of his father, a wealthy business magnate on Aquila, like most vanity babies Noah had been brought into existence above all to feed the source's ego. From early childhood he had been expected to behave precisely as his father saw himself, sit and learn at his father's knee and grow up to become his father's devoted protégé in the business.

So naturally, Noah had run away from home at fifteen. Caught a transport to Pandora and never looked back.

He was a criminal, of course. A 'trader' in polite company and a smuggler everywhere else. And while the guy came off like the buddy you watched the game and drank too many beers with on the weekend, he possessed a skill bordering on magic: he could find *anything*. If it existed in settled space, he could make it appear in your pack inside a week—as with all things, for sufficient credits.

In this instance he had far less than a week, but the item wasn't a particularly rare one and the compensation generous.

Caleb leaned over to shake his hand. "You know, just the usual—wine, women and song."

Noah laughed and took a swig from the mug Caleb had ensured would be waiting on him. "I do know it, man." His voice dropped as he leaned in and casually passed over the small, unremarkable-looking yet very advanced communications scrambler. Caleb dropped it in his pack and just as casually returned to his beer.

It wasn't that he planned to engage in anything overtly criminal, much less traitorous to the Federation. In fact, he believed Volosk and likely the Division Director knew about and expected such things. Black ops were 'black' for a reason, yet they also fell under government supervision and oversight. A difficult quandary.

Most things he did, most of the time, qualified as legal actions under Division's mandate, if not always under civilian law. But every so often a mission called for actions which…weren't. In such circumstances, his superiors winked and nodded and ignored the troublesome details, provided they had been sufficiently obscured. Hence the state-of-the-art communications scrambler—a necessary tool for those moments when even Special Operations didn't want a recording of what was said or to whom.

Noah's voice stayed low and conversational, barely audible amid the din of spirited patrons and generic pub background music. "I guess you misplaced the last one, huh?"

Caleb shrugged and sipped his beer. It really was rather good. "Eh, it blew up."

"What? Dammit, I'll have a *conversation* with my—"

"Not the scrambler—the ship it was in."

Noah's head cocked to the side. "Oh. Yeah, that does happen."

He had met Noah nine years ago. An influx of chimerals had begun flooding the streets on several of the smaller Federation worlds; he tracked the source to a drug ring on Pandora. Noah was little more than a freelance street merchant back then, hocking black market surveillance equipment, hacking tools and modified energy blades. Illegal, but nothing hardcore. The modded gear had come in handy, as had the inside information provided as a bonus.

After a few years, Noah earned enough credits to move his operation off the streets and began serving a more discerning clientele and their more unique needs. Caleb had called on him on occasion over the years, and now…well, they weren't friends. But in another life, they might have been.

"So how's Pandora these days? The last time I visited, holo-babes in the spaceport terminal were selling head trips which would make you believe you sported three cocks and twice the women to fill with them lounged in your bed. Oh, and the bed floated upon a golden nebula in the stars. God knows what they were selling in the markets."

Noah laughed in wry dismay as he motioned the bartender for a refill. "Trust me, Caleb, you do not want to know what they're selling in the markets. I don't mess with such insanity, nothing but trouble."

"As opposed to the trouble you already get in?"

He shrugged. "Yeah? Still, it's all good. Business is good. Life is good. Nobody's tried to kill me in at least a month."

Caleb chuckled in spite of himself. "I guess that's all you can ask for, right?"

Noah sighed wistfully. "No…you can ask for a beautiful, witty, intelligent yet minxy woman in your arms every night, a mansion on a hill—or better yet in the sky—and the best bodyguards to protect you when someone *does* inevitably try to kill you. For starters."

Caleb raised his mug to clank against Noah's. "I'll drink to that."

6

Miriam sat at her desk and tried to focus on reviewing next week's schedule. For a moment, she failed.

She prided herself on superior compartmentalization skills...yet hours after the Board meeting, she couldn't seem to shake a lingering unease. Disappointment. *Annoyance.*

Being overruled gave her no pleasure, particularly when the facts were on her side. Egos coupled with narcissistic insecurity had won out over logic and reason once again. Hopefully they wouldn't come to regret this decision, or the dozens before it.

With a private groan she sat up straighter and returned to her calendar. *Schedule.*

The christening ceremony for the new cruiser *EAS Thatcher* was on Monday, followed by a status meeting for Project ANNIE. She had various staff meetings on Tuesday, then Phase II testing review of new biosynthetics for special forces in the evening. Wednesday she left for the TacRecon Conference in St. Petersburg.

Her mouth twitched involuntarily. She had tried to get Richard to go in her place—it was more his area of expertise anyway—but he was elbow-deep in the damn Trade Summit.

She didn't want to go to St. Petersburg, where memories of David lurked around every corner and across every street. Even the places they had never visited held shadows of the stories he had told of his childhood.

She would need to visit her father-in-law while there. David had made certain his father received the latest in stem cell rejuvenation treatments, though the elder Solovy had accepted little else in the way of financial assistance. As a result, at one hundred sixteen years old he was built like a boxer and working low-altitude field construction ten hours a day.

It would be uncomfortable and melancholy. He would ask after Alexis, say, 'I've always loved that little girl,' leaving unsaid the insinuation *as opposed to how I feel about you.'* Her position of prominence meant nothing to him. In his own twisted way he would forever blame her for David's death, ignoring the fact that David had joined the military six years prior to meeting her. He would inquire as to whatever man she must have moved on to by now, oblivious to the reality that in twenty-three years she hadn't moved on; that she had no intention of *ever* moving on.

After two miserable hours she would excuse herself and return to her five-star hotel room, order her 250-credit room service, allow herself one glass of sherry and occupy her mind with vitally important matters of galactic security until she was too tired not to sleep.

She didn't want to go. But she'd do it anyway, because it was her job, and because she didn't trust anyone else other than Richard with the responsibility. At least next year the conference location rotated out to somewhere—anywhere—other than Russia.

She blinked to push aside the dangerously sentimental thoughts, opened the ANNIE briefing and proceeded to dive into breakdowns of recurrence quantification analysis, time series prediction, stochastic controls and most importantly, dynamic security feedback loops.

Nearly two hundred fifty years after the Hong Kong 'incident,' synthetic intelligences of all types were still locked down and circumscribed on every world, but nowhere more so than in the military. The Alliance didn't curtail the advancement of non-cybernetic synthetic technology; they merely kept it corralled inside safety fences, as it were.

ANNIE (Artificial Neural Net Integration and Expansion) represented the most advanced Alliance-sanctioned synthetic neural net to date. It also promised to be the safest, most secure Artificial ever constructed, for they had had centuries to perfect every control and safeguard.

Yet believing such to be true was exactly what had resulted in the Hong Kong incident in the first place. So she intended to double- and if necessary triple-check the dynamic security feedback loop protocols.

She had made it through an entire third of the file when her secretary pinged her eVi to inform her the Minister for Extra-Solar Development was in the lobby asking to see her.

She frowned in annoyance, and a bit of surprise. She didn't care for people dropping by without an appointment, but the man was influential enough she couldn't afford to rebuff him. "Give me two minutes before you send him in."

The layers of screens vanished; she went to the cabinet to fix a cup of tea. By the time the Minister walked in she was in perfect form and smiling with poised grace.

"Minister Karolyn, so good to see you again."

"And you, Admiral." He half-bowed from the waist. She dipped her chin and gestured him toward the chair opposite her desk.

There was only one conceivable reason for the visit—but she never made assumptions where politicians were concerned. "What can I do for you?"

He nodded and adjusted himself awkwardly in the chair. "I apologize for the unannounced visit. I found myself in the area this afternoon and thought I might drop in." Her left eyebrow raised the slightest bit. "I wanted to take the opportunity to impress upon you in person how much we want to see Alexis in the Deep Space Exploration directorship. She's a stellar candidate who can bring new energy and initiative to the department."

Her lips pursed briefly. "She would unquestionably do so, and I regret she was unable to accept your generous offer. But if I may be honest? This seems rather a lot of effort for a position which, while prestigious, is not one I consider to be world-altering. I imagine you have other qualified candidates."

"Yes, obviously." He fidgeted again, though this time it didn't seem to be related to the comfort level of the chair. "If I may also be honest, Admiral, I'm getting a fair amount of pressure to make sure your daughter is named to this post, and soon."

She suppressed a frown, but barely. It concerned her if political forces had taken an interest in Alexis without her knowledge. "Pressure? Wherever from? Alexis is hardly politically connected."

"That's the thing about political pressure, ma'am. One rarely can see from where it truly originates. All I can say is someone higher up than me very much wants your daughter in this job. So if you were able to reach out to her again and reiterate the degree of interest, I'd greatly appreciate it."

She sipped her tea, both to buy herself a moment and to center her thoughts. She wasn't eager to divulge the abysmal state of her relationship with her daughter to a stranger, much less a politician. But if there was any chance of Alexis accepting the position, she wanted to help make it happen. It would be good for her...eventually, it might be good for them. "Minister, do you have children?"

"I'm a bachelor, so not as far as I'm aware of." He smiled.

She didn't. "I see. You will not have experienced this yourself then, but like many children, my daughter developed a mind of her own before she was two years old and has never lost it. She stopped taking my advice around the time...." A shadow passed across her face she couldn't fully disguise.

The security office on Le Grande Retraite was as bright and clean as the rest of the orbital luxury resort. A young lieutenant in a spotless uniform greeted her at the entryway with a salute. "Commodore Solovy. It's an honor to meet you."

She leveled a dismissive glare at him. "This is not a social call, Lieutenant. Take me to my daughter."

His posture wilted as he stammered out a response. "Y-yes, ma'am. We put her in one of the interview rooms. I, um, gave her a juice. And some popcorn."

She fell in beside him. "And the young man?"

"Uh, he was of age and no laws had been broken, so we weren't able to detain him." He stopped in front of a doorway and glanced at her, then hastily opened the door and stepped back.

Alexis tossed a kernel of popcorn in the air and caught it in her mouth. Her feet were clad in braided flip-flops and kicked up on the desk, legs crossed at the ankle. She was all elbows and knees, half a child and half a woman. Her hair was bound in long pigtails draped over her shoulders and down her chest—strange, they somehow made her look older, not younger. Perhaps it was the sharp, spirited fire in her eyes. David's eyes.

"Mom. Here to throw me in the brig?"

"I am here to take you home."

Alexis gave a melodramatic sigh, rolled her eyes in exaggerated annoyance and pulled her feet off the desk. "Fine, whatever."

She turned to the lieutenant. "Thank you for taking care of my daughter, Lieutenant. I do apologize for any inconvenience she may have caused you."

"She was no trouble, ma'am." He jumped when Alexis tossed the bag of popcorn to him as she passed.

"Thanks for the snack, mes'ye."

Miriam didn't say a word until they reached the ship. She set the autopilot then shifted in the seat. "What were you thinking? You are fourteen years old and had no business flying off-planet without supervision."

"It's not like it was far off-planet...." Her hand jerked toward the viewport dominated by Earth's profile.

"How did you access the ship? The security should have prevented you from flying it."

Alexis snorted. "Please. I hacked full access to it weeks ago. It actually recognizes me as its primary owner now, you know."

"Not for long it doesn't. You will— "

"Did you even know I was gone until they called you? You didn't, did you? You spent another night at the office, doing whatever the hell it is you do there."

She felt her jaw tighten, but made certain her voice remained even. "I trusted you were mature enough so I didn't need to check on you constantly, trusted you would respect your curfew and not, for instance, steal the family ship and run off with a boy four years older than you."

"Nick? He's a tupïtsa, and entirely too easy to impress. I was bored with him before we got to the station."

"That is not the point. The point is I was mistaken. You aren't worthy of my trust."

"Bullshit. The point is—"

"Do not speak to me in—"

"The point is you will do everything in your power not to have to spend time with me. I'm nothing but a nuisance in the way of your damn career—but hey, it's fine. Say the word and I'll be out of your hair forever. I've got things to do anyway."

She opened her mouth to retort...then closed it.

How could she tell her daughter it was a knife in the heart every single time she looked at her? That she saw David in the light in her eyes, the way she walked, her voice, her smile and even her frown?

That she could hardly bear to be in the house where he was a ghost in every shadow and a whisper in every corner, yet couldn't bear to let it go for the same reason? That she sought refuge in work because it was the only place where she could pretend there wasn't a hole in the world? Where she could at least try to make sure he didn't die in vain?

She couldn't, of course.

"Don't be absurd. You are my daughter, and I care about you. But with the implementation of the armistice there's a tremendous amount of work to do. A lot of changes are on the way. Someone has to ensure matters are handled properly."

"Chto za khuynya! I don't understand why you agreed to the armistice in the first place. We should have blown Seneca into space dust."

"Alexis, please mind your mouth. Cursing in Russian is still cursing."

"I certainly hope so. And my name is Alex."

She gritted her teeth in frustration, inhaling a deep breath to swallow her initial response. "'I' did not agree to the armistice—you know better. The Prime Minister and the Assembly did, because the simple fact is we were taking too many losses. It was against Alliance interests to get into a long and messy quagmire."

"A 'quagmire'? Is that what you call them murdering Dad? That's cold, Mom, even for you."

"Don't you dare say such a thing. Your father died a hero."

"So everyone keeps telling me. You know what? He's still dead. They should be, too."

Yes they should be. But David wouldn't want—wouldn't have wanted—it. "I'm afraid their fate isn't up to me. But one thing which is up to me is your punishment. You are on home restriction until such time as I feel you've learned to be responsible. You can go to school and activities I have approved beforehand. Otherwise, the security system will not allow you to leave. If you get into trouble while at school, you will be holoing your studies for the foreseeable future."

"I'll just hack it."

"Young lady, I have people working for me who are far better hackers than you. You will not."

Alexis shrugged, threw her feet up on the dash and crossed her arms over her chest. "Right. Absolutely. You've got me."

Naturally, she had hacked the security system within the week; the tougher encryption subsequently added, two weeks later. And after that.....

She gave the Minister a tight, formal expression. "Well, she hasn't taken my advice in quite some time. In any event, if you legitimately want her to accept the position, I'm afraid asking me to press the matter is not the tack you want to take. I think it best if you reached out to her directly."

He exhaled in a suggestion of weary acceptance and stood. She stood with him and accepted his outstretched hand.

"Thank you for your time, Admiral, and your frankness. I'll likely do that."

"Certainly, Minister. My door is always open." It was a bald-faced lie, but one she had uttered at countless dinner parties and conferences, and she delivered it as smoothly as any greeting.

Once he had departed, she drifted to the window. Fall came early here, and the sun had already begun its descent into the waters.

Perhaps her suggestion to the Minister hadn't been such a good idea after all. *Please, Alexis, don't tell the man to fuck off.*

She thought on it a minute, then turned on a heel and went down the hall to Richard's office.

A checkerboard of screens decorated his desktop surface and an aural hovered in front of his right eye. When she walked in he shut off the aural and smiled, though it was a weak attempt. "What's up?"

She didn't respond immediately, instead pacing halfway across the room, hands clasped behind her back, before stopping to look at him. "You took Alexis back to the spaceport the other day, right?"

"Yeah, I caught her on her way out. Why?"

"Did she by chance say anything about the Deep Space Exploration offer?"

He huffed a brief laugh. "Not anything you want to hear."

Her eyes squeezed shut in a grimace. "Excellent. The Minister just left my office. He's rather eager—disturbingly so, actually—for her to accept the post. I told him he should contact her, but now I'm not convinced it was the correct thing to do."

He gave her an understanding smile, this one genuine. "Well, I'm not sure it really matters. She left Earth yesterday morning."

She sighed softly. "Of course she did. Listen, there's something else. Karolyn said he was receiving political pressure to name Alexis to the post. I don't suppose you've heard any chatter about that?"

"Miriam, I'm shocked you would imply we spy on domestic political affairs."

"No you're not."

"Ha...no, I'm not. To answer your question, not a peep."

"Damn. I know you're underwater right now with the Summit, but if you get a few minutes could you dig around a little? It bothers me that politicians are meddling in her affairs without my—"

"Approval?"

"*Knowledge.*"

His hands rose in surrender. "Okay, I'll look into it. It may take a few days."

"Thanks, Richard. I'll let you get back to work. Try to get some rest though—you know next week is going to be worse."

Despite Miriam's advice, it was almost twenty-two hundred before Richard walked in the door to his home in the foothills above Lake Sammamish.

Intelligence agents were now integrated into the official Alliance delegation to the Summit, the convention center staff, invited guests and rather voluminous press covering the event. By Monday morning on Atlantis (which for added fun was around three in the morning in Seattle) all his assets would be in place, and everything they saw, touched and interacted with fed to his office via an instantaneous quantum entanglement communication network.

He was met at the door by a kiss and a tumbler of whiskey.

He happily accepted the kiss but looked askance at the whiskey. "Will, I have to be back at the office in seven hours."

"And thus you need to relax and unwind in the most efficient manner possible." Will nudged him toward the living room while still holding out the glass. He sighed, felt a small percentage of the stress escape with the breath, and acceded to both the nudge and the glass.

He sank into the couch, grateful—not for the first time—for a home which was truly a refuge from the madness. The glass at his lips, he took a long sip and relished the smooth fire of the whiskey as it scorched down his throat. "You know, I could get used to this 'manservant tending to my every need' routine."

"Well, don't." Will chuckled while he dimmed the lights and crossed the room to settle onto the couch beside him. "My next project starts in three weeks, though at least it's a bit closer, on Demeter. Building a performing arts center, if you can believe it. But you can live the dream until then if you like."

"I like...." He made an effort to smile and rub Will's shoulder, but his head fell back against the cushion and the smile gave way to a groan. The Summit hadn't even started yet and he was already ready to tear his hair out. Although to be fair, much of the stress of the day had resulted from the ridiculous volume of bureaucracy involved in placing agents inside the official delegation. One of the best things about intelligence work was the lack of bureaucracy—but not this time. It paled in comparison solely to the sheer politics involved in placing agents in the press unit.

He tried again to push the hassles to the back of his mind. *Refuge.* "I absolutely believe it. Demeter fancies itself the next Romane, some kind of mecca of wealth and refined luxury or other. But hey, it's close enough you'll be able to come home most weekends, right?"

"Most, hopefully." Will rubbed his chin with his fingertips, which usually meant he was bothered by something.

Richard straightened up a little. "I'm sorry work happens to suck at the exact moment you're home and have actual free time. If I could do anything to change it, I would."

Will shook his head. "No, I know. I mean I understand. This is life, and we have all of it to be together. It's...listen, why don't you just *go* to Atlantis? It'd be easier than trying to control the circus from your office eighteen hours a day, and hey, at least you'd get a little sun."

He stared out the windows lining the opposite wall, comforted by the knowledge there was a beautiful view out there in the darkness. "Because if the EASC Naval Intelligence Liaison shows up at the Summit then someone might think we were engaging in covert spying activities—and we wouldn't want that."

"Yes, and otherwise they'll never suspect any such thing."

"Oh, certainly not." He sighed and took another sip of the whiskey. Will had been right; it was helping. "It's the game we play with our adversary. Both sides pretend to be upstanding, sincere and earnest. Both sides secretly try to undermine the other at every opportunity. The status quo continues."

"*Or* you could simply say 'to Hell with the whole damn thing' and go have a drink together." At Richard's incredulous glance, he shrugged. "Look. Earth controls sixty-seven worlds, already more than they can manage. The Senecan Federation wanted independence and they got it. They're thriving and successful and have a lot to offer. I for one would jump at the chance to work on several of the projects they're pursuing. But I can't, because I'm from Earth—"

"—and because you're married to me."

"Which is a price I'll gladly pay every day for the rest of my life." He squeezed Richard's hand to emphasize the point, then leaned forward to rest his forearms on his knees. "I'm merely saying we don't need to keep carrying around all this animosity. The war ended twenty-two years ago."

"Twenty-two years is the blink of an eye for the people involved. Some wounds don't heal so quickly."

"You're talking about Miriam, and Alex."

He cast his gaze to the ceiling. "Without a doubt. And thousands, Hell, millions of others…I don't know, maybe I'm talking about me, too. I mean, I lost my best friend, and several damn good ones. I don't consider myself as walking around bearing a grudge, but if faced with the option, I'm not sure I'm ready to be friends with the Senecans."

Will's nod bore conviction. "I get that, I do. My uncle died in the war. He was a good man, and my aunt has never gotten over it. And I hate I never had the chance to know David." He paused, the telltale twitch of his mouth a hint he was pondering whether to continue. "But I still think everyone might benefit if we found a way to put aside the past and move on."

Richard closed his eyes, but there was a smile on his lips. Will would have made an even better diplomat than he did a construction project manager…but it was only a sign of how much he cared. He laughed and finished off the glass of whiskey. "Except me—I'd be out of a job."

Will leaned in closer. "That's fine. I'll support you, and you can be *my* manservant."

7

SCYTHIA
EARTH ALLIANCE COLONY

Alex exited the levtram and crossed the elevated terrace at a hurried, clipped pace. She made a passing attempt at reminding herself she wasn't technically beholden to a schedule, but soon abandoned the effort. This stop on Scythia represented a detour, in time if not so much in location, and she intended to treat it as such.

The request for an in-person meeting had been waiting on her when she woke up this morning. She almost declined, but in truth she was right *there*. Her planned route took her less than a hundred parsecs north of Scythia's system. It still meant a delay of several hours in reaching her ultimate destination, but Astral Materials had proved a lucrative client. It would be folly to snub them.

Her gaze lingered on the glittering teal waters which stretched beyond the terrace as she neared the Astral offices. The gentle but dramatic tides intruded as much as eight hundred meters inland at their high point. This had led settlers to situate the coastal city largely on a series of elevated platforms, thus allowing them to enjoy the scenic and fertile environment free of constant water damage and its insidious, corrosive effects. The platforms eventually met the sloping coastal plain, and the city continued to spread across drier land; the prime real estate was above the sea, however.

The glass doors of the mid-rise building opened on her approach. It wasn't her first visit, and she proceeded directly up to the Astral Materials executive suite on the 5th floor.

Isas Onishi greeted her as she entered, presumably having been alerted to her arrival. "Ms. Solovy, it's a pleasure as always. Shall we go to my office?"

A pleasure so long as she continued to make him money, anyway. She shook his hand brusquely and encouraged the movement toward his office. "Yes, please. I'm afraid I don't have long."

"I understand. You're a busy woman, as I am a busy man."

She didn't hold out for an invitation to drop into one of the chairs facing his desk. Floor-to-ceiling windows spanning two of the four walls provided a stunning view of the ocean and evoked a sensation of floating. Onishi was doing very well for himself.

"Your Lacertae discovery continues to impress, Ms. Solovy. It's going to help us build the safest, most durable space stations in the galaxy."

"Glad to be of service." *The earnings bought me a new lattice layer for the* Siyane, *three top-of-the-line scanners and a supply of long-range probes, so quite glad.* "What can I do for you?"

He settled into his chair opposite her. "I'm giving you first refusal rights on a new contract. Spectrum surveys of M11 have identified an interesting L red dwarf hosting four planetoids. The system shows strong spectral lines of a magnesium/chromium isotope, one which should be paramagnetic. We need someone to confirm the findings and determine if, as we hope, the planetoids contain harvestable concentrations of the metal."

"Interesting. What's the timetable?"

"That's why I was glad to learn you were in the area—you'd need to get out there in the next couple of days. We're not the only ones in possession of the survey data, and both Palaimo Metallurgy and Surno Materials are doubtless planning their own expeditions as we speak. If we want discovery privileges, we have to move fast."

Alex groaned inwardly. M11 was in the *other* direction from Metis, well to the northwest past Arcadia. "Fee?"

"Forty thousand credits up front and irrespective of your findings, ⊃20,000 on proof of harvestable material and another ⊃40,000 if we succeed in claiming the system."

Her mind leapt to what the proceeds could translate into: a more efficient power allocation optimizer for the *Siyane* and two new ware customizations for her eVi she'd been researching, for starters, with forty thousand or so left over for savings and whims. Kennedy kept mentioning them taking a vacation to some new resort on Atlantis....

But she had her own plans. The whole point of being a free-lance scout, and an unusually successful one, was the freedom to set her own schedule. To go where she wanted when she wanted. To serve no boss and owe no obligations outside negotiated contracts.

And she wanted to go to Metis. She wanted a new mystery to unravel.

She managed to look regretful. "I'm sorry, Mr. Onishi. I'm booked for the next month."

He regarded her from across the desk as his fingertips drummed on its surface. Five seconds ticked by…he dipped his chin. "And if I tack on an additional twenty percent to the fee?"

Her lips pursed, buying herself a breath to reconsider. "That's very generous of you, and I appreciate the vote of confidence. Unfortunately, there's simply no way for me to rearrange my schedule."

Onishi threw his arms in the air and slid his chair back. "I shouldn't be surprised you're booked up. I suppose I'll have to engage someone else, then, as time really is of the essence. Terrence Macolly perhaps. He's submitted competitive bids on several recent contracts."

She smirked as she stood. "If you're willing to accept a sloppy investigation and unreliable data, go right ahead. If you want it done in a professional manner, hire Santino Dominguez instead."

"He's even pricier than you are."

"True, but he gets results." She gave Onishi a half-smile. "Don't tell him I said so, though."

"My lips are sealed." He walked her to the door of the suite, still courteous despite her rejection.

She accepted his outstretched his hand again; no reason to alienate a well-paying client. "Please let me know when another opportunity arises. Hopefully my schedule will be more accommodating in the future."

"I'll do so, Ms. Solovy. Safe travels to you."

R

Alex stared at the billboard hovering above the glass doors.

She'd been headed for the exit with single-minded purpose when the colorful holo brought her to an abrupt halt and demanded her undivided attention. It accomplished this feat by blasting a promo for a 'special acoustic performance' by Ethan Tollis at the Seaspray Amphitheatre on the adjacent platform.

Tonight.

Damn Kennedy for seeding her subconscious with thoughts of Ethan the other day. She scowled at the promo, eyes narrowed, until it cycled to the next ad, and tried to pretend she wasn't checking the local time.

Seven hours from now. Of course if she were to stay for the show, it would be far longer than seven hours before she was again en route. More like tomorrow...afternoon.

It was as if the gods themselves were conspiring to entice her away from Metis. First the Deep Space Exploration job offer, then the Astral Materials contract and now *this.* A rather vivid image of what staying promised to bring flared in her mind—a final, deliciously prurient temptation.

But she would not be deterred. She squared her shoulders in a show of defiance, exhaled...and turned away from the billboard. By the time she hit the terrace, she had resumed her hurried, clipped pace. She had a nebula to explore.

SENECA
CAVARE

Caleb had gotten as far as the hallway to his apartment when the alert flashed in his eVi. As soon as he saw the header he opened the file.

> **Cavare Police Department**
> **Harassment Report: 1628 - 02.09.2322**
> **Complainant:** *Dr. Jesse Valente*
> **Suspect:** *Mr. Francis Gerod*

Summary: Complainant stated that Mr. Gerod, a coworker at Hemiska Research, physically assaulted her this evening as she was leaving work.

According to her statement, she and Mr. Gerod had a heated disagreement during a staff meeting. He followed her out of the building, and when she refused to converse with him he yanked her arm roughly. She escaped his grip, but he pursued her to her vehicle and slammed the vehicle door shut before she could climb in, nearly crushing her hand. She retrieved a stunner from her bag and pointed it at him until he backed away, at which point she departed.

Complainant displays bruises on her left forearm (visuals attached) consistent with a handprint. She stated that she did not initially report the altercation because she "prefers to handle problems on her own." She reconsidered after realizing if Mr. Gerod came to her home, he posed a threat to her four-year-old twins.

Complainant doesn't wish to file charges at this time, but wanted to ensure there was an official record of the incident.

Status: Officers interviewed Francis Gerod at 1840 tonight. He admitted to having an "unpleasant encounter" with Complainant but denied he intended to harm her physically. He claimed he was upset about problems at work, but once he cooled off he recognized he had overreacted.

Mr. Gerod received a warning and was informed a second incident would result in arrest and formal charges.

The alert had been sent due to a flag Caleb maintained in the Senecan security network. It was one of many he'd placed over the last fifteen years. Some were on people he'd investigated in the past, individuals he suspected were dirty but who hadn't yet made enough of a mistake to get caught. Those flags were designed to alert him when that mistake occurred. Others were on people he cared about—or had once cared about, as was the case here—and were designed to warn him if they might be in trouble.

Jesse wouldn't want him protecting her. As she had admitted in the police statement, she took care of her own problems. But he hadn't asked her permission.

Caleb went inside his apartment long enough to grab a nano-bot injection to speed the metabolizing of the alcohol in his bloodstream. The evening at the bar with Noah had been entertaining, but he needed to be sober when he reached Francis Gerod.

⁂

Gerod lived in a townhouse on the outskirts of the Tellica University campus. The man's file indicated his wife and two young children lived there as well. In deference to the children, Caleb didn't intend to break down the door...unless it became necessary.

Twenty minutes after he arrived and set up surveillance across the street, Gerod exited his townhouse and headed for the community parking lot behind the building. He was alone.

Caleb followed.

Though night had fallen in full, it wasn't inordinately late. Nevertheless, the streets were sparsely populated, a symptom of the family-friendly nature of the neighborhood. He slipped unnoticed into the lot and closed on Gerod as he approached his vehicle.

He had the man locked in an armbar and shoved into the vehicle's frame before the man knew he was there.

"What—"

Caleb used his body to keep Gerod pinned against the frame while he clasped a hand over the man's mouth. "You're going to want to not scream, or the arm that will then be broken will be the least of your concerns. Are we clear?"

Gerod nodded haphazardly. Caleb couldn't see the man's eyes, but he could feel the terror in his quivering limbs. He waited two seconds then withdrew his hand slightly.

"Wha-what do you want? I don't have any valuables with me!"

"I'm not here to rob you. I'm here to kill you. Unless—" his palm slammed back onto the man's mouth to stifle the cry "—unless you make me a promise and keep it for the rest of your life." He paused to let the information sink in. "Are you ready to hear what the promise is?"

Another wild nod.

His lips hovered at the man's ear. "You will never lay another finger on Jesse Valente. You will never threaten or in any way whatsoever cause harm to her or her family. You will be polite and respectful to her at all times. When you next see her, you will apologize for your rude behavior and assure her you bear no ill feelings toward her."

Gerod squirmed in agitation. He stood no chance of escaping Caleb's grasp, but he seemed to be protesting in some manner.

Caleb loosened his hand but didn't completely remove it. "I sincerely hope you're not planning on refusing to give this promise."

Spittle landed on his palm as Gerod began sputtering out a response. "N-no. I promise—I swear. It's just I don't know if I'll see her again so I can apologize. You see, I got a new job offer tonight. I sent my resignation to Hemiska a few minutes ago. So it all worked out! I'm not even mad at her anymore." His words increasingly ran together in a fevered outburst. "I-I'm thankful, really. That business at the office forced me to finally make the decision to leave it behind. But I would never hurt her. I was angry and scared I was going to get fired. But she's a nice woman. A little intimidating, honestly—but I respect her." He sucked in a frayed breath. "Please don't kill me."

Unseen from his position behind Gerod, Caleb rolled his eyes at the sky but made certain his voice remained suitably frightening. "I told you what you have to do in order to live."

"But I—"

"If you won't see her again, you will send her a nice, extended, groveling apology by the end of the day tomorrow. If you don't, I'll know." It would require a bit of hacking on his part, but the active police investigation should make it easier. "The police are watching you, and now I'm watching you. Never, ever forget it."

"I won't." Gerod tried to twist back, but Caleb tightened his grip and held him fast. The man didn't need to get a look at his face. "I promise."

"I'll hold you to it." He released the man from the grapple and stepped away.

Gerod stumbled around and peered into the darkness, but Caleb was already gone.

Jesse Valente laughed as her husband massaged her shoulders and murmured something in her ear. The tender moment was soon interrupted by a blur of motion as two squealing mops of blond hair barreled into them then whirled out of the room.

Leaning against a tree across the street, Caleb smiled, genuinely glad to see her happy. He mentally ticked off the items on his list and confirmed he'd checked everything. Dr. and Dr. Valente had a robust security system installed on the grounds and in their home—so robust he'd almost tripped one of the proximity sensors during his perimeter survey.

Satisfied, he departed for his apartment for the second time that night.

He had found one weakness in the security system, a gap in the sensors in the left rear of the property. Several trees had grown wide enough there that an intruder could climb up and reasonably leap onto the roof without setting off any alarms. When he got home he'd access the police database and add an instruction for a security consultant to be sent out to the residence, including a note to pay particular attention to the left rear area. While he was in the network, he'd also add a new flag for Francis Gerod.

Then he'd get some sleep, because, comm scrambler now acquired, he'd be leaving for Metis in the morning.

8

O livia Montegreu woke to the sensation of calloused fingertips dancing along her hip.

She stretched and rolled over, to be greeted with the smiling face of...she had never asked his name. Not as if it mattered. He was handsome and well-packaged and enthusiastic and couldn't be older than twenty-five.

He leaned over to kiss her, but she wound a hand into his hair and urged him lower instead. "Be a good boy and finish what you started."

He grinned as he kissed down her lean, smooth stomach, wasting little time in reaching his destination.

She closed her eyes and let her head fall to the pillow. *What a fabulous way to start the day....*

When she had finished, she nudged him off the bed with her toes. "That was lovely. You'll find your clothes laundered and folded in the entryway. The receptionist in the lobby will call you a cab if you need one."

He stood, nonchalantly wiping the excess moisture from his lips. "Can I see you again?"

She was already on the way to the shower and didn't bother to turn around. "Oh, I doubt it."

Forty minutes later she was seated at her desk, legs crossed elegantly beneath the burnished copper surface. A black silk sarong contrasted against her pale blond hair combed straight to drape down her back. It was all meticulously crafted to project the desired image.

She regarded the nondescript man standing across the desk from her with the slightest tilt of her head.

"Kill her."

He nodded, unsurprised. "Yes, ma'am. Should I pin the blame on anyone in particular? Maybe Trenton's group?"

"No. I want everyone to know this one came from me."

"Understood, ma'am. I'll inform you once it's done."

"No need; I assume you are capable enough. Simply *do* it."

The man's throat worked, his composure faltering. "Of course, Ms. Montegreu. Is there anything else?"

"I hope not. Go." She flicked a perfectly manicured hand in the direction of the exit. He spun on his heel and hurried toward the door.

She rolled her eyes in irritation, but it was for show. Gesson was a competent enforcer, a crafty overseer and most importantly, not overly ambitious. On uncovering evidence the woman in charge of managing new chimeral distribution was skimming off the top, he had first confirmed the evidence then reported it directly to her. She was confident he would handle disposing of the embezzler with similar efficiency.

Once he had departed, she carried her hot tea over to the windows to inspect the morning.

New Babel's mornings looked suspiciously like its nights, on account of its distant blue dwarf sun and the heavy cloud of dust and gases from the surrounding nebula. It was hardly the most hospitable of planets, but it had two things going for it: an abundance of heavy metals which made industrial construction cheap and fast, and a natural barrier via the nebula against both electronic surveillance and warfare.

As such, it had become a home base for a wide swath of criminal organizations and black market entrepreneurs. There was no government to speak of and even less regulation; the strongest organizations built what they needed when and where they needed it.

The result was a chaotic architecture of high-rises, slums, factories, markets and red-light clusters...well, much of what occurred on the streets of New Babel would qualify as 'red-light' on other worlds. Here it took on a whole new meaning.

Her office stood in stark contrast to the dark, grimy, overcrowded city beneath it—quite deliberately so. The entire penthouse suite was spacious, minimally adorned and spotless. A décor of natural marble floors, white mahogany furnishings and copper and glass complements served as a declaration to all who entered that she existed above and apart from the masses below. Like her attire, appearance and bearing, it projected only and entirely what she desired to convey: refinement, prestige, exceptionality. But above all, *power*.

A soft chime in her ear reminded her it was time for the call. She stepped into the triple-shielded, soundproof QEC room hidden behind the visually seamless right wall of her office. Ten seconds later a holo shimmered into existence in front of her.

It revealed a man of indeterminate age, handsome and clean-cut but average in every way—medium skin tone, medium brown hair, medium height, medium build.

That is, until he looked up and met her gaze. Piercing, sea-green eyes hinted at intelligence and cunning, along with an indefinable spark which hinted at something else altogether. The overall effect was to transform what had been an ordinary man into one who radiated dynamism, charisma and authority.

She smiled darkly. "Marcus, it's good to see you again."

He raised an eyebrow in mock appreciation. "And you, Olivia. May I say you are even more beautiful than the last time we talked."

"You may say it, but you need to work on your sincerity a bit."

He shrugged. "It's a finite resource, and I need to save it for the constituents. What's the status?"

"We received the materials day before yesterday. They're stored in a secure location until it's time to deploy them. The team has been selected, every member screened by me, and is leaving tomorrow to train on Cosenti. The lead expects to have the final details worked out by late next week."

"Traceability?"

"Ah, Marcus, always concerned first and foremost with covering your own ass—I know, I know, your ass must be covered for later phases to work. I get it. To you? None. To me? Virtually none. The only conceivable link is the lead, and his cover is so deep it will take Senecan Intel months to begin to peel back the layers in the highly unlikely event he's identified."

"Will he break under coercion?"

"It won't be an issue."

The muscles in his jaw flexed. "Oh, really?"

"Oh, *really*. I have it covered. Regardless, he and the rest of the team know nothing of you. No one save me knows anything of you. That was the agreement, and I honor my agreements."

"True…" a hand rose to knead at his chin "…you *are* the sole link to me."

She *tsked* him reproachfully. "If you try to kill me, you will not succeed."

"Oh, I'm sure. And I won't need to try, because you are nothing if not power-hungry, and this little project of ours will bring you more power than you ever dreamed of."

"I can dream of a lot."

"And you shall have it all—so long as you make certain Palluda goes down cleanly."

She rolled her eyes in irritation, and this time meant it. "Marcus, who is the most dangerous, most effective, most Machiavellian criminal magnate in settled space?"

"That would be you, my dear."

"Correct. Don't question my methods, don't question my judgment—and most of all don't question my competency—and we will continue to get along just fine."

His chin dipped in acquiescence. "I have been properly chastised. We'll talk again after Atlantis."

ATLANTIS
INDEPENDENT COLONY

Jaron Nythal stepped out onto the rooftop landing pad and felt a smile grow on his lips. A warm breeze, salty air and bright yellow sun welcomed him like the arms of a beautiful woman. He was going to enjoy this trip.

He pulled his jacket off, draped it over a shoulder and strolled across the pad toward the railing at the edge of the roof while the rest of the Senecan delegation disembarked and saw to the luggage and cargo. Until the Director arrived on Sunday evening he was in charge of the delegation, which meant someone else would get his luggage to his room.

He rolled his shoulders to work out the kinks. The transport was fast and secure, but it was still a government vessel and nineteen hours was a *long* time.

His smile only widened as he reached the edge and the splendor of Atlantis spread out beneath him. A tiny planet covered wholly in water, it should have lain unnoticed and undeveloped. But the pleasant temperatures and calm weather of its equatorial region had caught the eye and imagination of a developer tycoon who found himself idle after many successful ventures and with money to burn.

The outcome was a fantasy retreat unlike any other in settled space. Winding pathways suspended a mere two meters over the crystal blue water connected islands of condos, gardens, golf courses and beaches. Only small shuttles and personal vehicles were allowed in the airspace stretching four hundred meters above the waters to allow for a variety of recreational activities, from sky gliding to paracruises and wave skimming.

Casinos, pleasure houses and vacation resorts competed with— or was it complemented?—state-of-the-art conference and convention facilities. Taking advantage of its unaffiliated status and convenient location nearly equidistant between Earth and Seneca, within ten years of opening the first hotel Atlantis had become the most popular destination in the galaxy for both corporate and government conventions.

The breeze began to wash away the grime of travel; he rolled his sleeves above his elbows to hasten the effect. He intended to make every effort to find plenty of time around the preparations and even the Summit itself to enjoy the finer pleasures Atlantis had to offer. He already had a series of high-credit escorts lined up for the room at night—more than one on several nights—but not all of Atlantis' offerings could be indulged in from a hotel room.

The flash of red at the corner of his peripheral vision banished the train of thought and brought a dark scowl to his face. And then there was *that*.

He supplied the decryption code, scanned the message and deleted it almost as soon as it had arrived. It contained suitably cryptic phrasing, but the point came through clear enough.

Payment had been received. Final preparations were underway. The assignment would be completed at the time and in the manner the other party deemed most efficient. If all went well, Jaron would never know the man (or woman) had ever been at the Summit. That is, except for the irrefutable evidence thereof they would leave in their wake.

He'd return to Seneca a richer man, though the new funds paled in comparison to the wealth he expected to soon follow. Yessiree...he should be able to set his wife and kids up in one of the swank new townhomes in the Pinciana neighborhood, with enough left over for a private condo retreat for himself downtown. It was a long way from his parents' tiny apartment tucked behind their 'herb' shop shouting distance from the *kasō shakai*, the underworld slums the rest of Cavare pretended didn't exist. A long way indeed.

Of course if all didn't go well, he'd be facing forty-years-to-life in prison at best, permanent disappearance into the black hole of a covert intelligence detention facility at worst. It wasn't the first high-stakes risk he had taken in his life…but it certainly carried the greatest consequences, whether win or lose.

The scowl lingered as he yanked his sunglasses off and looked around for his secretary. She tromped outside the transport cargo hull, arms flailing about to point at crates of equipment while she issued orders to the staff.

He tossed his jacket into her chest and headed for the lift. "I'll be in the Prep Room until dinner. Be a dear and bring me a drink, one of those strong tropical concoctions." He paused mid-step, considered the message again and glanced over his shoulder.

"On second thought, go ahead and make it a double."

Matei Uttara departed the commercial transport amidst a throng of passengers. It wasn't difficult to blend in with the diverse array of tourists and businessmen and women. Some were here for networking, some for relaxation, others for assorted pleasures of a daring but not truly dangerous variety. He imagined some were here for all three.

His attire was nondescript, his hair cut to the chin and dulled to a dirty brown beneath a summer cap common on the resort world. His movements were casual, his bearing relaxed as he let himself be carried along by the crowd of travelers. His pace and gait varied at random intervals such that even the best pattern-recognition ware would be unable to spot anything anomalous.

He passed among giggling children accompanying their parents to the family resorts and young people already drunk on hormones and synthetic liquor. He surrounded himself with other visitors as he made his way to the levtrams and nonchalantly snuck in the last seat of a full tram headed in the correct direction.

As he exited the tram an attractive but intoxicated woman bumped into him. She stumbled, grabbed onto his arm and smiled lopsidedly up at him. He returned the smile while he reached underneath her hairline and pinched a nerve behind her ear. As her limbs relaxed he nudged her to send her momentum back toward her companions. He faded away into the crowd as one of them complained he wasn't going to carry her all the way to the condo.

The hotel was busy but not so thick with people as the transport station. He chose a family of five and trailed them through the lobby to the front desk, where he checked in under an invented identity using an untraceable credit account.

His room was a modest affair on a middle level of the hotel adjacent to the conference center hosting the Trade Summit. The conference center had already heightened their security, and the security at the hotel was sure to soon become tighter than pleased him. But by staying here he could avoid transport complications which had foiled less talented men than he; also, it provided him ready access to staff corridors and maintenance shafts, should the need arise.

He settled in with a decent steak dinner from room service, then sat cross-legged on the bed and spread the blueprints of the conference center and hotel in the air around him. They rotated in a slow circle as he studied them.

Periodically he reached up and paused the flow to study one more closely. He intended to know the location of each and every one of the staff corridors and maintenance shafts throughout the complex.

He planned to get a tangible feel for the layout in the morning, when the area would still be dominated by tourists rather than Summit guests. The first two days of the Summit he would attend as a credentialed reporter representing the small but growing trade exazine *Celestial Industrials Weekly*, one of dozens of vultures hovering on the periphery of the proceedings and stalking the halls. He would schmooze and linger and talk to people, but not to any one person for so long as to make an impression.

At the end of the second day, his identity and tactics shifted. On the third and final day of the Summit, he would complete the job he had been engaged to do, again slip into the crowd, and vanish.

9

A lex opened her eyes to the best surprise.

The brilliant red and pink glow of the Carina Nebula filled the wide viewport above her bed. The vivid colors shone with a dazzling splendor only nature could create. She wound her hands behind her head and settled back onto the pillow to drink in the sight.

It was good practice to drop out of superluminal speeds for a few minutes at least once a day to diffuse the particle buildup. She spoiled herself by arranging it so the deceleration occurred just before she routinely woke up, and was often treated to lovely vistas as a result—but few so spectacular as this one.

There were no colonized worlds in the vicinity due to the imminent (any time in the next five hundred or so years) supernova of Eta Carinae. As such, one rarely had cause to linger so near to Carina. What she knew to be over a million stars clumped into multiple open clusters to glitter crisp and bright through the nebular cloud. She grinned, captivated, and watched until the sLume drive re-engaged and the stars blurred away beyond the bubble wall.

With a contented sigh she crawled out of bed and splashed water on her face. She slipped on an athletic tank and shorts, twisting her hair up in a knot on the way up the circular stairwell to the main deck. After a brief check of the cockpit to make sure nothing unusual had occurred overnight and she remained on course, she grabbed a water, put on Brahms' *Academic Festival Overture* and hit the treadmill.

Staying in shape while spending most of her days on a ship with under two hundred square meters of living space wasn't easy. Prenatal genetic tuning for physical hardiness and agility—a gift from her parents by way of the Alliance Armed Forces—made it easier to be sure, but even the best genetic enhancements didn't replace simple physical activity.

Nearly a quarter of the port wall was taken up by a treadmill, pull-up bar, pulley-based weight machine and pilates pad. It wasn't mountain hikes or barefoot beach runs, but it mostly got the job done.

Then she activated a full-sensory overlay of Discovery Park at sunset, and it effectively *became* a barefoot beach run. Almost.

A heavy sheen of sweat coated her skin by the time she slowed the treadmill to a stop, lowered the music to a pleasant background level and headed downstairs to shower.

One could make a reasonable case for the utility of every item on the main deck. But there was simply no denying the truth that the lower deck represented pure personal extravagance. She didn't feel the slightest bit contrite about it either; it was her money and her ship.

Still, she occasionally had to giggle in wicked delight at the full waterfall shower, oversized garden tub, cushy lounge chair and queen-sized bed with a view of the stars. Her own personal retreat, tucked into the void of space.

She sat at the kitchen-area table and munched on a banana and peanut-butter toast while she checked her overnight communications.

First up was a cool note from her mother letting her know she would be going to St. Petersburg to attend a conference in a few days, and would tell her grandfather 'hello' for her.

She ignored the tone of the message and smiled to herself. She had always rather liked her grandfather. He was simple and down-to-earth in a way few people were these days. Grumpy as all hell, but in a loveable way. A brief pang of guilt struck when she realized it had been more than four years since she had seen him. She really should try to rectify the lapse once she returned to Earth.

She was about to delete the message when she noticed it included an attachment. Puzzled, she opened it, only to find a sterile listing of Alliance command postings for the previous month. A frown tugged her mouth downward as she scanned down it while wondering if her mother had attached it in error—except that was an absurd notion, because her mother didn't make mistakes.

The name leapt off the list as if it were scripted in meter-high fluorescent neon colors.

EAS Juno: Lieutenant Colonel Malcolm Jenner

She sank back in the chair, chuckling a little at the irony. He had left her because she spent too much time in space, and now he was serving in space. God, he must be miserable. He had never been able to grasp why she loved it so much, no matter how many times she had tried to explain it, had tried to show him what a wonder the stars were.

Maybe she should send him a brief message wishing him luck…but some wounds were best left untouched, the better to fade away. In truth, he hadn't left because she spent too much time in space—he had left because he believed she didn't love him enough to spend *less* time in space and away from him. That wasn't the way she had viewed the issue, but in declaring such he had made her realize it didn't much matter, because the relationship was doomed to failure. He would never *understand*.

She didn't know what her mother imagined she was accomplishing by sending the attachment. Whatever. She munched on her toast for a moment, thoughts adrift in memories, before straightening up and forcing herself to refocus on the task at hand.

Her brow crinkled up in bewilderment at the next message. It contained a personal note from the Minister for Extra-Solar Development asking her to reconsider the Deep Space Exploration position, increasing the offered salary by twenty percent and offering to meet with her this week to discuss her needs.

Okay, seriously?

A somewhat disbelieving laugh escaped her lips. She didn't deny she felt flattered at the special attention; she had a great deal of confidence in her abilities, and her record spoke for itself, but *damn*.

She chewed on her bottom lip and pondered what in the hell might be the reason behind the lavish adulation. She didn't care for mysteries. Well, it would be more accurate to say she didn't care for mysteries she couldn't solve…but perhaps this mystery could be solved merely by the application of the universal law that politicians were *svilochnaya peshka*. Mollified by the thought, she shrugged and sent back a gracious decline.

The only other message of value came from Kennedy. It detailed her enchanting dinner with the eco-dev executive and proclaimed she was absolutely positively head-over-heels in love. This guy was the one. No doubt about it.

"What is this, the third 'true love' this year?" The woman went through men like most people went through flower arrangements. She responded with as much, then put away her plate and walked over to the data center.

The heart of the main deck consisted of a long table, rectangular except for rounded edges. Along the starboard wall were a set of embedded screens, a small desk and a workbench. A waist-high holo control panel, linked to both the screens and the table, spanned the gap at the cockpit-facing end. A plain cylinder twenty centimeters in diameter hung suspended from the ceiling to hover a meter and a half above the length of the table.

Both the cylinder and the surface of the table were made of a platinum-germanium based n-alloy. The inert, nonreactive platinum provided an ideal tableau upon which to display the data transmitted flawlessly through the zero-dispersive, semi-conductive and highly refractive germanium.

A series of commands entered in the control panel rendered a full-spectrum image of Metis above the center of the table. The EM bands gleamed in the traditional rainbow hues but stretched far beyond the range of visible light to cover the spectrum.

She reached into the display. One by one she pulled out each band and flicked it to the side, until eight discrete images bordered the center one. She couldn't help but smile; the images now resembled nothing so much as an old-fashioned painter's palette. Fitting, as to her it was pure art.

She leaned against the workbench behind her and let her eyes drift across the palette. It was time to get serious about this expedition.

10

***

Matei Uttara moved with deliberate aimlessness through the milling guests in the foyer of the ballroom. Dimmed lighting, standard protocol for dinner parties across millennia, gave him some measure of freedom in his movements. He took care not to abuse the privilege.

The current conditions—here, now, for the next seven to eleven minutes—most closely mimicked the environment he expected to encounter the following evening. Politicians, businessmen and press engaged in polite, formal mingling, everyone save the intelligence agents concerned solely with the impression they created.

Beyond the threshold eighteen dinner tables were arranged with careful precision, separated by a wide aisle cutting down the center. The aisle served as a clear demarcation of the factions present: Alliance to the left, Federation to the right. Even the corporate representatives and media were required to declare their allegiance for all to see.

The road to peace had quite a few more steps to be trod. Yet cracks in the symbolic wall were manifesting, courtesy of several brave souls among the attendees.

Political boundaries leaked like a sieve when it came to popular culture, but visible differences still existed between Alliance and Federation citizens. The inhabitants of Earth and the First Wave colonies preferred rather baroque clothing as the current fashion; ensembles tended to include multiple hues or a vibrant, often garish accent piece. Those hailing from Senecan worlds favored dark, more muted attire or a single dominant hue. They saw it as befitting their self-proclaimed no-nonsense, pragmatic nature.

The distinctions faded as one moved up the political ladder of course, for political culture remained traditionalist everywhere. Still, you could see it in the details if you knew how to look. For instance, among the brave souls chipping at the wall was Thomas Kalnin, the Alliance Deputy Minister for Textiles, whose bright fuchsia lapel kerchief in an otherwise conservative suit contrasted with the subdued sepia pantsuit of his conversation partner Sara Triesti, head of the Senecan Trade Biomedics Subdivision.

The crowd thinned a bit as those on the periphery began to wander toward their seats. He took a half-pace back into the shadows to survey the room.

The set of wide doors in the foyer constituted the primary method of ingress and egress to the ballroom. Halfway down the left wall were two doors used by the service personnel; one led to the kitchen, the other to supply stations then a maintenance corridor. The area bustled with activity as wait staff hurried in and out making final preparations.

Far less obvious was an unmarked door in the right wall, just in front of the dais that stretched the width of the room. It led to an engineering hub for the various screens, lighting and invisible acoustic enhancements. A single technician staffed it during events. Beyond it lay another maintenance corridor—but this one opened into a labyrinth of passages which spread through the convention center. He expected this to be his exit.

Director Kouris entered alongside his adversary-turned-partner Minister Santiagar. They would not linger amid the patrons. Not this evening. He could feel the subtle shift in the atmosphere, the intangible pressure on the guests to disperse, to take their places as rapt observers of the performance to come.

He watched Kouris and Santiagar move across the ballroom toward the seats of honor, aides trailing them in parallel clusters. The 'aides' included three Alliance and two Senecan intelligence agents identified the day before along with a dozen of their brethren elsewhere in the delegations.

There was danger in waiting until the final event on the final night to act. He would not be granted a second opportunity. Nevertheless, his instructions were to let the Summit play out, to let this very public spectacle of diplomacy run its very public course.

The reason for the instructions had not been provided, but it wasn't his concern. He knew quite well his role. He was to be the Bishop's Opening in a galactic chess match.

His white pawn stopped to acquire a drink at the bar before heading to one of the tables. Mr. Nythal had proved adequate in furnishing necessary access and information regarding certain codes and procedures, but was of little additional use. Yet another matter which was not his concern.

His concern reached the head table, and the pressure on the crowd to alight became suffocating. He discreetly slid into the throng of reporters flowing to the media tables.

⁂

"Welcome everyone, to our banquet this evening. Friends, guests, press, we invite you to enjoy some of the famed Atlantis hospitality. Fellow Summit attendees, you've all worked extremely hard these last two days—it's time to relax for a couple of hours with a fine meal and finer wine."

Jaron was already relaxing with something considerably stronger than wine. He took a long sip of the Polaris Burst cocktail while shifting to the right in order for the waiter to place a spinach salad in front of him. The first of—was it five courses or six? He couldn't be bothered to recall.

The dynamic voice demanded he return his attention to the stage. He truly hoped the man wasn't intending on talking through every one of however many courses there were. The Alliance Minister was annoyingly charismatic, exhibiting an earnest demeanor which oozed sincerity and optimism. Director Kouris had spoken at the opening night's dinner. It had been a direct and businesslike speech, as was his manner—supremely competent and utterly uninspiring.

The Minister stepped out from behind the coral-veined marble podium. It served no real purpose beyond an oversized holder for a glass of water, but podiums were a tradition which for some reason never seemed to fade away. If the man needed the crutch of speech notes, they resided on his whisper. His easy, natural mannerisms made it unlikely, though.

"We won't hide from the truth of Earth and Seneca's troubled past. To ignore it would be to devalue the sacrifices of those who lost their lives in a war both sides believed to be just. But we cannot alter the past. We can only move forward."

Santiagar paused to sip his water, and Jaron leaned in to chuckle at the punch line of a joke being shared by his table companions. He hadn't caught the setup, but it hardly mattered.

Mid-level members of the Senecan delegation surrounded him at the white-clothed table. While the Summit was by most accounts going well, few on either side were ready to mix socially yet. From a hierarchical perspective, he surmised this was the 'auxiliary' table—occupied by those on the fringe of real power.

He swallowed a frown in the fiery burn of the cocktail. By right he should be seated next to the Director, but he had been bumped in favor of the Chairman of Elathan Pharmaceuticals, with the admonition that this *was* a trade summit, after all.

"For though we have our differences, we are all members of the human race. We share thousands of years of history. We share a heritage, for Earth is the motherland for each of us."

Jaron nearly choked on a bite of ciabatta and quickly covered his mouth with a napkin. The Minister's eyes shown with the fervor of a true believer. It was revolting.

"We are here this week to take our first steps on a new path. A path which will bring greater prosperity to the citizens of our galaxy, no matter the affiliation of the world they call home. Director Kouris shares my commitment to forging this new path, and I give him my deepest appreciation and thanks."

The arrival of the soup dish provided him an opportunity to surreptitiously glance over at the press contingent. He didn't know what he expected to see—a ninja in a mask with a saber strapped to his back? He hadn't the faintest idea what the man looked like, or even if it was a man at all. Perhaps he might at least spot a steely gaze or an indefinable aura surrounding a *dangerous person*. But he could discern nothing. No sign or clue as to who among the two dozen reporters was the wolf in the fold.

He did however notice the vision in red crossing the room on her way to a corporate table near the corner. Silver hair cascaded down sculpted shoulders to frame a plunging neckline and ample cleavage.

Santiagar had abandoned the podium to stride along the front of the dais. His hands animated the energy of his words. "I believe, as the Director believes, commerce between private corporations and individual entrepreneurs should not be curtailed by political boundaries. Both the Alliance and the Federation espouse the principles of free enterprise and economic liberty. The time has come to practice what we preach."

Jaron gestured to one of the junior attachés seated at a lesser table to come over. When the young man—Cande-something—reached his side, he leaned in to mutter in his ear. "Do me a favor and see that a Velvet Fantasy is delivered to the lovely lady in red over there. And make damn sure she's made aware it's from me."

"Yes, sir. I'll take care of it." The man—Chris Candela was his name, he thought—nodded and scurried off. Jaron relaxed back in the chair and pretended to gaze with interest at what mercifully appeared to be the conclusion of the speech.

"Tomorrow we will be presenting a series of real, concrete initiatives which will relax trade restrictions on a number of consumer goods, opening new markets for Alliance and Senecan companies alike. In addition, I'm pleased to announce Director Kouris and I have agreed to meet again next year in what we hope will become a regular conference devoted to expanding galactic commerce."

The Minister stopped at the perfect center of the stage and smiled with assured conviction at the audience. "Here's to new beginnings."

As Santiagar descended the stairs to shake Kouris' hand, Jaron looked over his shoulder to catch the eye of the lady in red. She raised her drink to him with a small dip of her chin and a seductive smile.

Diffuse lights transformed the waters to a glowing turquoise beneath the translucent walkway. Tiny ripples danced in the mild breeze cooling the air after what had been a warm, sunny day. Glare from the many hotels, restaurants and clubs fashioned an eerie blue-filtered aurora in the night sky.

The Summit banquet had concluded three hours earlier. Afterward the attendees had practically trampled one another in their eagerness to scatter throughout the resort colony and partake in their sin of choice.

The reputation of the man Matei followed was not that of a sinner. Those who knew him regarded him as squeaky-clean to a fault, which would be why he walked alone rather than joining any of the roving groups of his coworkers. It would also be why the man was heading toward the less well-lit area of the entertainment quarter, where his carnal lapse was unlikely to be witnessed by those same coworkers.

Matei trailed his target into a sizeable crowd spilling out of a large theatre. The façade was festooned with garish flamingos, frolicking dolphins and a strange yellow-and-orange flying creature, all intertwined with neon magenta crystals. The marquee advertised a full-sensory interactive circus performance.

Past the theatre the crowd dispersed somewhat, and with a right turn shadows began to fall across the illuminated walkway. Progressively seedier bars competed with body art parlors, sensory booths and 'leisure' clubs. He quickened his pace.

As they passed the entrance to one of the more popular clubs and the foot traffic briefly increased, he bumped against his target. "Sorry, excuse me." A clumsy grasp of a fleshy upper arm masked the pinprick of the microneedle.

The man didn't even glance at him. "It's fine."

Matei blended back into the passersby to continue following three meters behind. Twenty steps later the man's gait became erratic, then slowed to sway unsteadily.

He sidled in beside his target and placed an arm around the man's waist for support. "Easy there. I think you've had a little too much to drink."

Unfocused eyes looked over groggily. "Wha...you...." The eyes drifted closed as the man sagged into his arms.

He held the slumping figure upright and guided him to an offshoot alley, then down two more alleyways, until the discordant sounds of the quarter faded to a low buzz. They moved around the corner of the rearmost building and he let the man collapse against the wall. A few incoherent mumblings escaped, but by this point all motor function control had ceased.

Matei squatted down and placed a hand under the man's chin to hold his head up. "Okay, smile for the camera." His ocular implant scanned the facial features and hairstyle; he had to hold an eyelid open to get a retinal imprint. The man sank to the ground while he turned over a palm and scanned the fingerprints. Lastly, he yanked a single dark brown hair from the scalp and pressed it between the glyphs on his index fingers to extract the DNA sequence.

Satisfied, he reached in his pack and pulled out a ball. It was a mere four centimeters in diameter, made of an ultra-dense alloy and attached to a length of fine woven rope. He wound the end of the rope around the man's ankle and knotted it securely.

The man had slipped into a fully catatonic state. Matei lifted him enough to shift him to the edge of the narrow walkway. After injecting the man's neck with another needle, he straightened up and nudged the body and the ball over the edge into the water.

Here in the deep recesses of the entertainment quarter there were no lights in the walkways or neon lights adorning the buildings. Within seconds the body vanished beneath the inky blackness.

The rope was constructed of a special water-soluble metamat fiber. It was coated with a resin designed to dissolve over three days, after which the rope would disintegrate and the bloated body rise to the surface. The injected solution acted to keep the core organs minimally functioning long past when the man had drowned, thus delaying the apparent time of death.

In the bright daylight sun and crystal waters, the corpse was certain to be discovered. To the world it would look like the man committed suicide shortly after committing the heinous act he intended to perform the next evening.

He picked up the pack and retraced his path through the alleyways, where he rejoined the revelers. He wound his way back toward the hotel, where he would spend the remainder of the night transforming himself into Chris Candela, junior attaché to the Senecan trade delegation.

11

BORDER OF SENECAN FEDERATION SPACE

Caleb sat on the floor in the open space of the main deck tinkering with a spare circuit panel. It was a trick he had learned as a teenager when he had spent a summer placing monitoring stations for the Park Service in the mountains outside Cavare. Occupying your hands with a detailed task became a form of meditation, allowing your mind to work through concerns in the background.

His hands worked to separate the main and below deck temperature control circuits; his mind pondered Volosk's oblique suggestion that he might, if he wanted, take Samuel's place in Division.

It wasn't a question of whether he thought he could do the job. It was a matter of whether he wanted to do the job. Samuel hadn't been confined to a desk in his last few years, but he had certainly spent less time in the field. Caleb *liked* the way things were now. He liked the chase, the intrigue…the simplicity. There were no politics to worry about and no bureaucratic entanglements; there was only the mission. He hadn't—

—alarms began pealing in the cabin, the high-pitched wails bouncing off the narrow walls to clash in a discordant clangor.

He leapt to his feet and lunged for the cockpit—in the small cabin it wasn't a great distance—dropping into the seat as he brought the alerts front and center of the HUD.

The primary alarm alerted him to the fact that a particle beam had missed the ship by thirty-eight meters, sent off-kilter by the passive defense shielding. Weapons fire *skimming the hull* was the first warning of other ships in the vicinity?

They must be sporting hardcore stealth, and since they were firing on him unprovoked they were definitely mercs. Drop out of superluminal for ten damn minutes and he's getting shot at….

"VI, identify hostiles and ready weapons."

The medium-pitched female voice responded in its pleasant, forever-placid tone. *"Tracking hostiles."*

The VI represented the top-layer interface for the onboard CU which monitored and manipulated the various ship systems. In 1.7 seconds the CU used the trajectory of the beam to extrapolate the attacker's location and analyzed the energy readings in the region to identify the unique signature of the vessel.

A red dot appeared on the HUD's regional map.

Having used the information to match similar energy signatures in the area, two additional dots quickly joined the first one. The three dots flew in formation and closed rapidly.

"Let's do this, you bastards. VI, autopilot off."

"You have navigation."

He engaged the safety harness then activated the manual-guided controls and yanked the ship upward into a sharp arc. He sailed above the pursuers, locked on and fired at the lead attacker.

Particle beam weapons were standard fare on merc vessels, because they were comparatively cheap, standardized and mass-produced. However they weren't particularly agile, with limited on-the-fly adjustability and a non-negligible recharge time.

He'd noted earlier how Division hadn't scrimped on the ship's hardware, and was never more grateful for it than at this moment. The dual neodymium-crystal pulse laser weapons his ship wielded exhibited far greater responsiveness than particle beams. They realigned each pulse to account for the movement of the target and were capable of firing continuously for upwards of twenty seconds before needing to recharge. Granted, each pulse carried rather less force than a particle beam shot—but in practice the continual fire more than made up the difference.

Twenty seconds of fire was enough to rip through most vessels' primary and secondary shielding, much as it was doing right...about...*now*.

The lead ship ripped apart into jagged metal shards, followed shortly thereafter by the bright white nova-like implosion-explosion of the sLume drive. His ship shuddered in his hands as the shockwave passed over it.

He concentrated back on the HUD and the two outstanding attackers. The rush of adrenaline in his veins focused his thoughts and created the illusion of time stretching out. Intellectually, he knew nanobot regulators in his bloodstream were honing and directing the adrenaline to enhance the effect. Physically, he only knew his eyesight became sharper, his reflexes faster and his decision-making clearer.

He'd exploited an advantage with the initial shot; they hadn't known he could track them. Now they did. Predictably, the two ships began zigzagging while attempting to track his own erratic path.

Maneuvering to slide behind them, he flipped the ship around and set the weapons to track one of the them until it gained a reliable lock then automatically fire. Unfortunately, while he did so the other attacker got a lock on him. The ship jerked in a violent wrench from the instantaneous impact of the particle beam. The shielding held but after two hits now stood at thirty-seven percent power.

He tried to make his movement as unpredictable as possible. It was one of the reasons why humans remained better pilots than CUs. Even seemingly random variations by a CU were able to be predicted to a reasonable probability by another CU; an Artificial might be another matter, but building a synthetic neural net into a ship remained impractical, not to mention highly illegal. The decisions of a human acting on instinct under combat pressures, however, could never be predicted with any degree of accuracy. Or so the scientists said.

Of course this meant he couldn't predict their movements either. The weapons would fire within a picosecond of achieving a lock, though—and everyone paused at the controls for a picosecond or two. He was sweeping below and aft of the attackers when his weapons locked and the second vessel followed the first into the beyond.

He made a snap decision and pushed the ship's speed to one hundred five percent maximum. The mercs—one merc now—were fast, but not that fast.

He had been traveling at seventy-five percent max sub-light speed when the attack occurred, and they had been gaining on him. Still, on the assumption the pilot of the final ship would spend at least a few seconds reeling from the close-proximity explosion and the fact all his companions were now dead, he figured he stood decent odds of escaping in those critical few seconds. Given the depleted state of his shielding, better odds than surviving another hit.

"VI, divert non-critical power to impulse."

"Eighty percent of environmentals and utilities power diverted."

He amped the speed an additional twelve percent. It wouldn't be maintainable for long without blowing out the engine—maybe ten minutes—but it should be long enough to lose the merc and transition to superluminal.

"VI, divert communications power to dampener field."

"Communications is classified as a critical system."

"I'm aware. Divert communications power to dampener field."

A slight pause. *"Dampener field at 97.2 percent strength."*

He sped 'north-northwest' toward a region of denser interstellar gas and dust. Concepts like "north" had no real meaning in space, true. Nonetheless, the intrinsic human need for directional bearing had led to the development in the early days of extra-solar space travel of a heading scheme based on Earth's location relative to the center of the galaxy.

Eight minutes later he decreased his speed to ninety-eight percent max, sent the diverted power flow to the dampener field and began altering his route. He'd veer about for a couple of hours and approach Metis from a different angle than his previous trajectory. As a precaution.

The air in the cabin started to get uncomfortably cold. He withstood it for another fifteen minutes, tucking his arms against his chest to maintain body heat. When his jaw shivered so violently he accidentally bit his tongue, he decided the success or failure of his escape had by this point surely been decided.

"VI, return power to normal distribution."

"Standard power flows restored. Primary systems nominal. Two thermal blankets are located in the aft supply cabinet should you require them."

"Thank you, VI. I'll be fine." The breath he had metaphorically been holding since the attack began escaped in a very real expulsion of all the air from his lungs as he sank deeper into the chair. No longer required to focus on escape, evasion or keeping warm, the last of the adrenaline dissipated. He was left with little to do but sit there and attempt to wrap his head around what had just happened.

How had they tracked him? For all practical purposes ships were not able to be tracked while superluminal. Theoretically the warp bubble could be detected, but to track it one would have to be traveling at the same precise speed on an identical trajectory. Even then, the minimal maneuverability coupled with the vast distances being covered made it effectively impossible to follow a ship in superluminal through a miniscule change in trajectory.

At sub-light speeds his ship was virtually invisible from greater than 0.1 AU; the odds of a band of mercs randomly encountering him at such close proximity in deep space were so low as to be nonexistent. Certainly, merc bands loitered in space waiting on targets all the time; but they did so in populated, high traffic areas and preyed on far larger, less stealthy vessels.

Lycaon was almost 0.6 kpcs behind him, Gaiae more than 0.7 kpcs to the southeast—and neither of those worlds were exactly hotbeds of activity. There was essentially nothing between here and the borders of explored space except the Metis Nebula.

"VI, initiate an analysis of all systems and a nano-scale scan of the interior and exterior of the ship."

"What am I to look for?"

"A tracking device or item capable of sending out a signal, but I'll settle for anything which doesn't belong. Also, run diagnostics on the dampener field and let me know of any errors."

"Acknowledged. A scan at such a level of precision will take 3.62 hours."

"Understood. Inform me of any anomalies as soon as you find them."

He didn't expect the VI to find anything amiss. Security on Division's wing of the spaceport was as tight as that of Headquarters; tampering with the ship would have been quite difficult, though he had to acknowledge not impossible.

For the moment he had no choice but to operate under the assumption the ship was clean....

So how the hell had they found him? And more relevantly, why had they been so eager to vaporize him on sight?

12

M atei stepped through the wide doors and into the foyer of the ballroom.

His position was two-thirds of the way down the receiving line for the dignitaries, a prelude to the final gathering of the Trade Summit. It was the appropriate station for a junior member of the Senecan delegation—after the diplomats and CEOs, before the administrative personnel.

The disguise wasn't perfect. There were limits to what even glyphed cybernetics could do, the most significant one being they couldn't alter bone structure. That had been one of the factors in choosing the victim though, so it wasn't a major issue. Silica-cellulose injections added sufficient depth to his cheekbones and prominence to his chin; block-heeled shoes added the extra four centimeters.

His skin had darkened two shades, eyes hued to light green and hair tinted to a chocolate brown and cut to match Candela's style. Foam padding beneath the borrowed clothes provided the extra thirty pounds to his lean frame.

A friend or family member of Mr. Candela wouldn't be fooled—but the man had no friends among his coworkers, and his family was kiloparsecs away.

Matei had made public appearances over the course of the day only when necessary, during which he remained quietly invisible among the Summit attendees. Here, he had positioned himself in line between two Alliance officials; he would not be expected to speak to them.

As the line continued its slow procession forward, the polite greetings and repetitive small talk began to rise above the low din of those who forewent the receiving line. The line was an odd, anachronistic formality, a tradition he thought had perhaps become malformed somewhere along the way. Nevertheless this night it was to his advantage, for the man he impersonated would not otherwise be allowed to get so close and he might have been forced into a more risky strategy.

The woman in front of him took another step, and he entered the critical zone. He didn't look around—not for security or agents, nor for cams or sensors. He knew where they were and had factored them into the plan.

In the next step he triggered the release of nanobots into his bloodstream which secreted a specially formulated epinephrine compound. It heightened his senses by twenty-two percent and sped his physical reaction times by thirty-six percent above already genetically and biosynthetically enhanced capabilities.

He spotted Mr. Nythal sitting at a table to the right, his eyes a little wide as they scanned up and down the receiving line with a drink in hand for easy access. If the man spooked security with his vaguely panicked expression, they would have…words.

The next advancement brought him to the Atlantis Governor. He smiled politely and shook the woman's hand. His voice, though not loud, was clear and crisp so as to be easily overheard and later recalled by those in the vicinity.

"A pleasure to meet you, ma'am. Chris Candela, Seneca Trade Division."

She smiled as all politicians do, possibly with a tad greater warmth than most since she oversaw a resort world. "I hope you've enjoyed your stay here, Mr. Candela."

"Very much so, thank you."

The Senecan Trade Director was occupied talking up the trophy wife of a Senecan dignitary and didn't even glance at him as they shook hands. All the better.

Without altering his gait or demeanor he stepped face to face with Alliance Trade Minister Santiagar and extended a hand in greeting.

"Chris Candela, Seneca Trade Division. It's an honor, sir."

His eVi activated the virus which had been quarantined in his data cache for the last week and directed it through his cybernetics into his hand. As he shook Santiagar's hand, he shifted his grip so his index finger made contact with the Minister's index finger on release.

Like every person in society above the poverty level, the Minister's index finger contained the conductive fibers necessary for interaction with a variety of screens, panels and the millions of other electronic devices which pervaded the world around them. The fibers at a minimum connected to the man's eVi, which at a minimum connected to his brain.

In Santiagar's case, the files indicated his body contained a reasonable amount of additional cybernetic enhancements. The minimum would have sufficed, but the enhancements removed all chance.

There wasn't even a vibration or tingle when their conductive fibers made contact and the virus passed from his fingertip into the Minister's cybernetics. He smiled, dipped his chin in appreciation and moved on.

He made a point to have his pace appear aimless while winding between the milling guests toward the plain door in the right wall.

The first gasps of horror and panic began to echo behind him as he slipped through the door.

METIS NEBULA
OUTER BANDS

Caleb frowned at the Evanec screen again.

Static wasn't something one commonly encountered in the twenty-fourth century. Yet static was precisely what he was looking at.

Upon entering the golden-blue wisps of Metis this morning, communications had begun to deteriorate. First the exanet feed had stuttered for a few minutes then died. Being cut off from the endless avalanche of media populism and celebrity gossip and pseudo-political intrigue was mostly a welcome respite, but it did nag at him that if anything of actual import were to happen, he'd remain ignorant of it for a time.

Next the Evanec had started to flicker in and out, and after an hour the ship couldn't establish a connection to Senecan security channels or anywhere else. It shouldn't be a problem, seeing as he wasn't expecting to be engaging in ship-to-anything communications deep in the void of space...though the static *was* a bit unnerving.

Finally, his eVi's communication system fell silent. Locally stored messages remained, but any attempt to send or receive a message or ping the network resulted in a chilling response:

Connection unable to be established. System is not connected to ex-anet infrastructure. Messages will be queued until able to be delivered.

Well. Should Division feel the need to alter his mission, he wouldn't get the memo. Should they need him for a more urgent mission, he wouldn't get that one either, which bothered him a marginal amount more. If something happened to Isabela and he didn't know...but he'd only be here for a few days. It would be fine.

His gaze drifted to the viewport. The Nebula's luminous, misty haze formed an eerie, even ghostly environment. Not frightening as such; only dust, gases and the charged particles of the pulsar wind inhabited the sky, and they wielded neither sentience nor intentionality. Rather, it created the impression one had crossed over into an ethereal, incorporeal plane of existence—an effect without a doubt magnified by the disconcerting silence of a formerly ever-present and quite loud civilization.

He assumed the particular makeup of Metis' EM signature interfered with transmission protocols, both governmental and commercial. Given communications were 'classified as a critical system,' he imagined the VI might be somewhat concerned about the matter.

"VI, do you know the reason for the interference in communications?"

"Though no single emission is strong enough to interfere with our systems, the overall EM makeup of this region is nonetheless diffracting all external signals to the point their integrity is lost."

"How so?"

A pause, far longer than normal. *"I cannot determine the precise mechanism at this time."*

Though cognizant it consisted solely of qubits, he felt a strange urge to reassure the VI. "It's fine, it doesn't matter."

"I will continue to analyze the problem."

Wave diffraction was a common enough occurrence, if not often to such damaging effect. Space in its natural state did not always cater to human preferences. On his return he'd submit a log of the interference, and within a few months the Senecan security protocols at least would be adjusted to counteract it. So long as the region stayed uninhabited, the exanet purveyors weren't likely to give a shit.

He played with the Evanec settings for a while, but refining the bands merely seemed to make the problem worse—not that 'null' could really be made worse. Resigned to the fact he did not possess the ability to improve matters, he relaxed in the pilot's chair and surveyed the situation.

Whatever the source of the anomalous readings which had sent him here, it was a solid day to day and a half away based on the rate of increase in the signal strength. The probe had traveled more than a hundred parsecs farther into the Nebula than his current location.

Still, for obvious reasons he took things slowly. This was unfamiliar territory with unknown factors at work and no safety net should something go wrong. While he would be the first to go in with guns blazing where the circumstance called for it, this one did not. So he moved carefully, scanning and recording for future analysis by those more scientifically minded than he.

⌇

He was standing up to go make a sandwich when the physical sensor blinked an alert. He eased back into the chair and magnified the screen.

Buried in the shadow of backlit clouds, 0.01 AU away, floated a small planet. The initial scan indicated moderate gravity and a reasonable atmosphere, albeit one consisting of toxic air and volatile weather patterns, which didn't come as a surprise. What star did it belong to? The pulsar? It wasn't common for pulsars to have planets, though it did happen. Perhaps it was a rogue, ejected from orbit in the eons-past supernova explosion.

He called up his astroscience files, projected them to an aural and scrolled down them in an effort to recall—

—a flicker...no, an *absence*, a dark gap in the nebular clouds, caught the corner of his eye. In a breath he shifted to full alert.

There was no logical explanation for why his senses were instantly hyper-focused and nanobot-aided adrenaline already rushed through his veins. But preternatural instincts was one reason the government paid him a rather generous salary.

He swung around to sweep the area in a broad arc, and came up empty. The sensors detected only the noise Metis radiated. Yet a moment later a well-defined *void* was distinctly silhouetted against a dense fog of dust, illuminated by the pale golden glow of the Metis interior. He checked the scans again. Nada.

The sensors told him the region was empty. His eyes told him otherwise. His ocular implant strained to zoom in and focus on the distant shadow; he would have a headache later. He tensed as the silhouette solidified in his vision into the outline of an artificial construct. He'd call it a ship, but….

Then it whipped about and accelerated toward him and he decided it was most definitely a ship. Aerodynamic and tinted an inky black, it resembled nothing so much as a bird of prey preparing to swoop down upon him.

"Son of a *bitch!*" How the bloody fuck had those mercs tracked him here? This vessel was supposed to be stealthy. It *was* stealthy. The scans of the ship had come up squeaky clean. No bloody fucking way could they have tracked him—except for the fact they very plainly had. He slid into the heavier gas clouds to his right, using the visual and EM cover to strafe to the side of his adversary.

Based on the trajectory and speed when the ship had been visible, he estimated the amount of time until it drew even. With a jerk across the controls he emerged from the clouds and fired on where it should be.

His instincts served him well; the other ship tacked away as an explosion blazed bright against its hull—it plummeted and swerved into a dense clump of dust—

—the laser lost tracking. Terrific. It must have one hell of an aversion shield.

No time to ponder it, for he promptly became the target of the return flare of a pulse laser—silver-white in hue, suggesting ytterbium crystal construction. Not a particle beam…and Alliance-produced? Odd.

In a smooth motion he accelerated in an arc up and over the attacker and entered a wall of thick nebular gases. He strafed horizontally before sinking down into the cover, hoping to sneak around and catch his adversary from underneath.

He exited the cloud to find the enemy due ahead and waiting for him.

Didn't see that coming.

He jerked up at a fifty degree angle and away—

—but it was too late. The ship quaked beneath his hands from the impact of point-blank pulse laser fire.

He managed to get off a staccato of fire while in full reverse, though it was unclear if any of it hit. The attacker's weapon did not lose tracking. A relentless pulse stream tore through his shields, then the outer hull. The rear of the ship plummeted into a wild spin as alerts flared across the HUD bank.

Letting loose a string of curses in half a dozen languages, he wrenched out of the spin and set a trajectory for the nearby planet. It had obviously been placed here *just* so he could crash on it.

He surrendered the controls to the CU long enough to pull on the environment suit and carry the helmet back to the chair. The helmet annoyed him; it cut off his senses and narrowed his perspective, and he wasn't putting it on until it was required to continue living and breathing.

On retaking the controls he worked to approach the planet at an angle which stood a marginal chance of not turning the ship and him to flaming meteoroids. Concentrated as he was on flying a vessel which seemed to have lost most of its tail section, it took a few seconds for him to realize the incoming fire had ceased—possibly on account of the fact he was *clearly* already dead.

The turbulence of the planetary atmosphere sent the ship into violent convulsions. He threw everything into holding her steady, but he was fighting a losing battle.

Then the HUD went dark.

Then the aft section of the ship exploded.

*Goddamn pain-in-my-ass mercs...*with a groan he pulled the helmet on and secured the seal to the suit, punched the evac and dove for the hatch.

꙰

It went without saying that there were no atmosphere corridors onto the small, barren planet buried within Metis.

Alex fought to maintain control of the damaged *Siyane* in the buffeting atmospheric forces. Visually she was blind, for the viewport revealed only the whirl of an impenetrable caramel-colored dust. She relied on the bank of displays to track altitude and angle of descent and to search the topography for a safe place to land. She needed to inspect the damage, and she just wasn't crazy enough to open the engineering hatch while in space when she was fairly certain the lower hull had been blown wide open.

The fiery bloom of an explosion thirty degrees to starboard cut through the dust and haze. A harsh breath escaped between gritted teeth. She should feel satisfaction at the attacker's destruction. Bastard had the gall to shoot her ship!

But extinguishing life wasn't actually something she routinely—or ever—did, and deep down it hadn't been her goal. She'd merely done what was necessary to defend herself. It was one of many lessons her father had impressed upon her once she was old enough to comprehend them.

Alex, if an attacker means you harm, you cannot hold back. The attacker will seize advantage of your attempt to preserve their life. They will take yours.

The simple and stark truth was the other ship fired first, giving her no choice but to destroy it before it destroyed her.

Still, her heart leapt of its own accord when a pinpoint blip appeared on the radio, mid-infrared and electronic sensor screens. The pilot had escaped prior to the vessel's disintegration and currently plummeted toward the planet's surface. Presumably they wore a suit and a chute and would land intact, for all the good it would do them.

Her initial relief at the sign of life dissolved into dismay. Without a way off the planet or any rescue incoming—assuming their communications capabilities were as nonexistent as hers had been since entering the Nebula—whether in two days or two weeks, the pilot was as good as dead.

"*Gavno!*" This person had tried to shoot her down, and would doubtless have left her to die had they succeeded. Likely a merc, assuredly a criminal and clearly dangerous; in all probability a killer who deserved to die.

But not by her hand.

She wasn't a killer...though for perhaps the first time ever she almost regretted it.

Groaning in exasperation at an obstinate conscience, she yanked the ship into a rough trajectory toward where the pilot should be landing. It took some doing; the ship gyrated like a teenager on a chimeral high at a rave. When the opportunity came to inspect the hull she expected to find a royal shit-ton of damage.

But for now the exterior plasma shielding continued to hold. She forcibly drove the ship downward, weaving a path toward the projected impact point. She had to dodge the wreckage of the enemy ship twice as it cavorted wildly and wrenched apart from the pressure of the atmosphere and the pull of gravity.

Finally the air cleared—so to speak. Sand-saturated winds whipped through the sky, and physical visibility increased only to meters. She zeroed in on the weak electronic signature of the pilot's suit while keeping an eye on the ground sensor; given the presumed damage to the lower hull there was no guarantee the collision warning still functioned.

She had slowed almost to a stop before the vague outline of a tensile-fiber chute billowing in the wind came into view.

Last chance to bail, Alex. Land beyond that hill on the topo map there and make sure you have basic functionality. Then hobble to Gaiae, repair your ship and get on with your life.

She rolled her eyes in annoyance and settled to the ground with a modicum of grace. After scanning the system monitors to make certain nothing threatened to go critical for the moment, she stood and pulled on her environment suit. She grabbed the Daemon from the cabinet and primed it prior to activating the hatch. Twenty seconds later she stepped onto a rather rudely unwelcoming world.

She struggled against punishing winds to approach the chute and the prone form tangled in it. Goddammit, was she going to have to go back and get a blade and cut the *suky sranuyu* out?

In a flurry of motion the pilot somehow disentangled from the chute and crawled to their knees. *Guess not.*

The chute rose in the air to be caught by the wind and shredded to ribbons. The pilot stood, faltered for a second, then righted themselves and focused on her.

A deep male voice bearing a lilting, melodic timbre came over her suit's vicinity comm. "Listen, whoever you are, I'm sure we can work something ou—"

She steadied the gun with both hands and fired.

PART II:

CAUSALITY

*"Civilization begins with order, grows with liberty,
and dies with chaos."*

— *Will Durant*

13

M iriam double-checked the file index a final time. She wanted to be able to review her notes during the flight for the session she would be chairing at the TacRecon Conference, on the economic viability of continuous passive planetary-wide hyperspectral scanning. They had been sent to Reference Confirm this morning and needed to be ready by the time she arrived at the spaceport.

With any luck the notes would occupy her for the entire flight, and she'd have no opportunity to dwell on the destination. She allowed a quiet sigh to escape as she reached for her jacket.

The sound of the door sliding open caught her by surprise. She could count on one hand the number of people who dared enter her office unannounced. If the entrant wasn't on the list....

Richard's eyes were starkly bloodshot even from across the room. He clearly hadn't been getting much sleep the last several nights. "Turn on the news feed."

"I was just on my way out the door for St. Petersburg."

"You're not going."

She arched an eyebrow. She didn't want to go of course, but he had very little say in the matter.

An aural materialized in front of him; he leaned against the front of the desk and shifted it out so she could also see it. "The data stream from the QEC to Atlantis. Now *please*, turn on the news feed."

"Very well." A finger press to the edge of her desk and a large panel embedded in the far wall burst to life.

"—Atlantis security and Alliance officials are refusing to provide any information regarding the incident. However—"

Her eyes flew to the aural Richard had generated.

Trade Minister Santiagar confirmed to have suffered a catastrophic overload of cybernetics resulting in stroke and brain hemorrhage

"What?" She hurried around the desk and positioned herself beside him for a clearer vantage. "Are you certain?"

"—guests at the dinner recount seeing nothing unusual as the Minister joined the Senecan Trade Director and Atlantis Governor in greeting attendees, and say he abruptly began shaking violently then collapsed—"

remote injection of self-replicating virus suspected, confirmation expected within seven minutes

He ran a hand roughly through his hair. "I'm afraid so."

"—the ballroom has been cleared and everyone present is being detained, though officials assure us it is only precautionary—"

surveillance scans identify an individual exiting the room through a service door 1.8 seconds after initial manifestation of symptoms

"—we realize several other networks are reporting that Minister Santiagar has died. We don't want to jump the gun and report something which turns out to be inaccurate—"

"Is he dead?"

He merely nodded.

individual was tracked into maintenance corridors but disappeared from surveillance cams during level transition 26.4 seconds after incident

"—responses from both the Earth Alliance and Senecan Federation representatives are confused and conflicting, making it difficult—"

review of visuals confirm individual physically interacted with the Minister 7.8 seconds prior to incident

He blew out a sharp breath. "Means it was an official guest. There will be a record."

"One of the Senecans?"

"Or one of ours."

"—again, we are reporting an incident at the final event of the Trade Summit involving Alliance Minister—"

"Don't be ridiculous."

"Miriam, it's my job to be suspicious."

82.6% certainty individual is Christopher Candela, listed as a junior attaché for the Seneca Trade Division

Her jaw clenched, causing a painful jolt as her teeth clacked together. "I told you."

"—we are now able to confirm that Earth Alliance Trade Minister Mangele Santiagar has died. The cause of death is still undetermined—"

Her eVi began signaling a cascading avalanche of alerts and incoming data. A red alert force-loaded on her whisper.

Board meeting in twenty minutes. Level V Priority.

Richard pushed off the edge of the desk and killed the aural. "I got it too. If you'll excuse me, I have nineteen minutes to pull together everything we have into some sort of coherent form."

She was already crossing back around her desk and waved distractedly after him. She sat down, took a deep breath and began issuing orders.

ℛ

Barely controlled chaos ruled the conference room as she walked in. A cluster of advisors surrounded General Alamatto at the head of the table, and several military officials huddled by the windows gesturing in animated whispers. The holos of the remote members jerked and flickered as they handled interruptions and rushed to prepare. Aides hurried around in a bustle of activity which closely resembled pointless circles.

Miriam simply crossed the room and took a seat. Her shoulders locked straight as she opened three small screens and proceeded to study their contents.

Richard hurried in, both hands interacting with two separate aurals and only belatedly remembering to make sure his uniform shirt was tucked in properly. She spared him a tiny, sympathetic smile but didn't otherwise acknowledge his presence.

Alamatto cleared his throat loudly; it barely registered above the din. Again, to no avail. In frustration he slammed his palm on the table.

"If we can bring this meeting to order…" he paused as those present scurried into some semblance of order "…thank you. First, I'd like to note that in addition to the regular Board members, we have present this evening Major Lange from Security Bureau and Colonel Navick from Military Intelligence in person and Defense Minister Mori and Deputy Foreign Minister Basak via holo."

He waited for the last person to settle on a location to stand. "As you're all aware by now, approximately thirty minutes ago Trade Minister Santiagar collapsed and died while attending the Trade

Summit on Atlantis. I don't want to misrepresent any of the facts, so I'll let those closest to the situation bring us up to speed. Major Lange?"

Lange was a tall, wiry blond with pale blue eyes which connoted his strong Scandinavian ancestry. Miriam had worked with him on occasion and found him professional, if cold, and highly competent.

He nodded brusquely at the General. "Thank you, sir. The incident occurred while Minister Santiagar and other senior officials greeted guests in an official receiving line before the closing banquet. Including staff, seventy-nine individuals were in the ballroom at the time, as well as another sixty-five in the entryway and hall area." He flicked his wrist and a three-dimensional schematic of the ballroom and immediate surroundings materialized above the table.

"The ballroom was locked down six seconds after the Minister collapsed, the wing of the convention center containing the ballroom twelve seconds later. All exits from the convention center were staffed and monitored within two minutes." The schematic zoomed out to encompass the entire building and the exits lit up in red.

"All spaceport departures are being held and searched beginning five minutes after the incident. Atlantis security has been extremely responsive. Despite the frivolous nature of the colony, they are a well-trained and professional department and I have every confidence in their ability to support our investigation."

He took a sip of water from the glass an aide had placed on the table. "Alliance doctors treated the Minister on the scene. He displayed no vital signs upon their arrival and was declared deceased after six minutes. Initial analysis indicates he suffered a cybernetics malfunction which triggered a neural stroke and brain hemorrhage. No other attendees have experienced health issues. Nonetheless, officers on the scene are investigating every possibility, including biological and chemical weapon dispersal, food tampering and remote cyberbomb delivery."

He gazed around the long table and to those standing along the walls. "Any questions?"

Admiral Rychen, the Northeastern Regional Commander based on Messium, spoke up. "What about the guests? A lot of people were in the room. Could someone have slipped in?"

"We're obviously still questioning the attendees, but we have confirmed everyone present was on the official guest list or approved staff. At least one person present departed before the lockdown was complete, but I'll let the Colonel speak to the matter." He nodded to Richard, who stepped forward as Lange backed away.

Richard coughed a tad awkwardly. She knew he wasn't fond of speaking in front of large groups, preferring to work in the background if not the shadows. But matters were what they were.

"Yes. Though preliminary, examination of the Minister's body suggests his cybernetics were sabotaged by a self-replicating virus, resulting in a forced overload designed to damage the brain."

"So he was assassinated then?"

He glanced at the Defense Minister. "Yes, sir. It appears that way. We are pursuing every lead, but the primary suspect at the moment is Christopher Candela, a junior staffer in the Senecan delegation." He displayed a visual of an unremarkable-looking man with dark brown hair. Looks were often deceiving these days, but the man seemed to be in his late twenties.

"Mr. Candela was seen greeting Santiagar in the receiving line several seconds before the Minister collapsed. He left the room via a service door immediately thereafter. EAMI agents initiated pursuit and tracked him through multiple corridors before he vanished from surveillance cams, likely due to a cloaking shield. By that point the lockdown *had* been completed..." Richard was too polite to look over at Lange "...and the fields placed on the exits will disrupt cloaking tech, so it is unlikely he will be able to escape the net. An exhaustive search of the conference center is ongoing."

"Goddamn Senecans! I *knew* this Summit was a trap."

Alamatto grimaced at the holo of General O'Connell. "General, we don't yet know anything for certain. Please, Colonel, continue."

"Yes, sir. Nine individuals attending the Summit did not attend the dinner: three reporters, five corporate executives and one of our low-level staff members. We've confirmed they didn't leave Atlantis prior to the dinner and are in the process of tracking them down."

O'Connell spoke up again, though he appeared to be making a marginal effort at restraint. "How did an assassin get past your background checks, Colonel? I was under the impression EAMI had their spies all over this damnable Summit."

Miriam smiled to herself. Like many people, the General assumed Richard was a pushover due to his mild, nonthreatening demeanor. He was incorrect.

Richard focused in on O'Connell. "We are and one didn't. While we have limited ability to blacklist Senecan government personnel, we do have extensive files on each of them. Christopher Candela is as clean as they get. Family man, hard worker, upstanding member of society. A little quiet and keeps to himself, but zero history of trouble. Never been arrested, never affiliated with extremist groups or vocalized anti-Alliance sentiments. Frankly I would be less surprised if you accused my hundred sixty-four year old grandfather living in Bonn of being an assassin."

O'Connell snorted. "That simply means his government put him up to it. If you ask me, this was an act of war."

The Deputy Foreign Minister looked down her long, pinched nose at him. "That remains to be seen...General, is it? We will naturally be demanding answers from the Senecan government. This man might have acted alone, or as an agent of a terrorist organization. It's far too soon to be throwing around declarations of war."

"Well, ma'am, how about you just let me know when it *is* time, all right?"

The glacial stare which came in response would have frosted the room had the woman been present in person. The Defense Minister stepped into the tête-à-tête to redirect the conversation. "Have we implemented additional security measures yet?"

Miriam acknowledged the Minister with a miniscule nod. "Absolutely. Security at Alliance buildings galaxy-wide has been increased to Level IV, military bases to Level III. As a precautionary matter all military leave has been canceled and personnel recalled. Heightened security is in place for the Prime Minister and Assembly Speaker as well as their families and homes. Protective details are currently being dispatched to senior administration officials and Assembly members."

She gave a rare, wry smile. "And as we speak the dust is being brushed off the strategic plans for a number of military scenarios." She should know, she expected to be spending the next twelve hours preparing recommendation briefs on them.

Alamatto gave the room a formal nod. "If there are no further questions, we'll adjourn for now. All updates should be forwarded to my attention. I'll be flying to Washington to brief the Cabinet shortly. Unless there are significant new developments, the Board will meet again at 0800. Dismissed."

14

SIYANE

A lex lugged the unconscious form to the jump seat, deposited it unceremoniously and engaged the safety harness.

Mesh straps emerged from the wall and snaked around to pull him upright in the chair, hands snug against his sides. She activated a web normally used to secure cargo; the subtle silver glimmer barely registered against the gunmetal fabric of his environment suit. She code-locked the web.

Only then did she disengage the suit's seal and remove the helmet from her captive. A mop of soft, loosely curly black hair tumbled across his forehead and along his neck. She ignored it to scan the manufacturer imprint inside the helmet.

~ 2321, Seneca SpaceEX, Ltd. ~

The accent, of course. "Well that's just fucking...great."

She carried the helmet over to a cabinet on the opposite wall and dropped it in a drawer, stripped off her own environment suit and stowed it, then sat down in the cockpit chair. Her toes propelled the chair in agitated circles while her fingers drummed a staccato rhythm on the armrest.

This did not fit in her schedule. Not repairing a gaping fissure in the hull and certainly not babysitting a prisoner. Why did she have to go all honorable and rescue him? She could have simply kept going and everything would have been fine....

Admittedly, there would still be the small matter of the hole in her ship. And he would be dead.

She spun the chair around to face him. The Daemon rested on her thigh, but her hand maintained a loose grip on the trigger. With a flick of her thumb the nervous-system suppressor field keeping him unconscious dissipated.

It took only a few seconds for the man's eyelids to begin to flutter, long black lashes beating against tanned olive skin. An additional second ticked by.

His head snapped up. Bright indigo eyes met hers, startlingly clear and alert. She forced herself not to flinch and to meet his gaze coolly.

"You're Senecan."

He glared at her with what she took to be cocky contempt, almost as though he hadn't noticed he was rather extensively restrained. "Are you insane? Why the hell did you shoot me? I didn't even have a weapon!"

She didn't answer right away, instead eyeing him appraisingly. Advanced if utilitarian environment suit. Beneath the suit, hints of a lean but athletic build. A taut posture which evoked the impression of a panther poised to spring, restraints be damned. Well-defined but not angular facial features dominated by vibrant, piercing irises.

In sum, every pore of his being oozed one thing…

…okay, *fine*. Every pore oozed two things. The first was irrelevant.

The second was *dangerous*. She arched an emphatic eyebrow. "Somehow I don't think you need a weapon in order to kill me."

He didn't argue the point. "And why should I want to kill you?"

"I don't know, you tell me. You're the one who opened fire."

"Merc raiders attacked me on the way here. I thought you were one of them. Are you?"

"No."

"Well I'd say 'sorry,' but seeing as how you shot down my ship then shot *me*, I'm not feeling particularly generous at the moment."

She shrugged with intentional mildness, a counter to the intensity of his stare. "Self-defense. What are you doing here?"

"Studying the pulsar. What are you doing here?"

"Just seeing the sights. You're lying."

"So are you."

"Maybe. I'm also the one holding the gun and the key to those restraints."

"Fair point." He paused as an odd shadow flickered across his eyes…then chuckled with surprising lightness. "I'm sorry, but I can't tell you what I'm doing here."

She nodded deliberately, as if she were contemplating a philosophical assertion, and decided to play a hunch. His lilting and very distinctive accent had vanished, replaced by the generic intonation heard on the largest independent worlds. Such a talent was uncommon, and typically found in a very specific skillset.

She crossed one leg over the other and relaxed a bit in the chair, though the Daemon remained on her thigh. "Hmm. Well, I suppose that means you're likely either military, intelligence…or a criminal."

Her eyes narrowed in pointed accusation. "I bet you're a criminal. A human slave trafficker, or maybe a gunrunner, arming the violent gang wars on the independents? Or are you a drug dealer…yep, I bet that's it. I bet you sell hard chimerals to kids so they can burn their brains out, but not until they—"

He growled in palpable frustration. "I wouldn't do that. *Ever*."

She grinned smugly. And she was quite proud of herself. "So military or intelligence, then."

Her gaze ran down and up the length of his body again, this time for dramatic effect. "And I highly doubt the military would let you keep that mess of a haircut, so intelligence it is."

His brow furrowed into a tight knot at the bridge of his nose; the muscles of his jaw contracted beneath cheeks shadowed by the hint of stubble. He looked at her as though she resembled some sort of alien creature, perhaps with slimy tentacles swirling about her head, but remained silent.

She took the silence as confirmation. "Why is Senecan Intelligence interested in the Metis Nebula?"

He blinked, and with the act his expression morphed from dismay to wary detachment. "This is unclaimed space. I have as much of a right to be here as you do."

"Wasn't what I asked. Why is Senecan Intelligence interested in the Metis Nebula?"

"I still can't tell you, especially not when you're Alliance. What are *you* doing here?"

Her mouth twitched before she managed to squelch it. "What makes you think I'm Alliance? This is a civilian vessel."

"Oh, you're not military—though you're not far removed from it—but you are definitely Alliance."

"Why?"

"The way you said 'Senecan.' Like it was a curse."

She met his penetrating stare with her own cool one. "It is."

"Lovely." The left corner of his mouth curled up in a brazen smirk. She instantly disliked it. "In fact, I'd put credits on you being from Earth."

"There are sixty-seven Alliance worlds. Why would I be from Earth?"

"Earthers exude this arrogance, this pretentiousness—as though even now, nearly three hundred years after colonization began, they're still the only people who really *count*."

"That is not true." Her toes swiveled the chair again. Her gaze drifted away from his to stare at the ceiling. Seconds ticked by in silence; she felt him watching her.

Finally she rolled her eyes in reluctant exasperation. "Okay, it's totally true—but not me. I don't feel that way."

His self-satisfied smile noted he could give as good as he got, and knew it. "So you are from Earth."

Dammit. "That's irrelevant. What's your name?"

"Samuel."

"I'm sure. Well, *Samuel*, make yourself comfortable. I'll be back in a little while."

His expression turned imploring. "Can I at least get some water?"

"When I get back." She leveled an unimpressed glare in his direction but gave him a wide berth as she passed him and headed down the circular stairwell.

⟁

First things first. She double-checked the status of the plasma shield to make certain it was holding. Getting sucked out onto an inhospitable planet sporting unbreathable air and limited atmosphere absolutely didn't fit in her schedule. Satisfied with the readings, she lifted the hatch to the engineering well and descended the ladder.

The dull sallow of the planet's surface could be seen through a roughly three meter long rupture in the hull. The reassuring plasma shimmer kept the interior free of the churning sand and harsh wind.

A smaller gash twisted diagonally from the midpoint of the rupture up to the base of the right internal hull wall. The wall had been ripped open to expose the housing for the plethora of conduits, filters and cabling which powered the ship. The external hull, partially visible behind the mess, sported merely a hairline crack.

From one perspective, this was quite good news—more structural integrity, less hull to repair. On the other hand, it meant the laser had likely danced around wreaking havoc in the gap until it dissipated. Even absent closer inspection she noted several of the photal fiber weaves were shredded in multiple places. Dread pooled in her gut at the thought of what systems they might belong to.

With a sigh she maneuvered around the rupture in the floor to the open gap. She crouched and peered into the aperture, rocking absently on the balls of her feet. Once she got in there it would be hours just cataloging the damage. Perhaps she should get her captive a little water first....

What *did* Senecan Intelligence want in Metis, anyway?

She had picked up some rather unusual spectrum readings on the long-range scans before being so rudely interrupted by laser fire. Had someone else already found the same thing—or more?

"Puzzle it out later, Alex. Prioritize: Water, damage assessment, repairs." She stood and climbed out of the engineering well, went upstairs and rummaged around in the kitchen storage for a field water packet.

'Samuel'—she doubted it was his real name—regarded her as she approached. His acute gaze made her strangely uncomfortable, but she did her levelheaded best to not let it show. She gave him an irritated look and shoved the water packet in his face.

"Something wrong?" he inquired as he accepted the straw.

"*Yes,* something is wrong. You totally wrecked the undercarriage. God knows what it's done to power and navigation. We're going to be grounded for days thanks to your handiwork."

He lazily sucked on the straw, eyes twinkling in blatant amusement. Annoyed, she yanked it away and stepped back to cross her arms stiffly over her chest. "I'll be below for the next few hours cataloging the damage."

She pivoted and left before he could respond.

AR

The damage was even worse than it had appeared at first glance.

She lay on the narrow strip of flooring that wasn't ripped open and stared at the wrecked tangle of conduits and cabling. The blast had shredded twenty centimeters of one of the three lines going to the impulse engine. With the inflow reduced by a third, it was questionable whether the engine had the power to escape the atmosphere.

Even worse, fully half the conduits feeding the plasma shield were damaged—which meant the likelihood of it failing in the vacuum of space was...high.

She never would have made it to Gaiae.

Half a dozen other somewhat less critical problems were immediately evident, thanks to the fissure occurring along one of the primary cabling paths. Aft navigation controls had suffered measurable damage. Splinters of the mHEMT amp for the dampener field decorated the floor.

And all this was ignoring the obvious, irrefutable fact that the undercarriage of her ship had been torn to shreds.

She only hoped the pulse laser hadn't vaporized too much of the hull material, and once the ragged shards were smoothed back out the hull would be able to be resealed. She kept reserve components for the internal electronics and extra conduit coils; spare sheets of reinforced carbon metamaterial? Not so much.

She opened a work list in her eVi and began. The end of the gash closest to the ladder seemed as good a place as any. She shimmied along the edge of the open wall, periodically crawling half into the exposed aperture for a closer inspection. Goddamn it was a mess.

When she finally finished cataloging the damaged components along with severity and criticality, she started constructing the most efficient order of repairs. At least the internal systems resided farther inside and hadn't been damaged—electronics, mechanical, temperature control and water recycling were all fine. So too was the crucial LEN reactor powering them.

Crawling out of the opening, she found an undamaged section of the wall, leaned against it and drew her knees up to her chest. After a deep breath she projected the work list to an aural, expanding it until it no longer required scrolling. The result stretched for more than half a meter.

She made a couple of notations and adjusted the order. Realized she had made a mistake. Corrected it. Corrected it again.

She was tired. Too tired to begin repairs tonight for certain.

Then there was the matter of her prisoner. His restraints secured him for the time being, but long term he constituted a significant problem. A damn Senecan intelligence agent. Dangerous, clever and wearing an arrogant smirk that was going to annoy her real fast.

She wished he had just been a merc. Even the smart mercs were simple and straightforward, with easily discernible motives usually involving credits. This guy represented far more of a mystery, making him even more dangerous than his profession already did. And while in any other circumstance she would simply go on her way, the option wasn't currently available to her.

A groan emerged from the back of her throat as she banged her head against the wall. Anywhere else and she could hand her prisoner over to the authorities, pay a premium for materials and have her ship back in near-to-good-as-new-shape in a day, two days max. But here on this forbidding planet in the middle of nowhere, there were no communications, no supplies and no authorities.

She was on her own.

R

Several hours did in fact pass before she reemerged from the depths of the ship.

Caleb didn't spend the time dwelling on the unfortunate reality that he had been 'captured,' as it were. It was regrettable, but he hadn't exactly been at his best, on account of having plummeted eighteen kilometers through a violent, punishing atmosphere with a centimeter of fabric and a nanopoly faceplate protecting him then crashed onto a barren, unforgiving wasteland.

Instead he carefully studied his surroundings.

By the time she returned, he'd identified the functions of the controls within line of sight, noted several crucial junction points and potentially useful screens and—actually first—determined the nature of the encryption on the restraint web. The cockpit appeared blank and unadorned save for a single chair, which meant it was the most advanced area on the ship. Virtual and impenetrable.

The overall design of the interior conveyed a sense of understated, elegant functionality, with as much attention paid to comfort as to utility. Definitely not a military ship. No, this vessel was of private origin and very, very expensive. Corporate perhaps, though it didn't *feel* corporate. It felt personal.

Once he completed the visual inventory his thoughts shifted to formulating a plan of escape. Well, not so much 'escape' as freedom; it would be counterproductive to abandon the only viable means off the planet.

But he had to admit he was impressed, and more than a little curious. Not about why the most advanced scout ship he'd ever seen was running around Metis. Clearly Alliance interests had discovered the same anomaly as his government and dispatched an investigator.

No, mostly he was curious about what this woman—mechanically savvy and with undeniable flying skills, acerbically sharp, ill-tempered, caustic…and rather stunning in an uncommon, confounding way—was doing piloting it, much less who she might be. At least he would be able to answer the latter question soon enough.

The woman retrieved a new water packet from the kitchen area in the aft of the deck and once again approached him. Her arms glistened from a thin sheen of sweat, while grease and fluids streaked her pants and shirt. Tangled strands of *very* dark red hair had slipped out of a twisted knot to tickle her cheeks and jaw.

She was making a valiant effort to come off as cold, aloof and even threatening. But he read the exhaustion in the stiff way her feet hit the floor with each step and the tense cording of the muscles in her long, slender neck.

She extended the packet straw toward his mouth. The motion was less rude than earlier; he rewarded the good behavior by giving her a quick smile as he accepted the drink. After a moment he nodded, and she stepped back.

Her expression was flat with weariness. "I'm going to get some sleep."

He gazed earnestly at her, looking as hopeful as he could manage. "No food?"

"You won't starve before the morning."

True enough. "What if I have to, um, use the facilities?"

"*Pozhaluysta, ya zhe ne tupïtsa.* Your suit has provisions for that."

His eVi identified the unfamiliar words as an Earth-based Russian dialect. He priority-cached Russian into the translator then shrugged within the confines of the restraints, a dry chuckle on his lips. "No, of course you aren't a moron, but I had to try."

She managed to look highly unimpressed as she turned away. "If you say so. Sleep well."

"What are the odds?"

Halfway down the stairs she paused and gestured toward a screen embedded in the wall. The lights dimmed to a faint glow.

He called out after her. "Thank you…." But she was already gone.

He waited another ten seconds, his posture relaxed and nonchalant in the uncomfortable jump seat. Slowly his eyes drifted downward.

Even in the low light he recognized the strand of her hair which had fallen to rest on his thigh. He took a deep breath and cracked his neck.

It was going to be a long night.

15

"I don't suppose you can tell me what the hell is going on here?"

Michael Volosk nodded with proffered conviction, though his inner thoughts were decidedly less confident.

This was his worst nightmare, if not only his. A prominent Alliance diplomat was dead, and all signs pointed to an official member of the Senecan delegation being responsible. He didn't need to be a politician to recognize the clusterfain of trouble it meant.

Intelligence Director Graham Delavasi dropped his elbows on the desk and waited expectantly for answers he didn't have.

The man's bushy salt-and-pepper hair had strayed onto the wild side, an indication he too had been awoken in the middle of the night. He wore faded denim and a wrinkled polo and kept a giant thermos of coffee in easy reach. There were no aurals around him and no screens active on the desk, which was his way. When he met with someone he gave them his full and undivided attention, for good or ill.

Delavasi had always been a bit of a renegade, wielding a blunt demeanor unusual in the intelligence trade and even more unusual among the political ranks he now technically belonged to. He had risen to a position of power due in large part to a keen intellect, a sharp eye for bullshit and unassailable integrity. Michael admired the man; didn't always like him, but admired him.

He met the Director's gaze. "The Alliance Trade Minister was the target of what looks to be an assassination hit during the Summit's closing dinner. The scene remains in a state of flux, but the evidence indicates the hit was in all probability conducted by a member of our Trade staff."

"Have we executed the son of a bitch yet? Because that may be the only thing standing between us and the full might of the Alliance military showing up at our doorstep."

The data stream from his agents on Atlantis continued to scroll on his whisper; he checked it a last time to make certain it held no better answer. "No, sir. Neither my agents, the Senecan security detail, Atlantis police, nor Alliance security have as yet been able to locate Mr. Candela."

He cringed at Delavasi's disbelieving glare and rushed to reassure the man. "It's simply a matter of time. Atlantis is locked down hard. He won't escape." His hand came to rest at his chin; it was a tic and usually meant he was bothered by something...which he was. "I recognize the undeniable seriousness of the situation, but sending in the military would be a rather disproportionate response, wouldn't it?"

"Assassination of a government official is an explicit violation of the armistice. Now that may not matter to everyone, but I guarantee it will matter to someone with more authority than good sense." Delavasi took a long swig from the thermos. "Who is this guy anyway?"

"He's nobody. A low-level staffer in Director Kouris' office. He's worked in the Trade Division for three years, prior to which he served as an intern for the Parliament's Commerce Committee. Graduated 3rd honors from Tellica with a degree in economics. Has a wife and a new baby. His record is spotless, and he has a reputation as a competent if unexceptional employee. There's no history of political activism or fringe activities. He didn't even vote in the last election."

"Enemies? What about his family, his wife's family? Any potential for blackmail or coercion there?"

"We're looking into it." 'We' had started looking into it three hours earlier at one in the morning when he had been awoken by a flurry of alerts and left Shera sleeping in their bed, and it likely would be days before 'we' knew anything for certain. The Director no doubt recognized this.

Delavasi sighed and sank into the high-backed leather chair. "Bloody hell, Michael, this is a disaster. Nobody wants open conflict with the Alliance. Well, maybe a few fire-breathing Parliament backbenchers and some wackos on Caelum who want an excuse to shoot over the border. But nobody who matters wants another war—and the Chairman *definitely* doesn't want one. He put a lot of political goodwill on the line in pushing for this Summit."

Michael frowned. "Could that be what this is about? Perhaps it's not actually about the Alliance at all, and instead an attempt to discredit the current administration and destabilize the government."

"Damned if I know. Which is a problem, seeing as I'm the Intelligence Director and thus expected to know the justifications of lunatics and devils. But I do know something isn't right here. This smells from top to bottom and I need answers. You'll have all the men you need. Find out what's going on."

"Absolutely, sir. The official delegation should be cleared to leave Atlantis in the next few hours. My men on the ground have already begun private interrogations and will continue them during the flight home. Agents are at Mr. Candela's home now and en route to extended family locations. My best analysts are scouring every aspect of his past for clues as to what might have led to this action."

He paused to take a sip of his own coffee. "As soon as the delegation arrives we'll begin whatever extended interrogations are required at HQ. I intend to personally interview the Assistant Trade Director first thing, as he was in charge of planning and staffing."

Delavasi's eyes creased, drawn inward by the furrow in his brow. "That still Jaron Nythal?"

"I believe so."

"Be careful with him. He's a slippery bastard."

"...care to elaborate?"

Delavasi kicked his chair away from the desk and slowly spun it around. "A couple of years ago—back when I had your job—we took down a spy network operating in several of the high-profile corporations. They were selling secrets acquired via their 'special' access to certain government agencies to the Zelones cartel. Nythal was Corporate Liaison in Trade at the time, and was on the periphery of the scandal. I couldn't make any allegations stick to him, but he was entirely too smooth for my taste."

Michael chose his words carefully. "He would need to be fairly smooth to parlay with the corporate bigwigs, wouldn't he?"

"Without a doubt. Nevertheless, the man was...wrong. I'm just saying be on your toes when you talk to him, and don't assume you're getting the whole story merely because he's on our side."

"Understood."

Delavasi stood and grabbed a gray trench coat lying rumpled on the window sill. "Now, lucky me, I get to go tell the Chairman that *yes*, it appears one of our people did assassinate the bloody Alliance Trade Minister, and *no*, I don't have any evidence he can present to the Alliance government to show it was an isolated act by a lone crazy."

He gave Michael a slightly worn smile as he pulled the coat over his shoulders. "Don't worry, I'm not throwing you to the wolves. I know you're all over it, and it will take a little time to get answers—a sentiment which I will also convey to the Chairman."

"I appreciate the support, sir."

The first steel-hued rays of sunlight broke across the horizon beyond the office window as he stood and shook the Director's hand. It was going to be a long day, and probably not the last.

16

F reshly showered. Hair pulled back in a ponytail and twisted up out of the way. Clean workpants, pockets empty and ready for use. A fitted shirt that wouldn't catch on any jagged edges. Grip-soled slip shoes for ease of movement in the narrow spaces of the engineering well.

Her battle armor. For repairing her ship below—and facing the unknown above.

Alex blew out a long breath and scrunched her face up at the mirror. She only hoped her mental preparation equaled the physical prep. She gave a sharp nod to her reflection and headed up the stairs to the main deck.

Her prisoner resembled...well, someone who had crash-landed on a barren planet then spent the night tied up in a utility jump seat. The hint of stubble had graduated to full shadow, tousled locks to a wild shock of curls. But his eyes were unsettlingly bright and alert as he watched her cross the cabin.

She flopped into the cockpit chair, Daemon back in her hand, and regarded him with a critical eye. "So. *What* am I going to do with you?"

He was ready for her, too. "I've been thinking about that. Let me assure you I'm not a threat to you. It's clear you're my only ticket off this rather inhospitable world, and as such it is against my interests to harm you. So you can remove the restraints, for one."

An eyebrow arched. "So you can kill me, dump my body and steal my ship?"

One corner of his mouth curled up; damn that was going to get annoying. "I'm quite certain your ship won't leave the ground unless you're piloting it. Every control in here is locked and keyed to you. Further, I imagine the navigation system requires regular interaction with your eVi to function."

"True enough. But you could hold me hostage and force me to fly you wherever you wanted to go."

He shrugged within the restraints. "At least you wouldn't be dead."

"Very funny. Until we got where we were going."

His jaw tightened into a rigid line. Before, it hadn't appeared 'square' as such. Now though, she thought she could probably cut a steak with the edges.

The flicker in his eyes hinted he hadn't meant to display frustration so visibly. She watched as he willed his jaw relaxed. "*Why* would I want to kill you?"

"Because I know Senecan Intelligence is after something in the Metis Nebula. Because I know what you look like and what you do, and that *is* a threat to you. Because then you'd have a shiny new ship as bounty."

His mouth opened, presumably carrying a snap response. Instead of delivering the response though, it closed in silence, then after a pause opened again. "Okay, those are…fairly decent reasons." He looked at her with what might be mistaken in civilized company for honesty. "But I'm *not* going to hurt you, especially not when you're the daughter of an Alliance Admiral. I have no desire to start another war."

What? He couldn't possibly….

Of course. He'd have access to the extensive files the Senecan government doubtless maintained on their adversary. Hell, he likely kept the files in his internal data cache and had the tech in his ocular implant to do a retinal scan from at least a meter away. She must have merited a footnote:

> *Alexis Mallory Solovy: Born October 17, 2286, San Francisco, Earth. Father: Dead Martyr. Mother: Cast-Iron Bitch.*

She snorted in mock appreciation. "Neat trick you got there. Still not good enough."

He exhaled softly. Something akin to disappointment flitted across his face.

"*Okay.*"

With a flick of his wrist the restraints vanished. He had unlatched the safety harness and stood before she had blinked.

She and the gun were both up in the next blink, her hands clenched tight on the grip. "*How* did you?"

His hands were in the air, palms open, and he made no move to approach her. The tone of his voice remained scrupulously even. "The web field was DNA-coded to you, obviously. You left behind a strand of hair last night. I used it to create a hack and unlock the web." His shoulders raised in an exaggerated shrug; freed from the restraints it became a far more expressive motion. "Intelligence? It's what I do. If it helps, I didn't get much sleep."

Her response consisted of an icy glare.

He sighed. "Look, the point is, I could have killed you in your sleep, but I didn't."

Her finger only tightened on the gun's trigger. Her thumb hovered over the stun toggle. "Because you need me to do the repairs and, as you noted, fly the ship."

"True. But you are not getting me back in those restraints."

"Oh really? I might just shoot you again."

He glanced around the cabin. "In here? I don't think so. You'd overload half your systems."

"You have no idea the kind of—"

In the space of a breath he had crossed the distance separating them and spun her around into a vise grip from behind. Somehow, the gun was out of her hand and in his. He locked her arms between them and raised the gun to her temple.

She was thoroughly disgusted with herself. One, because she had been standing too close to be able to react, even if he had moved *ridiculously* fast. Two, because she was having to work unexpectedly hard to focus on the gun pressed against her temple rather than the body pressed against her back. *Get your head on straight, life-threatening situation here!*

His voice resonated low and dangerous at her ear. "Just so we're very clear. If I want to kill you, I can kill you."

She growled through gritted teeth in response; she would not show weakness. "Motherfucking Senecan *scumbag*."

"I'm flattered. Now, I'm going to—" His grip loosened as he began to move away.

She wrenched an elbow up and slammed it against his forearm. His arm jolted back, and her elbow continued upward to catch his eye socket. Her left leg swept around to knock his feet out—

—he dodged the sweep by a centimeter and rolled out of reach, coming to his feet three meters away with the gun raised.

He smiled at her, and seemed almost amused. "I'm impressed. That was close."

Her expression was a black hole from which no amusement dared escape. "So what now? You tie me up?"

He bit his lower lip, and a dark flare glimmered in his eyes. "Don't tempt me."

Her face screwed up in disbelief. He was making a *sexual innuendo* while holding her at gunpoint? What did he think this was?

As he stood there though—pointing a gun at her—his expression turned serious. If asked, she'd say it was earnest, even...well, it didn't matter how it looked.

His voice returned to an even and controlled tenor. "I need you to listen to me very carefully. I need you to hear what I am saying. If you try to hurt me, I will respond in kind. Otherwise, *I. am. not. going. to. hurt. you.* Not now, not later, not when we get to wherever we go. You have my word."

He paused for effect then slowly crouched down, his gaze never leaving hers, and set the gun on the floor. He stood up, palms open in submission, and kicked the gun over to her.

Her gaze also did not stray from his while she retrieved the gun and holstered it to her belt. Then she simply stared at him. She didn't know exactly what she hoped to find. Some sign, any sign, of deceit or artifice maybe, or....

He waited patiently.

It would be counterproductive to spend all morning standing on the deck staring at one another when there was a gaping fissure in the hull in need of repair. She made a snap decision.

For the moment, she would take him for what he appeared to be: a smart man demonstrating a realistic perspective on matters and a healthy self-preservation instinct. For the moment, it reduced the threat he represented to a manageable level.

"If you touch anything, I will kill you."

He nodded in ready acceptance of the edict.

She exhaled an exaggerated breath, rolled her eyes and strolled past him. "Want some breakfast?"

ᴙ

She contemplated him over a buttered croissant. Having shed the environment suit, he wore a faded slate-hued Henley, soft black utility pants and an air of calm self-assurance. He casually nibbled on a slice of grapefruit, having taken only a single bite of his own croissant.

Puzzled—by more than one thing concerning him, but currently his lack of an appetite—she frowned at him. "I expected you to be hungrier, seeing as you didn't eat anything last night."

His lips tweaked up. "I, uh, sort of did eat last night."

Her eyes widened in indignation as realization dawned. "You *didn't.*"

"Forgive me, I really was hungry. After I finally broke the encryption on the restraints, I might have opened a few of the kitchen cabinets until I found the energy bars. And helped myself to a few."

The idea of him wandering around her ship in the middle of the night, getting into whatever he cared to and probably brandishing his damnable smirk while he did.... Ugh, she wanted to strangle him, and only the likelihood of him killing her for the effort stopped her. *It's only the kitchen, Alex.* But it didn't have to be only the kitchen. And that wasn't the *point.*

His expression and demeanor projected an affable, nonthreatening persona. His actions a mere few minutes ago told another story. Her brain struggled to process the discordant information, to reconcile what she knew to be true with the man sitting across the table from her.

"I swear, I should have just shot you again."

"I know, I touched something. But it was before your warning, so you can't fairly hold it against me." He shrugged and traded the grapefruit for the croissant.

"You were *physically restrained.* I would have thought my wishes had been made clear." She pinched the bridge of her nose in irritation. "Fine. Whatever. So here's the deal. I need to keep an eye on you, but I also need to be below doing repairs. Therefo—"

"What damage could I do up here? You know I can't access any of the controls."

Her response was a harsh laugh. "If it's all the same to you, after your magic trick on the restraints—and the fact you spent last night running rampant all over my ship—I'm going to err on the side of caution. I'm sure you understand. Therefore, you're going to come down to the engineering well with me, sit in the corner and not bother me while I work."

"Okay."

"Okay? That's all I get?"

He relaxed back in the chair and began licking excess butter off his fingers. "I think you'll find I'm rather easygoing when I'm not tied up."

"I'll be sure and remember that—"

It was all she could do to keep from slapping a hand over her mouth. She had been momentarily distracted by…things, and the words had simply slipped out. She stuffed the last of her croissant in her mouth and studied the crumbs adorning her plate, trying to ignore how the statement might have *arguably* sounded. And it didn't really, not unless you thought about—*no*.

Seconds ticked by, and the moment mercifully passed.

She looked up to find him regarding her…mildly? Displaying slight curiosity perhaps? Even bearing a relaxed posture and amiable expression, the intensity of his gaze unnerved her. She gave him a tight smile and busied herself gathering their plates.

She carried the plates to the counter and stowed them in the sanitizer, then glanced back over her shoulder. A splash of water to the face and a hand through the hair had improved his appearance a surprising amount, but had done nothing to remedy the darkening bruise beneath his right eye.

With a quiet sigh she went to a cabinet in the starboard wall. Beneath the medical station was a drawer containing basic first aid supplies; she removed the wrapper on a small gel pad.

"Here."

He barely looked up in time to catch it before it whacked him in the face. She stifled a cringe.

The pad suspended in the air between two fingers, he tilted his head curiously and raised an eyebrow the tiniest bit.

"For your eye."

"Ahh." He chuckled. "You did nail me pretty good."

She made an effort to not appear amused, though she kind of was. "Stick it on for five minutes and be done with it already. Or don't. Makes no difference to me."

17

"**H**ey Noah, over here, man!"

Noah Terrage picked his way through the crowd in the direction of the voice. Twice he had to maneuver past slumped bodies, kids zoned out on head trips and oblivious to the world around them. Those people who remained upright were shopping, often for the same.

"Dude, you got any Skies?"

He ignored the beggar, other than to surreptitiously nudge him to the left and into the crowd.

The Boulevard was not his favorite place on Pandora. To anyone visiting it for the first time, the name would be taken as an ironic joke. Booths and fabs lined both sides, stacked at least eight deep. The open way through no longer ran down the middle; instead it veered left, then right, in a seemingly random pattern resembling a path of one of the trippers who frequented it. Multi-sensory signs and giant screens blaring out jarring, discordant rhythms jammed the overhead space to entirely obscure Pandora's rather nice sky.

Yet beneath the chaos did exist an actual boulevard, stretching fifty meters in width and paved with marbled stone. At least, that was the rumor. No one had seen it in thirty years.

So, no, The Boulevard was not his favorite place. Still, occasionally his business necessitated a visit. He didn't deal in chimerals, but there was a lot more for sale here than merely chimerals. More to the point, there were dealers here who dealt in a lot more than merely chimerals.

He slid in around the storefront to where his contact rested on a lounge stool and leaned in close so as to be heard over the raucous din. "Emilio, my man. How's business?"

Emilio shook his head, sending long, glittering green braids swooshing through the air. "Same old. Want a beer?"

"Ah, wish I could, but I'm tight on time. Got to gather with a needy client on the Prom in twenty. Next time?" It never hurt to remind Emilio he had a diverse and well-paying clientele.

"I hear ya. Hang on a sec, I'll get your gear." Emilio slipped behind the shimmering barrier which separated the 'store' front from the supply area, but returned in seconds.

A handshake and Noah palmed the small, innocuous-looking gadget and slipped it in his hip pack. He instructed his eVi to transfer the funds to Emilio's account. And like that, the deal was done.

He patted Emilio's shoulder. "Pleasure doing business with you, as always."

"I'm gonna buy a top-shelf *illusoire* with the proceeds, man."

"Enjoy, then!" He laughed as he slid out of the booth and back into the crowd.

⋅ℛ⋅

The city which comprised Pandora's inhabited region constituted a two hundred kilometer swath of gleaming metal and bright lights. There existed dark areas of Pandora, but they resided below even the Boulevard.

People assumed Pandora was unruled, out-of-control chaos, a patchwork of merchants and clubs and black markets. In truth, it had been constructed and continued to be overseen by a loose association of wealthy entertainment moguls. Which individuals participated in the association was a closely guarded secret, presumably because they held important positions in society.

They built out additional infrastructure when it became needed and ensured the power grid and transportation system continued to function. They kept the slums corralled in small, well-defined areas and made sure the criminal cartels didn't gain too powerful of a foothold in the commerce of the planet. Agents of the cartels existed on Pandora without a doubt; some of them even had significant business ventures, but they ranked no higher than the successful independent entrepreneurs.

Pandora was a world where anything went, where you could buy anything and sell anything, where you could live out your wildest fantasy or spend forty years in a haze of parties and booze and chimerals and sex—or do both. And it was an illusion.

Oh, you could do all those things, to be sure. But the world was an artificial creation. A planet-sized theme park where the machinery of the rides was kept hidden from public view.

Noah knew this because his father acted as a minor player in the association which controlled Pandora. In the weeks before bailing on his father's grand plan for his life, he had hacked and made copies of his father's personal and business records. For insurance, for blackmail if necessary, and out of mild curiosity at what he would be leaving behind.

He'd never used the information to his advantage, at least not overtly. But simply being aware of the 'men behind the curtain,' as it were, gave his life here a certain unreal quality. Like he had been immersed in a nineteen-year-long deep-dive full-sensory head trip. It gave him freedom and, it could be argued, encouraged a level of recklessness and imprudent behavior he might not be inclined to engage in if any of this were *real*.

Still...it was all good, he thought as he stepped off the levtram and into The Approach.

Most of the districts on Pandora were named some variation of a thoroughfare; there was also The Channel, The Promenade, The Avenue, The Passage, and so on. Their names gave no clue as to their character or quality, however. Visitors arrived clueless, but enterprising street urchins stalked the spaceport, willing to size up what a visitor had come to find and what they could afford and send them in the right direction—for a few credits, of course.

His apartment was located in The Approach, which only meant it lay in the region between the transport hub and the most popular entertainment district. It actually did have a lot of character, inhabited by a chaotic jumble of artists, merchants and runaways who had decent funds in their account—which he supposed, even after nineteen years, included him.

He unlocked the door and slipped in his apartment, grateful for once no one frolicked in the hallway, as he did need to work this afternoon. His proffered excuse for not hanging out with Emilio hadn't been a lie, as such. He did need to meet a client on the Prom in twenty; it happened to be in twenty hours, not minutes. Emilio was an okay guy, but his cohorts weren't. And besides, he'd just as soon not loiter on The Boulevard any longer than he had to.

He grabbed a water from the fridge and stepped in his work room. A floor-to-ceiling cabinet lined the left wall, full to the brim with components, spare parts and pending orders. The far wall contained four shelves of equipment and tools. He sat down at the workbench along the right wall, spun around to retrieve the other components from the cabinet, then sat back and contemplated the pieces spread on the table in front of him.

The item he had picked up from Emilio represented the final component for a special order of custom equipment. Individually, each component was innocuous: a neck wrap, a contact pad to access the tiny fibers at the base of the neck which connected to a person's cybernetics, a quantum data transmitter and a data buffer. Combined, they created an extremely powerful and quite illegal tool.

When worn by an individual, the item allowed the person to interface directly with a remote synthetic neural net ('Artificial' being the somewhat derogatory but widely used term). The buffer was a necessity because even a heavily cybernetically-enhanced human brain couldn't begin to process the data streaming from a neural net in real time; absent one you risked frying your cybernetics from the overload of data.

Artificials were required to be registered and pre-approved by regulatory authorities, who certified the mandated security blocks were in place and sufficient. Even on the most free-wheeling independent worlds they were carefully monitored. And remotely interfacing with one—which thanks to quantum transmission might literally be halfway across settled space—was strictly forbidden. A person walking down the street, or more likely sitting in a corporate boardroom, sporting secret access to zettaFLOPs of mental power went several steps beyond the unfair advantages tolerated by society.

Seeing as it really was a dangerous tool, he wouldn't normally be comfortable either constructing or selling it. In this case, however, he knew the client personally and felt certain she didn't intend to use it for galactic domination. No, he suspected she simply wanted to see what it was like to effectively meld with the mind of an Artificial...and because she *could*.

18

SIYANE
METIS NEBULA, UNCHARTED PLANET

Caleb sat on the bottom rung of the ladder, arms draped over his knees and hands clasped loosely together.

She lay half-subsumed beneath the tear in the wall, working to re-secure a long strip of threaded cabling in the narrow space between the interior wall and exterior hull. She hadn't said more than two words since they had come downstairs, the two words having been 'stay there.'

He had already analyzed what he could see of the hold. Though the rather significant damage muddled matters somewhat, he had quickly classified the engineering section as an advanced but mostly standard layout for a ship of this size, albeit featuring several unusual customizations.

This conclusion he had come to in the first two minutes; thirty-seven minutes later, there was only one thing left in the hold for him to analyze.

"So you're a treasure hunter."

It was the most rational conclusion. The instruments and panel readouts on the main deck were geared toward measurement and detection of element concentrations, spectrum spikes and notable astronomical phenomena. They covered too broad a range for a purely scientific expedition; and besides, a double Masters in mechanical engineering and stellar astronomy yet no doctorate suggested she was far too practical to be a scientist.

The ship displayed a complete lack of corporate branding anywhere, and the last employer listed in her file was from eight years earlier. Taken together with the fair number of personal extravagances, it meant she had to be independent.

The muffled response came from within the aperture. "I'm an explorer."

"That's what I said—a treasure hunter."

She grunted in exertion and a section of cabling snapped snugly against the wall. "And *I* said for you not to bother me."

He gave an exaggerated shrug, though he doubted she was able to see it. "Right, my bad."

A few seconds passed. She groaned and slid into the open to glare at him in obvious annoyance. "I find undiscovered planets, resources, astronomical events, other anomalies, and sell the information to whoever can make the best use of it."

"To the highest bidder."

"If they're legitimate and meet the correct profile? Usually, yes."

"That's cold. Ruthless even."

She exhaled. It was less a sigh and more a forceful expulsion of air from the lungs. He took note of the way the firm muscles in her stomach expanded then contracted beneath the thin, pliant fabric of her shirt, but decided it would be best to ignore the smooth rise then fall of her chest.

"No, it's not. Everyone is better off as a result. Without my work, no one knows about the resource. With it, others are able to develop new tech, new materials, even new worlds. I'm merely improving civilization."

He burst out laughing. It was genuine and unplanned and he just couldn't help it.

She straightened her arms behind her and sat up, the better to direct the full power of her glare at him. "*What.*"

The white-blue light of the screens hovering in the otherwise dark hold transformed her irises to liquid silver. He blinked and tried to ignore the startling effect—which was somewhat difficult if he was to continue meeting her gaze. Ignoring every attractive quirk of hers might be harder than first thought.

But he wasn't here to get laid; he was here to get off this planet in one piece. Building an amicable relationship furthered his goal, but he suspected coming on to her would result in another elbow to the face. For starters.

Of course, he probably shouldn't tease her either. *Ah well, too late now.* "You are not out here, on this very unique ship, to 'improve civilization.'"

Her eyes widened in offense. But he merely regarded her with amusement, and the severe countenance melted away.

She rolled her eyes at the low ceiling, but her shoulders snapped straight into a proud posture. "I sleep well at night, comforted by the knowledge what I do helps rather than hurts. But...no, perhaps it's not my *primary* purpose."

Then she frowned, and it occurred to him maybe she hadn't intended to say so much—which meant she thought she had revealed something about herself she hadn't wanted to.

She dropped to the floor and slid back under the wall. "Now would you *please* shut up?"

He needed some time to ponder what the accidental reveal meant, anyway. "Certainly."

R

She was eyeing him over her sandwich—roasted penzine, which his data cache told him was a small fowl native to Erisen, and Swiss cheese on dark rye bread. "Why are you out here?"

His lips pursed together, his own sandwich poised in midair. Damn she was persistent. "I still can't tell you, except to say it wasn't supposed to involve violence."

"How comforting."

He shrugged, annoyed she doubted him, then annoyed at himself for being annoyed. He should really be more in control of the situation than this. "What do you want me to say?"

"What you're doing out here."

He dropped the remains of his sandwich to the plate in frustration. She raised an eyebrow in response, which only made things considerably worse. He looked around the cabin, eager to change the topic of conversation. "So do I get to sleep in the chair again tonight?"

She shook her head in the negative, then jerked it in the direction of the starboard wall. "There's a guest cot, pulls out of the wall. There's even a privacy screen. You'll be snug as a bug in a rug."

He chuckled at the odd, quaint-sounding idiom. "A what?"

"It's just something my—" Her eyes darkened and she practically leapt out of the chair to carry her plate to the sink. "Never mind."

He frowned, as much at her abrupt change of mood as his unexpected desire to make it better. No, it was the proper reaction; a cheerful mood meant harmonious interaction and the absence of guns and hand-to-hand combat. "Thank you, I'm sure it'll be fine. Not quite the luxurious nest you have downstairs but—"

The loud *clang* of a plate against the sink's surface cut him off. His frown deepened; he made sure his voice sounded neutral and non-threatening. "Is everything okay?"

She spun around to lean on the counter, an indecipherable look on her face. "Look, I'm not used to having someone out here with me, in my space and asking questions and—particularly a suspicious and dangerous spy who tried to kill me."

"I didn't try to kill you." At her dubious glare he grimaced. "Okay, I might have tried to shoot you down. But you *did* shoot me down, and you don't see me holding a grudge. Second ship blown up in two months, but whatever, it's fine, they're only ships."

"To you, maybe."

For the briefest moment, her expression became totally unguarded and open. Until this instant, he hadn't realized the cold, hard demeanor was a mask she had donned for him, or possibly for everyone. This though...*this was beautiful.*

He smiled with what he hoped conveyed sincerity. "Your ship's important to you, I imagine."

"You could say that." The unguarded, beautiful expression lingered for another breath before fading away behind the mask.

He stood, plate in hand, and headed over to the sink as well. "You've obviously put a lot of time and money into it." He leaned in to stow his plate right as she reached across to grab the hand towel.

For a solid two seconds they both froze in place, shoulders touching and faces centimeters apart, too close to even focus on the other. He was suddenly consumed by the thought of how damned *hot* the air felt for a supposedly climate-controlled room.

She snatched the towel off its hook and stepped back, and the spell broke. He busied himself with stowing his plate...and slowing a racing pulse.

As the afternoon faded into evening, she gradually started talking, responding to his casual inquiries in a more conversational tone and even volunteering information from time to time. What she was doing and why, details on the mechanics in the engineering well and other parts of the ship.

He responded by sharing where appropriate. He talked about what his experiences had and hadn't taught him about ships, some of the more interesting designs he'd seen and so on. Building rapport with his captor.

It was late in the evening ship-time when she sank against an undamaged section of the wall and looked at him. Damp strands of hair had glued themselves to flush cheeks; grease had smudged along her neck.

"Can you cook?"

He shrugged in careful nonchalance. "I've been told I'm not half bad at it, yeah. Why?"

She climbed to her feet and wiped her hands on by now filthy pants. "I'm going to take a shower. You can cook dinner."

"You realize in order to cook I'll have to touch something."

"I grant you a specific, limited exception."

"Fair enough. But how do I know how to work the stove, or where the food is?"

She shot him an odd look as she passed him and climbed up the ladder. "You're a smart guy, and seeing as you're apparently already familiar with my kitchen, I assume you'll figure it out."

And he did figure it out, because he *was* a smart guy...and was already familiar with her kitchen. By the time she came up the stairwell the aroma of steaming vegetables and roasting potatoes filled the cabin.

He glanced over upon her arrival and nearly dropped the wok mid-toss.

She wore flimsy little gray shorts and a black tank top. The tiny straps exposed a sculpted collarbone and delicate hollow at the base of her throat. She was toweling dry her hair, which turned out to be quite long when it wasn't tied up in a ponytail or knot or whatever she did to it. Burgundy locks fell in soft waves to frame those remarkable cheekbones, then down along her neck to tease alabaster shoulders before draping midway down her back. Beneath the shorts slender but toned legs seemed to go on *forever*.

He swallowed and promptly gave up on ignoring any and all attractive traits of hers; it was far too much work. It had been some time since a woman had legitimately taken his breath away.

"Um, stir-fry okay? I wasn't sure...."

She smiled, and for yet another moment her expression was genuine and unguarded and easily as beautiful as before. She appeared completely unaware of the effect she was having on him. "Definitely. It smells delicious."

He tried to match the tenor of her smile. "Excellent." The steam started stinging his eyes; he returned his attention to the stove and hurried to make sure the potatoes didn't burn while mentally berating himself for getting all goo-goo eyed and flustered like he was fourteen.

He sprinkled pepper on his vegetables. Thanks to the flash freezing they had retained much of their flavor, but Senecan dishes tended toward spicy, and he had acquired the taste. "Caleb."

Her fork paused at her lips. "Hmm?"

"My name. It's Caleb." *Why* was he telling her?

The corners of her mouth rose a fraction. "Better."

That was why. Shit.

She took a sip of water. "I knew a Samuel in elementary school. He was a bully, tried to beat my friend up."

"What happened?"

"I beat him up instead."

"Naturally."

She shrugged. "It worked. He left us alone from then on. Caleb what?"

"Marano."

Surprise flashed across her face. "You're just telling me?"

Apparently. "I could be lying again."

"True. But you're not."

Was it painted in neon letters on his forehead? "No, I'm not. You fancy yourself good at reading people?"

"Hell, no. I'm terrible at it." She continued eating, but her motions slowed as her eyes unfocused. "Caleb Marano: Born June 3, 2283, Cavare, Seneca. Father: engineer for the Senecan Civil Development Agency. Mother: freelance industrial architect. Younger sister Isabela, age thirty-two: professor of biochemistry. Parents divorced in 2301. It says you're an assembly line manager for Terrestrial Avionics—which is a lie, of course."

Her gaze sharpened back on him. "And that's it. There's no public record of what you've spent the last twenty years doing. But there wouldn't be, would there?"

"How did you access the information? I assumed your communications were down as well."

"They are. There's an exanet backup in the ship."

"The *entire* exanet?"

"No, not the entire exanet, don't be ridiculous. Merely some repositories I find useful."

He nodded and speared a potato wedge. "Well, now you know as much about me as I do about you, Alexis Solovy."

She studied her glass of water with a startling intensity. "It's Alex."

His voice softened as hers had. "Better."

No response followed, and when the silence verged on uncomfortable he ran a hand through his hair. "So, what's the state of the repairs?"

She grimaced a little, her body language shifting subtly. "Full power's restored to the impulse engine, and I've replaced all but one of the conduits to the plasma shield. Probably another half-day on the smaller problems before I can turn to the hull itself. I'm going to try to weld it back together. Hopefully sufficient material is left, plus whatever I can scrounge up, to close it."

"I can help with that—I mean I'm not bad with a welding torch and a metamat blade."

She regarded him with a guarded expression. "We'll see." Then she stood, grabbing both their plates and taking them to the sink. "Dinner was very good, thank you." She glanced over her shoulder. "You can use the shower if you'd like. I'll clean up."

"Thank you. I am feeling a bit ripe at this point."

"Just—"

"I know." He laughed lightly as he started down the stairs. "Don't touch anything."

ℛ

She was standing at the data center when he returned. A number of screens floated above the table, bright with graphs and visuals. Actually, he realized, there were no screens, only the data. The table itself must be a conductive medium.

Her focus on the information displayed, she didn't notice him. He took advantage of the opportunity and paused at the top of the stairwell to watch her.

Her right hand reached up and three fingers glided fluidly over one of the graphs. The lines shifted color and position in their wake.

Now he could see. Starting at her fingertips and running along the inside of her arm, across her shoulder blades and up to the nape of her neck where they disappeared into her hairline, wove a pattern of elaborate, intricate glyphs. They pulsed a vibrant white glow when she touched an image or data point and faded after her fingers lost contact.

Most people who had extensive glyphs brandished them like a badge of honor, tattooing them in bright glittering colors to declare the extent of their cyberization for all to see. Hers, however, vanished when not in use; until now he had been unaware they existed, and he was a rather observant guy.

He smiled as he watched her blow up a waveform to dominate the space above the table. The glyphs indicated not only was she absorbing the data into her cybernetics, she was likely manipulating it internally and sending it back to the table. Her movements displayed a seamless connection between her and the information she studied. He suspected he was witnessing her in her natural habitat.

Best for her not to catch him watching though. He cleared his throat and ascended the last stair. She glanced at him but didn't clear the displays.

He joined her but kept a respectful distance by leaning against the nearby worktable. "Thank you for the shower. To say it was needed would be a colossal understatement. I, uh, couldn't do anything about the clothes. I don't suppose you have any…?"

She shook her head, a hint of a twinkle in her eyes. Though in fairness it may have simply been the reflected glow of the graphs. "Sorry, no. Haven't had any boys sleep over recently."

"Now that is a tragedy."

Somewhat to his surprise, she laughed. "Perhaps, but everything has a price."

He wanted to ask what she meant, but that question lay several steps further away in their precariously thawing relationship. Instead he gestured at the table. "What you got?"

"Full-spectrum scans of the Metis interior, at least as far as my instruments were able to penetrate before…well it wasn't as far as I'd like. The nebular dust is maddeningly dense, particularly when you consider how old its supernova is. Nonetheless, I picked up some unusual readings."

"How so?"

She flared her palm and one of the graphs zoomed in. It showed a single line exhibiting multiple, regular peaks. "This is the pulsar beam. Firmly in the gamma spectrum, and with a spin of 419 revolutions per second it's clearly a millisecond pulsar. So question one, where's its companion?" She worried at her lower lip. "If the companion's radius is small enough, its signature might be hidden in all this dust or on the other side of the pulsar, but...anyway, so that's curious."

She nudged the graph off to the top right corner and magnified another graph to the center. It overflowed with data, multiple overlapping waveforms of differing widths and colors.

Two fingers reached into it and pinched the thickest waveform, a line of deep purple. "So this is the gamma synchrotron radiation. It's by far the strongest reading." She flicked it off to one side where it shrank into a small square, then pinched a more diffuse but thick line blue in color. "The pulsar wind, gamma bleeding into x-ray." It landed above the purple square.

After their removal a pear-colored line dominated the graph. She spared a quick glance at him; he studied the graph with interest and didn't acknowledge it. "Ionized particles left over from the supernova. This is the glow we see." A flick and it minimized below.

The graph was now virtually bare. She pushed away two thin lines of dark and light orange. "Random infrared and microwave readings from whatever."

A single, tiny line of dark crimson remained. Thin and semi-transparent, it marked a nearly horizontal path across the graph. She crossed her arms over her chest and rested on her back leg. "Then we have *this*."

He kept his tone scrupulously neutral. "Radio emissions I presume?"

"Tremendously Low Frequency—TLF—technically, but they don't even have a proper term for a wavelength this long. This wave is propagating at a frequency of 0.04 Hz. *Nothing* emits at so low a frequency."

A soft breath fell from his lips, and the response with it. "Not 0.04 Hz. 0.0419 Hz."

Her eyes shot to him and flared a lustrous argent hue. "What?"

He focused on the graph, difficult though it was. "Can you expand the period shown?" A glance at the top right corner of the spread. "Say to ten hours?"

"*Okay.*" Her stare bore into him as her right hand slid along the graph. The crimson line now undulated in long, smooth waves.

"Now superimpose the pulsar beam on top of this one."

"No fucking way."

"If you don't want to it's fine, I—"

"I mean *no fucking way.*" She yanked the pulsar beam graph out of the corner and dropped it in the center. It wasn't a surprise to him, and he assumed no longer a surprise to her, when the pulse spikes lined up perfectly on the crests of the crimson line.

"That's why I'm here."

She still stared at him instead of the graph. "Explain."

"Last month we sent in a prototype, state-of-the-art probe for testing. Among a few other things, it returned this congruence. My government would like to determine what it is."

"But you're not a scientist. Why send in a black ops agent?"

"Well, the thought was the level of precision strongly suggests it's artificial, and thus it might be hostile…." He sighed. *Shit.* "I never said I was a black ops agent."

She gave him a wicked grin. "Not until now."

She had managed to fit in manipulating him in between sophisticated data analysis. Impressive.

He brought a hand up to run through his hair, still damp from the shower. "Well played. Anyway, given the concern it might be hostile they were reluctant to send civilian researchers. And while I'm not a scientist, I know my way around spectrum analyses and whatnot better than the average *black ops agent.*"

Her gaze had finally returned to the graphs, and his returned to her. "Is this what you're here for?"

Her voice was soft, almost whimsical. "Maybe."

"Look, you don't have to tell me, but there's no reason to hide it."

She half-smiled. "Not what I meant. The Nebula caught my eye. I knew there would be something to find…I didn't necessarily know what it would be."

Her expression shifted even in profile. "Did you learn what it was? You know, before you tried to shoot me down."

"No. I had only been here a few hours when you *blew my ship out the sky.*"

"Right." She rolled her eyes a little. "I'm sorry about that, by the way. In the same circumstances I'd do it again, but I *am* sorry."

He looked at her askance. "Um, thanks?"

"Certainly." The graphs abruptly vanished; the cabin darkened in the absence of the holographic images. "I'd like to get an early start in the morning, so good night."

"Good night...." He frowned, taken aback by the sudden shift in tone and quick exit. In a few brief seconds she had waved the lights dim, descended the stairwell and disappeared.

Then he was alone and unrestrained on the main deck of her ship.

He noted the previously identified stations, controls and junction points. While the security on them was doubtless more complex than his restraints had been, he suspected he could hack at least some of them.

But he didn't need to, and gained nothing by doing so. The repairs weren't complete; if he tried to fly away now he'd just get himself and her killed. And given their 'relationship'—if one wished to call it such—was improving, odds were decent once the repairs were complete she would in fact drop him on an independent world and be on her way.

So instead of hacking her ship he unfolded the cot from the wall, pulled the privacy screen over, took off his shoes and lay down. The cot wasn't too bad; he'd slept on far worse.

He laced his hands behind his head and pondered how she had managed to get him to tell her his name, his profession and his mission, all in less than a day.

It went against one of the mandates of his job: never reveal anything more than is necessary to finish the mission. On the other hand, he was in a compromised position and reliant on her to get out of it. In such a situation exceptions could be made.

Even so, he should get on his game. *Though....*

As long as he didn't kill her and she didn't kill him, this would likely end with him making it back to settled space in one piece.

Therefore, other than ensuring she felt enough goodwill toward him to not throw him out the airlock—which seeing as she had gone out of her way to rescue him in the first place, he suspected was a fairly low threshold—he really didn't need to play her.

He had been trained to always be looking for an opening, for a weakness he could use to his advantage to cripple the enemy and complete the mission. But she wasn't an enemy. She wasn't even a mark.

So he decided he was marginally comfortable with her knowing a few truths. Which was interesting, seeing as he allowed very few people to know many truths at all about him.

Special circumstances and all.

Alex crashed onto her bed, relishing the sensual, almost carnal feel of her head sinking into the silky pillow.

After several deep, luxurious breaths she glanced up, and promptly scowled. The viewport above the bed often revealed twinkling stars or occasionally a glowing nebula, but at the very least the blurred shimmer of superluminal travel. Tonight it revealed a thick haze of sickly amber dust and little else, serving as a stark reminder she lay stranded on a nasty uncharted planet with a broken ship and a confounding…she didn't even know what he constituted now.

Why had she let him see the scans? Worse, why had she *explained* them to him?

Because he was putting on a very convincing act of being friendly and nonthreatening? Of course he was convincing. It was his job to convince people he could be trusted until he was ready to kill them or arrest them or dispense whatever justice he fancied upon them.

Because he was a good cook? While a rather nice surprise, it hardly qualified him for 'friend' status.

Because he was disturbingly good looking, with hair as black as the void between stars which sent her pulse aflutter when it fell across his brow? Because he had the bluest eyes she'd ever seen—the color of the uncut natural sapphires they displayed in geology museums—which sparkled from a thousand facets when he made a teasing remark?

Yep, that was probably why.

She groaned and rolled over to bury her face in the pillow. "I'm waxing poetic about a man. Kill me now...."

In a world of cheap genetic enhancement before and even after birth, handsome men were a dime a dozen. They'd never distracted her or done much of anything in particular for her, at least not from looks alone.

No way was she going to be led astray by a pair of pretty blue eyes. Especially not when they belonged to a Senecan, and a Senecan black ops agent at that.

She possessed enough self-awareness to realize her view of the world was slightly jaded and *perchance* cynical. Nonetheless, objectively she recognized being born on Seneca did not automatically make him an evil monster. Granted, hardly a galaxy-altering revelation. Seneca was an adversary, one toward which she bore deep-seated animosity for her own personal reasons. But most people living there were no different from everyone else, spending their time doing the things most people did and not torturing puppies or sacrificing virgins.

And even being a black ops agent didn't automatically make him an evil monster, though it did make him dangerous. Her mother was and her father had been military; Richard, Malcolm and a number of her acquaintances were military—and thus trained killers. She had no right to judge him for engaging in activities those closest to her would do, and had done, if asked by their government.

The experience of the day seemed to bolster the decision she had made this morning. He appeared to be a smart, rational guy and not a zealot or fanatic or psychopath. As such, he presumably realized getting along and not causing trouble for her would result in him getting out of this situation alive and unharmed, and anything he did to actually help would speed up said resolution.

Thus, she came to the conclusion that while she definitely couldn't *trust* him, she could perhaps 'trust' him a little for now.

She went through the reasoning two more times to make certain it was sound, logical and had nothing whatsoever to do with a pair of pretty blue eyes.

19

DEUCALI

L iam entered the pub as unobtrusively as possible. His tall, stocky frame placed a lower limit on his ability to be unobtrusive, but he did try.

The pub was located many kilometers from the base, in an upper-middle yet not quite upper class neighborhood. He had dressed out of uniform, wearing navy slacks, a crisp white button-down shirt and a navy blazer. Well, perhaps not far out of uniform. But he wore an unadorned navy cap over his distinctive ginger hair so as to avoid being recognized.

When one was a Regional Commander of the Earth Alliance Armed Forces, one possessed no 'peers' in the region—no one it was appropriate to go out with for a couple of beers, or watch the game or barbeque with on the weekend. No one to assemble with to watch the tides of war gather.

Maybe it was better this way, lest he give something away in a careless laugh or knowing nod at a crucial moment, but a man such as him did not have friends. Subordinates, professional colleagues, rivals and enemies. But not friends.

If he stopped to give thought to it, there did exist a time when he *had* had friends…teammates in primary, a few worthy cohorts in university ROTC. But that had been *before*. Before the war against Seneca, before his mother had returned home in a flag-draped coffin and gutted his father's spirit. Before he had sworn a vow to his mother's eternal soul and the God who shepherded it that he would have vengeance.

As an only child, since his father died in a construction accident seven years earlier he had no family of note either. He'd never married, unwilling to let another person inside his private affairs much less his private emotions. His spouse was the Alliance military, which was all he'd ever required. And it worked out for the best, as it meant the chance of bringing shame to his family had not needed to be a consideration in his decision whether to collude in recent events, and events soon to come.

He acquired a chair at a high table in the bar area and motioned for a waiter, remembering at the last second not to bark an order for immediate service. He ordered an Earth ale; since he was out of uniform he didn't need to publicly support the local economy, and Deucali's meager attempts at hops brewing left a good bit to be desired.

Deucali wasn't a particularly scenic world either. Its landscape had been painted in browns and yellows and decorated with dull waters and minimal mountain ranges. Nevertheless, it was rich in natural resources and boasted a calm, temperate climate, one reason it had been the first world colonized on the Perseus Arm of the galaxy and for a brief time the most distant colony in existence. The Alliance had established a strong presence here and for decades used it as a base from which to expand outward along the southern arc of the Arm.

After a hundred and ten years a thriving, self-sufficient economy was firmly established, even if much of it continued to be centered around military operations. The patrons of the pub were engineers, defense contractors and civilian managers, yet even they retained a rugged, down-to-earth aura. You wouldn't find glitzy balls or elaborate sensory circuses on Deucali, and he thanked God on an almost daily basis for their absence.

The waiter delivered his drink and a bowl of crusted bread, then vanished upon his disinterest in further purchases. The pub was busy bordering on packed, and he assumed the young man had others to service who would be freer with their credits.

He twisted the cap off the pure-bottled ale and rotated the chair toward the nearest exanet news screen in time to see Prime Minister Brennon walk to the podium.

Brennon was a sturdy, solidly built man, with a slightly lined face and slightly graying hair that could mean an age anywhere from sixty to a hundred sixty. He held himself as all politicians did, shoulders back and chin a notch high.

"As you no doubt know by now, yesterday we suffered a great tragedy in the loss of Trade Minister Mangele Santiagar. He was one of our brightest young stars, a dedicated public servant and a personal friend. He volunteered to lead the delegation to the Trade Summit because he believed

in the possibility of a peaceful future with the Senecan Federation and the benefits which could result therefrom."

The Prime Minister paused to look troubled. In the pub, most of the patrons shifted their attention away from the various sporting events playing out on the other screens; the previously lively room grew subdued. Though situated in nearly the opposite corner of settled space from Seneca, the strong military presence here meant even civilians on Deucali exhibited a strong patriotic streak.

"It was a good dream, one we all hoped would come to be. But it, and he, were betrayed by those who might have reaped its benefits—by the very Senecans he reached out to in a gesture of peace. He was savagely murdered by those who came forth in a costume of friendship but wielded daggers beneath their cloaks."

Liam took a sip of his ale. Politicians could always be counted on to turn a phrase when the fires of outrage needed to be fanned. Hyperbole and metaphor were powerful tools in the right hands. He doubted the PM was anything other than a vapid politician in an empty suit, but he certainly knew how to give a performance when a performance was required.

"The General Assembly has convened in emergency session and is discussing the best manner of response to this shocking outrage. Rest assured that our response, when it comes, will be measured, deliberate and commensurate with the crime committed against the Earth Alliance."

He paused again, his voice softening in tenor. *"For now, our hearts and prayers are with Minister Santiagar's wife, his children and all the members of his family. I grieve with them, as we all do, in their time of loss. Thank you."*

Liam gestured to the waiter for another drink. The pub had a nice atmosphere and safe anonymity. He decided he might linger awhile.

Perking up at the renewed prospect of further purchases, the waiter quickly reappeared to deliver his drink. Liam nodded to himself as he turned the fresh bottle up. He didn't know whether Santiagar had been a good man or a bad one, but it made no difference. He had been a sacrificial lamb to the mission.

Mr. Prime Minister, you ain't seen nothing yet.

COSENTI
INDEPENDENT COLONY

A chill breeze drifted in from the flatlands as Thad Yue instructed the bots to bring the crates down the ramp and move them into the unmarked hangar.

Eight crates in total were unloaded from the transport. Each one contained four autonomous VI-guided short-range Earth Alliance missiles tipped with high-density HHNC warheads. As missiles went they were lightweight and compact; even so, each crate required two of the industrial-grade mechanized bot lifters to be moved inside.

As soon as the last one cleared the ramp he signaled the transport to depart. The pilot had no knowledge of the contents of the crates, and probably didn't care to find out. Just another routine delivery from New Babel.

Cosenti was a tiny colony not far outside Senecan Federation space. Nominally independent, it maintained only the most basic governance infrastructure, and in practice the criminal cabals ran things here. It served primarily as a storage and staging location for smuggling illicit goods onto Senecan worlds, which was just as well, for its arid, infertile soil and flat landscape rendered it suitable for little else.

Although it sported fairly substantial defensive measures, if the Senecan military really wanted to they could wipe the colony off the map. Thus far they hadn't chosen to, presumably because they realized a replacement would spring up somewhere else within a month. The real source of illicit trade—chimerals, weapons, gear and all manner of cyber tools and unauthorized enhancements—was New Babel. And wiping it out would be another matter entirely.

The land outside the small town which constituted Cosenti's sole inhabited locale was populated by a patchwork of warehouses, flight hangars and plain structures of hidden purpose. Kilometers separated each cluster of buildings and perimeter drones guarded every region, programmed to eliminate any vehicle or person who did not possess the correct code. Various organizations controlled the buildings, but no markings, signs or other identifying features designated ownership. Visitors either knew where to go, or had no business going there.

By the time Thad walked in the hangar the others were already unpacking the crates. He watched several of them guide the smaller, more precision-oriented bots in securing the first missile beneath one of the fighter jets while the others readied the next missile.

The four jets dominating the hangar's open space had arrived two days earlier and were carbon copies of current generation Earth Alliance Navy ships. The paint on the Alliance logos and distinctive blue stripes shone like new. Which it was of course, having been applied about eighteen hours earlier.

This particular hangar belonged to the Zelones cartel, so named for the family who founded and ruled it for almost two centuries. Their rule had ended decades ago, though, with the rise to power of Olivia Montegreu. Formerly the chief lieutenant to Ryn Zelones, following his death under the suspicious circumstances typical of a criminal kingpin's demise, she had rapidly secured control of the cartel under her sole and absolute authority.

He had met the woman on several occasions, and found she more than lived up to her reputation—sharp, cold, beautiful and utterly, soullessly ruthless. It didn't represent a problem for him. He was confident in his ability to meet her admittedly considerable expectations.

The others didn't know for whom they worked; from their perspective he had hired them for a job, end of story. They were all independent mercs-for-hire, all skilled enough to actually be able to maintain their independence and all being paid quite well for the op. Still, he imagined their payment en masse didn't touch the cost of the fighter jets. Most were ex-military, a mix of Alliance and Federation, and brought with them the requisite knowledge and understanding of military procedure. None possessed sufficient morality to harbor any qualms about the nature of the op.

He came from a military background as well, having departed the Alliance armed forces in the wake of an *unfortunate* incident during ground operations on Elathan in the Crux War. Unfortunate indeed.

"Hey!" He shouted at the men docking the missiles. "Don't load up one side first, you'll tip the ship over." He received curt nods in return. The camaraderie level wasn't particularly high on the team, but it didn't have to be. They were all professionals.

"Janse, join me for a few?"

The tall, lanky man finished popping the lid on a crate then came over to where he stood near the hangar wall.

Janse's skin was as black as unburnished onyx, a rarity in a world where racial and ethnic distinctions had blurred to the point of virtual meaninglessness. The man liked to claim his family were aboriginals living in the Australian outback until twenty years earlier. It was a blatant lie—he had been a third-generation hoverflyer racer before becoming a mercenary—but one which served to enhance his already fearsome reputation.

Thad projected an aural in front of them displaying the flyover layout of Palluda's single city. "I'd like to go over the targets and assignments again. No need for us to be crashing into each other on our flight paths."

"Yue, if there's one thing I know how to do, it's how to *not* crash into other vehicles in close proximity."

"Be that as it may, you're not the only pilot and I don't want to take any chances. Now I'm reasonably happy with the target choices, though I would like to fit this industrial machinery building in if we can." He pointed to a flat, rectangular building near the top left corner.

Janse leaned against the wall and shrugged. "Thirty-two missiles man. No more, no less. Unless you've figured out to make missiles blow their payload then keep going, turn left and detonate again, you'll have to trade something for it."

Thad allowed himself a small smile. "Well, let's do a walkthrough and see what we can find."

20

Alex glared at the two lengths of fiber conduit in annoyance. Also a trace of disgust.

They insisted on entangling one another every time she tried to secure them in place alongside their brethren against the hull wall. The aft navigation line really shouldn't be so cranky about the whole situation. True, she had removed it from where it typically rested to repair the section which had been sliced almost in two; that was no excuse for it not to go nicely back where it belonged.

The dampener field conduit on the other hand, being a recent addition, didn't natively integrate into the cabling layout of the other systems in the first place. In Seattle she had had the time and tools to devise a relatively elegant arrangement which kept it safe and secure. Well not from errant pulse lasers obviously, but at least from normal dangers. Here, though, she was using spare supplies and jury-rigged fixes and…

…they just *wouldn't fit*. No matter what she did, it ended with a jumbled pile of conduit in her face. She blew out a breath through clenched teeth.

"Hey, could you come help me a minute?"

No response.

Maybe he couldn't hear her over the music. She worked better and faster when music played in the background, and the last two days had needed every edge available to her. She gestured toward the small embedded panel by the ladder to mute it.

"Caleb, you got a second?" His name rolled off her tongue with surprising ease.

Still nothing. She frowned, suspicion flaring about what nefarious deeds he might be engaging in while alone on the upper decks of her ship. She was two seconds away from crawling out of the aperture and sneaking upstairs to catch him in the act when he leaned into the hold at the top of the ladder—

—wearing nothing but a towel wrapped loosely around his hips. Loosely and *low* around his hips. His head tilted into the hatch opening. "What do you need?"

Long, lean muscles rippled subtly beneath tanned skin, confirming her earlier assessment of a well-built, athletic but not overly muscled frame. It was the type of body one developed from an active, physical lifestyle rather than a weight bench. A neat pattern of dark hair tapered in from his pecs to trail down the center of his abdomen and disappear beneath the towel. The Greek/Italian genetic heritage of the initial Senecan colonists asserting itself no doubt, and more chest hair than the current fashion. Then again she'd never particularly cared for the prepubescent look. And it wasn't as if it appeared unkempt or….

She arched an eyebrow to stare at him with exaggerated incredulity.

"What? I'm washing my clothes, remember?"

Right. Should not have forgotten. "Right." She gave him a tight, close-mouthed smile. "You know what, it's fine. I've got it."

"Are you sure? Cause I can—"

"No, that is *o-kay*. Really. You just concentrate on getting dressed."

He returned her smirk. "All right, but don't say I didn't offer."

Offer *what*, exactly?

He vanished from view, leaving her to drag a hand raggedly down her face. "Well, where was I? I think I was…connecting one thing…to another…thing…of some sort…."

His yell echoed in the hold. "Are you talking to me?"

"Nope!" She cringed and slid into the aperture, dropping her voice to a murmur. "No sirree, not at all. Merely having a little chat with my libido, ordering it to kindly go back into hibernation before it gets me into far more trouble than I need…."

She stared at the two lengths of fiber conduit sagging freely in the open space in annoyance. The trace of disgust she reserved for herself. *Not getting led astray, dammit.*

In a fit of redirected energy she shimmied deeper inside the gap, suspended one line out of the way using her toes and right pinky and balanced the other in place with her left knee while she secured it. The final line then fit taut along the outer row.

There.

Diagnostic screens hovered in front of her when he climbed down into the hold—mercifully fully clothed, she noted through the translucence.

"So should I hang out back here again, or what?"

She raised a finger. "Hold one sec, confirming all the power flows are stable."

"Holding."

After a few seconds she killed the screens to find him leaning against the opposite wall, one ankle crossed over the other to match his arms. She regarded him a moment. "You seriously want to help?"

"Yes. Absolutely."

"Okay. Grab a welding torch and metamat blade from the cabinet, get suited up and head outside."

His mouth twitched while his eyes did the damn *sparkly* thing. "Dare I ask why?"

"I suppose. Right now the plasma shield is extended out about two meters beyond the body of the ship to encompass all the shredded pieces of the hull. I'm going to pull it in to the rim. You'll heat the shards, shear off the jagged edges and bend the pieces as flat as possible against the hull, after which I will re-extend the shield and we will try to mend the hull back together."

"Sounds reasonable. And what are you going to be doing while I'm braving the elements?"

"I'm going to be telling you which pieces to work on, how much to shear off and when to stop, of course. From the comfort of my insulated, heated ship."

"Of course..." he gave her a positively evil look as he pushed off the wall and went to the supply cabinet "...I'm likely to get all sweaty and need to wash my clothes again afterward, though."

She snorted and reached for her water bottle. "Don't think so. Just strip before you put on the suit—" his head had already begun whipping around "—in private, please."

"Hmm, should have thought of that myself."

He ran a fingertip along the contour of the blade then slid it easily into a notch on his pants and quickly checked over the torch. The fluid, efficient motions left no doubt as to his proficiency in their use.

For a few minutes she had almost forgotten what he was. A mistake on her part.

"Let me know when you're suited up and I'll open the airlock. Once the internal hatch has closed, the external one can be opened by pressing the panel beside it, and a ramp will extend to the ground."

"Got it." He nodded sharply and ascended the ladder.

She stretched out on her stomach at the edge of the hull rupture. With no sun in sight, as the pulsar would provide no day-night cycle, the meager yet ever present light came solely via the glow of the Nebula.

The wind had died down somewhat compared to the gale forces it had exhibited during her arrival, and fine dust particles danced about in the air. The overall effect bore a slight resemblance to the heavy, misty fog of a winter Seattle morning, albeit doused in pale sallow paint. She loved to go for a run on such mornings, when the dew blanketed so thickly it bowed the tree limbs and turned the grass silver and the fog brought silence to a noisy world.

"Ready!" His shout echoed down from the main cabin.

She waved at the panel behind her to open the airlock. A moment later Caleb arrived under the ship from the left, gloved hand already flicking on the torch as he glanced up at her. "It sucks out here. You know this, right?"

"Hell yes I know. I had to drag your unconscious body through it, remember?"

"Well, you didn't *have* to. You could have, for instance, not shot me, and instead asked me politely if I'd like to come aboard where it was warm and cozy."

Her eyes narrowed in feigned non-amusement. "Easy for you to say now. Start with this long piece here."

"Yes, ma'am." He pulled the blade off the belt of the environment suit and raised the torch to the piece in question.

"Smooth the ragged corner, but only a little. I don't want to lose any more material than necessary. Okay, now heat it along the bend. Not too much or it'll melt!"

"Don't get your panties in a twist. I've got this." He eased the sheet of metal up toward the hull and her. His tone was conversational. "Carbon-based metamaterials become pliant at around 1340°C and don't begin to lose their atomic structure until 1920°. The torch is set to 1460°, which will create malleability without damaging the integrity of the material."

"They teach you that in spy school?"

The metal shimmered as it met resistance at the plasma shield, and he lowered the torch. He stood less than a meter beneath her, only the shield and the faceplate of his helmet separating them. "Engineering school."

He looked up at her, the curl of his lips clearly visible through the faceplate. "*Yes*, I have an engineering degree. Try to contain your shock. Where to next?"

She worked to keep her expression neutral and unaffected. So he possessed skills beyond subterfuge and selective removal of criminals from the gene pool. And culinary endeavors. It didn't change anything.

She pointed to the narrow piece at the end of the rupture closest to her.

"This one."

21

In the late 22nd century, a number of social philosophers asserted their belief that the expansion of humanity beyond the bounds of the Sol System would usher in a new era of civility and order. With unparalleled prosperity and a galaxy to explore, we would at last put behind us petty foibles such as crime and violence in favor of higher, more noble pursuits.

But through the Renaissance and the discovery of the Americas, the Industrial Revolution and the taming of Earth, the invention of computers and the advent of space flight, human nature had remained fundamentally unchanged. It was foolhardy to believe this latest advancement would bring about some profound transformation in the souls of men.

In reality, those predisposed to violence did not give it up; they simply developed more sophisticated methods of going about it. Avenues for physical and mental pleasure only became more refined and powerful, and thus an ever greater temptation. Physical addiction was now able to be cured easily enough—but many didn't *want* to be cured.

Through gene therapy, stem cell manipulation and biosynthetic treatments the medical profession cured the great diseases of the body: cancer, Alzheimer's, muscular dystrophy, paralysis, the list was endless. Diseases of the mind, however, proved to be another matter entirely. The brain represented the most complex organism ever to exist, and impossible to tame. Morality could not be spawned by tweaking a few genes or shutting off a few neurons. Not yet.

So though humanity conquered the very stars, it remained unable to conquer the darkness within. Thieves, rapists and murderers continued to occur in roughly the same percentage of the population they always had. The weak continued to be preyed upon by the strong in the prolific shadows not policed by any government.

The Zelones cartel was the strongest criminal organization in settled space because its leadership had always understood certain core truths and harnessed them to maximum effect. Some people desired nothing more than to spend their lives on a synthetically induced high and merely needed the chimerals to do so. Cutthroat businesspeople needed thieves and hackers. Thieves and hackers needed tools and funding. Bullies and thugs needed targets and outlets for their aggression.

One who could not only recognize these opportunities but channel and exploit the disparate needs was as a puppeteer pulling the strings of the world.

Olivia Montegreu knew this, because she was one of the puppeteers. It wasn't arrogance on her part, but simple truth. The veil had been ripped away and the lie at the heart of 'civilized' society bared to her a very long time ago.

She had watched her older sister—weak-minded, impressionable, helpless to take care of herself—eschew their upper-middle class life to hook up with a gang and get addicted to a particularly nasty chimeral. The drug of choice created a state of utter bliss for half an hour that felt like days, then swung in the opposite direction for twice as long. Her sister spent two years as a literal sex slave to the gang's local leadership before she ended up dead in a back alley in the slums of Buenos Aires, naked and strangled.

Olivia had watched her parents wail and gnash their teeth and pull at their hair, then resume living their lives. She had watched the authorities take statements and nod in feigned sympathy and close the case as 'gang-related.' She had watched the world proceed onward, as if nothing at all had happened. One family, one girl, one death among the multitudes.

Six months later she joined the same gang. The 'Montserrat Matónes,' they called themselves. In reality they were financed by an arm of Zelones, one of thousands of such street-level interests, but not even the leaders realized it.

At first she played the innocent, impressionable young girl her sister had been. She slept with who she needed to but carefully avoided the chimerals in copious supply. She made herself useful and displayed enough capability to get close to the leadership. In time she learned the details of how the gang worked. Though it gave the impression of being an unorganized group of thrill-seekers and dropouts, it did have structure and rules. They procured chimerals from a larger, more powerful group; they were given targets for shakedowns and small-time thefts.

Once she was satisfied she had learned everything she could, she slid a gamma blade into the base of the Matónes leader's neck while he fucked her. She killed his lieutenant when he found them—he *had* been the one who strangled her sister, after all. Then she took over leadership of the gang.

The year was 2229, and she was sixteen years old.

Olivia instructed the pilot to wait with the ship at the Krysk spaceport. She didn't expect to be long, and did not require a chaperone.

She was meeting the head of the Ferre 'corporation,' in all likelihood alongside a retinue of his lieutenants, at their headquarters in the center of downtown. On New Babel she traveled with a small entourage of bodyguards and lieutenants; it was expected and projected the correct image. Here on his turf, Ilario Ferre would doubtless do the same. It wasn't a problem. In fact, she was counting on it.

The sweltering heat from the midday sun burned against her bare arms. She wore a sleeveless, lightweight white tunic and loose, breathable linen-style pants to temper the heat.

The oldest and largest Senecan-allied colony, Krysk offered a robust urban infrastructure. As she walked along the moderately busy sidewalk, she looked to the world like any other young, fresh-faced professional; perhaps a mid-level marketing executive or entertainment director. For she spent a notable percentage of her considerable annual income on cutting-edge cellular regeneration therapies, and would appear to the world—as she had for more than eighty years—in her late twenties.

No one she passed had the slightest idea one of the most powerful people in the galaxy walked among them. A face scan by a high-end ocular implant might have revealed it, but anyone who tried would find themselves inexplicably unable to capture such a scan.

The invisible, nanometer-thick shield coating her skin blocked any and all intrusions of her body and cybernetics and scrambled the signals of any such attempts.

Her destination was located in an unremarkable midrise just off the main thoroughfare. It claimed to house a company called Fotilas Services, which she suspected didn't exist beyond a government filing, if that. Senecan Federation regulations were after all notable primarily for their absence.

She gave the receptionist, a woman with flowing mahogany curls and skin the color of sun-bleached toffee, a charming smile. "Would you tell Mr. Ferre his twelve o'clock is here? I'm expected." While the receptionist frowned and readied a protest, she added a courteous nod to the camera hidden in the ceiling.

A second later the woman cleared her throat and stood. "I'll show you to the conference room, ma'am."

The room was deep in the complex. A windowless affair consisting of a conference table and little else, no inner workings of the business would be on display in this venue. As the receptionist stepped in to announce her presence, Olivia nonchalantly ran the bracelet circling her right wrist over the small embedded panel in the wall.

Ilario Ferre greeted her with a glib smile and a firm grasp of her hand. "Ms. Montegreu, so kind of you to come all this way..." he glanced behind her, a puzzled expression ghosting across his face "...is it only you? You have no escort?"

"Do I need one? Given all these armed guards here—" she motioned toward the half dozen enforcers lining the walls of the room "—I imagine I am quite safe from anything less than an invasion."

To his credit he recovered quickly, dipping his chin in appreciation. "And of course you are. You must forgive me, my father took paranoia to an art form. Old habits and all. Shall we sit?"

She followed him to the table and took a seat opposite him. Immediately a door opened at one end of the room and a young man and older woman entered. Ilario nodded as they joined them at the table.

"My mother, Alaina, and my cousin and first lieutenant, Laure."

She was familiar with both of them from her files. Alaina, she gave a respectful but curt nod; Laure, a tiny smile.

"Now I know you are a very busy woman, Ms. Montegreu, so let's get straight to business, shall we? I confess to being intrigued by the idea of a strategic partnership between our interests. I think we both have much we can offer the other."

A strategic partnership—it was the ostensible purpose of her visit. The Zelones cartel *was* the strongest criminal organization in settled space, but its reach was not absolute. In point of fact, its presence was weakest on Senecan Federation planets, where an entrepreneurial culture encouraged the rise of homegrown, enterprising 'freelancers' and where the wholesale change in government twenty-two years earlier had muddled their network of contacts.

Ilario without a doubt knew this, which was why her overture had likely been perceived as logical and natural. But what he did not know was there was chaos on the horizon, and she did not intend to share the spoils.

Her expression turned predatory. "Yes, *about* that. I think the better choice is for you to simply work for me."

The man almost choked on the water he was sipping. "Ms. Montegreu, I don't mean any disrespect, for your, shall we say, *business* prowess is legendary. But my family does not work 'for' anyone. We are doing rather well in the Federation, which I believe is a good deal more than you can say. Now I am willing to entertain discussions of a mutually beneficial arrangement, but nothing else."

Her lips pursed together in a show of thoughtfulness. She allowed the silence to stretch a breath longer than was comfortable, then shrugged and stood. "Very well."

She lifted her wrist to eject two aSTX-laced blades from her bracelet and into the necks of Ilario and his mother. The toxin would paralyze their respiratory muscles, suffocating them even before they bled out from their throats being sliced open.

The laser fire from the guards bounced harmlessly off her personal shield. A thought and she activated the EMP she had staged when she touched her bracelet to the panel by the door. Most of the guards were still within three meters of the walls, and the EMP fried their cybernetics along with much of their brain matter as a side effect.

One guard had been moving toward her and escaped the EMP. Likely deducing—correctly—that physical restraint was the only way to neutralize her, he lowered and squared his shoulders in preparation for tackling her. She slid the gamma blade hilt out of her pants' pocket and activated a two-meter long blade which sliced him in half at the waist. She took a step back to avoid the blood spurting out of the body and returned the blade hilt to her pocket.

Physical violence had been an occasional necessity over the years as she climbed the ranks. These days she employed people who would happily engage in it on her behalf, but there were times when a more personal touch was required. She didn't particularly enjoy it; nor did she particularly loathe it. Violence was simply a tool, and in this instance the most expedient tool available to her.

Her gaze locked on Laure Ferre. He sat at the table beside his dead cousin and his dead aunt, deep green eyes wide but not panicked as he stared at her. He presumably had by now deduced, first, if she wanted him dead he would already be so, and second, if he tried to harm her his status would change. His file indicated he was intelligent and quick on his feet, but not so narcissistic as Ilario.

"You work for me now. The Ferre organization is now a wholly-owned subsidiary of the Zelones cartel. For the time being you will be allowed to continue doing business as you have up until now, subject to a few minor adjustments. Someone will be in touch with the details. Are we clear?"

A harsh, ragged laugh bubbled up from his chest, but he nodded. "Yes, ma'am." His eyes roved around the room, taking in the massacre, then back to her. "I, um, look forward to being a part of your team."

"Glad to hear it." She pivoted and walked out.

22

Alex had sandwiches and sliced fruit ready by the time Caleb returned from showering. An environment suit protected a person from the elements outside the suit; it did not create a comfortable environment inside the suit, and three hours in it had left him a sweaty, sticky mess.

He settled in one of the chairs at the small dining table while she brought the plates over. "Thanks. So what do you think? Is enough material remaining to seal the hull?"

"I honestly don't know. You saw, there were definite gaps, but I keep a few spare mats I can use." She looked across the table at him. "Eat fast so we can find out."

"Right." She was smiling, so he added a light chuckle. It was still a guarded one though, only hinting at reaching her eyes. After a bite of his sandwich he decided to ask about something which had bugged him on the trip out of and back into the ship: the silence. "I can't help but notice you don't seem to have a VI on board."

"Nope."

"Are you uncomfortable with the idea of giving a VI access to the systems?"

"Not at all. I simply don't need one to tell me the status of my ship." She paused, and a smile which felt somehow private tugged at her lips. Her left hand nonchalantly gestured in the direction of the embedded panel behind her.

As they had the last two nights when she went to bed, the lights dimmed; a second later they returned to full strength. The strains of a synthwave ballad began wafting through the cabin. A frown, and the volume decreased.

Her right hand brought the sandwich to her mouth as the left waved toward the cockpit. The glyphs along her wrist pulsed faintly.

"It's a brisk -54° outside, while in here it's a cozy 23°. The system repairs are essentially complete: the plasma shield is up to 93%, and the self-healing hydrogel on the damaged conduit should bring it to 100% by morning. The impulse engine reports all systems fully functional.

"The LEN reactor is expending 12% of its output capacity on keeping us alive and comfortable...and it's a little cranky at having to work harder on account of there being two of us." She winked at him—sending an unexpected wicked shiver down his spine—and took a bite of her sandwich.

"Most impressive. I don't know if I've ever seen such extensive wireless interconnectivity from cybernetics alone, no hardware adjunct."

"Planet-side there's almost always too much interference for it to work reliably. The invisible yet teeming cloud of electronic signals permeates everywhere, clogging the air with noise. Here though, it's just me."

"And, as the reactor noted, me."

She gazed at him a moment, and he could *see* thoughts flitting across her eyes. He wished like hell he knew what they were. "And you."

Her gaze darted down to acquire an apple slice. "Bet you didn't think I was a warenut, huh?"

"I still don't. I would say you have simply optimized both yourself and your ship for maximum capability and performance."

She shrugged but seemed pleased by the response. "More or less."

He took another bite—despite her admonition, neither of them were hurrying through lunch—and cocked his head to the side. "This music...Ethan Tollis, right?"

"Yep. You've heard of him?"

"Of course. Music doesn't respect political boundaries. But it's a different style than what you've usually had playing."

"He's a friend."

He arched an eyebrow in genuine surprise. "You're 'friends' with one of the most successful prog synth musicians in the galaxy."

She nodded, her mouth full. "Mmhmm."

Hmm, indeed. She came off as so serious, so focused and no-nonsense, he would've thought she'd have no patience for artistic types.

She caught him staring at her. "What?"

"Nothing." He didn't try to hide the mischief in his eyes. "*Good friends?*"

"What is that supposed to mean?"

"It's not supposed to mean anything. I'm merely asking how good of friends you are."

"Very funny." She took a sip of water. "If you're asking me if I slept with him, it is so far beyond your business."

He laughed. "So yes, then."

She sighed in clear annoyance and picked up her sandwich, only to set it down again to glare at him. "*Fine.* I met him after university while I was doing an externship at Pacifica Aerodynamics. He was a struggling coffeehouse musician at the time. We dated for around a year. I took a job on Erisen, we parted friends. A few years later he hit it big. I was happy for him. End of story."

The notion of her *dating* a musician threw him for even more of a loop. It appeared he had quite a bit more to discover about her—but he'd ponder it later. "Interesting. You keep in touch?"

"We catch up every now and then."

He really shouldn't rile her up; it was not conducive to him making it off this rock alive and in one piece. But he couldn't help it. When she got annoyed or flustered her nose crinkled up and sideways and her mouth contorted into the oddest shapes. It looked so....

"And by 'catch up' you mean?"

She glared at him again and...yep, there it was. *Adorable.*

"Are you done? You look like you're done." She reached across and snatched his plate away, stood and marched to the sink.

He grinned to himself and began clearing off the rest of the table. "You know, feel free to ask me embarrassing, invasive things about my life. I'm good with tit-for-tat."

She glanced over her shoulder at him. "Why bother? Whatever you said would be a lie."

Ouch. The lighthearted mood instantly evaporated. "No, it *wouldn't* be."

"And I could tell the difference...how?"

He opened his mouth, then closed it. He gave her a pursed smile that wasn't. "You probably couldn't."

Her shoulders notched upward to emphasize the point. She turned back to the sink to stow the dishes.

He didn't think he had ever been shamed so thoroughly and to such stinging effect by a few casual words. He sank against the table, taken aback by the rebuke...and by how badly he wanted to change her mind.

⟋R⟍

They lay on their stomachs at right angles to one another in the engineering well. She heated an edge of intact hull while he heated a torn section and brought it to meet her edge; she aligned them and they held the pieces in place until they cooled and bonded together.

The conversation since lunch had been polite but strained, and fairly minimal. He struggled to find some way to get back to the comfortable interaction they'd been playing at having all morning. Because it had been nice.

He nodded in appreciation as the metal melded seamlessly together. "This is seriously high-quality material, not that I'm surprised. Maybe the Trade Summit was a success, and we'll get access to material of this caliber."

"What Tra— oh yeah, that political circle-jerk. Yes, let's decide to sell doilies and mantle ornaments to each other, it'll make everything better."

He followed her lead and scooted to the next section. "It's been twenty-two years, it's arguably time to at least try."

She didn't respond, acting as if she were focused on heating the metal at her fingertips and positioning the now pliant material. She kept her gaze on it when she finally spoke. "My father was killed in the war."

Well this *topic isn't likely to bring back the lighthearted atmosphere. Way to go.* His voice was carefully soft. "I know."

She let go of the metal to screw her face up at him. "What?"

He attempted a self-deprecating smile. "Hey, even us backwater Senecan rubes study history. The Kappa Crucis Battle is famous, it...well it was an important event in the war." The battle turned the war in Seneca's favor and ultimately led to the armistice. She knew this. It didn't need to be said.

He took on an officious tone as he recited from memory, having reviewed the entry a mere two nights ago when studying her file.

"Commander David Solovy, commanding officer of the Earth Alliance cruiser *EAS Stalwart*, successfully blocked the Federation fleet's advance for twelve minutes, giving a number of Alliance vessels, the staff of a nearby monitoring station and nearly all of the *Stalwart* crew time to safely escape. It is estimated he saved the lives of over 4,000 Alliance men and women before the *Stalwart* was destroyed."

"4,817." It was less than a whisper.

"I'm sorry, Alex."

"Why? You weren't to blame." Her gaze rose to meet his in challenge. "Unless you were there—were you?"

"No. I was sixteen, and finishing primary."

The taut raise of her lips was somehow the antithesis of a smile. "Well there you go. Clean hands."

"It was war. A *lot* of people died—on both sides."

"Which made it so much easier for a thirteen year old to understand." She reached over and tried to wrench his piece up to meet the hull. It wasn't sufficiently heated and refused to budge, leading to a harsh, frustrated expulsion of air from her lungs.

"I'm not saying it...." He squeezed his eyes shut in equal frustration. He was doing this all wrong, and in serious danger of wiping out whatever goodwill he may have built up. After a moment's pause he tried a different tack. "You were close to your dad?"

She shot him a fierce glare; her eyes blazed silver ice. He resisted the urge to retreat into the corner to get further away from the glare. He thought he would do almost anything to not be the recipient of such an expression ever again.

"*That* is none of your business."

So yes, then. He gave up any attempt at a kind, sympathetic tone of voice; it clearly made no difference. "Right. Of course. My mistake."

They worked in silence after that, save for the occasional instruction or question. It was efficient, for they had naturally settled into a productive routine. Even with the weight of uneasy tension hanging ignored in the air, they undeniably worked rather well together. He wanted to diffuse the tension, but under the circumstances silence seemed the least damaging choice.

Since his position forced him to move backwards through the hold, he hadn't been focusing on what lay behind him. Therefore he wasn't as prepared as he probably should have been for her abrupt shattering of the heavy silence.

"Dammit!" She dropped her torch to the floor and rose to her knees, only to sink back on her heels and drag a hand down her face. "It's not enough. We'll keep going, but there's not sufficient material to seal her up. Not even close." With a visceral growl she sent the torch skidding across the hold.

While his own self-interest led him to wish for a friendlier, more amicable situation, he had to admire her intensity and spirit. Far too many people hid behind holos and aurals and sensory overlays to project an air of cool aloofness and detached disinterest. This woman though...she had *fire*. And even when directed at him, it was something to see.

He sat up and leaned against the nearby wall. Once he saw the entire area, he didn't dispute her assessment. A much smaller but still substantial opening ran along much of the center. The metal converged in only two locations, and they had already used all the spare mats.

He raised a hesitant eyebrow. "The shield's at full power now, right? Will it hold in space?"

"Maybe, but I'm not particularly anxious to test the theory out in the void. Are you?" It sounded like another challenge.

His head tilted as though an idea had come to him. In truth the option had occurred to him immediately upon seeing the enormous rupture in the hull the day before, but he hadn't known if it would be needed, and if it were needed whether it would be feasible. Now, however, their options were rapidly dwindling.

"What about my ship?"

"What *about* your ship?"

"The hull was made of an amodiamond metamaterial. It's similar enough to yours to patch the gaps, isn't it?"

She huffed a breath that was almost a laugh. "Well, yes—but I kind of blew up your ship. Or have you forgotten?"

"Oh, I have absolutely not forgotten. But we're okay to fly in-atmosphere? If we can locate some of the wreckage, I'm sure there are intact pieces large enough to salvage material from. Especially since we don't need very much."

She regarded him in surprise…and perhaps a measure of appreciation. "That's a really good idea."

He smiled, relieved more than he cared to admit to be the recipient of a softer, gentler expression. "Great. Now we just have to find the wreckage."

She was already climbing to her feet, renewed vigor in every motion. "It shouldn't be too difficult. I dodged the remains of your ship most of the way down. Navigation ought to be able to extrapolate a landing zone from their trajectory."

When she reached the first step of the ladder she paused. "You know what, I'm certain it will. Let's go ahead and finish this work while we're in the groove. We'll go hunting in the morning."

He watched her retrieve her torch from the corner where it had landed and return to her previous spot on the floor, then joined her and flicked his torch on.

"We have a groove? I mean, *I* felt like we definitely had a groove thing happening, but I didn't know for sure if *you* thought we had a groove."

Her eyes cut over to him, now dancing with mirth rather than ice. "Are you going to help, or is droll commentary going to be the extent of your contribution?"

He bit his lower lip, and was intrigued to see an odd flare in her eyes before she directed her attention to the hull. "I can't do both?"

"Nope. It's scientifically impossible."

He sighed for added effect. "Ah well. I guess I'll help then."

"Thank god."

As they settled back into the routine, this time with considerably less tension in the air, he pondered her rapid and dramatic shift in mood. Unquestionably the prospect of locating additional materials for the hull would be a welcome development and should cheer her up, but not to so great an extent.

It took him a few minutes to figure out the answer, though in retrospect it seemed blindingly obvious given what he had ascertained about her thus far.

He had provided her the means to make her ship whole. To fly again.

23

"It's the same principle as the dampener field, except blocking signals from getting in rather than keeping them from getting out. We don't need to reinvent the wheel, merely reapply the principles in a slightly adjusted manner."

The young engineer looked at her as though she had sprouted a second head. She checked, she hadn't. "Well? I'm not forgetting some fundamental rule of chemistry, am I? Quantum physics? Electronics?"

"Um, no ma'am, not as—"

"Kennedy's fine." She smiled at him in the ghostly light. The prototype lab was of necessity windowless and dark, save for the scattered glow of dozens of screens and interfaces.

"Yes, ma'am. Kennedy. Ma'am. It's just the dampener field doesn't block everything, even at its strongest. It only tamps down the strength of the waves. For reverse-shielding to work, it'll have to be impermeable."

"True, but the energy the dampener field blocks is on the order of terajoules. The energy we want to block here is far smaller."

"Right. Good point." He ran calculations on the screen in front of them. The blue and teal glyphs coating his arm pulsed brightly to splash color in the air. "It shouldn't be too difficult to create a strong Faraday cage using a silver-based nonlinear metamat. We could—"

"And we should do that—but not now. For this project to be successful it has to be easy to install and inexpensive, relatively speaking, not another costly lattice which has to be painted on."

He stared at her. "A cheap virtual shield blocking the *entire* spectrum?"

"No, I'm not that crazy. It has to protect against directed signals, not space radiation or anything. I think it doesn't need to be a Faraday cage at all. It simply has to disrupt specific signals, after all. We disrupt signals all the time."

His eyes widened and looked to the ceiling for inspiration. "We can certainly design a shield to diffuse or disrupt incoming waves. But it would disrupt the exanet as well, including messaging, and I, um..." he chuckled to himself, then blushed "...don't think our customers would like that, right?"

She patted him on the shoulder in encouragement. She loved nerdy engineers; they were so pure. In point of fact this was the root of the problem she had sought him out to solve. But she had wanted him to work through the variables and come to it on his own, because now he would feel *he* owned it, too.

"You are absolutely correct, which is why I need you to figure out a way to allow exanet signals in without creating a hole big enough for the evil pirates to sneak through. What do you think? Can you do it?"

His brow furrowed and his gaze bounced around the lab. "Well, it will have to be adaptive and semi-intelligent, so we're looking at some manner of active ware in its core and—"

She laughed and began backing away. "Just let me know when you have something."

He nodded distractedly, his mind already lost in a magical mathematical world.

In truth she needed 'something' rather fast. The Board presentation had gone better than expected, and they had requested practical design plans as soon as possible. But the fastest route to those plans was to get a techie intrigued by the challenge then give them the room to be brilliant.

She stepped out the glass doors of IS Design's offices onto the broad sidewalk, only to grin in delight. Light, fluffy snowflakes danced about in the air to become a luminous gold in the refracted evening rays.

She pulled her hat snugly over her ears and started off, though not too quickly. Her apartment was eight blocks away in the heart of downtown, and she decided to enjoy the walk.

Erisen had been her home for eleven years now, but having grown up in Houston and attended university in Pasadena, she still found herself a little enamored by snow. It made everything feel...softer. Gentler. Brighter. It was okay to be a child again when in the presence of snow.

Halfway down the next block she lingered at the window of a shoe boutique, futilely as always. She was going to Houston for her parents' anniversary in two days and required eye-catching attire to wear to the party. In her parents' vernacular, 'party' meant gala extravaganza involving five hundred guests, a private orchestra and delicacies shipped in from half a dozen worlds. And while Erisen's fashion offerings had matured to a point, retailers tended toward the practical attire required by a cold and snowy climate.

Alas. Maybe she should head to Earth early and swing by Manhattan first. She wouldn't want her parents' friends thinking Erisen was some backwater hick world, because at a hundred seventy-two years old, it wasn't. Much.

Her eVi indicated an incoming message, and a frown tugged at her lips when it opened. Miles, the eco-dev executive, would like to take her to an art exhibit the next evening. She pondered it a moment while crossing the street, and abruptly stuck her tongue out to capture a falling snowflake.

Once the initial thrill of a new romance had worn off, she was finding him increasingly high maintenance. He had turned out to be a horrific skier, which could have been cute if he hadn't been so damn whiny about it. He prattled on about his work incessantly, which could have been interesting if his work didn't consist mostly of lobbying. And while he was quite handsome, his mouth did this odd downturn thing in response to whatever you said; it made him look churlish.

With an eye roll she sent back a decline and excuse. The excuse was easy, as she legitimately wasn't available on account of needing to get ready for the trip home. Whether he interpreted it as a more permanent decline...well, she would worry about that on her return.

Another one bites the dust. She laughed to herself, fully aware she had done it *again*, but opened a compose anyway.

> *Alex,*
>
> *...or not. He's entirely too needy, and on the verge of petulant. Oh well, tomorrow is another day.*
> *— Kennedy*

She sent the message as a gleam to her left caught her attention. The last moment of the sunset over the mountains tossed glittering beams into the snow-filled sky. It looked—

> *Message unable to be delivered. Recipient is not connected to ex-anet infrastructure. Message will be queued until it can be delivered.*

What?

The person behind her collided into her, and she barely caught her balance in time to prevent a tumble to the ground. She mumbled a "sorry" and moved out of the way.

Distracted by troubling thoughts, she managed to wind through the busy pedestrian foot traffic to the low ledge marking the barrier between the sidewalk and a small sculpture park. She sank against the ledge.

There were a few instances when one might be cut off from the ubiquitous exanet infrastructure. Spelunking beneath a couple of kilometers of solid heavy metals, for instance, or catching a front-row seat to a supernova explosion. Not much else…other than being dead, of course.

The *Siyane* was equipped with the most robust radiation shielding available, but even it had limits.

Oh Alex, what are *you doing?*

24

The *Siyane* skimmed fifteen meters above the ground, cutting through a harsh wind toward the only reading for kilometers which showed any signs of being artificial.

Alex pointed at the screen taking up the uppermost-right quadrant of the cockpit display. She had given him view rights to the HUD, because it was simply practical to do so. "Keep an eye on this readout while I try not to crash into any sudden mountainous objects. Let me know when it spikes."

Caleb nodded from his position leaning against the half-wall separating the cockpit and the main cabin. "Gotcha."

They had spent the previous evening stretching the hull material as far as possible and called it an early, tired night. This morning they had set out in the direction of the region the navigation system identified as the likeliest crash site zone. They'd been flying for more than an hour to reach the edge of the region; for obvious reasons she flew conservatively.

He had baked muffins after they had lifted off, then showed up in the cockpit and casually handed her two.

Muffins. He had utterly confounded her with *muffins*. Banana nut multigrain muffins, to be precise. The man's arsenal of weaponry was truly impressive.

She found her mind wandering to what other weapons he might have in his—*Jesus, Alex, get your mind out of the gutter. It's far too early in the morning for those sorts of thoughts.*

"Hey, got a spike."

She blinked hard and glanced at the display. "Yep." She arced toward the flashing signal. When they were in range she slowed to a crawl until they could see the wreckage among the blowing sand.

He moaned and sagged against the wall in apparent despondence. "My baby...."

"Look, I said I was sorry. There's nothing else—"

"She was a loaner. I'd had her all of a week."

"Unh!" She leaned over and punched him in the shoulder. "Very funny."

"Ow." He rubbed his shoulder gingerly. "So what's the plan?"

She studied the hazy outline of the wreckage. "It looks promising. The wind is nasty strong though, so we'll tether ourselves to the hull. I say we take turns slicing off a piece and bringing it to the airlock. I'd like to end up with at least three square meters, as solid and flat as possible." She leaned in closer to the viewport. "Given the state of the wreck, it may mean a lot of small pieces."

"Works for me."

The ship's landing gear settled to the ground, and she cut the engine. "Let's get to it."

She rejoined him after depositing a sheet in the airlock, her fourth such trip. They had accumulated a nice stack of material by this point, but she didn't want to come up short and have to do this all over again. The wind made every step a challenge, and the swirling dust reduced visibility to a few meters. "Goddamn this planet sucks."

He chuckled over the vicinity comm. "You don't have to tell me—I'm fairly certain I've been telling you. But that's not even what bugs me the most about it."

"And what does bug you the most about it?"

"How is it even here? What is it orbiting? We're a *long* way from the pulsar, and there's no indication of another star in the vicinity."

"Perhaps the answer's in that unusual radiation. I don't know. Regardless—"

A powerful gust swept across them from out of nowhere; the crashed ship rocked precipitously, several loose sections tearing off to disappear into the sky.

The punishing wind ripped the piece of hull he had just severed out of his hand. Its jagged edges sliced right through the line tethering her to her ship on its way to oblivion.

The velocity of the wind increased yet more and began to push her relentlessly backward. She reached to grab onto the wreckage, and had succeeded in doing so when a fresh gust whipped in and her tenuous grip slipped on the metal surface.

His voice was low and steady. "Hang on. I'm going to—"

"I *can't*!" The gust shifted direction, and she felt herself being blown sideways away from the wreck—

—his arms wound around her waist and gripped her against him. She didn't understand how he managed to reach her. Somehow he had.

"It's *okay*. I've got you."

Her pulse raced, pounding in her ears above the howling wind. A wave of dizziness crashed over her with the rapid flood of adrenaline. She gasped in a breath. "Don't let go."

His faceplate dropped forward to rest on hers. "I won't. I promise."

Her eyes rose to meet his. She was shocked at how frightened he looked. Those beautiful irises had darkened to a raging midnight blue surrounding pinpoint pupils. Rigid lines of clenched muscles cut beneath his cheekbones.

But the tone of his voice remained calm and confident. It made her feel safe...as did the firm grasp of his arms around her. It seemed his deceptively lean build hid a great deal of strength. She sucked in several deep breaths until her pulse began to slow. "Thank you."

He grinned, if a little shakily. "Couldn't lose my pilot, now could I?"

"We should probably...head to the ship."

"You want me to carry you?"

And the cocky wit returns. She glared at him through the faceplate, though any annoyance was contrived at best. "That's quite all right. How about we just tie my line onto yours instead."

"Okay, but don't say I didn't offer."

"Noted." She hoped the helmet hid the smile which insisted on pulling at her lips as she reached around him to secure the frayed end of her line to his. "Let's each get a piece and head in. I think we have enough." She jerked the knot tight and pulled back to face him.

A second passed, then two. Her pulse decided to reverse direction once more. She swallowed. "You can let go now."

He laughed softly. "Right." But he waited another full second before loosening his grip and taking a half-step away.

She spun toward the wreck, only to grumble in frustration. "And my blade's gone."

"S'ok. You can take...this one." He finished cutting off a small piece and handed it to her, then went for the last one. Once he held the final slice in his hands, he paused to stare at the remnants of his ship.

"What is it? Is there something else you wanted to try to find?"

She saw his shoulders drop fractionally, though the sigh wasn't audible. He looked back at her. "Nope. We're good."

She smiled to herself as the metal cooled to meld together into a nearly seamless sheet. The materials weren't identical; as such, the hue underwent a noticeable shift at the...well, seam. Still, it would do. More than do, honestly. She had to admit, she was impressed by the Senecan-manufactured metamat. It wasn't better than hers, merely different. But not bad different.

She began heating the next section. After laying out the recovered material and matching the pieces to the remaining gaps, they had divided up the repairs to save time. His work the previous afternoon had more than convinced her he knew what he was doing. She trusted him to get it right, which was saying a fair amount.

"So I was thinking. Once the repairs are finished, we should go check out those anomalous readings."

His torch froze above the hull. "You think so?"

"We should consider it at least. At this point we're practically there, we might as well drop by. I mean it's why I'm here, it's why you're here. It won't be much trouble to check it out."

Her torch created a bright glare, and beyond its halo she couldn't see his expression at the opposite end of the hold. She *could* see him set his tools on the floor. A reply was several seconds in coming, however.

"You're right. It is why you're here, and why I'm here. So what does that mean? If it turns out to be important, do I get a copy of the data?"

She didn't even hesitate. After all, 'I've been thinking' meant she had previously identified the parameters and analyzed all the branching considerations. "Yes."

His response was also quick, though she suspected for a different reason. "You mean it? Why?"

She returned to the still-ragged edge of the salvaged material. "Because I don't gain anything by keeping it from you. You'll know what the phenomenon is, at least in general terms, because you'll be there. I suspect unlike my typical clients, your bosses won't demand detailed scientific analyses and spectrum charts before acting on the information, so you'll already have everything you need. I won't gain any advantage by being a bitch and I'll lose...." Her hand paused two centimeters from the shard.

"You'll lose what?"

Asshole, as if he didn't know the answer. "Comity."

He choked back a laugh. "*Comity?*"

She scowled at the torch. "Yes, *comity*. Goodwill. Friendly relations. You not trying to kill me. Call it whatever—" She yelped as the flame grazed her fingertip, and quickly extinguished it lest she set the ship on fire.

"Alex, you have to know by now I'm *not* going to kill you."

She sucked on the scalded finger to buy a second or two. "Of course I do. I was trying to be humorous. Failing miserably apparently. Not a huge surprise, it was never one of my strong suits." He didn't comment further, and she flicked the torch back on and turned to the hull—

—then realized he had come over and crouched on the balls of his feet against the wall beside her. Damn he could move quietly.

She eyed him without actually looking at him; a corner of his mouth tweaked up in response. He was entirely too cute for his—or her—own good when he did that.... Surprised at her own reaction, she wondered when precisely it was his smirk had stopped being annoying and started being cute. The evening before? This morning with the muffins? Just now?

"I don't believe you."

She blew out a breath, flicked the torch off *again* and rolled onto her back. "You understand why, don't you?"

He nodded. "Because it's my job to be a chameleon, to become whatever I need to be in a given situation in order to complete the mission—or at least get out alive, as the case may be. And I'm very good at my job, which I imagine you have surmised. Therefore, you have no way to be certain whether or not I'm simply acting the part of the easygoing, agreeable, helpful, funny, charming stowaway and will slit your throat the minute it benefits me to do so."

She shrugged, and didn't bother to deny he was all of those things. "Kind of sums it up, yeah."

"And I don't see how there's any way for me to convince you otherwise...especially when I'm not even sure myself."

"*Not* helping."

He cringed visibly. "That came out wrong—I'm sure I'm not going to slit your throat. I meant...it's been so long since I've truly been myself around someone else, I'm not sure I even remember how to do it anymore."

She frowned. "That's kind of tragic." The frown deepened. "Unless this is just another layer of the act, designed to win my trust when the easygoing, agreeable, helpful, funny, charming routine wasn't getting the job done."

He groaned and sank the rest of the way down to the floor. "Totally valid point. It's impossible for me to talk my way out of this."

"Yep. Sorry." She shifted onto her stomach and activated the torch. *Again.* "Okay. Thought experiment. If you weren't in dire straits, if this wasn't a 'situation,' if it had nothing to do with a mission and instead you were on vacation, what would you be doing right now?"

"Kissing you."

Fuck.

His voice had dropped in pitch and volume, and its lilting tenor washed gently over her like a lover's caress. She bit her lower lip hard enough to draw blood, but did her damnedest to not display any reaction. Her tone remained casual and nonchalant. "Oh, so the real you is a modern-day Casanova, traversing the galaxy and wooing a damsel in every port?"

She glanced over to find his eyes twinkling devilishly and his mouth wearing a far too kiss-worthy smirk again. *Fuck.*

"That's *not* what I said."

She nodded and focused on the hull, the metallic tang of blood stinging her tongue. "My mistake. And what would the real you do when I said 'in your dreams' and shoved him on his ass?"

He sighed loudly, doubtless for dramatic effect. "He'd return to his post and help you finish the repairs so we can go check out this anomaly...."

She looked back at him, an eyebrow arched, and gestured toward the other end of the hold expectantly.

He rolled his eyes and pushed off the floor. "I'm going, I'm going." *Fuck.*

⁀ℛ⁀

Caleb prepared dinner while she ran through the preflight checks—twice for good measure by the looks of it—then at last they departed what had been, all things considered, a rather unfriendly planet. The atmospheric traversal was rough, but on such a small planet it took only minutes.

The ship held together, everything stayed in the green, and he saw a wave of tension leave her even in profile. Her posture relaxed and her jawline softened markedly as she spun the chair around to face the cabin.

"I'll engage the sLume in a few minutes once the impulse engine builds up some negative mass. We'll run superluminal overnight, and when we drop out in the morning we should be close enough to the pulsar to get far more definitive readings. What's for dinner?"

"Seared salmon with wilted spinach and lemon rice. You genuinely do have a fine selection of food aboard."

"As much time as I spend out here, hell yes I do. Is it ready?"

"Two seconds. Impatient much?"

She smacked her lips and danced her toes along the floor, impatiently. But she seemed more at ease than he had ever seen her. And why not? She was flying again, which he suspected meant a great deal.

The blatant flirtation earlier had been a gamble, though not necessarily a failed one. Time would tell. He had worried it may backfire and push her away, but it appeared not. Why had he done it? Because it felt...right. The situation was now quite a bit different from his initial assessment on his first day of freedom. *Quite* a bit.

He positioned the salmon on the plates and served them up with great formality. "And now it's ready. Oh Great Starship Captain, your dinner is served."

"Smart ass." But she wore a smile as she came over, gestured to dim the lights and settled into the chair. Now the smile did reach her eyes, and the result took his breath away.

"Well, yes." He buried his reaction in a chuckle as he joined her. She had already dug into the spinach. "And how is it?"

"Ymmmm." Her eyes closed, a blissful expression spreading across her face, and he found himself wondering if she looked this way when she.... *Wow. Best save those thoughts for when you're alone behind the privacy screen.*

"It's delicious, which I'm sure you know. I suppose being multi-talented is a job requirement for becoming a spy."

"I—" He paused, fork in midair, his brow furrowing up a little. "Not cooking skills necessarily, but yes, I suppose it is."

"How did you? Become a spy I mean."

Hmm. Test time was it? His instinct told him to spin a web of half-truths around the truths and lies; it was his modus operandi.

He recalled their earlier conversation. He hadn't been lying—much—when he said he wasn't sure how to be himself around someone else, but he was fairly certain it didn't involve lying when the truth would suffice. She knew what he did for a living. So long as he refrained from revealing state secrets, talking about it held no danger.

He finished his bite of salmon and smiled the slightest bit. "They found me. I was about to graduate from university with degrees in history and engineering physics. I was going to build orbital communications arrays. See, I had this idea for a new kind of adaptive array which could intelligently shift its orbital distance depending on the signal load and transient needs. It would require coordination of—it's not important. Anyway, a week before graduation a—" *not that, not yet* "—man representing the Intelligence Division approached me."

He shrugged mildly. "Something I had done, or maybe everything I had done, had attracted their attention. And I said yes."

"Why?" She was observing him rather intently, bright gray eyes dancing in the dim lights. It might have felt like an interrogation, except he wanted to tell her.

"I didn't want to end up stuck in a corporate job for the next eighty or a hundred thirty years. I enjoyed engineering well enough, but I also loved the outdoors and working with my hands. I had good people skills, and orbital hardware construction isn't known for its vibrant social scene. *This* though, it offered adventure. New places, new goals, new challenges on every mission. I would never be bored."

He paused to take a bite of rice. "And before you ask, I don't regret it. There are downsides I didn't foresee at the time, but I'm not sorry I chose this life."

"Hold that thought." She slipped away in the direction of the cockpit, he assumed to activate the sLume drive. It occurred to him he was busy spilling forth his life story to her...but he found he couldn't summon up the urge to stop.

A few seconds later he felt the almost imperceptible shift in the purr of the engine beneath them and the glow of the Nebula blurred outside the viewport. She didn't return to the table immediately, and he sensed her move behind him to the corner of the kitchen area.

It came as a pleasant surprise when she showed up at the table holding a bottle of wine and two glasses. "I think escaping that godforsaken planet is worth a little celebrating. Want some?"

It was so easy to get lost in her eyes, and for a moment he let himself. "I'd love it."

She broke the gaze to sit the glasses down and pour the wine before returning to her chair. "What about your parents, your sister? It wasn't difficult having to lie to them?"

He took the time to enjoy the first sip of the wine. A chardonnay, chilled to the perfect temperature. Deep golden in color, it drew in the light until a glow emanated from within. Also, it tasted delicious. Then again it would.

"We weren't close—I mean my sister and I are fairly close now, but she was still a young teenager then. And my parents...well, they weren't a consideration." He sighed. "Probably sounds cold and heartless, doesn't it?"

She had finished her dinner and settled back in the chair, legs comfortably crossed and the glass of wine in her hand. Her hair, damp from her shower, cascaded messily across her shoulders. She grimaced at the glass; it didn't appear to be vicariously directed at him.

She took a long sip, then contemplated the wine as it swirled languidly in the glass. "Perhaps, but I understand how it can happen. My mother and I don't exactly get along, and haven't for years."

His head tilted a fraction. Curiously, but nonthreatening. "Why not? If you don't mind me asking."

She glared at the ceiling. "What does it matter why not?"

He flinched at the sudden sharpness in her tone. Goddamn but her parents were a touchy subject.

"It matters to you."

He almost frowned, taken aback by the intimateness of the words coming out of his mouth, not to mention the sincerity of them. He had fallen so far off his game it was laughable. Except he wasn't actually playing the game any longer, was he? Nope, apparently he was not.

She didn't seem to notice his mental gymnastics; her words dripped with bitterness, but again it didn't appear to be directed at him. "It really doesn't...."

He nodded slowly and sipped his wine, letting the silence linger. Finally he sat the glass on the table and idly ran a fingertip along the rim. *Already shared far more than you meant to, might as well go all in. What the hell.* "My mother's a nutcase."

"I thought your mother was an industrial architect?"

"The two are mutually exclusive?"

She merely shrugged in response.

"She is—or was anyway. Had a decent career and several prominent buildings to her name. Then one night, out of the blue and after twenty-four years of marriage, my father walked out on her. Said he simply didn't love her anymore and needed to find some happiness for himself.

"She had always tended toward the emotional side, but so long as he was there she stayed stable and fully functional. But...I don't know. I guess she viewed him as her whole world. When he left, she just...broke."

He stared at the bottle a moment, grabbed it, refilled his glass and took a lengthy sip. "She quit working, quit sketching, quit doing much of anything at all. Even now, she mostly sits in the house and waits for him to come back."

"Do you think he will?"

"After twenty years? No."

"Well, what does he say?"

"Don't know. Haven't spoken to him since the night he walked out."

Her eyes creased at the corners as she regarded him over the rim of her glass. "I'm sorry."

She sounded like she meant it, but he supposed he carried a bit of parental baggage himself. "I'm not. He showed his worth when he left."

Upon first being given the advice to 'never have anything you can't walk away from,' he had been skeptical. After all, wasn't it the very thing he hated his father for? He had resolved the matter by developing a corollary rule: *Never let someone get close enough to depend on you. That way they don't get hurt when you walk away.*

He didn't share any of those thoughts aloud, of course, and they fell silent again. He watched her without *watching* her. It was evident she struggled with something. Her gaze drifted around but failed to focus on anything while she absently twirled the stem of her glass between two fingers. Her lips pursed together as if to prevent words from spilling forth without prior approval.

He hoped she viewed his confession for what it was: an honest, unpremeditated sharing of a less-than-pleasant part of his life— because apparently he intended to spill forth his entire damn life story to her—rather than a manipulative feigning of vulnerability to get her to open up in return. He *had* done such on more than one occasion; this wasn't one of them.

She refilled her glass and appeared to come to a conclusion. Her gaze finally settled on him.

"The answer to your question yesterday is yes. My father and I were very close. He taught me to fly, he taught me to love the stars. Work took him away a lot, but he always came home with some new adventure for us to embark on. He was...." Her voice drifted off, but then she blinked and straightened her posture.

"After he died, my mother shut down emotionally. She had never been a particularly affectionate or doting mom, but she became a robot, a cold automaton throwing herself into her work for eighteen hours a day. At a minimum."

She took a deliberate sip of wine. "Looking back, I realize she was grieving and it was the only way she knew how to deal with the pain. But I was thirteen years old and I was grieving, too, and she wasn't there to comfort me, to tell me it would be okay. She wasn't even there to silently dry my tears. She wasn't there *at all.*"

Her shoulders raised in a half-hearted shrug. "I rebelled. She reacted harshly. I rebelled more. She tried to exert military-style control over my life, and did not succeed.

"And that's it. We tolerate one another, but we never really made up. We never talked about it. And we most *certainly* never talked about my father."

"Maybe it's not too late."

The laugh she gave rippled with cynicism. "I tried once. Before I left for the job on Erisen, I took her to lunch one day. I apologized for some of my more...*extreme* behavior in the wake of Dad's death. I told her I understood now she had been grieving as well. And though I was only a child, it had been selfish of me to act as I did, and I was sorry if I had made her life more difficult at an already difficult time."

She stared into her glass, but her gaze seemed focused on someplace very far away. "She responded by saying I was still a child—note, I was twenty-five at this point—and I should never presume to believe I was capable of understanding anything she had gone through or anything she had or had not *felt*." A quick gulp of her wine. "And as for my behavior, while it was disappointing as she had expected better from me, it amounted to nothing of real consequence."

"No..." her head shook with an air of finality "...I'm afraid it is much, *much* too late. Whatever emotions the woman may have once possessed, they departed the premises long ago."

"I'm sorry. You didn't deserve such a reaction."

"Maybe, maybe not. I was quite the recalcitrant teenager." She took a deep breath and slid her chair out, leaving the nearly full glass of wine on the table. "And on that lovely downer, I'm going to call it a night. But...."

Her eyes found his. "Thank you."

He met her gaze with his full attention. "For?"

She gave him an almost wistful half-smile. "Being honest."

He had told her she probably couldn't tell the difference, but perhaps she truly could. He didn't know whether the possibility comforted or terrified him.

He instinctively leaned forward, his hand moving toward hers. It paused halfway to its destination.

She hesitated halfway to standing, her expression now completely unreadable to him. "What?"

Stay.

He withdrew his hand and eased back in the chair, though his attention didn't leave her. "Nothing. Good night, Alex."

25

I t was one-thirty in the morning when Michael, freshly showered and wearing pressed khakis and a crisp forest green shirt, walked in the incident command center at Division HQ. His wife was a saint, and as soon as this crisis passed—if it passed—he owed her a nice dinner out, if not a weekend getaway.

He smiled at an agent who handed him a steaming mug of coffee and let his gaze run calmly across the room. Most of the Summit delegation had been brought directly here from the spaceport upon their arrival; a few lower-level staffers cleared of involvement or knowledge were allowed to go home for now.

The agents tasked to Atlantis having exhausted their avenues of interrogation during the nineteen hour trip to Seneca, his best interrogators had taken over upon the delegation's arrival. Several of the senior Trade Division officials were, shall we say, *displeased* about being detained. They shouldn't have hired an assassin as an employee, then.

Karin Pitrone, the team lead on Atlantis, spotted him and came over. Her stride appeared purposeful and her shoulders rigid, though she must have been awake for going on fifty hours now. He gave her a sympathetic smile, which she acknowledged only by a tight nod.

"You asked to speak to Assistant Director Nythal, sir? He's in Interview Room 3 whenever you're ready."

"Thank you, Karin. No time like the present." He was kept apprised of events via a constant stream of updates over the last two days and didn't need further briefing.

Jaron Nythal sat on the edge of his chair, his hands drumming a rapid rhythm on the table while his eyes darted around the empty room, then up to Michael as he entered. A half-empty cup of coffee sat to his right, a crumb-filled plate to his left. Dark irises almost masked the dilated pupils.

Michael recognized it had been a long few days for everyone and would understand if the man was running on caffeine and adrenaline, but he just wasn't sure it had been the best idea for him to take amps before the interview. He recalled Delavasi's warning regarding Nythal; he already understood what Delavasi had been getting at.

He made certain none of those thoughts tainted his expression as he smiled professionally. "Mr. Nythal, I'm Director Michael Volosk with the Division of Intelligence. Thank you for agreeing to meet with me. I realize the situation is far from ideal for everyone involved, so I appreciate it."

Nythal cracked his neck. "It's fine...Volosk, is it? I'm still in shock over what happened. I can hardly believe it. We all had high hopes for the Summit, and it's a shame it went down this way. It truly is." He dragged a hand through sleek black hair. "So what do you need from me?"

"Merely a bit of information." Michael cleared his throat and sat down opposite his 'guest.' "I won't take any more of your time than is necessary. What can you tell me about Christopher Candela?"

Nythal shrugged. "I didn't really know him."

"I understand if you didn't know him socially, but he served as a staffer in your department, and you oversaw administration and coordination for the Summit. You approved his attendance, correct?"

"Well, yes. But you must realize, there were thirty-seven people in the delegation. I can't be expected to know each of them individually. I can tell you Mr. Candela's record was clean. He wouldn't have been permitted to go were it not."

"I'm sure." He really wished the man hadn't doped himself up, as it made it difficult to judge and interpret his body language. He considered putting the man on ice until he'd returned to a baseline state...but there was a lot to do and little time to do it in. "Do you have any personal impressions of him you can share?"

Another shrug. "He was...young. Eager to please. Seemed intelligent enough, but we hadn't asked anything of him yet. My *impression* of him is he didn't make much of an impression."

"What about during the Summit? Any out-of-character behavior?"

Nythal leaned into the table and clasped his hands together. His thumbs continued to dance erratically. "Look, Mr. Volosk. I stayed busy two ways from Sunday during the Summit. I barely noticed what my personal secretary did, much less some no-name lackey."

Michael maintained perfect composure, offering no hint of annoyance. "Of course you did. Do you remember the last time you saw him?"

Nythal blew out an exaggerated breath and crashed back in the chair. "Uh, I think I saw him at the dinner Tuesday night. Wednesday though? I attended meetings all day."

"And around the time of the incident?"

His gaze drifted around the small room as if deep in thought. "No, I don't think so. I mean I was in the ballroom, so I suppose my eyes might have drifted across him, but...."

Now Michael did show annoyance, with deliberate intent. He'd let the man play out his routine. Now to remind him he wasn't actually in control of his situation. Nythal was a government official of moderate stature, certainly, but one didn't get far in the intelligence business without learning to disregard political niceties. Granted, once you rose to a department directorship you needed to begin to practice them again, but not in this particular circumstance.

"Fine. Did he have a reason to be in the receiving line? He doesn't sound like the type of person who would want to glad-hand dignitaries."

"Maybe it was a secret dream of his. I don't even know if he'd ever met Kouris—"

"What was his job at the Summit? It doesn't appear as though he did much of anything."

"He was an attaché, he...got shit for us. Ran errands. Made notes, whatever."

"How many *attachés* did you have serving you?"

"Um, four, five? I don't...remember...." The lines had begun to deepen around his sagging eyelids. The amps were wearing off.

"Seems like a little too much bureaucratic padding to me—this isn't the Alliance. What about the following individuals: Alice Terre, Gerald Michaels, Treyson Rivers, Brandon Chao?"

"Wha—what's special about them?"

"They also participated in the receiving line and greeted Minister Santiagar prior to his collapse. We'll need to review their files and activities as well."

Michael sat at his desk, the door closed. A few moments' respite. His hands rested at his chin in a thoughtful pose. And he *was* thoughtful.

He'd conducted half a dozen interviews at the request of his agents, spent hours reviewing summaries of three dozen more interviews and viewed the footage of the incident from every angle and the cams of the pursuing agents. He'd confirmed the logs of every exit and patrol on Atlantis.

The man in the receiving line *was* Chris Candela. Scans of both Kouris' and Santiagar's hands minutes after the incident recovered trace DNA. Yet the man pursued into the service corridors displayed evasion and subterfuge skills which nothing in Candela's life history indicated he should possess.

Worse, he was gone. Despite an ironclad lockdown on the facility in under two minutes—due as much to quick-moving Alliance security as anyone else's actions—and a meter-level grid search, no trace could be found of the man.

The exit logs stared back at him from the screen above his desk. Eventually they had been forced to allow the uninvolved guests and bystanders to depart. The official Summit attendees were accounted for, save Candela. The nine attendees not present at the final dinner—an Alliance staffer, three reporters and five corporate executives—were interviewed on-scene and provided viable reasons for their absence. After follow-up they had been cleared and allowed to depart as well.

He exhaled softly, feeling every gram of the weight though it didn't show in his posture or the bearing of his shoulders. Diplomatic relations with the Alliance hung by a dangling strand of a thread. If they could provide hard evidence of this being the act of a lone crazy, they stood a chance of at least regaining an uneasy détente. Otherwise, their claims of non-involvement came off as weak and impotent. But damned if he could find any such evidence.

He traded the exit logs for the rapidly growing file on the life and times of Chris Candela.

He had seen many criminals in his years in Division. Dangerous men and even more dangerous women. Small-time hucksters and savvy crime lords. Spies, gangsters, assassins, insurgents and wanna-be-revolutionaries. True believers and soulless mercs willing to kill children for the right price.

Candela was none of these things. While the possibility continued that something in the man's past, some event they had yet to uncover would open a Pandora's box of secrets, it became increasingly unlikely with each passing hour. Even if—

His eVi blinked red, and a second later a brief message flashed into his vision.

We found him.

ℛ

The body had floated onto a beach filled with frolicking children mid-morning Atlantis time. Once the children were corralled for counseling and the scene secured, a thorough forensic investigation was conducted onsite before moving the body to a medical facility.

The examination indicated a time of death between late afternoon on Wednesday and mid-morning Thursday; two-plus days in the water made a more precise TOD impossible. The cause of death was determined to be drowning. All evidence indicated that upon escaping the convention facility, however he accomplished it, he had simply dived off a walkway and let himself drown.

Oceans did not constitute a significant feature of Senecan topology. They existed of course, but were shallow and unexceptional, and generally far too cold to frolic in. It was conceivable Candela didn't know how to swim. Unlikely, but conceivable.

It remained a mystery how he escaped the lockdown. But he clearly had—after which, by all indications, he committed suicide.

The evidence at this point was near to irrefutable. And despite herculean efforts and their most earnest protestations, they had nothing they would be able to show to the Alliance government to prove the assassination was anything other than a premeditated act on behalf of the Senecan Federation.

26

T had Yue led the fighters into Senecan Federation space. He had swung down a bit to the south so should they be tracked, they would appear to be approaching from the nearest Alliance military base on Arcadia. They were unlikely to be picked up until they reached Palluda however, as other than one tiny Alliance colony the region to the south of western Federation space was a desolate wasteland devoid of life.

At 0.2 AU out from Palluda they dropped out of superluminal. He signaled the other fighters to move into a tight standard Alliance approach formation, one they had practiced several times in the last week in the skies above Cosenti.

From here on out, everything needed to proceed according to the script.

"Activate transponders."

Acknowledged.

"Switching to Alliance encrypted communications protocol. Confirm."

Confirmed.

He consciously added a crisp abruptness to his tone. "This is Vengeance Alpha. Operation Vengeance is a go. Initiate jamming of orbital sensors on my mark. And...mark."

Palluda became visible in the viewport moments later. It was a smallish planet, two-thirds the size of Mars, and the lone habitable world in the system. Nevertheless with a location solidly in the goldilocks zone and a stable orbit, it was a bountiful if ordinary garden world.

The colony had been founded ten years earlier as an agricultural outpost. It supported a population of under thirty thousand, for bots did most of the work tending the vast kilometers of farmland.

A single town sat in the center of the cultivated land. Thankfully the first atmosphere corridors had begun operation six months earlier— corridors which helpfully included transponder monitoring, though no connected security measures.

"Bravo, Charlie, Delta, on me. Prepare for corridor transit."

The corridor ended to the southwest of and outside town. Only the most basic defense system protected the colony, consisting of two surface-to-air turret lasers and a single patrol drone. He planned to knock out the drone immediately, and custom jamming ware would disrupt the STA turrets.

His ship emerged from the corridor and the distant outline of the town came into view. The other three fighters followed him out as he banked east.

"Vengeance, you have your targets. We are weapons heavy."

R

Thomas Harnal was deeply engrossed in watching Ava Loumas saunter across the street. As such, he didn't see the patrol drone until it crashed to the ground three meters in front of him.

"Ah shit!" His arms cartwheeled in the air as he was thrown backward to land on his ass on the sidewalk. He looked up to discover Ava staring wide-eyed at the scattered wreckage of the drone and the deep crater it had created.

He laughed gamely and climbed to his feet. "Well, there's my brush with death for the day, eh?"

She glanced over at him, a perplexed frown animating her pretty features. "Oh...Norm...Tom? That's your name, right? Are you okay?"

She didn't even know his name. His shoulders sagged. "Yeah, I'm fine." He looked back at the crater marring the park grass. "I wonder what happened to make it fail? Maybe the—"

A sonic boom reverberated, so close the ground trembled beneath him. His eyes jerked up to see two fighter jets zoom overhead. The distinctive navy Earth Alliance emblem was clearly discernable— they were flying *that* low.

He hated the Alliance. Alliance soldiers killed his grandfather in the Crux War. He had never met his grandfather, but his mom said he had been a great man, which was good enough for him.

A fireball plumed into the sky from the vicinity of the spaceport. Three seconds later the sound of the explosion reached them, a low rumble vibrating along his skin as it built to a malicious *growl*.

In a burst of adrenaline-fueled bravery, he grabbed Ava's hand and started sprinting in the direction of the town hall. His dad worked for the Agriculture Bureau; he should be there if he wasn't on his lunch break.

"Come on! We have to warn them the Alliance is attacking!"

Gerald Harnal sat at his desk, picking at a sandwich while he reviewed the quarterly production reports. The whole-grain hybrid fields were doing really well, which was fortunate since the food corps on Krysk were requesting an increase in shipments next quarter.

No matter how smart, how fast or how resilient humanity grew, they still needed food to survive. Sure, using adaptive cybernetic subroutines most people could now survive longer without food, so long as they had water. But the limit had only been stretched to four months at the outside, and no one wanted to live in such a state for any length of time, much less months.

So the seeds to feed humanity continued to be planted, nourished, reaped and transported across the galaxy.

He knew he was a small cog in a very large machine, but he liked to think he did his part. His great-great-great-grandparents had been farmers on the Oklahoma plains, and in his own way he carried on their proud tradition.

Nevertheless, it—

—his eVi flashed red and pushed an emergency pulse into his vision.

Dad Alliance ships are attack—

He never saw the missile, nor the ship which fired it.

The town hall appeared to implode from within, then expel an enormous red-gold wave of fire to consume all in its wake. The heat rolled over them like a blast furnace.

"Dad!" Thomas fell to his knees in horror. "No, Dad…."

Ava was pulling on his arm, trying to drag him back up. "Come on, we should get somewhere safe."

"But my dad…he might still be alive and need our help…."

She glanced at the collapsed, destroyed building at the end of the square. It bowed in to the center, where jagged pieces of synthetic stone piled twenty meters high. Black smoke billowed out of every surface, licked by bright yellow flames.

"I don't think so, Tom. I'm sorry. We need to move!"

He gazed at her, eyes wide and desperate. It felt like a dream, everything hazy and sluggish. Ava was talking to him…and his father was dead. Slowly he nodded and struggled up.

She tugged him around the rubble. "Come on, let's go to the school—they've got a storm shelter!"

They stumbled through huge chunks of debris and upended vehicles and veered left toward the school. People were running in every direction, some panting, others screaming. A few merely huddled on their knees beside bodies.

Behind them the jets could be heard approaching again—or maybe it was different ships, more ships. The beam of one of the defense turrets chased them as they passed overhead.

He saw the beam trail off in the air to the right. Why didn't the lasers hit the ships? The government had promised they were state of the art.

Someone crashed into him from behind, and he remembered to start running again.

Ava's hand felt sweaty and clammy in his. Not at all like he had imagined it would feel. *But she was probably scared, right? That was why it wasn't soft and warm and gentle.*

To their left the community center smoldered in ruins. A gust of wind blew a cloud of ash and smoke onto them; he accidentally inhaled some of it and doubled over in a coughing fit.

"Tom, *please*, we have to keep going!"

Ava was crying now. Her tears cut wet streaks into the ash coating her face, but her gorgeous green eyes, stark with terror, shone through the smoke.

He tried to stand, but another coughing fit crippled him.

She stared at him, panic bubbling forth. "I'm sorry, Tom, I don't want to die. I have to go!" She let go of his hand and took off running.

"Ava, wait...." His voice was hoarse and cracking and there was no way she heard him above the cries and screams and thunder of collapsing buildings.

He crawled to his feet and stumbled after her. She seemed far ahead of him now. He saw her join a group of people scrambling up the stairs and fighting to squeeze through the doors all at once—

—the front of the school erupted in a pillar of fire.

His steps slackened to a halt. *It was a dream. It had to be.* Only in a dream would Ava finally talk to him, then have the life stolen from her.

"Ava?"

A column of thick black smoke flowed down the street toward where he stood. He let it wash over him, no longer caring if he could breathe.

AR

New Babel
Independent Colony

Olivia observed the feeds from the jets on a large screen above her desk as their fourth and final run began. The perfectly manicured nail of her left index finger tapped a slow, measured beat on the surface of the desk; it was the only sign of tension in an otherwise calm and poised demeanor.

She waited until the first of the final two missiles had been loosed by each ship. Twenty-eight high-powered precision Alliance missiles had done quite sufficient damage to a nascent village of thirty thousand. She entered a code on the control panel beneath her right hand. The custom ware installed on the jets to jam the defense turrets ceased to function.

Five seconds later Charlie fighter exploded. Confused chatter burst forth in the other three cockpits.

"Wha—? How'd that laser hit?"

"Jamming is down. I repeat jamming is down! Evasive maneuv—" Bravo took a missile to a wing and spun out of control to disintegrate on impact with the ground.

"Abort! Delta, abort!"

But they were too close to the town and its meager little defense systems.

"Eject!"

She checked, concerned for a moment at least one team member had somehow managed to eject. The eject mechanisms were supposed to be disabled, but mistakes did happen—and would be paid for if they did. Area scans identified no chutes, however.

She listened as Thad Yue grumbled in the final seconds before his fighter caught a laser from one of the turrets and exploded as he pulled ineffectually on the eject lever. *"Qu si, gāisǐ biǎo zi."*

Her eVi helpfully provided the translation: *Go to Hell, you fucking whore.*

A wry smile grew on her lips as she shut off the screen. "You first."

She had told Marcus traceability wouldn't be an issue and she had meant it. Yue had been the sole team member who knew the operation was under her direction, but they all knew they weren't working for the Alliance. Modern interrogation techniques were quite effective, no matter the will of the captive. She simply could not risk the slightest chance of any information being revealed to either Alliance or Senecan agents.

Therefore none were allowed to survive.

She sent a brief pulse to Marcus, one whose meaning would never be construed as incriminating.

As requested.

27

T he *Siyane* dropped out of superluminal into an ocean of light.
Like most plerions, Metis grew brighter as one neared the center despite the lack of visible light from the pulsar itself. Alex had been prepared for it, and spectrum filters were in place over the viewports above and beyond the strengthened radiation shielding. Even so, she had to blink away halos while her eyes adjusted to the increased brightness and her ocular implant adapted to the new range of signals it now received.

The wispy, amorphous nebular dust of before was gone, replaced by sweeping, dramatic cloud formations in vibrant shades ranging from crisp gold to rich cornflower blue. They towered in thick pillars, resembling the storm wall of a galactic hurricane and spilling forth as crashing waves upon a shore.

It was magnificent. A stunning tableau of brilliant color and radiant luminance.

"Well that's not something you see every day."

She tore her attention away from the scene to look over her shoulder. Caleb stood behind her chair, hands perched on the headrest. His attention was directed out the viewport, but sensing her gaze he looked down.

He wore a spirited grin, one which only broadened when he saw her own expression of delight. Dear lord, when it was genuine his smile could illuminate a world.

Things had been different between them this morning...more comfortable, more naturally at ease. It was as if giving full voice to the unresolvable conundrum of their circumstance enabled them to, if not break through it, at least put it aside for the time being.

She returned his smile before returning to the vista. Silently she framed and captured a number of visuals using the external cameras, including several excellent candidates for future additions to the wall in her loft. Satisfied, she leaned forward and rested her chin on her palms to simply stare out and soak it all in.

Moments such as this made everything else worth it. The difficult choices, the judgmental frowns and even scorn of others, the fading away of friends and lovers, the isolation and solitude and, every now and again, perhaps loneliness…

…of course she wasn't alone right now, was she? She found—somewhat to her surprise—she was okay with that.

After a soft exhale she sat up and straightened her posture. "Time to get to work." She glanced back and found him watching her instead of the view. *Huh.* "All the sensors are wide open. We can monitor the readings along the top of the HUD, though not to the level of detail we can analyze later at the data center.

"The pulsar resides about half an AU in that direction." She gestured to an area fifteen degrees port. "Physically it's quite tiny, only a few kilometers wide, yet obviously the pulse is very strong."

The top far right screen showed the rapid, spiking frequency of the gamma flare. "We won't be able to get any closer than 0.15 AU or the radiation shield will be overwhelmed. But we don't have to. We can see everything we need to from here."

She leaned back in the chair and kicked her feet up on the small dash lip, crossed her arms against her chest and watched as the screens lit up to display new readings. Thirty seconds, a minute passed in silence, her focus wholly on the screens.

Finally she looked over at him. He had taken up a position beside the half-wall of the cockpit. "See anything interesting?"

He huffed a laugh. "If you're seeking an opportunity to put me in my place, now would be a fairly good one."

She merely shrugged, and he sucked in a deep breath. "Well, for the most part the readings match the earlier ones you took. The TLF radiation is definitely stronger now, but…it seems a little off-kilter. I can't put my finger on why."

Her lips smacked together, though she was impressed he picked up on the oddity. "Yep. Sure does." She swiveled to contemplate the far left screen for a moment, then stood and went to the data center. In a few seconds she had redirected the feeds to the table. She pulled up a large physical map of the region and began superimposing the various electromagnetic waves.

The gamma flare, not surprisingly, lined up directly on the location of the pulsar. The synchrotron radiation also originated at the pulsar to spread in all directions. Same for the pulsar wind. The visible light was diffuse throughout the region, having no clear origin point—consistent with a late-stage supernova remnant. The minor infrared and microwave readings were a bit haphazard, clumping around the pulsar but peaking at several other locations as well.

The TLF radiation…. "It's not coming from the pulsar."

He had joined her at the table, and stood near enough if she shifted her weight their shoulders would brush against one another. Yet for the moment the unsettling effect of his rather close physical proximity was outweighed by the sheer magnitude of the impossibility in front of her.

"Impossible. It lines up *perfectly* on the gamma flare."

"I know. But it's not coming from the pulsar." She zoomed the map in. "It intersects the pulsar, but it's coming from…there." 'There' was a region of thick nebular clouds 0.2 AU to the right and behind the pulsar. "And…" a thought and the entire table updated with new data "…I think the pulsar's orbiting that location."

He ran a hand through his hair in consternation. In its wake loose curls spilled down across his forehead, sending her pulse *subito accelerando*, to put it in polite terms. She willfully blinked the sensation away.

He seemed completely unaware of the effect he was having on her. "Which would mean it's a binary system, just as you suspected. Can you detect a companion in here anywhere?"

"Nope. I mean it's *possible* it's one of these infrared or microwave markers. Still, they don't really line up correctly for it."

"Well if the companion's a white dwarf—given the age of the Nebula it would make sense—it might be difficult to pick up, right?"

He continued to impress her with his knowledge of astrophysics concepts; it was layman's knowledge, but very well informed layman's knowledge. He was certainly turning out to be quite a bit more than simply a black ops agent.

"Sure, but from this position it should be detectable. Hmm…the pulsar's in a tight orbit. If I had to predict, I'd expect the companion—"

She pivoted and headed to the cockpit. But instead of resuming her seat, she stood so close to the viewport her nose almost pressed to it. Her eyes roved across the scene, pupils dilating and contracting as she repeatedly adjusted the focus of her ocular implant.

"Come on you little star, shine for me...."

Abruptly she spun back around. "Let's go over there."

He was leaning on the edge of the data center, ankles and arms crossed loosely as he regarded her with a look of...she couldn't classify it. But his eyes sparkled and one corner of his mouth was curled up the tiniest bit, causing a flutter in her chest beyond the excitement of the discovery.

One of his eyebrows arched in question. "Over...where, exactly?"

She laughed as she settled into the chair. "Sorry, guess I didn't actually finish that sentence. Not used to having company." She gestured about ten degrees starboard. "Over thereish."

It took them more than an hour to find the companion, despite the fact it was in the end precisely where Alex had thought it would be. It took so long partly because the companion traveled in a bright, dense mass of nebular dust which masked any visual cues, partly because it was smaller than it should have been—roughly the size of Europa—and partly because it was *impossibly* cool.

The *Siyane* hovered 1.5 megameters above the white dwarf. Deep red in color (despite the name), it pulsed at a leisurely period of thirty-six seconds. Seven different ways of measurement told her it radiated a temperature of 910 K.

"That's not possible."

"And that's the fourth time you've said so."

She shot him a glare. "It's the fourth time it's been true. The coolest white dwarf ever measured is 2440 K, and it is a helluva lot closer to the center of the damn universe than this is. A temperature so low means it's almost as old as the Big Bang—and *that* is impossible."

"Excellent." He shrugged. "So...we go back home and win the Nobel Prize in Astrophysics?"

She burst out laughing, and felt the tension which had been building within her, and thus in the cabin as well, since locating the dwarf melt away. "Maybe, yes."

She dragged a hand down her face and blew out a long breath. "Okay, fuck it. I've measured and recorded everything. Floating here staring at it isn't going to solve any mysteries. On to the next questions: what are they orbiting and why?"

He frowned a little...in concentration, she thought. When he frowned the bridge of his nose drew together until his eyebrows were virtually horizontal. Two fierce streaks of discontentment.

After a second he glanced over and caught her watching him. The frown curled upward into a half-grin. "Yes?"

She looked as innocent as she could manage. "Nothing. You have thoughts?"

"If I remember correctly, nobody ever gets worked up about whatever binary stars are orbiting. It's usually some arbitrary center of mass they happened to be drawn around."

"All true. But you forgot one thing—the TLF radiation. There's nothing arbitrary about it."

"Consider me chastised. So we go check it out?"

"We go check it out." She swiveled the chair to the viewport and began pulling away from the strange, impossible dwarf star. "We're likely half an hour out from any visuals." She gazed at him wearing a hopeful, imploring expression. "Make me a sandwich?"

R

She had taken a mere two bites of the quite tasty penzine and Swiss cheese sandwich when it dropped forgotten to the plate in her lap. "What the...?"

The nebular clouds had thickened precipitously as they neared the epicenter of the binary orbit, until it was like traveling through fog in a muggy swamp. Flying by instrumentation was a skill of necessity, so it wasn't a problem as such. It had become disturbingly eerie, though.

The cause of her bewilderment however was not the fog, but rather the spectrum analyzer output. Two minutes into the dense clouds it had begun displaying new frequencies, at first in the background then strengthening until they dominated the noise of the Nebula and even the pulsar.

She sensed him at her shoulder and pointed at the screen.

"What the hell?"

"Indeed."

She had tuned the analyzer as broad as practicable to capture any unusual readings across the spectrum. Now it was capturing exactly that.

The primary spectrum display updated every two seconds with a measurement of amplitude over frequencies ranging from 0.01 Hz to 10^{30} Hz. It showed a deeply concave shape, featuring strong peaks at both extremes and a severe dip along the middle, except for a narrow but massive spike in the upper terahertz range. Every update saw the peaks grow in power.

Below the primary a smaller display mapped the measurements over time. It showed a continual series of deep red, light orange and purple spikes—precise, well-defined and increasing in a perfect linear function as they drew closer.

He dropped his hands to the headrest and leaned into her chair. "Okay. The two extremes are the signals we already knew about, right?"

"The lowest band is in fact our mystery TLF. But I filtered out the gamma flare and synchrotron radiation on account of them being so noisy. I wanted to be able to spot new anomalies. And it seems I have."

"The gamma wave really isn't from the pulsar?"

"Nope. And it's a harmonic partial of the TLF wave."

"What's the source of the terahertz?"

"No idea."

His voice dropped low and acquired a carefully measured tenor. "Alex, slow down."

"Why, you want to see if the rate of increase slows?"

"No, I'm sure it will. I want you to slow down because I think we should approach more cautiously."

"Right...." She decelerated to half speed. To neither of their surprise, the sequential graph increases slowed proportionally.

"You think the signals are artificial."

"I do."

"You know a number of astronomical phenomena produce very exact, fixed waves, including pulsars." As she spoke, she sent the terahertz and gamma bands to new screens of their own. At the greater detail the level of fidelity was astonishing.

"Uh-huh. Is the dampener field on?"

"It is. But I can probably kick the power up a bit."

"Strikes me as a good idea."

She glanced up at him. He had again moved to lean nonchalantly against the half-wall to the cockpit, one ankle thrown over the other, the picture of casual interest. But the rapid twitching of the muscles in his now rigid jaw and the steady flexing of his left hand told another story.

For the first time in days, he radiated *dangerous*. She didn't feel threatened, not by him—which was interesting. Yet he clearly felt threatened by whatever lurked in front of them.

She shifted her attention back to the viewport. Her direct line of sight was free of HUD screens so she would have an unobstructed visual of their course. "The clouds look to be thinning out. We may get a glimpse of something interesting soon."

Three minutes later the nebular clouds didn't just thin out, they effectively evaporated away—

"Holy mother of god...."

She threw the ship in full reverse to slide backward into some measure of cover while diverting all non-critical power not being used by the radiation shielding to the dampener field. The lights in the cabin dimmed and the temperature control could be heard shutting off.

Then she sank into the chair, instinctively reaching up to grasp Caleb's hand as it landed on her shoulder. He didn't let go; neither did she.

A halo of thick clouds—similar in color to the gold and blue of the Nebula but of a distinct form and illuminated from within—roiled like a thunderstorm billowing forth out of...nothing.

The halo framed a ring of seamlessly smooth metal the color of lustrous tungsten-carbide and perhaps a hundred meters in width. The ring itself spanned more than a kilometer in diameter. Its interior was filled by a luminescent, rippling pool of pale gold plasma.

Emerging from the pool was a ship. It was approximately half-way through—which they could tell because it was plainly evident the vessel was identical to the other seventy plus ships filling the space beyond the ring.

Each ship was twice again as large as any human-made dread-nought. Made of an inky black material and laced with bright red fluorescents, they resembled nothing so much as mythological titans of the underworld.

Behind the columns of dreadnoughts were a dozen ships of a different style. Less angular yet still unmistakably synthetic, these ships were long and cylindrical and were woven through with pulsing yellow-to-red filaments. One end expanded to become a claw-like structure, out of which hundreds...no, thousands of small craft streamed.

The small ships were almost insectile in form. Multiple—at least eight or nine—spindly arms appeared to be comprised of a material similar to the dreadnoughts. Yet this material was pliable, for the arms twisted and writhed around a glowing red core. The craft poured out of the birthing ships then flew to the dreadnoughts and docked into their hulls in tight lines.

It was a caricature of the most extreme 'space monster' horror films popular in the early days of space exploration. Vids had made millions capitalizing on worries of what fearsome and powerful aliens may be encountered in the void of space. As humanity continued to expand, they never encountered such aliens—or any aliens at all—and in time the fad had passed.

But now they were here.

Her voice trembled at a whisper; she didn't seem to have enough breath for proper speech. "What *is* this?"

His was lower and darker, though not much stronger. "It's an invasion."

The dreadnought finished emerging from the pool of light and began moving toward the end of the flawless columned formation as the nose of yet another ship broke through the plasma.

She swallowed hard to dislodge the lump in her throat. "Where are they coming from? The ring's obviously artificial, but the interior doesn't look like a black hole, or a white one. It looks...no, that would be impossible."

He squeezed her hand; she wasn't sure he even realized he was doing it. "I think we've fairly well redefined 'impossible' today already."

"Ha. Yeah. Okay. It reminds me of conceptual drawings of a brane intersection—a dimensional border."

"Wow. And I thought I'd learned to expect anything."

She worried at her lower lip. "Regardless, it's clearly a portal of some kind. I wonder what's on the other side."

"If I had to guess, I'd say *they* are. You're recording all this, right?"

She spared him a smirk. "Visual and every band since we arrived."

He spared her a smile. "Of course you are."

She stared at the mouth of one of the birthing vessels, watching in fascinated horror as the spidery ships spewed forth. Extrapolating from the apparent number docking on each dreadnought, there must be at least half a million of them—and their generation showed no sign of slowing. A quick scale overlay confirmed while they appeared tiny against the dreadnoughts, each one was nearly the size of the *Siyane*.

His grip on her shoulder tightened. "We need to go, before they notice we're here. We have to warn someone."

"We have to warn *everyone*."

PART III:

RECURSION

"I do not believe in a fate that falls on men however they act; but I do believe in a fate that falls on them unless *they act."*

— *G. K. Chesterton*

28

CAVARE, SENECAN FEDERATION HEADQUARTERS

"So it's war, then."

Chairman Vranas didn't scan the room to search for confirmation. Or if he did, it wasn't with sufficient flair as to be noticeable. From his seat at one end of the long oak table taking up most of the room, he likely could assess the inclinations of the others without so much as a shift of his gaze.

The Senecan Federation government prided itself on being efficient, utilitarian, tasteful and modest—quite deliberately everything the Earth Alliance bureaucracy was not. As such, the conference room was large enough to hold the conference table at which conferences took place. No more, no less. Its walls were lined with sophisticated EM shields and assorted flourishes, but as they were hidden away they didn't spoil the image of minimalistic functionality.

Vranas notched his chin upward in a show of confidence. "We can't allow the Alliance to paint us as weak—not when we are stronger than ever. Twenty-two years ago we matched them on the field of battle and won our freedom. Today we are far more capable. Today we possess the capability to achieve unconditional victory. Field Marshal Gianno?"

The head of the Military Council nodded brusquely; she also wasn't one to waste effort on unnecessary motions, albeit for different reasons. "The presumed source of the Palluda attack force is the Alliance base on Arcadia. We've finalized a plan to destroy the base and cripple their short-range incursion capabilities. Authorize the operation, and we can engage within twelve hours."

"Arcadia is a large, established colony. It will be heavily defended, won't it?"

Gianno gave a condescending glance in the direction of the Parliament Minority Leader while not actually turning her head. The Senator had a reputation as an alarmist, typically with little justification to back up the accompanying histrionics.

"Of course it will be, which is why we're dispatching the entire 3rd Wing of the Southern Fleet. The offensive will be swift, massive and overwhelming. It will immediately weaken their ability to launch attacks into Federation territory, as their next closest base is another kiloparsec away—and it borders far more fortified space." Her tone broadcast not annoyance, but rather disappointment at having to *explain* what she meant by 'crippling their short-range incursion capabilities.' The Senator remained oblivious to the implied insult.

The Chairman smiled, the corners of his mouth so nearly reaching his ears he could be accused of preening. "A clear show of force will send an unmistakable message that the Senecan Federation is not to be trifled with."

"They'll declare war on us for certain after an attack of such magnitude!" The Minority Leader's voice had already risen to a keening level.

"Certainly. But they will be the ones who do so. We are merely responding to an incursion and assault upon one of our colonies. It will be the Alliance who starts the war—a fact we will not allow anyone to forget. Marshal, the operation is authorized."

Graham Delavasi cringed and didn't bother to hide it. "So…what is our ultimate objective? Say we kick their asses all the way back to Earth—what then? We take over? Is that what we *want*? Because I was under the impression we wanted to minimally govern a loose association of worlds by mandating a core set of democratic principles and capitalistic standards—or was it just me?"

"Don't be ridiculous. We have no intention to take over ruling the Alliance. We shall simply defeat them convincingly enough to cow them into not committing aggression against us again."

"Oh, I see." He ran a hand through too-bushy hair; he had found it was uniquely suited for such tics. "Well, not as if anyone cares at this point, but my assets within the Alliance report the highest levels of the bureaucracy are in a state of confusion. No one can figure out who authorized the Palluda attack, and no one is stepping up to take responsibility. They're trying to keep the discord under wraps lest the government appear weak—but it seems all is not well in the Brennon administration."

The Chairman shrugged. "It hardly matters. Alliance forces came onto our soil and attacked a peaceful colony, and that cannot stand. All the better if their leadership is squabbling amongst itself. We may be able to win this war in short order."

He bit back an annoyed sigh. Vranas had been a mid-ranking senator during the Crux War and spent his time serving on commerce committees and the like. A week ago he had been championing the virtues of peace; now he was rattling sabers. Though an assertive, confident leader, the man knew almost nothing of the military, and like many politicians had a case of selective amnesia when it came to the ugly realities of war.

Graham had fought in the war, spending two years leading stealth tactical interdiction squads behind enemy lines. It was an experience which had led him to jump on the intelligence post offered at the war's conclusion. Combat was messy, violent, terrifying, costly and tragic—truths few people at the table appreciated.

These days much of the 'fighting' occurred between ships at a distance of megameters from their targets, making it even easier for noncombatants to lose sight of the underlying reality. Especially politicians. They viewed war as a sterile and clean affair, a remote non-sensory circus performance holding little in the way of real consequences.

Nevertheless, he held his tongue. His post earned him some influence and his blunt manner was common knowledge—but he was far from the most powerful person in a room filled with powerful people. Instead he watched as the Chairman straightened up in his chair and nodded perfunctorily, a signal the Cabinet meeting was drawing to a close.

"We will not issue a statement until the operation on Arcadia is complete, at which point I plan to address the media and explain the necessity of removing this blatant threat to Federation security. If as expected the Alliance subsequently issues a declaration of war, then—and only then—will we reciprocate. Senators, I assume the Parliament will be in a position to pass a counter-declaration swiftly when the time comes?"

The Majority and Minority Leaders each indicated agreement.

"Thank you everyone for coming. Dismissed."

⁂

EARTH
VANCOUVER, EASC HEADQUARTERS

Miriam found Alamatto sitting placidly at his desk, shoulders squared and head high as he performed a stellar imitation of reviewing materials on said desk. Her entry had doubtless been announced sufficiently in advance for him to compose himself.

"Admiral, what can I do—"

"Close the door."

If he took offense at what was clearly an order, he gave no indication. It wasn't insubordination, strictly speaking; he may be her boss but he did not outrank her. The door slid shut in a faint whirr.

She motioned him silent with a terse slash of her hand. "You and I have our differences, but I've consistently respected your military judgment. If anything I've found it too conservative. But this is beyond the pale. How could you authorize such an action?"

"I di—"

"We killed *children*, Price! I recognize why you saw fit not to inform me of your intentions, as I would have objected in the most strenuous terms—"

"Miriam, I didn't authorize the strike."

"I am not gullible, Price. Neither am I a fool."

All the air left his lungs in a laborious breath; with it his shoulders sagged and carefully fabricated expression collapsed. Stripped of the poise, he appeared a beaten man, small in the oversized chair. "I swear to you—I did not authorize the strike."

Her head tilted a mere fraction. "There is no one else who *could* authorize such an action."

He forced out a jittery laugh and gazed up at her. She had not availed herself of any of the chairs opposite his desk, and the height advantage added to the impression she was now in charge here. It was not an inaccurate impression.

"The Prime Minister can. Arguably. At least he retains a Statement of Position from his Attorney General saying he can."

Her mouth descended into a small frown at that. "Brennon? He has no military experience—why would he keep you out of the loop?"

"Maybe because he knows, like you, I would object. He's denying responsibility, though he doesn't need to. But who else is there?"

"Defense Minister Mori might counsel Brennon to take this sort an action, but he wouldn't stick his neck out so far as to attempt it himself." She paced along the front of his desk, hands clasped behind her back. "Have you considered the possibility we're dealing with renegade officers further down the chain of command?"

He sank lower into the chair. "Oh, Miriam...."

"You know there are segments of the officer corps who continue to harbor significant animosity toward the Federation."

"I've always counted you among them."

She made it a point to keep her personal feelings separate from her professional judgment, to project an impression of objectivity. She liked to think she was in fact objective. Still, the world expected her to harbor a degree of animosity toward the Federation, and it had not been difficult to oblige them.

"In some respects I am. But I am also a realist. I've seen the costs of war and do not desire to repeat them. And I would *never* provoke a war by blowing up a school full of children, thereby painting us as the evildoer from the start."

"Technically they provoked it with the assassination."

A dismissive wave landed in his general direction. "An assassination of a mid-level diplomat is hardly reason enough to start a galactic war. Sanctions for certain, perhaps a blockade—but not war. However, others may have seen it as an opportunity to right old wrongs. Others who are more hot-headed than rational." *Unlike me* went unsaid. "It is possible the assassination spurred such individuals to take matters into their own hands."

"Rogue officers—even entire units—committing offensive operations without authorization because they're *angry*? What a disaster…."

He went over to his cabinet, poured a glass of water and gulped down half of it, then scowled at the glass as if he had expected it to provide something far stronger. "It will look like I can't control my own officers, like I'm unable to command discipline and obedience from the rank and file. Brennon will have my head."

And he should, because you cannot. Price had invariably proven a weak leader, too eager to foster harmony and accord and unwilling to make the difficult decisions or stand behind them on the rare occasions when he did. It was a management style which had served him well enough in a time of peace, yet was wholly unsuitable for the discord which marched in lockstep with armed conflict.

Whether at Brennon's 'request' or due to his own implosion, the prospect of him lasting the year in his current post was low and decreasing by the hour. She began making plans to distance herself from him, quietly and without fanfare. She would not actively work to bring him down, but she owed him no duty to fall upon her own sword on his behalf.

"I believe the Prime Minister has more pressing concerns at the moment than your head. Most notably, the fact that we appear to be on the verge of another war. The Senecan Chairman is consulting his senior advisors as we speak—and I don't believe we should expect a peaceful outcome."

He stared at her, bleak desperation in his eyes…and she realized any self-assurance which resulted from his position, family heritage or even experience had abandoned him with the advent of the crisis. He looked as frightened as an FNG on his first orbital drop.

"I'm meeting Brennon and the cabinet in six hours. What do I tell them? What do I say?"

She smiled thinly. "Only you can decide your best course of action. If you are asking my advice, I suggest you tell them the truth."

29

"**W**ould you shut up for two seconds and *listen* to me?"

Alex cringed at the frayed edges and shrill pitch of her voice. She sounded hysterical. Hell, she felt hysterical. If it weren't for the fact she'd never been hysterical in her life—other than on the day her father died—odds are she would be hysterical.

They had run. They were still running.

She hadn't wanted to engage the sLume drive at first, worried the notable expansion and contraction of the fabric of space might be detected, and god only knew how fast those *alien* ships were capable of flying. But she'd thrown so much power at the dampener field on their retreat the field's module had overloaded and fried out. Thankfully the silica-sapphire matrix filter caught the backflow and prevented any damage to the LEN reactor.

Figuring an unmasked full-power impulse engine was likely to attract at least as much attention as initiating a warp bubble, she had relented and switched over to vanish at superluminal velocity. Thus far no alien ships had trailed her to blow her out of space.

Beyond its designated requirements, feeding more power to the sLume drive did not result in greater speed. The limit to how rapidly it propelled her and her ship through space was built into the design of the drive, and no amount of power in creation could make it go any faster. So she'd also turned the heat and lights back on.

She would lessen the frequency she dropped out of superluminal. Two days in between particle dumps should be *fine*, so long as she did so far outside any outpost of civilization. She'd run the sLume at 100% instead of the 95% she typically did to minimize wear and tear. Together with high-tailing it out of Metis at full speed from the start rather than meandering around on impulse as she'd done coming in—and the fact she intended to acquire herself a goddamn superluminal travel waiver for inside the Main Asteroid Belt—and she should be able to trim nearly a day and a half off the trip home.

Three and a half days had never seemed so long.

But it wasn't three and a half days. As soon as she escaped Metis communications would return. She could warn people. She could get the information to her mother, who could get it to those who mattered, and they could...deal with it.

The Earth Alliance armed forces were very capable. Certainly they were very large. Not state of the art, but reasonably advanced. Were they strong enough? She imagined it depended on how many ships were still to come through the portal. Perhaps if the Alliance cooperated with Senecan forces—she cut a glance over to evaluate the state of her Senecan companion.

His jaw had locked in place, and his eyes were flaring as hot as the bright blue core of Messier 32. But his expression was one of...of pained *patience*, which only made her want to strangle him more. At least he had acquiesced in one respect—he shut up. She should probably start talking before her two seconds ran out.

"I am not trying to allow genocide to be committed upon your 'people.' I am not leaving them to the wolves, to those...things, okay? I *realize* Seneca and its friends lie directly in the way of any path to Earth and are located substantially closer to Metis."

She forced herself not to pace in a manner which might be interpreted as hysterical. "The instant communications return, you can comm your boss or your President or Chairman or whatever it is you call him or her. Comm whoever the hell you desire. Send the visuals—send the entire fucking data set. Talk to them for hours. Whatever you feel you need to do to prepare them is fine by me. I want you to warn them.

"*All* I am saying is I'm going to Earth, and I'm not taking a two-day detour to Seneca on the way."

He sank back with a sharp sigh against the wall behind the data center, where she had been pulling in the information captured and trying to begin to organize and categorize it while they raced at maximum speed away from the center of Metis and its otherworldly portal and army of monster ships.

That was earlier though. Before the argument.

He had assumed they would be heading to Seneca forthwith to warn his government of the danger in person. A logical enough assumption she supposed, given Senecan space extended practically to the outskirts of the Metis Nebula and thus its inhabitants may be in a wee bit of clear and present danger.

She wasn't going to Seneca. She didn't care to go there when things were peachy, much less when aliens were knocking on the door. For one, on Seneca she'd be dependent on him and not even remotely in control of her situation. For another, she possessed a direct line to the highest ranks of the Alliance military; she needed to get to Earth and if necessary yell and scream at her mother and her mother's bosses and anyone and everyone else required until they understood the *magnitude of the fucking problem*. And she had no time to waste.

The shock of witnessing an invading army of unimaginably powerful aliens emerging through an unfathomably advanced portal had left them both on edge and not exactly at their best. When he had expressed his assumption regarding their destination, she had protested. He had misinterpreted. Words had ensued.

After seeming to search her face for a moment, as if for reassurance of the truth of her statements, his chin dropped to his chest. It was followed several seconds later by a weak nod. "Okay. I hear you. And I'm...sorry I accused you of being insensitive."

"I believe the term you used was 'soulless'?"

"Right." A desperate-sounding breath escaped his lips. "All of those ideas sound reasonable, and I'll likely do most of them. But what then?" He looked up at her from beneath long lashes, his gaze less hard but no less troubled. "Where does that leave me?"

She dropped her hands to the rim of the table and leaned into it, allowing her eyes to drift down rather than hold his. "Look, if you want I can drop you off on Gaiae. I know it's small and the residents are kind of creepy, but it has a spaceport and regular transports. You can get home from there. It'll cost me four hours or so, but I'll compensate somehow."

Unable to resist any longer the pull of his stare boring into her, she raised her head to again meet his gaze. "I'm sorry, but we have *no* time. It's the best I can do."

"Thank you. I—Gaiae will be fine."

The corners of his mouth twitched but exhibited no definitive direction, forcing his jaw to relinquish its clench of death. His Adam's apple bobbed a heavy swallow. "You said 'if I want.' Is there an alternative? Are you asking me to go to Earth with you?"

She opened her mouth to respond...and let it close. That was precisely what she was doing, wasn't it? *Well.*

"Yes, I suppose I am."

"Why?" A few hours earlier the tenor of his voice would've been playful, even teasing, when uttering such a question. Now it was somber and dark, weighed down by responsibility and the dread which came with terrible knowledge.

Why, indeed. Her eyes slid away from the intensity of his stare, and she made a show of inspecting the checkerboard of data sets spread out above the table. "Two voices are better than one. I stand a better chance of not being deemed crazy if you back me up. Yes, I recognize I have hard data to back me up. Still, you'd be shocked at how little bureaucrats respect hard data."

"Is that all?"

Stop. Please. This was a conversation she was so far from ready to have. "Don't be an ass."

"I'm not being an ass. I'm simply asking if there's another reason why you want me to go with you."

She ignored him and expanded the set containing the visible light images. "I need to get this data into some semblance of order so we can send it along as soon as we're clear of the Nebula. It's still in raw form and a jumbled mess right now."

After a moment's pause—she didn't know what he may have done or what expressions he may have displayed during the moment, because she didn't look at him—he joined her at the table.

"We need to do a lot more than organize it. I barely comprehend half of this, and most people won't understand any of it. Presentation matters. We need to structure the data so it tells a story, one which is compelling and easy to understand in a couple of minutes."

Her eyes cut over at him. "We?"

For the briefest second the trademark smirk returned. "Don't be an ass."

"Touché."

He sighed and squeezed the bridge of his nose, then pulled her gaze in once again. "Listen. I would...I would *like* to go to Earth with you. I don't know if I will be able to do so. There's a good chance once my superiors see this information they're going to ask me to come in. And while I enjoy a significant amount of freedom in my job, in this situation I won't be able to say no."

She nodded, possibly too quickly. It felt too quick. "Of course. We'll play it by ear. If it takes them a while to decide I'll need to drop you on New Orient instead, but I can make it work. It's fine."

It wasn't fine at all, but she told herself she had far more important problems to worry about right now. Like how to break the news to the world—or at least its rulers—that the elusive aliens everyone had been searching for had at last been found, and they most decidedly did not appear friendly.

30

ARCADIA
EARTH ALLIANCE COLONY

Arcadia's orbital defense array detected the approaching ships at a distance of 0.2 AU beyond its outer atmosphere.

The detection was expected. The commander of the 3rd Wing made no attempt to hide the force's arrival, as it was futile to try. A flight of stealth electronic warfare ships deployed in an advance position and began scrambling the array sensors, introducing errors into their targeting mechanics. A number of bolts from the enormous plasma weapons nevertheless reached the frigates forming the bulk of the Wing.

Long, dark and sleek, Senecan Federation frigates stretched for one hundred forty meters. They were constructed of a lustrous amodiamond metamaterial which absorbed and reflected the steel blue glow of their powerful twin impulse engines. Plasma shielding and reinforced layered p-graphene lattices deflected and dispersed the majority of the high-energy plasma, though in the opening seconds two frigates suffered critical damage from direct hits and were forced to disengage. The remaining frigates targeted the orbital weapons infrastructure and drew its fire while three fighter squadrons launched from the Wing's carrier ship.

The Arcadia Earth Alliance Forward Naval Base went on full alert the moment the defense array picked up the approaching ships. Fighters were scrambled to guard the mouths of the nearby atmosphere corridors and patrol the surrounding airspace. Eight SAL turrets ringing the facility activated and began searching for targets.

The Senecan squadrons didn't take the corridors however, for to do so would have been to fly directly into a massacre. Instead they battled the punishing atmosphere in nine flights of four, each flight closing in on the base from different directions and altitude.

Arcadia's topography was mountainous and lush, and the base lay nestled in a vale at the northern end of a long valley. The valley entrance was heavily guarded by automated systems, and four of the eight SAL turrets were positioned along the gap in the mountains. Drones dispatched with the 2nd flight broke off to engage the turrets, while the accompanying fighters followed three seconds behind to eliminate the automated defenses.

Senecan fighter jets possessed exceptional maneuverability, even in-atmosphere. Constructed of a hyper-light honeycombed metamaterial and sculpted into sharp edges and acute lines, they sacrificed non-electronic defenses for speed and agility. The jets raced over the mountains bounding three sides of the base, braked to a near stop at the crests and dropped into the vale, pulse laser weapons firing in long arcs through the surface facilities.

The offensive did not go unchallenged; in fact it was met with considerable resistance. Alliance fighters engaged the attackers in the sky above the base. Ships on both sides suffered catastrophic damage, the fiery wreckage often causing yet more damage to the facilities upon impact with the ground.

Alliance fighter jets featured considerably sturdier hulls than their Senecan counterparts. This meant, though more difficult to destroy, they were also slower and less agile. Several attempts to chase down the Senecan ships led to mountainside collisions when an Alliance fighter was unable to execute the hairpin maneuver its quarry performed to clear the treacherous terrain.

Over 8,300 troops were stationed at the Forward Naval Base. Most of them were noncombat servicemen—ship and equipment technicians, engineers, administrative officers—and the remainder were troops who rotated through in tours on the frigates and supply and patrol ships which called the base home. Thus for fully ninety percent of the base personnel, there was simply nothing they could do to repel the attack.

Many of the personnel present realized this and bunkered down in the most fortified area of the facility, an underground storage warehouse. In the end this kept the loss of life disproportionately low when measured against the destruction inflicted.

Nevertheless a few soldiers, caught in the throes of battle-rage, charged onto the field of battle wielding shoulder-fired SALs. But even ocular implant-aided human eyesight could not hope to track the movements of a Senecan jet. One hundred percent of the shoulder SALs missed their targets; seventy percent of the wielders—exposed and in the open—perished.

With the automated turrets eliminated, the sixteen Alliance fighters were relentlessly whittled down by the superior Senecan numbers. When the last one fell, twenty-six Senecan fighters remained to wreak havoc on the base facilities unimpeded. In thirteen minutes the attackers disabled or destroyed every structure more than forty square meters in size, save the massive headquarters building. They settled for blowing out all its windows and leaving two thirty-meter craters in its core.

Mission parameters successfully completed, the Senecans bugged out, taking the easier corridor routes on departure. The orbital array weapons had by this point been obliterated by the frigates and they faced no resistance as they exited Arcadia's atmosphere and docked with their carrier.

All told, the 3rd Wing of the Senecan Federation Southern Fleet lost two of twelve frigates and ten of thirty-six fighter jets. Though the Arcadia base was not a Regional Command Center, as the closest military facility to Federation space it constituted a strategically and politically important location. In twenty-seven minutes it had been, for all intents and purposes, eradicated.

31

B y mid-afternoon the *Siyane* finally left the Nebula behind for the comparatively empty void of space. They had worked late into the previous night, a visceral, slow-burn panic driving her and him both forward.

Alex had wanted to study the data captured, to try to understand what these aliens—or at least their ships—truly were and what they might be facing. Caleb, being the practical sort, had pushed her to first catalog, organize and summarize the data, so if nothing else they would be able to send the information out to others as soon as the ability to do so returned.

Being still more practical, he had also forced her to sleep for a few hours—even if 'sleep' meant crawl in bed and proceed to toss and turn for the bulk of those hours. She couldn't say whether he had taken his own advice and gotten any sleep himself.

Breakfast had been fruit and warmed-up bread consumed at the data center; lunch, neglected. They slowly pieced together a coherent package which could be delivered alongside a brief summary and nightmare-inducing visuals, and waited for their connection to the rest of the galaxy to reappear.

She raised a somewhat erratic eyebrow across the table at him. "So do you think we should lead with the panoramic shot of the seventy-eight superdreadnoughts or the enormous close-up of the synthetic tentacle creature from Gehenna?"

He chuckled in response; it came out half-strained, half-weary and half-genuine. "When I was six years old, my dad called himself taking me camping in the mountains outside Cavare. I woke up in the middle of the night to find this *kartinga*—you've probably never seen one, but it's sort of a cross between a tarantula and…an enormous locust—hanging in the air a few centimeters from my face. I say we lead with the tentacles. It'll make a stronger impress—" He broke off mid-sentence. "We're coming back online."

A second later her eVi lit up in a deluge of comms and data deliveries. Far more than usual came in marked 'urgent' or 'priority' or 'important,' and she had to override the force-loading mechanism before she got blinded by pop-ups.

She picked out a recent message from Kennedy, because why not.

Alex,

Well, this is going to bollocks up all our fun, isn't it? Whatever it is you're doing that has you off the grid, stay clear of this mess, will you?

— Kennedy

What? With some reluctance she selected the most recent communication from her mother. It was marked 'priority,' but hers were always marked 'priority.'

Alexis,

Wherever you are, you must realize it's best if you come home now, for your own safety.

— Miriam

"Okay, what the hell is happening?"

He held up a finger to silence her, irises jerking across an unseen whisper. She ignored her remaining forty-seven messages to watch him.

Finally his eyes focused on her. They looked...complicated. "I think you'd better turn on a news feed."

"What is going on?"

"I don't even...just turn on the news, okay?"

"Right." She gestured toward the embedded screen on the opposite wall and tuned it to a generic Alliance news feed channel.

"Again, we are reporting that in response to what they say is confirmation the Earth Alliance was responsible for the attack on Palluda, the Senecan Federation military has retaliated by destroying the Alliance Forward Naval Base on Arcadia."

"They did *what*?"

"A spokesperson continues to deny the Alliance was involved in the Palluda incident or that it was in retaliation for the assassination of Trade Minister Mangele Santiagar last week. However, they—hold on, we're getting word the Prime Minister is about to speak. Let's go live to Earth Alliance Headquarters."

She sank back onto the edge of the data center as dread pooled in her gut, already sensing whatever followed was, in fact, going to bollocks everything up.

"*Ladies and gentlemen, citizens across Alliance space. As announced yesterday, we have irrefutable evidence one or more Senecan Federation officials perpetrated the tragic assassination of Minister Santiagar at the Trade Summit on Atlantis.*

"*Likely anticipating our reaction, today the Federation has opted to falsely accuse the Alliance of attacking one of their colonies and use it as a pretext to launch a violent and destructive incursion against strategic Alliance assets. I am saddened to report over six hundred men and women lost their lives on Arcadia, a number which is likely to increase.*

"*Let me assure everyone the Alliance was not responsible for the unfortunate incident on Palluda. Nevertheless, at this point it is obvious Seneca intends to provoke us into renewed war by any means necessary. We must and will defend all our citizens from aggression. Therefore, moments ago the General Assembly approved a formal Declaration of War against the Senecan Federation. We will begin mobilizing forces immediately. I will speak further as events warrant. In the meantime, follow the »SFWar feed for the latest information. Thank you.*"

"You have got to be kidding me. We disappear for five days and the galaxy goes insane? Now there's an armada of alien ships at our doorstep and we've decided to start a war against *each other?*"

He was pacing in agitation around the cabin, but didn't respond. In fairness though, she hadn't technically asked him a question yet. "Why would the Federation assassinate our Trade Minister?"

"They didn't. Why would the Alliance respond to a minor assassination by blowing up an entire colony?"

"What do you mean, they didn't? And weren't you listening? I don't know what happened on Palluda, but the Alliance isn't to blame."

He stopped pacing long enough to glare at her. "Alex, I've got classified reports coming in which state it was Alliance fighter jets bearing Alliance transponder codes and using Alliance communication protocols firing Alliance missiles on Palluda. Politicians lie."

"Of course they do. But Earth doesn't want war with Seneca. I mean some people do, but the politicians can barely keep track of the colonies they do govern. And they'd never take such drastic action before spending three months debating it and forming four commissions to study it first. The real question is why Seneca so badly wants war with Earth."

"They *don't*. We got everything we needed in the armistice: to be left alone to go our own way."

She arched an eyebrow in challenge and pushed off the table to meet him at eye level. "Maybe you're no longer content with your little corner of the galaxy. Maybe you desire more influence and power."

Frustration crept into the creases of his eyes. A muscle beneath his left cheekbone twitched. "*I* don't desire anything. If my *government* desired more influence it would start by persuading the nearby independents to join the Federation. Think about this logically, please."

"Oh, now we're applying logic to government practices? Tell me then, *logically*, why would your government assassinate our Trade Minister?"

"They wouldn't. They didn't. There's always some nutcase championing a cause he's willing to die for, but all the information crashing into my head indicates it was absolutely not officially sanctioned."

"Well it's not like they'd own up to it once the Alliance has called their bluff."

"By destroying a farming colony? That's low, even for them."

"So you say. Regardless, attacking Arcadia makes it quite clear Seneca does want war with Earth. They sent half their damn fleet to destroy one base—hardly a defensive action, wouldn't you agree?"

"Not when it's to disable the military facility posing a proximate threat to Senecan worlds and the presumed source of the Palluda offensive." His brow drew into a tight knot above eyes squeezed shut. "My god, for being one of the most intelligent people I've ever met, you can be blindingly stupid!"

Her mouth fell open in shock. Or outrage. Possibly both. "How dare you—"

Both hands rose in surrender. "You're right. My bad. I'm sorry I said it." His expression said he was sorry for *saying* it, but little else.

He took a long, deep breath and seemed to forcefully will a portion of the tension out of his limbs, the pose of his shoulders and the set of his jaw. "Perhaps we should not fight our respective governments' war for them here on the deck of your ship, and instead remember the real threat we're facing."

For a few brief moments, she *had* forgotten. Now the crushing weight of what they had seen descended on her anew. She could feel her posture falter from it. "The invading army of giant alien monster ships."

"Yeah, those."

"*Dammit*, Caleb. How are we supposed to get anyone to listen when they're busy blowing each other up?"

His mouth opened, only to snap shut as he resumed pacing. He lapped the cabin once, twice before slowing to run fingertips along the top of the couch.

She watched his lips quirk around as his eyes darkened, a shadow passing across them and refusing to leave. It occurred to her she watched him a lot. Watched him move; watched his lips move. She needed—

"Stupid...."

"Oh you are not seriously calling—"

His focus jerked over to her, sparks of light dancing behind the shadow. "Not you. I...I really am sorry. You're not stupid—in fact you're kind of brilliant. You said it: there's an armada of alien ships at our doorstep, and we've decided to start a war against each other? That's not merely stupid, it's improbable beyond all reason."

She frowned. "I agree it does seem rather ridiculous. But I've learned not to underestimate the sheer idiocy of government bureaucrats."

"*Exactly*. Politicians can be counted on to make rash, short-sighted decisions." His pace regained speed, purpose now animating his steps between the kitchen table and the couch.

Curious, she watched—again—and waited, until his gaze returned to her. "Look, the information I see is as close to the raw, unvarnished truth as you can get. It is not propaganda and it is not sugar-coated and it says my government did not assassinate the Trade Minister."

She blew out a harsh breath. She wasn't eager to rehash the earlier argument, but she also didn't intend to give in. "Well one of your government officials did."

"Yes. Granted. And maybe he was simply a lone crazy and that's all there is to it. But then the Alliance blows up a farming colony, except they say they didn't—and you're right, it is out of character for them. And now in a matter of days—far too quickly for cooler heads to prevail—we've gone from improving relations to all-out war. And I have to wonder if anyone has stopped reacting long enough to ask *why*."

The world had flipped upside down upon the sight of the invading alien army, and once more at the revelation of this nascent war. Did that make things right-side up again? For a moment she couldn't decide if he was a genius or delusional—or whether she even remained capable of telling the difference. "You think someone is manipulating events in order to provoke a war? You might be a tiny bit paranoid."

"I know. I'm just suggesting that coming into this from the outside it appears damn suspicious. Which brings us back around to the question, why now?"

She suddenly felt an intense desire to get off the crazy train and return to reality, such as it was. "It's possible the Trade Summit provided the first real opportunity. Or perhaps the answer to 'why now' is the Summit. There are plenty of people in the Alliance, and I imagine plenty on your side, too, who don't want better relations between Earth and Seneca."

He seemed to *still*, as if all the energy of his movements came to rest within him. "You're one of them, aren't you?"

The sharpness of his gaze speared into her. It left her feeling naked and exposed, but she refused to look away. "I didn't say that. I only...Caleb, I don't want *war*. I never did." She swallowed. "Well not for a long time now anyway."

He smiled with unexpected softness. His eyes softened to match, transforming his expression to one of gentleness. "Okay."

His shoulders rose in a weak shrug. "And you're probably right. It makes more sense for the Summit to be the trigger, and not anything to do with the aliens. It nonetheless means something's fishy. We're walking into an even bigger mess than we thought—and we're about to toss a bomb into the middle of it."

32

SENECA

CAVARE

Michael pulled the collar of his jacket up to his ears as he exited the restaurant. A cold front had moved in over the course of the afternoon, and the night air now carried a stinging chill.

Nonetheless, he chose to walk the dozen blocks back to Division HQ. He needed the brief solitude—if one considered being surrounded by hundreds of pedestrians going about their business solitude—to get his head focused in the right direction. The dinner had been a brief but necessary departure from work, if only to make sure his father was doing well. Which he was. His father perpetually insisted Michael didn't need to worry over him; it never stopped him from doing so.

With the arrival of hostilities—a full-on war as of this evening—his teams were being pulled off the Summit investigation and re-tasked toward Alliance missions. Pretty much everything about the assassination still struck him as *wrong*, but he tried to convince himself it hardly mattered now. Events were moving fast; before long the assassination would be merely a footnote as the incident which kicked off a series of incidents which kicked off another war.

Though he had a few people embedded in the Alliance infrastructure and its periphery, for the most part such long-term espionage missions fell under the purview of other sections of Division. Special Operations tended to undertake focused, directed actions in lieu of passive spying. Going forward those actions were to be targeted at Alliance interests. He bore no particular ill will toward the Alliance or its citizens as a rule, but war was war—and the visuals of Palluda were certainly disturbing enough to stir up a case of righteous indignation.

He wove through the crowd materializing when a levtram arrived and its passengers disembarked. For the moment, life continued on as normal in Cavare, and the streets thrummed with citizens working, playing and transitioning between—

His eVi signaled an incoming livecomm request from Caleb Marano. Huh. In the chaos which had been the last week he'd had no chance to wonder about the Metis Nebula mission. He started to put the agent off…but once he got to the office he expected to again be overwhelmed for many hours.

"Agent Marano, it's good to hear from you. As soon as you can get back to Seneca, your services will definitely be in demand."

"The war, of course. We'll talk about it in a bit, but I'm afraid there's a larger problem."

His pace slowed. "Larger than a war? You found something in Metis?"

"You could say so. I found an army."

"An *army*? I'm going to need you to be more specific."

"A sizeable army of alien warships gathering. I'm sending a few visuals."

"Now is not the time for—" An image of a tentacled ship of obsidian metal with a red glowing core appeared on his whisper. It was followed by one showing an uncountable number of identical such vessels docked in rows along the hull of a massive— there was no scale reference, but he sensed it was massive—carrier ship. A final image pulled out to reveal dozens of such carrier ships.

He came to an abrupt stop in the middle of the sidewalk, hardly noticing as pedestrians jostled against him then continued on their way. "I sincerely hope you are joking."

"Would that I were. I—"

"Are you seriously telling me an alien civilization is hiding in the Metis Nebula, and we've somehow missed this fact until now?"

"Not exactly. There's no signs of an actual civilization. You can see a large portal ring behind the ships in the last image—they're coming through it."

"From where?"

"No idea. Perhaps from some other region of the galaxy, or another galaxy. Perhaps from somewhere else. For obvious reasons it wasn't feasible to approach close enough to determine much with respect to the portal."

He exhaled, long and slow. Things were never simple, were they? His job often required him to adapt quickly to rapidly changing circumstances, but *damn*. "Do you have any hard data on the ships or their inhabitants? These visuals are powerful, but as you can imagine our superiors are currently rather preoccupied. I could use some additional data to attract their attention."

"I do. I'm sending a full report detailing all the findings to your account."

"Excellent." He resumed walking, albeit at a reduced pace. "What kind of numbers are we talking about? Does the last image constitute the entire force?"

"The larger ships were still emerging through the portal when I left. I didn't want to risk detection before getting this information out—hmm. The report bounced. It's being blocked."

"Really? We've strengthened the defense grid on account of the conflict, but your ship's authorized so transmissions from it should be allowed."

"Well...I'm not on my ship."

"Where are you?"

"On a civilian vessel."

"Agent Marano, did you blow up another ship?"

A notable pause. *"Not intentionally."*

He groaned. The man's reputation was unmatched in Division; he had a fifteen-year-plus record of successful missions, including several no one should have been able to pull off. But he was proving to be a tad expensive. "Division's resources are not unlimited. You realize this."

"I do, sir. It was unavoidable."

"I'm sure it was. You said you were on a civilian ship?"

"Yes. It is registered under an Alliance designation though."

"I imagine there's quite a story—" He frowned as an unwelcome possibility occurred to him. "You're not being held under any coercion, are you?"

"No, it's nothing like...no, sir." He thought he detected a trace of amusement in the response.

"Well civilian or not, chances are it'll still be blocked. We can't risk remote electronic attacks so the defenses are casting a wide net." He paused. While not officially sanctioned, the use of comm scramblers was at times a necessity in their line of work. "You don't have any method of sending from a different designation?"

There was a longer pause this time, as if the matter was under discussion. *"No, sir. Not at this time. Can you obtain a waiver? I can provide the ship's serial number designation if necessary."*

"I can, but I'll need to certify it Level IV. Is it worth it?"

There was no hesitation in this response. *It is.*

"Okay. Send me the ship ID and I'll put in the request right away."

"Sent. Sir, regarding the war? It seems as though—"

He drew to a stop once again as the ship ID came in. "Caleb, are you *certain* you're not being held under any coercion?"

"Quite certain. Why do you ask?"

"Because you're on a ship belonging to the daughter of a very powerful Alliance Admiral—were you not aware of this?"

"Ah, that. Yes, I'm aware. It's a long story, but she's not acting on behalf of the Alliance military. She's a civilian."

"Is she now. Nevertheless, I'm sure you will utilize any opening which may occur as a result of your current situation, yes?"

"Absolutely. It's just...yes, of course."

"I've filed the request. It shouldn't take longer than an hour. If this report is as serious as you indicate, I'll advance it up the chain with all due speed." He sighed, his shoulders sagging briefly from the placement of yet more existential weight upon them. "Aliens, truly? As if everything hadn't already gone to clusterfained Hell and back...."

"I had noticed. Is this war supposed to make any sense? Because from here it simply doesn't."

"Not so far as I can tell, but no one's asked my opinion on the subject."

"We can talk about it further when—do you need me to come in, sir? Provide perspective or an eyewitness account to go with the report?"

"Normally I would say yes, but your, um, rather unique situation complicates the issue. It's an opportunity I'd hate for you to lose. I tell you what—hold tight until we have a chance to review your report. This alien threat is likely to fall to the military to handle, in which case they may want you to consult, or you may be able to turn your attention to other matters. I'll get back to you as soon as I know something."

"Understood. I would implore you to treat the contents of the report with the utmost urgency, but I suspect the report will accomplish that for itself."

The connection ended, and he paused at the side entrance to HQ. The visuals Marano had sent were horrifying, almost incomprehensibly so. They were otherworldly, as if out of a nightmare....

A nightmare which now made the real horrors of the actual war waiting for him inside those doors seem almost welcome by comparison.

ℛ

"Graham, the eve of war is not the appropriate setting for your brand of humor."

Delavasi leaned back in the chair and crossed his arms against his chest. "Chairman, even I wouldn't attempt such a joke tonight of all nights."

Vranas stared at him, skepticism ranking high in his expression. "Aliens."

"And not the fluffy bunny kind. It's best if I just show you." He sent the report to the screen above Vranas' desk. "These images came in from one of our SpecOps agents three hours ago, but they're over a day old. Apparently communications into or out of the Metis Nebula are difficult, as in impossible."

The Chairman sank into his chair as most of the color drained from his face. "Those are…what's the scale?"

"The dreadnoughts measure approximately 2.4 kilometers in length and 410 meters in width. There are seventy-eight of them in the visuals, but they were apparently still emerging from that ring structure when our agent departed the scene so he could get the report to us. As for the smaller ships, there are easily hundreds of thousands."

"And this is in Metis? But there's nothing in Metis."

"Agreed. Clearly the portal originates elsewhere. Where that might be is anyone's guess."

Vranas guzzled his bottle of water and activated a holo. "Field Marshal Gianno. Apologies, but I need your immediate attention."

The leader of the Military Council and Commander of the Armed Forces crystalized into view. She stood at a bank of screens bright with data, but turned to face them. "Chairman. Director Delavasi. What can I do for you?"

"I'm sending you a file. Take a moment to review it then we'll discuss the matter."

Graham stood to pace along the rug in front of Vranas' desk while they waited. It didn't take long.

Unlike Vranas or even Graham himself when Michael had initially shown him the report, Gianno's expression remained as neutral as when she had answered the holo. The woman gave new meaning to the word 'unflappable.'

"Well this represents a complication. I don't relish fighting a war on two fronts. Am I looking at the most up to date information we have?"

"You are."

"Is the Alliance aware of this development?"

Graham nodded. "If they aren't yet, I believe they soon will be." Vranas' eyes shot over to him in question; he gave a weak shrug. "It's complicated."

Gianno opened a new screen and scrolled through data too detailed to be read over the holo. "The 2nd GOI Platoon on New Riga can be inside Metis in a day and a half. They're heavily armed, fast and very covert—and should it be necessary they're unmatched in a fight. We need updated intel and a location on these ships."

The Chairman raised an incredulous eyebrow. "They can stand up against those dreadnoughts?"

She gave the tiniest little smile. "Well, as much as anyone can. Perhaps more relevantly, they can bug out faster than anyone can. The report states communications aren't working in Metis?"

"Correct. I've set one of my Tech groups working on it, but it's not looking like an easy fix."

The tiny smile had already faded to a tiny frown. "The lack of real-time intel is going to be problematic. I'll instruct the team to send back drones with updates for the time being, until we devise a better solution. Chairman, on your order I'll initiate the operation now."

Vranas let out a long, heavy exhale and stared at the foreboding images, then nodded. "Authorized."

"Very well. Director, is this Agent Marano available to accompany the team? His experience in Metis and observing the ships firsthand would be valuable."

Graham rubbed at his forehead then ran the hand through his hair. "I don't believe he's in the region at the moment, but I'll request he report to New Riga promptly."

"Thank you. It will take around twelve hours to ready the mission. If he can't be there in sixteen, we go without him."

33

Caleb was leaning against the back of the couch when she came upstairs. The expression on his face was as weighty as when they'd discovered the portal and its travelers. She paused at the top of the stairwell. "What is it?"

"I heard back from Volosk."

"And?"

His eyes closed with a slow exhale that screamed weariness. He looked tired in a way she had never seen. Of course, she probably did, too.

"Alex, I need to get back home."

"Why, so you can join the war effort?" *Damn that sounded snippy. She hadn't meant it. Unless it was true.*

"So I can do my *job*. Listen, I don't want this war any more than you do—almost certainly less—but they didn't ask me."

"And the army of invading aliens?"

"My top priority—my only priority. They want me to join a team heading into Metis for a more extensive investigation. Which is a good thing—it means they're paying attention to the threat."

She flinched and spun away, toward the kitchen. Tea. She needed tea. It kept her mother absurdly calm, no reason it shouldn't do the same for her, right? Her pulse pounded in her ears, causing his voice to sound distant, all echo-y and muffled. Why did she feel as though she was about to panic?

"No." Her voice was so soft she hardly heard it above the *pounding*.

Silence lingered for aeons.

"No...what?"

"No, you can't go home right now. We passed New Orient hours ago and are well into Alliance space." She half-turned to him, leaving herself the option to retreat again. "At this point I can't afford to turn around. I'm sorry, you'll have to come with me."

He blinked at her. His jaw solidified into a chiseled line. His lips pursed together. He blinked again. She could *see* his eyes darken, until they were the color of the Pacific under a moonless night sky. "So I'm still your prisoner after all."

"There's no reason to look at it that way…."

"Not really seeing another way *to* look at it."

"I told you before, I need you with me when we get to Earth."

"You need me. Tell me Alex, how exactly do you *need* me—and don't even try the 'two voices are better than one' line, because that is *bullshit*."

She wished then she were the recipient of an expression of pained patience, as it beat being the recipient of the expression he wore right now by several parsecs. But she had no answer for him. She couldn't have an answer for him.

"I guess you're still my prisoner then."

"Well. That's…outstanding." The tight muscles along the line of his jaw flexed. Abruptly he pushed off the couch and started down the stairs.

"Where are you going?"

"To take a shower. A long one."

"But you already—"

He paused mid-step, but didn't even glance up at her. "I. Don't. Care."

She watched him disappear down the stairwell. *Terrific move, Alex. Top notch.*

She walked slowly to the cockpit, tea forgotten. She sat and toed the chair in aimless circles and tried to puzzle out precisely why she had done it and what she had expected the result to be. But she hadn't expected any result, because she hadn't thought. Instead she had panicked and reacted instinctively.

Which wasn't like her at all. She felt…detached, untethered. Like the firmament of the world had been yanked out from beneath her, leaving her adrift without an anchor. It was odd, since she usually felt *more* grounded in space, on her ship, sailing amongst the stars. Now though, her beloved stars had become the enemy. And she was on the verge of turning an ally into another one.

But when he reappeared upstairs half an hour later, she couldn't bring herself to retract her declaration. She told herself once he cooled off it would be fine. "Listen—"

"Don't."

"I only—"

"And I said *don't.*"

Okay, not quite cooled off just yet.

He practically stalked over to the data center. "Give me access to the raw data. I'm going to search for anything else to help the team heading in."

When she didn't respond, his gaze rose to find her. Her brow had furrowed in uncertainty at him.

"Alex, give me access to the raw data."

The tone of his voice brokered no argument, permitted no resistance. She found she was standing and walking over.

She entered a sequence in the holo control panel then reached across and activated the interface in front of him. Their shoulders touched, and she looked up at him; he didn't look down at her.

She swallowed and backed away. "You can access whatever you need from there. I'll be over here working...if you have any questions."

34

T he ballroom gleamed from a ceiling adorned in thousands of fiber-optic icicles. The orchestra occupied a circular raised dais in the center of the room so their dulcet strains could be heard throughout the space without overpowering any portion of it. The bar and buffet lined the left wall, split in the middle by the cake—an enormous affair which spelled out 'Happy 50th Anniversary.' It should provide sufficient pieces for the 640 guests. She had underestimated.

War may have been declared the day before, but it had not yet hit the radar of *this* social scene. That much was certain.

Kennedy entered the room fashionably late, having just arrived on the suborbital from Manhattan where she had picked up her dress, her shoes and her date. The dress was sea foam lace, the shoes translucent strappy heels and the date the CEO of a startup solar-power satellite firm. He also happened to be an old friend from university, and more than happy to entertain her when she came to town…or Earth for that matter. It was a shame she had never managed to fall in love with him, because he genuinely was quite a good time and a good friend on top of it.

She leaned in close on his arm. "Oh my. I haven't lived here in twenty years, I don't recognize any of these people—except the famous ones, obviously. You run in these circles, help me out, Gabe."

He chuckled. "Well, to the left is your brother, alongside his dashing husband. And there toward the middle near the orchestra are your mother and father. If I'm not mistaken, they're talking to the Alliance Attorney General and the District Governor."

"They are such ass-kissers. And you're a smart ass." She sighed and rolled her shoulders gamely. "I suppose we should go speak to them. But I see Tara Singleton over there eyeing the cake—we're escaping to her at the soonest available opportunity. Oh, and drinks first."

He gestured for her to lead the way. "You know, if you dislike your parents so much, why did you travel over three hundred parsecs to be here?"

"Because it is *expected*. Because I deplore making a scene, even by my absence. And because I don't dislike them—I'm merely bored by them."

Her parents were intelligent enough people. Capable and shrewd. In their years together they had served as excellent stewards of the family fortune, growing it by over forty percent while investing handsomely in the economic and environmental improvement of the Texas coast and Louisiana delta.

But they didn't *do* anything. They didn't *make* anything. The family fortune existed solely due to the genius and sheer determination of her great-great-grandmother, whose design of a commercially viable Woodward-Mach impulse engine opened the solar system to colonization and development. Sixty years later the sLume drive opened the galaxy to the same and rendered the impulse engine a commodity, but those were a very lucrative sixty years.

Though her great-great-grandmother had died in a construction accident during the early days of the Jupiter orbital habitats, her devoted husband had ensured her legacy endured. Yet each generation since had been less impressive. Her great-grandfather helped improve the radiation shielding necessary for interstellar travel, while her grandmother and granduncle contented themselves with managing—but not improving—deep core oil drilling in the Gulf. Her uncle was a representative in the Earth Alliance Assembly and served on several environmental committees. Her father...he simply married well.

"Dad, how are you?" She smiled broadly as she hugged him, careful not to spill a drop of her drink in the process. As she pulled back the smile remained firmly in place. "Mom, you look ravishing, as usual."

"Oh, but you put me to shame, Kennedy dear. What a stunning gown, truly. And Mr. Hamilton, isn't it? I believe I saw you on the cover of Galactic Entrepreneur Weekly recently, yes?"

He bowed at the waist to kiss her hand, ever the gentleman. "It was an honor to be mentioned."

As he rose, Kennedy extended a hand to her parents' companions in turn. "Governor Samus, it is so good to see you again. We met once, at the party my parents gave for my university graduation—I don't presume you would remember, of course."

"And of course I do." The woman accepted her hand with refined elegance. As a politician, it presumably was her job to remember everyone she met lest they later prove relevant. "You had a bright future then, and it is my understanding you are not disappointing. Your father and mother both have been bragging on you nonstop."

Her smile grew into genuineness. Just when her parents threatened to annoy her beyond reproach, they went and reminded her they loved her. She gave her mother a small, heartfelt nod in appreciation and turned to the distinguished-looking man standing beside them.

"Forgive me, I spend my time these days slaving over ship schematics on Erisen, far from the center of power...."

The man tilted his head in respect, then met her gaze. Sharp, piercing eyes which almost matched her dress but sparkled far more intensely met hers. "I would not expect you to know me even were you to frequent the Earth social scene, for I am only a humble public servant. Marcus Aguirre, Ms. Rossi. It is a pleasure."

"The pleasure's mine, I'm sure." She directed her most diplomatic smile at him, though she found his gaze a tad unnerving. "What brings you to my parents' little celebration? Given current events, I must say I'm surprised your presence isn't required in Washington or London."

She ignored Gabe's subtle elbow to her side. She wasn't insulting the man; she was curious. No, that was a lie. She wasn't remotely curious, but rather making conversation until she found an opportunity for escape.

Aguirre's mouth curled into a dark sneer for the briefest second; it was gone before she could be sure it had even been there, replaced by a grim frown. "Such unfortunate circumstances we find ourselves in. I had hoped we had at last moved beyond the need for war, but alas. When I leave here I will be traveling up to the EAO Orbital to join the Prime Minister in meeting with the governors of the colonies closest to Federation space. It will be a late night, I'm afraid—but I didn't want to miss the occasion."

"How do you know the family? Are you from the area?"

"Kennedy dear, I'm sure the Attorney General doesn't—"

He gestured her mother silent. "In a manner of speaking. My family benefited from your parents' Gulf rehabilitation initiatives in the second half of the 23rd, enough to pay my way through university until I earned a scholarship. I am showing my appreciation in the smallest possible way."

"Well…" she paused to sip on her drink "…I imagine that is a very good story. I would love to hear it—but I must excuse myself for a moment first to speak to my brother. It was a pleasure seeing you again Governor, and meeting you, Mr. Aguirre. Mom, Dad, enjoy your party."

She grasped Gabe's hand firmly in hers and delicately yanked him away. Once they had put a safe distance between them and her parents she leaned in to whisper in his ear. "While I speak to Ian, you get us fresh drinks. And use your powers of persuasion to ensure they're strong, *please*."

PANDORA
INDEPENDENT COLONY

The Promenade was not the wealthiest district on Pandora, but it was close. The entertainment engaged in here included no less depraved activities than what occurred on The Boulevard; it was merely engaged in via far more refined surroundings by guests in far more refined clothing.

Gleaming mid-towers rose alongside the walkway, all constructed of a brushed chromium and all lit in a soft blue-white glow. The walkway appeared suspended twenty meters in the air, but in reality an invisible membrane extended out beyond it, ready to catch anyone who fell off the side due to clumsiness or intoxication. A small sign of the men behind the curtain.

Noah didn't feel much more comfortable here than he did on The Boulevard, but his father had at least made sure he knew how to act, and dress, in places such as this. He straightened his blazer and joined the fashionable denizens strolling toward their evening's entertainment.

His destination was a club not far into the core of The Promenade. *Distraire* was a mid-range establishment striving to become something greater. As such, it tended to attract clientele seeking the same thing.

Mia Requelme fit the bill perfectly: a feisty young entrepreneur striving for more rarified heights. He admitted to being a bit surprised she'd agreed to come to Pandora...but he supposed any ghosts she harbored were by now either dead or long vacated.

Over a decade ago she had been a street rat here—a hacker and thief working for Eli, a lieutenant in the Triene cartel. Noah had looked out for her when he could, though his resources were pretty meager back then. Then one day she had simply vanished. He'd feared she was dead, especially since most of Eli's operation got taken out around the same time.

But two years later she contacted him out of the blue, searching for some specialized items. Come to find out she had gotten away, gotten out from under Eli—somehow—and was running a home tech supply business on Romane. She ran a good deal more than that now.

He found her at the bar, slender legs crossed beneath a midnight black dress and significantly exposed by the slit which cut up it. A mane of even darker razor-straight hair fell across a toffee-hued shoulder. She sipped on a martini and scanned the crowd for him. Her mouth curled up ever so slightly when she spotted him.

He slid in beside her and dipped his chin in appreciation. "You are looking most stunning this evening, Mia."

Her tongue ran lightly along subtly glossed lips. "What can I say, I clean up well." Her gaze ran over him appraisingly. "As do you. I must admit, you are cutting quite a striking figure yourself these days."

His grin sported a wicked flair as he accepted the drink the bartender placed in front of him with a nod. "I do try. So how is business on Romane?"

"Profitable. How is business on Pandora?"

"...entertaining."

She laughed, but her eyes were serious; then again, he remembered, they almost always had been. "I guess we've both gotten what we wanted."

"I guess so." He slipped the interface, secured in a small case, out of his jacket pocket and into her hand. She'd paid him upfront so there was no need for an exchange of credits. It disappeared into a small black bag made of the same shimmery material as her dress. "Dare I ask what you intend to use this for?"

"I have an Artificial. I imagine it's clear what I intend to use it for."

"Hmm. Is it registered?"

She regarded him over the top of her martini in a manner indicating she questioned either his intelligence or his sanity.

He gave her a mild chuckle. "Right. Silly of me to ask." His own eyes grew serious—briefly. "Just be careful, okay?"

She signaled the bartender for another drink. "Noah, darling, I am always careful. I value the life I have now quite highly." After the bartender departed she shifted to face him. "So, what do we do now?" The glimmer in her eye suggested she had something in mind.

Though she was only a year or two younger than him, back when she had lived on Pandora he'd thought of her as a little sister; someone to be protected. The times he had seen her in the years since had been friendly but businesslike, and brief. Now, though...she clearly no longer needed protecting, and appeared more than his equal. And my god but she was a stunner.

He smiled, this time with a wicked flair of another sort, and leaned into the bar and closer to her. "I tell you what. First, I'd like to buy you dinner. Then, perhaps a little dancing. And later, if all goes well, I'll show you a side of Pandora you never got to see when you were living on the streets."

She arched an eyebrow, but her lips curved gracefully upward. "Oh? And where might that be?"

"My apartment, of course."

35

Caleb lay on the cot and stared up at the ceiling, barely visible in the dim light. He wanted to hit something. Anything. Instead he stared at the ceiling.

For one, hitting anything—the wall for instance, or one of the tables—would result in a loud noise sure to bring her running. And he did not want to bring her running. It had been late into the evening when, scarcely able to keep her eyes open, she had finally retired downstairs and given him the solitude, the space to think, he desperately craved. For another...well, that was plenty reason enough.

A portion of his brain busily formulated a plan to get to Seneca. Despite the dramatic nature of the report, he worried his government didn't truly understand the seriousness of what they were facing. He had discussed the situation with the leader of the investigation team heading to Metis, a Major Fergusson. The guy seemed sharp enough, if a typical special forces type. Still, he needed to be there, else they were liable to get everyone killed. Or worse, with no one reminding them to keep their eye on the ball, get distracted again by the bloody war and lose sight of the real threat.

He groaned to himself. He was a patriot, as far as it went, but it wasn't as though he cared for politicians, bureaucrats *or* military leaders. The war was idiotic, a fool's errand likely to end in tragedy for far too many involved. Or worse—again—a trap they had all been ensnared in, one certain to leave them easy pickings for the aliens when they showed up to feast on humanity.

He felt like a traitor, relaxing here on this ship while others ventured out to confront an unimaginable threat. Granted, he was the one who had alerted them to it. But he should be doing more.

After six days on the ship he was familiar with the functions of the vast majority of the controls and screens. He at most required her very minimal input to fly wherever he desired. He had no doubt he would be able to force her into providing him access to the controls, and without even harming her—assuming she didn't fight him like a possessed hyena.

Which she would.

Thus, in order to take control of the ship and get himself to Seneca or even an independent world, he'd probably need to hurt her.

And he didn't think he could do that.

No matter how angry at her he was right now—which happened to be quite angry—he didn't wish to cause her harm. He understood she had legitimate reasons for acting as she did. And though she clearly bore personal animosity toward the Senecan government if not its people specifically, he doubted she actively wished them ill. She was doing what she thought was necessary. It simply happened to conflict rather directly with what he thought was necessary.

He definitely didn't *want* to hurt her. But more to the point, he wasn't at all sure he was even capable of doing so...

...because he was emotionally compromised. Badly.

His training, his rules of engagement, his experience and the teachings of his superiors and his mentor all told him he should take control of this vessel and use it to get wherever he needed to go. Only he wasn't going to do it.

Another in an already fairly long line of rules discarded in the face of Alex Solovy.

Two hours later he still lay awake. He pondered the nonsensical, suspicious events leading to this new war and how they might have occurred; he considered his options going forward. But mostly he brooded about the alien ships at their portal and the dark feeling of dread which had taken up permanent residence in his gut since witnessing them.

He heard her come up the stairs, her steps slow and a bit uneven. She didn't come over right away; it took a minute before her faint outline appeared on the other side of the privacy screen.

"Caleb, are you awake?"

He considered whether to let his muscles tense, to confront her again or to hide behind feigned sleep. But the situation would be no better come morning.

"No."

There was no breath of amusement in response. "I'll drop you on Romane tomorrow." Her voice sounded flat and toneless, belying the significance of her words. "It's the last independent world still somewhat nearby. I've shifted our route and input the new destination.

"I'll have to backtrack a bit, but...it's fine. I've been able to put the report in front of some 'important' people on Earth, so they can wait another day for me. We should be at Romane by late morning. Of course you can take a hardcopy of the data and the report when you go."

He pulled the screen back, leaned against the wall beyond the edge of the cot and attempted to meet her gaze. Her eyes were so sleepy and unfocused it was difficult. Her hair was a tangled mess, tumbling to cover half her face and down over bare shoulders. She wore a white tank and navy shorts; the dark material was wrinkled and hung unevenly above her frankly *remarkable* legs.

He wanted very much to hug her. Instead he softened his expression. "Why did you change your mind?"

She gave him a tired, half-hearted smile. "Turns out I'm not very good at keeping prisoners." She couldn't keep up the smile, and it faded away. "I understand why you feel you need to go home—I understand you need to help protect your people. And you don't owe me anything so...."

"Only my life."

She made a valiant effort at rolling her eyes. "True, but I did try to kill you before I saved you, so it's likely a wash." She started toward the stairwell, but not before a sad, almost desperate shadow passed across her expression. "I'll let you get some sleep. I just...thought you'd like to know."

"Alex, why did you really want me to go to Earth with you?"

The words had spilled forth unbidden...and the answer suddenly seemed the most important words in the universe.

In her weariness she revealed a series of pained, frustrated emotions in her eyes and the quirking of her lips. Finally her shoulders dropped, as though she had given up. On what, he couldn't say.

"Because what we saw terrifies me, and I didn't want to face what it might mean alone. With you here, it all somehow seems a little less daunting. You...you make me believe maybe we have a chance. Intellectually I know you can't do any more than I can to stop what's coming but...but still you make me feel...safe."

She squared her shoulders and stood up straight. *Proud. Defiant.* "But it's fine. I'm a big girl, and I've spent twenty-three years facing challenges alone. I've got it covered." She nodded sharply to emphasize the statement and started down the stairs.

"I'll go."

She froze, one foot hovering above the second step, and whipped her head over to him. "What?"

What, indeed. "I'll go to Earth with you."

"Are you *serious*? We went through all this drama and angst—enough to fill a *smeshnoy* soap opera vid—and now you're just—"

He raised an eyebrow in challenge. "Do you want me to go with you or not?"

"Well yes, but—"

"Then quit bitching." He gave her the smirk he had already figured out drove her nuts.

She stared at him for a second—and burst out laughing. It was uncontrolled, weary and beautifully genuine.

When she had minimally composed herself she gestured to the cockpit. "I'm going to go revert our route back real quick...." Halfway there, she paused. The dim light faded to darkness near the cockpit, and her profile was a shadow against blurred stars.

"Thank you."

He merely nodded in response. After a breath he drew the privacy screen closed, lay back on the cot and closed his eyes.

What was he doing?

Following her, apparently.

When he had stood there and watched her, hair all tousled and tangled, gaze sleepy and unfocused, defenses worn away, defeated and near to broken but standing proud nonetheless...he had realized he simply wasn't ready to let her walk out of his life.

Okay. Going to Earth, then. To Earth Alliance Strategic Command, in point of fact—

His eyes flew open.

He had an idea.

"Sorry if I disturbed you, sir. I realize it's very late there—or very early, I suppose."

"It's fine, Agent Marano. None of us are getting much sleep at the moment. Has there been a change in your circumstances?"

"Of a sort. I'd like to propose a new option."

"I'm listening."

"First I have a question, and I'd appreciate your honesty when answering. Did our government authorize the assassination of the Alliance Trade Minister?"

"To my knowledge it did not. As far as I'm concerned everything about the assassination is wrong...but events have moved beyond it now."

"Perhaps not. One more question. Does the government desire war with the Alliance?"

"They do after Palluda. That kind of slaughter can't go unanswered. But before the attack? No."

"This war—I believe it's a trap, one which will leave us weakened and defenseless when the aliens attack."

"What are you implying?"

"I suspect we didn't assassinate the Trade Minister and I suspect the Alliance didn't attack Palluda. I suspect everyone has been tricked into going to war against one another. And I hope to find us a way out of the trap."

"Okay, now I really am listening."

"Thank you. I want to act as an unofficial, off-the-record envoy to Alliance military leadership. If I can prove to them we didn't start this war, perhaps we can end it."

"Well, that's a problem, because I don't have any proof—beyond the word of politicians—we didn't start the war. Don't get me wrong, I've tried like Hell to find it. But all the evidence points to Chris Candela as the assassin, which makes it damn hard to deny it was our doing with a straight face."

"You think he's not responsible for the hit?"

"I think I can't prove he's not responsible because the Minister's body became an Alliance state secret approximately two minutes after he ceased breathing."

"What if you could?"

36

T he QEC room always made Liam feel as though he was suffocating. It wasn't so much the size—while hardly what he would
consider spacious, it included a desk, a full-sized chair, a long wall for
holo projections and plenty of space to maneuver around. But the
three layers of six-centimeter thick sound-absorbing nanomaterial
together with the active phase cancellation waves reverberating in
the gaps between each layer created a hyper-silence in the air which
was both unnerving and stifling.

Still, it was a required accommodation for EASC Board meetings, and these days it may even be necessary.

A large holo projection filled the back half of the room, creating a near-real representation of the view from his 'chair,' were he
to be sitting in Vancouver. If he turned his head the holo followed
his eyes, in a complete 360-degree circle should he desire to see if
anyone stood behind his virtual presence.

As it had been for the last several meetings, the scene was rather chaotic. Aides bustled about and mini-conferences were
underway scattered around the room. In the past it might have
made him feel like an outsider, cut off from the real power. Today
though, he simply couldn't get worked up over it; he was in too
good a mood.

After all, he had his war.

He made an effort to tamp down the smile he realized was
growing on his lips as Alamatto called the meeting to order.

"Good morning. By now I assume everyone has transitioned
to wartime protocols and procedures within their organizations.
It's still early yet, but we need to stay in front of developments.
General Foster, if you would update us on the Arcadia situation?"

The Northwestern Regional Commander nodded solemnly.
In Liam's opinion, he should be handing in his resignation and

crawling off in shame after allowing such a humiliating defeat to occur on his watch.

"Yes, sir. The casualties have risen to 763, but I don't expect them to rise appreciably further. The damage assessment has been completed, and it is not good. We lost all the fighters stationed at the base and two of the four frigates which were groundside—the other two sustained significant but repairable damage. Seventy-two percent of the physical structures are a total loss. Temporary plasma shields have been placed around the headquarters building to enable it to retain some functionality. Most of the electronic systems were underground and are undamaged, thankfully."

"What's the status of the orbital arrays?"

"Sixty-four percent of the sensors suffered damage and are functioning at reduced capacity. Six of the fourteen plasma weapons—those facing the region the attackers approached from—were destroyed."

"It'll take months to replace those—and hundreds of millions!"

Liam rolled his eyes in the direction of the EASC Logistics Director. If ever there was a more whiny, pansy little bitch, he hadn't met them.

Alamatto acknowledged the Director but kept his attention on Foster. "In the short term, the diminished planetary defenses are our largest concern. It's my understanding a squadron is inbound from Fionava to provide active patrols in the system for now."

"Obviously this initial setback is unfortunate. However, given no declarations of war had been issued at the time, we must not view it as a defeat. But we *are* at war now, and the important thing is to focus on winning it, as quickly and bloodlessly as possible."

Liam leaned forward expectantly. "What's our first front? We should have already moved by now, in my opinion. The 2nd and 3rd Brigades attached to the Southwestern Command are at full strength and on alert, ready to engage against any target identified."

Solovy exhaled in the annoying, holier-than-thou way she had. "General, it would take a week for your ships to reach Senecan space. If you will send a squadron to Fionava to compensate for the one dispatched to Arcadia, that will be sufficient for now."

"Well what are we *doing*, then? Sitting around with our thumbs stuck up our asses?" Dammit, now that his war was here, he needed to be *in* it. He had lobbied for one of the northern regional commands several times in the last few years, but had been unsuccessful. Maybe with Foster in a weakened position....

Solovy looked positively smug. "Far from it. While Admiral Rychen's forces maneuver into position for strikes on Senecan targets—forgive me, General, perhaps you'd like to brief everyone?"

Alamatto smiled weakly. He seemed nervous and uncertain, even for him, and practically bowed in deference to Solovy. Liam briefly wondered what power plays may be at work in Vancouver.

"For several years Senecan Intelligence has maintained long-range passive hyperspectral scanners near significant Alliance assets, including Scythia, Messium, Erisen, Fionava, August and New Cornwall. They haven't succeeded at placing any in range of Earth, but nonetheless, this has been one area in which their technology is superior to ours. We haven't been able to do anything about the scanners, beyond obscuring signals where we can, for fear of provoking further hostilities. Obviously that is no longer a concern. Within the next two hours they will find every one of their scanners destroyed and their ability to eavesdrop on any strategic discussions or monitor troop movements effectively nulled."

Liam sighed. He had to admit it was a smart tactic. A little too sneaky and clever for his taste, but arguably necessary. "And after that?"

"Here are the plans for the next four days." A screen superimposed itself over the holo of the conference room. "For obvious reasons, this information will not be transmitted over the exanet, even secure channels, so please study it now."

Alamatto gestured to one of the 'guests,' EASC Special Projects Director Brigadier Jules Hervé. "Brigadier, thank you for coming. Would you brief us on the status of Project ANNIE?"

Goddamn Artificial. Mere mortals should not be playing at creating life.

"Certainly, General. ANNIE was not scheduled to go live for another four months, but given the current circumstances we are working to accelerate the timetable—" the woman glanced around the table to head off premature objections "—while maintaining strict safety protocols."

"During our testing, we've begun feeding it our existing data on the Senecan military—fortifications, assets, leadership, numbers—as well as historical data, and plan to compare its analyses with our existing tactical forecasts. We expect it to produce a number of refinements and likely valuable new insights. This will allow us to utilize some of its capabilities before formally bringing it online."

Rychen spoke up. "And what does 'bringing it online' mean, precisely? I assume we're not handing over the codes to the missiles, but what are we planning to do?"

Hervé adopted a more confident posture in her chair. She was an attractive woman, with piercing, intelligent blue eyes and rich mahogany hair wound back in a conservative braid. It was a shame she was a warenut.

"Certainly we will not be handing over the codes to anything bearing lethal capability. Once ANNIE is live it will receive real-time feeds of all military, war-related and surveillance data. It will also monitor news feeds and exanet traffic.

"To put it simply, it will look for patterns in the chaos. It will see what we cannot. We anticipate it to be able to alert us to impending attacks, secret troop movements and exploitable weaknesses in the enemy. For starters."

Rychen nodded. "That does in fact sound useful—and safe. Might we be overdoing the safety precautions a bit?"

"Well, Admiral, the thing about synthetic neural nets is they display a habit of developing a mind of their own, so to speak. It's best to keep them securely inside a high fence, because even if the core programming is perfect—which is a very big 'if'—synthetics have been known to rewrite their internal code on occasion."

Alamatto gave her an appreciative smile. "Thank you, Brigadier. It goes without saying we need ANNIE's capabilities as soon as feasible, but of course we can't sacrifice safety and security."

Once Hervé had excused herself from the room, Alamatto turned to Solovy. "Admiral, when is your daughter projected to arrive?"

"She should be planet-side midday tomorrow."

What?

"Good. We'll tentatively schedule an audience for day after tomorrow, say 1500. Needless to say, if her claims prove to be accurate they are a significant concern we must take into account."

"General, my daughter is many things, but fanciful is not one of them. I expect they will be exceedingly accurate. Unfortunately."

Alamatto appeared to wilt into his chair. "*Aliens*, on top of everything else...but let's not rush to any conclusions for now."

Liam pushed aside the strategic plans screen he had been re-viewing with half an eye—but before he could interrupt, the Logistics Director had.

"Excuse me, did you say 'aliens'? Is there something we haven't been informed of?"

Alamatto hurriedly straightened up; the expression on his face made it clear he hadn't intended to let that slip out. "Our scientists are still examining the initial data, and I don't want to send it to the larger group until they've evaluated it. It's not an immediate concern."

Liam jumped in this time. "Perhaps we would be a better judge of how immediate a concern it is."

"You will be fully informed before we make any decisions on the matter. We'll discuss it when the data is ready, and not before."

He scoffed but settled back in his chair. Aliens? Two hundred years of extra-solar exploration, and no extraterrestrial life with intelligence greater than that of a canine had been discovered. No ruins, no artifacts, no trace of sentient life. If 'evidence' of aliens had suddenly materialized now, it had to be an attempt at distraction on the part of the Senecans. The timing was too fishy for anything else.

And who the Hell was Solovy's *daughter*, anyway?

37

"E banatyi pidaraz, u etogo pridurka poehala krisha!"
Caleb heard the outburst from the lower deck and hastily finished dressing after his shower.

The morning had been a little awkward for them both as they tried to figure out what these new circumstances, this new phase of their...relationship, he supposed, meant for them. That and he struggled with what and how much to reveal regarding his new mission.

He was relieved to have devised a way to get in the game, to be able to act to avert disaster. Volosk was on board with the plan, which essentially involved him walking into enemy territory, straight into their seat of military power—and asking for their help. It was risky, daring, highly likely to fail and reasonably likely to get him arrested or shot.

But he didn't make a habit of failing. Or getting shot. Getting arrested had occurred a few times, and once or twice it hadn't even been on purpose.

The plan stood a better chance of succeeding with her help; in truth he had no reason to keep it from her. Yet he was no longer merely the prisoner-turned-stowaway-turned-traveling compan-ion, but again the intelligence agent. This was his job, and in his job secrecy and subterfuge were the order of the day.

Reveal only what you must; lie if you can.

Still, the current situation constituted an exception, right?

The argument continued unabated in his head as he went up-stairs and found her pacing in considerable agitation between the data center and the couch. "What's wrong?"

"*This. This* is what's wrong." He didn't think an aural was ca-pable of displaying anger in its generation—but if it could, this one would've done so. He crossed the deck to her side to read the message she had projected.

> *Ms. Solovy,*
>
> *Thank you for your report on possible anomalous activity in the Metis Nebula. As you are no doubt aware, all reports must be submitted via physical data disk in order to be officially accepted. Once we receive a physical copy from you, the Astronomical and Space Science Department will review the scientific findings and contact you should we need further information.*
>
> *However, as a courtesy to the EASC Director of Operations, I have briefly looked over the report. While startling and rather disturbing, according to Earth Alliance Assembly Regulation AAS 41767.239.0655k, any claims of alien discovery must be validated by an official envoy of the Earth Alliance government using approved protocols.*
>
> *After receipt of a physical copy of the report and analysis of its claims, if the Astronomical and Space Science Department finds them worthy of investigation, we will request authorization to assemble a survey team and deploy it to the Metis Nebula. Given the severity of the claims, we look forward to receiving the materials in a timely manner.*
>
> *Regards,*
>
> *— Dr. Aaron LaRose*
>
> *Director, Astronomical and Space Science Department*
>
> *Science Advisor to the Office of the Prime Minister*

"Well—"

"This is why I hate politicians. This is why I hate bureaucrats. This is why I refuse to have anything to do with the government or the military or anything which remotely looks like it might be connected to the government. Stupid, bloated, overwrought bureaucracy has lost the capacity for even rudimentary independent thought. Ugh!" With a visceral groan she threw herself onto the couch and dropped her head into her hands.

It took him a minute to get past his own stunned reaction and circle around to sit beside her. "Perhaps he didn't actually review the report—I have to believe if he did his reaction would be a bit more alarmed."

"Oh, I'd believe he reviewed it." Her voice was muffled against her hands. "But he's a government lackey. What else is he expected to do? He has a checklist full of procedures and every fucking thing which crosses his fucking desk must be corralled through that fucking checklist. It's the only thing which exists in his world—without it there would be *chaos*! And he's probably got a fucking checklist for that, too...."

She groaned into her hands. "I swear, I should just let them all die."

"Hey...." He reached over and gently pulled the closest hand away from her face, then lifted her chin so she was forced to look at him. "Possibly. But you won't, because you're a better person than they are."

"I'm really not. I can count on one hand the number of people in the universe I truly like or even particularly care about...well, maybe plus the other pinky if I have to add you."

"Do you?" It came out far more serious in tenor than he had intended.

She shifted her attention away, but her mouth curved up in what closely resembled a smile. "I suppose." He suspected it might have come out far more affectionate in tenor than she had intended.

Then she sighed, and the moment passed. "I can already see how it will all play out. I'll yell and scream and make an ass out of myself, and the bureaucrats will frown and hem and haw and suggest calm and caution, and I'll end up flipping off the EASC Chairman or the Defense Minister or, hell, the Prime Minister himself. And getting kicked out of the building isn't going to help the situation, but it'll hardly matter at that point...."

Abruptly her hands fell to her lap; she nodded sharply. "Okay. Pity-party over." She leapt up and strode over to the data center.

"I am responding to let Dr. LaRose know he will have his precious hardcopy by tomorrow evening. I am checking to make sure my *mother* is arranging me an audience with the EASC Board, because if anything is a matter for the military, this damn sure is."

She worried at her lower lip. "And I think I need to make the visuals of the scary tentacle ships bigger."

She eyed him over her fork piled high with pasta. He had managed to pull her away from the data long enough to sit down and eat something for dinner, though not until after he had whipped up the angel hair pasta with Campari tomatoes and spinach and the tempting aroma filled the cabin.

"What."

He chuckled, a little chagrined at having been caught. Her ability to read him was approaching uncanny levels. "You do realize you're bringing an enemy spy into Alliance military headquarters, right?"

She rolled her eyes in mild amusement. "You won't be recognized, will you?"

"I highly doubt it. No more than two dozen people in the galaxy are aware of what I do for a living—and I'm fairly certain none of them are on Earth. My official record shows me as an assembly manager for Terrestrial Avionics, as you discovered, but even it's a very old image."

"You've got fake identities, right? Can you use one of them? Samuel maybe?"

"Samuel isn't one, but yeah, absolutely. I can—"

"It isn't? Why did you use it with me, then?"

"It's just somebody I knew and was the first name to pop in my head."

"Hmm." She frowned. "Can we say you're a scout for a corp and we bumped into each other while investigating the Nebula?"

"I happen to have a ready-made identity for such an occasion. I can be Cameron Roark, minerals scout for Advent Materials out of Romane."

"How many fake identities do you have?"

"More than two, fewer than ten...." At her widening eyes he shrugged. "What? I'm a versatile chameleon."

Her expression darkened as she busied herself twirling more pasta around her fork. When she spoke, her voice had lowered noticeably in tenor and volume. "So we're once again back to the fact that I wouldn't know if you were lying to me."

He exhaled through pursed lips. "Normally I'd say no, you wouldn't...but you appear to have my number, don't you?"

She regarded him with such intensity he felt stripped, bare. "Do I?"

Still, he struggled past the instinct to mask himself behind a façade and forced himself to meet her gaze honestly. "A minute ago, I wasn't entirely truthful as to where the name 'Samuel' came from—and you knew it, didn't you?" Her mouth merely twitched in response, which was response enough.

"The truth is he wasn't just somebody I knew. He was the person who recruited me into SpecOps. He was my mentor and my friend for seventeen years, and he was murdered four months ago by anti-synthetic terrorists. The funny thing is, he wasn't even especially pro-synthetic. He was simply doing his job. I didn't mention it because...well, because I'm not ready to talk about it."

"I'm sorry, Caleb."

"So am I...but that's a tale for another day. Alex, I'm not lying to you—about anything. And if I try you catch me, so I may as well not try. But I can't prove it, I can only say it. And you can take it for...whatever you think it's worth."

It seemed as if her eyes were searching his very soul for traces of deception, and he wondered why he had ever thought he could lie to her. He straightened up in the chair. "Which is why we need to discuss something."

Her gaze didn't budge or falter. "Okay."

"You're right, I do need a false identity to get inside EASC, because there's no way they're going to let a Senecan intelligence agent walk in the front door. But I have an idea, one which stands a chance of bringing an early end to this war and uniting us against the alien threat. And I'd like your help."

"Good news. Richard's available to meet us tomorrow as well."

He stowed the last of the dishes and raised an eyebrow at her over his shoulder. She had responded enthusiastically to the plan, jumping at the prospect of being able to diffuse the 'stupid *khren-ovuyu* war.' She had proceeded to strategize and improve upon the plan and now had increased its odds of success considerably by bringing to the table someone who might actually possess the information he needed.

She continued to surprise him in the most unexpected ways, and he had been an idiot to think he should—or even could—do it without her.

"So, Naval Intelligence Liaison to Strategic Command, huh? Sure he won't shoot me on sight?"

"It'll be fine. He's a teddy bear."

"Alex, no one in intelligence is a teddy bear." The man was a necessary and arguably welcome player—but he would be an adversary, at least to start.

"Well he is." She turned to him when he joined her at the data center. "Listen. I've known him my entire life, and he is one of the few genuinely good people I've ever met."

"Okay. My life is in your hands, but okay."

"*Whatever*. Besides, he'll have no reason to doubt you because you'll be with me. I'll be talking about alien superdreadnoughts, and you'll simply be...."

"Alex's boy-toy?"

She laughed. "Um...."

"How many times have you visited Strategic Command wearing a random man on your arm?"

Her brow furrowed in a farce of deep thought. "Almost nev...once, maybe twice...three times at most. Definitely."

His jaw dropped open in mock indignation. "Then I *shall* be Alex's boy-toy. Now that I will enjoy."

She grinned playfully at him, and he found himself yet again drawn into her eyes. They reflected the light from the visuals above the table, transforming her irises to an incredible luminous platinum. Mirth danced in them like fireworks against a star-soaked sky.

Seconds passed before she tore her gaze away and focused back on the data. After a moment she flipped the position of two of the images, frowned, and flipped them again.

"The second way was better."

She didn't question his opinion and immediately flipped them back while chewing on her lower lip. "It's not as though the fate of the galaxy rests on the order of a couple of visuals. I only hope it's enough. Maybe when decorated by some high theatrics on my part...."

He grasped her shoulder and shifted her to face him. "I have no doubt you'll make them listen. You have a way of refusing to accept any alternative to getting what you want, and everyone else will find they've no choice but to fall in line."

A corner of his mouth curled up. "I mean, you got me here."

Her voice dropped to a murmur. "I did, didn't I?"

They were already standing *so* close. His hand, still resting on her shoulder, drifted up and slowly, carefully tucked her hair behind her ear…then lingered along the curve of her jaw. She didn't pull away, and the ticking by of endless seconds faded to insignificance.

The pad of his thumb drew softly over the hollow beneath her extraordinary cheekbone. With a breath she began turning into his hand, as if to place a kiss on his wrist—

—when a chime pealed through the cabin.

Her eyes were a little wide as she stepped back, but he couldn't be certain if he heard regret or relief in her voice. "And *that* would be the Gould Belt monitoring system…with the tightened security I'm guessing I need to check in."

He somehow managed to wait until she moved toward the cockpit before dragging a hand roughly over his mouth to stifle a groan, followed by a curse or two. He sucked a deep breath into his oddly constricted chest. *Jesus.*

She spent several minutes in the cockpit. He leaned against the wall, ankles and arms crossed loosely in a stellar imitation of casual relaxation, and waited.

When she finally returned to the table she was grimacing a bit and managed to avoid his gaze while not *looking* like she was avoiding it. "Security's even tighter than I expected—we'll need to check in half a dozen times before we get to Earth, but I set up the next few to be automated so I can get some sleep. Which…."

She glanced at the Metis report a final time, then shut it and the other data on the table down. "I should do. Busy day tomorrow, so I'm going to call it a night."

He didn't bother to hide anything in his eyes or his expression. His voice was soft but its tone unmistakable. "Are you sure?"

She huffed a breath that came out a ragged laugh and at last met his gaze, irises swirling liquid silver filled with unknowable thoughts. She almost smiled.

"Not in the slightest..." a retreat toward the stairwell "...which is why I *really* should."

He bit his lower lip, blinked and forced a smile. "Understood. Good night, Alex."

Her eyes closed for a moment. She nodded, seemingly to herself, and started down the stairs. "Good night, Caleb."

⟶ℛ⟵

Alex lay on the bed, still dressed, the bed still made, and stared at the ceiling.

What was she *doing*?

She ached to leap off the bed, vault up the stairs and claim the kiss stolen from her by the alarm. And whatever followed.

She wouldn't have stopped him; she had been moving into him, welcoming the embrace and its consequences.

She had no particular problem with casual sex. Though she'd never give Ken a run for her money, she had engaged in it from time to time. And given all the stress and tumult of the last week, god knows she could use some about now....

So why not follow through now? Why not leap off the bed, vault up the stairs and give in to the undeniable attraction and sexual tension which had been building for days—hell, since about five seconds after they met?

Because she was afraid.

It wasn't easy for someone like her, to admit even to herself she was afraid. Unless it was of an army of massive alien ships— and that hadn't been easy to admit.

But she was afraid.

She was afraid it wouldn't be casual at all. She was afraid if she fell into the ocean of those devastating blue eyes, she might drown. His easygoing demeanor belied an intensity simmering just beneath the surface, one constantly threatening to overwhelm her even from afar.

She was afraid if she allowed him *in*, if she opened up, if she shed the multiple layers of emotional armor in which she wrapped herself, she risked losing the very control over herself and her life she so treasured. Control she had cultivated for years, decades.

And when he inevitably left, she was afraid she would have lost her way.

38

Major Donel Fergusson stood at the wide viewport of the *SFS Aegea* and gazed out at nothing.

It wasn't actually nothing, of course. It was nebular gas and dust and particles. It glowed the color of lemonade with dashes of periwinkle.

It was a tactical nightmare. There were no distinguishing features, no points of reference and no shadowy recesses in which to hide.

In addition to the *Aegea*, the 2nd GOI Platoon consisted of four electronic warfare and two reconnaissance vessels. All the ships were well-equipped both offensively and defensively, but the majority of the firepower was concentrated in the *Aegea*. It also sported a suite of VI-driven probes and wideband passive sensors.

And though every ship possessed the finest in multilayer dampeners, the *Aegea* provided further protection in the form of an adaptive field. Dynamically generated and powered by a dedicated LEN reactor, it extended out in a five kilometer radius from the hull and blended all emissions within it into the surrounding cosmic radiation. 'The Bubble,' as the team referred to it, encompassed the entirety of the Platoon during normal impulse travel. In the absence of shadowy recesses in which to hide, it would have to suffice.

"Rather beautiful, wouldn't you say?"

He glanced over at Lieutenant Udine, who had joined him at the viewport. "Just looks like gas and dust to me."

The young man laughed. "My mother's a cosmologist. She'd faint on the spot if she heard you say that. I guess a bit of her perspective wore off on me."

"I didn't know we let dreamers into the special forces these days."

"Only on the sly."

"Well, I won't spill your secret, but you might want to keep it to yourself. Some of these soldiers may be inclined to break your spine if they catch you waxing poetic."

"I welcome them to try, sir."

"Ha! Good to hear." His gaze drifted around the bridge. The *Aegea* was thinly staffed, and everyone on board doubled as a commando, sniper, EMT or half a dozen other roles along with running the frigate. "Scans?"

"Expected EM signatures continue steady from the core region of the Nebula, sir. No deviations and no additional readings."

He activated the platoon-wide comm. "Re-engage sLume drives on my mark, destination 0.4 AU out from the portal, heading 22.4° NE. This will be our final superluminal traversal before reaching the target zone. Ready state on arrival. Two…one…mark."

The gas clouds blurred and faded, though it hardly looked any different to him. As they had already been deep in the Metis interior, the journey took minutes.

The 'scenery' which snapped back into focus shone considerably brighter than before and had organized itself into pillars of thick, nearly solid cloud formations.

"Status report."

"EM signatures match those provided, sir. TLF signal originating N 297.41° W, distance 0.39 AU. No anomalies detected."

"Recon 1, Recon 2: fan and approach TLF origin, full stealth. Slow and easy, boys."

Acknowledged.

He waited. Civilians imagined special forces missions were all gunfire and explosions—but whether in an urban incursion or deep space, eighty percent of any mission involved waiting.

Somewhere beyond the towering golden clouds sat an army of alien vessels. Once located, the team would take measurements and visuals from maximum safe distance. They would send a drone back out of the nebula to report contact. Then they would remain here, hidden in The Bubble, ready to track the alien force if or when it departed.

Unless the aliens were already gone, a far worse scenario. If they had departed the portal they could now be, quite literally, anywhere—in which case in order to track them, the team would first have to find them. Hopefully before the aliens massacred a world or did whatever it was they were planning to do.

He fully understood the size and scope of the enemy force which awaited. The power of the force he couldn't say, as the type or size of their weaponry remained unknown. But one thing he had learned over the years was every adversary had a weakness. Fortified ships were slow and unwieldy; small ones were fragile. Bombs could be disarmed, EM attacks shielded. In this case, enormous ships simply made for enormous targets—not that he intended on shooting at them. Not this mission anyway.

"Recon 1, Recon 2, report. See anything yet?"

He was met by silence. Sometimes their shielding was a little too good. "Comms, can you establish a connection with either of the recon units or their pilots?"

"Negative, Major. Recon units are not responding, nor are they showing up on scans."

Well, they wouldn't. "Keep trying. All ships, prepare to advance at 0.5 impulse. Stay inside The Bubble. I repeat, stay *inside* The Bubble."

Acknowledged.

The *Aegea* and its complement of electronic warfare ships flew silently into the pillar of nebular clouds. The viewport revealed only a bright yellow haze, thick as the fog rolling through Cove Bay when he was a child visiting his grandparents on the Scottish coast. He hadn't been to Earth since the First Crux War. If galactic events continued on their current path, he may never see Cove Bay again...which seemed a shame.

A bank of screens filled with broad-spectrum sensor readings created the illusion of sight as they advanced. The screens displayed the positions of the other ships (minus the Recon units), the locations of the pulsar, its companion white dwarf and the location of the portal, as well as a plethora of scientific data beyond his expertise.

"Major, we should clear the densest clouds in another thirty seconds or so."

"All ships, slow to 0.2 impulse. Again, stay inside The Bubble."

Acknowl—

"Sir, I'm picking up a—"

The last thought Major Fergusson had as the blazing white pulse incinerated the *Aegea* and the rest of the 2nd GOI Platoon was that the viewport's spectrum filters really needed to be upgraded, because this was just *too damn bright.*

39

SPACE, SOL SYSTEM

Alex spun the cockpit chair around when she heard him come up the stairs. He wore a smile; she returned it in full. If he had taken her retreat the night before as a snub, he wasn't showing it. They had quickly fallen back into a comfortable, easy, mildly flirtatious routine this morning. She was glad for it.

It wasn't the only reason she felt rather relaxed, all things considered. While normally she retained at most a vague, mild attachment to Earth as 'home,' in the current circumstances she had been relieved to enter the Sol System. Yes, it was home, but it was also the best defended stellar system in existence. If Earth's defenses weren't enough to keep it safe, nowhere would be safe.

"Final clearance granted. Looks like your alter ego ID held up. Ready to see the homeland?"

"I've seen Earth, Alex."

"In vids."

"In full-sensory overlay."

"Still not the same." She shrugged teasingly. "You'll see."

When they exited the Northeast 1 Pacific Corridor they were above the Gulf of Alaska. She veered south-southeast and slowed the angle of descent to run slightly off the coast.

The waters began a deep cerulean, but shifted to a paler cyan as they approached land. It being late fall, the massive glaciers had already begun descending from the mountain peaks toward the shore. Two icebergs were mid-calving from a glacier and the water was sprinkled with free-floating chunks of ice.

She watched him out of the corner of her eye as discreetly as she could manage. He had doubtless seen many worlds and more than a few wonders. He wouldn't be easy to impress...but it didn't hurt to try.

His gaze was riveted out the viewport, but his expression in profile appeared scrupulously neutral except for the faintest hint of a smile tugging at his lips—

—he sucked in a gasp, and the formerly neutral expression lit up in delight. She followed where his gaze led. A school of five orcas had broken the surface in dramatic fashion as they pushed through the ice slush and into the open waters. They danced and dove—then the largest one leapt out of the water, spinning through the air to land on its dorsal fin and send a cascade of frothing water over its companions.

She gave up watching him discreetly and grinned. "They were once nearly extinct. It took a lot of work to bring them back into the wild." She paused, simply enjoying his delight for a moment. "Seneca doesn't have oceanic wildlife?"

He shook his head. "What we call oceans are...well, not like this. Only about forty percent of Seneca is covered in water. It's a young planet, rich in metals due to the active stellar cluster, but indigenous species are limited and tend to be small. This is amazing."

Her attention drifted to the view once more. "I've always thought so."

The terrain soon gave way to tundra followed by the coastal forests of the numerous islands dotting the coastline. In minutes the northern edge of Vancouver Island came into sight; beyond it the midday sun reflected brilliantly off the first of the skyscrapers which stretched from North Vancouver to Portland. It was a beautiful fall day in the Pacific Northwest.

She swung to the east, dropped into an airlane and headed down the Strait toward the spaceport. He leaned against the half-wall and draped his arms across his chest. "Nice city you've got here."

"This?" She scoffed with feigned nonchalance. "This is nothing. The Northeastern Seaboard Metropolis stretches for over 1,000 kilometers along the east coast. But it *is* the largest metropolitan area in settled space, so it would."

"Uh-huh. You done showing off now?"

"You'll just have to stick around and find out." *Oops, that might have come out a little differently than she had intended....*

His voice became both softer and deeper in tenor. "Okay."
Yep, sure did.

She chose to ignore it while slowing and banking toward the rooftop docking platform.

EACV-7A492X to ORSC: Arrival sequence initiation requested Bay L-19

ORSC to EACV-7A492X: Arrival sequence initiated Bay L-19

ORSC to EACV-7A492X: Arrival clearance window 14 seconds Docking Lane 27

She eased in and lowered the ship to the roof. The clamps grasped the ship with a gentle *clang*.

The process was all automated for the next few moments as the lift descended to the L level and rotated to her private hangar bay. The force field shimmered as they passed through it, resolidifying once they were on the other side. A small jolt and the clamps locked into place in the hangar floor.

She shut off the engine and toed around to face him. "Shall we—" A blinking red light flashed in the corner of her eVi; she frowned but accepted the livecomm.

"Alexis, dear, I'm afraid the Defense Minister has arrived and requested a personal briefing. We'll need to push your meeting until 1430."

"Oh, for fucks sake, Mom."

"Now, I—"

"Was there something about 'urgent' and 'vital importance' and 'grave threat' and 'alien *yebanyy* superdreadnoughts' that you didn't understand?"

"Of course not. But I have many responsibilities which impact the safety and security of the entire Alliance, and we are *at war, and some—"*

"You mean you have a Very Important Job? I hadn't noticed."

"There's no reason for you to take such a tone with me. I can't exactly keep the Defense Minister waiting."

"*I'd* keep the Defense Minister waiting, if it was important enough. Probably even if it wasn't."

"Alexis."

"Fine. 1430. Don't postpone it any further." She cut the link and pursed her lips, grimacing at the effort of not punching the wall or spewing forth a tirade of expletives. She realized Caleb was looking at her expectantly, an eyebrow raised in question. Unsurprisingly, as he would have only heard one side of the conversation.

She glared at him, though not *at* him. "There's been a small delay. Let's get some lunch."

40

"Yes, I understand we need a larger production facility. But these things take time to build. Besides, I'm not happy with the chosen location. I don't enjoy the thought of flying halfway across the planet should I decide to pay a visit."

Olivia regarded the holos above her desk. "It will be cheaper and faster to simply seize an existing facility for ourselves."

The man in the left holo frowned. "It would mean bloodshed to do so...."

"*Obviously* it would mean bloodshed—inevitably everything always means bloodshed, it's merely a question of timing. If this war generates the level of chaos I expect it to, we need to position ourselves quickly. Hence, bloodshed now rather than bloodshed later."

Her nod foreclosed any further discussion. "It's decided. John, I need a list of the top four candidates in two hours. I'll arrange a team and the post-op additional security. That's all for now."

Not waiting for their sign off, she gestured away the holos, stood and stretched. She needed—

Her eVi indicated a priority incoming message. It was encrypted and coded, but Marcus wanted to speak, now if possible.

She scowled at nothing in particular. She didn't care to create an impression with him that she was at his beck and call, lest it set a dangerous precedent. On the other hand, events were moving rapidly and significant wealth was at stake. With a roll of her eyes she went over to the QEC room.

She had met Marcus almost fifty years earlier—though that hadn't been his name at the time—when she ran Zelones operations in South America. He had risen to the top of an upstart gang on the streets of Rio, one which had begun to impinge upon clearly demarcated Zelones interests. After a series of escalating threats did nothing to stop the encroachments, she had sent a squad of her best enforcers to wipe them out.

Marcus and his lieutenants killed the entire squad. He sent her a message to let her know of this—despite the fact he shouldn't possess her contact information. He then proceeded to come to her headquarters, kill, incapacitate or evade the entire building's security detail and her personal guards, and stroll into her office.

For one of the few times in her life, she had been genuinely surprised when he walked in. He couldn't have been more than fifteen years old, scrawny and gangly in secondhand threads. But the sharp, dynamic sea-green irises regarding her shone bright with intelligence, cunning and most of all confidence.

Her personal weaponry had not been so advanced then as it was now, but she pointed a quite lethal customized Daemon at him while she calmly inquired what she could do for him.

"I want out."

"Done. You've proven your point. Walk out the door, and no one will stop you. Keep walking, and no one will come after you. You have my word."

"You misunderstand, Ms. Montegreu. I want a new life—a new identity and a new background, one which is gold-plated and fool-proof. I want fifty thousand credits and a ticket to Miami and your vow you will never speak a word of this conversation to another soul."

She arched an eyebrow and rested against the front of her desk, though the gun remained in her hand. "And why ever should I agree to do such favors for you?"

A smile crept across his face, more chilling than any she had seen on the cruelest, most malicious killers. A shiver ran down her spine...but at least now she knew what she was negotiating with.

"Because then I will be in your debt. And at some time in the future, I expect that will be worth a great deal."

She had conceded to the transaction, arranged everything he had asked for and not seen a trace of him for more than thirty years. Then one day his face showed up on the news feed. It seemed he was being named the youngest ever Deputy Minister of the Justice Department for the North American Region.

She wouldn't have recognized him, so transformed was his appearance, but for the memorable sea-green eyes—and the name she had given him.

It was another fifteen years before he reached out to her and, in due course, offered her the opportunity to collect on an old debt.

ᴙ

He was turning around as he shimmered into existence on the QEC holo, a charming smile well in place when he faced her. "Olivia. My apologies for the short notice. Are the materials on their way to Earth yet?"

She likely looked far less charming, and didn't especially care. "Are you trying to micromanage my end of the operation, Marcus?"

"Not at all, Olivia dear. I do have a good reason for asking."

"I certainly hope so. The answer is no. The 'materials' aren't exactly the kind of items you leave sitting around on Earth for too long."

"Good. An opportunity has presented itself—to kill two birds with one stone, as the old saying goes."

"An opportunity?"

"A fortuitous coincidence. I need you to route at least a portion of the materials through a specific individual if possible. Ideally, have him be the one to deliver them to the necessary party on Earth. He's a smuggler and tech dealer on Pandora."

She glanced at the information he sent. "He doesn't work for me, not even indirectly. It'll take some doing. This is last minute, Marcus, and I don't care for surprises. Again I ask—*are* you trying to micromanage my end of the operation?"

"Again, *no.* This is a unique opportunity which has only just arisen."

"Fine. Dare I venture to ask why?"

"The details aren't important from your perspective and would require far too long to explain—but it will help ensure the blame is placed appropriately and the war continues unabated. That is what you want, Olivia, is it not?"

Of course it was what she wanted. The greatest threat to her business was and had always been *order*. Crime flourished in the friction generated by conflict, and the First Crux War had carved a landscape rife with fractures. While the Alliance and Senecan governments jockeyed for leverage, independent worlds were able to grow and thrive in the spaces in between, like weeds in sidewalk cracks.

Prior to a week ago, relations between Earth and Seneca had been steadily thawing. Left unaltered, mere inertia would eventually lead to true peace. The independent worlds would be 'persuaded' to return under the umbrella of a benevolent government. The spaces in between would vanish.

It would take decades, perhaps even half a century. But she would live for another hundred fifty years; decades mattered quite a lot to her. So yes, she wanted to alter the field of play.

She gave him a miniscule nod. "Very well. I'll see what I can make happen, but time is short. No promises."

"I understand. Do what you can."

41

VANCOUVER, EASC HEADQUARTERS

Earth Alliance Strategic Command was not nearly so pompous and decadent as Senecan propaganda painted it. Oh, it was certainly shiny and polished and self-important, yet there were no spotlights sweeping across the sky or garish colors decorating the walls or waterfalls spilling champagne. At its core it remained a military installation. The walls and floors gleamed brighter and the artwork appeared showier than what was found in Senecan government facilities; he imagined the cafeteria and break rooms stocked posher amenities as well. Still, the difference was one of degrees...and not so many degrees at that.

It wasn't as though Caleb was shocked or even particularly surprised. No childhood illusions were being shattered as they paused at the security scanner and Alex authorized for him—which he did have to stifle a chuckle at.

Technically speaking, she had just committed high treason against the Earth Alliance government. But she didn't view the world in such a way. To her, there were good people and bad people, and most of the rest weren't worth classifying. He had—he hoped—qualified for the 'good people' side of the equation, and that was the end of it. Government intrigue and games of espionage simply didn't impress her, something he found both amazing and delightful.

And while his training, rules of engagement, experience and the teachings of his superiors and his mentor all told him he should take full advantage of this opportunity and record, image and hack every item he could find or see...he didn't intend on abusing her trust. He remained observant, but observation would be the extent of his espionage. Besides, he had a mission.

"Capt—Ms—Solovy. Ma'am. The Admiral is expecting you. I'll inform Colonel Navick you've arrived."

"Thank you, Lieutenant."

Alex moved away from the reception desk to roll her eyes at him then grasp his hand and pull him toward a fish tank along one wall of the lobby. He instinctively sucked in a breath at the sensation of her hand in his. They had still only touched skin-to-skin a few times, the last one being the *intimate* moment the night before. Her palm was cooler than his, but not cold. It felt natural and confident—much like her, here.

She believed she didn't belong in this environment, saw herself as an outsider. Yet she strode through the halls as though she owned the place, and so unaffectedly so that he had no doubt she didn't know it. It merely reflected her inherent self-assurance and sense of worth, which oozed out of her every pore. It was impressive to witness.

"Richard...." Her hand left his, and he immediately felt the sting of its absence. He turned to see her embrace a man in BDUs save for an officer insignia on his shoulder. The embrace was warm and friendly to a degree he'd never seen her be. Until now he hadn't realized she was to some extent still always on edge around him. Seeing her this relaxed and at ease jarred him.

The man appeared in perhaps his sixties and was handsome in an average, unassuming way. He did have kind eyes.

"This is Cameron Roark, a professional colleague. He works for Advent Materials." The lie rolled off her tongue with impressive ease, but her eyes twinkled as she gazed at him. And like that he was back on the inside. It made him far happier than it should.

The plan, as finalized by them on the way over, was for him to maintain the fictitious identity to start. The alien threat constituted an even higher priority than diffusing the war, and they agreed she needed to focus first and foremost on the Metis report. Once they had been assured the Alliance was moving ahead with a clear action plan—and her mother and Navick had become somewhat comfortable in his presence—she would ease into a discussion of the war and his true identity and purpose. And if things didn't go according to plan...he'd improvise.

He grasped the outstretched hand of Colonel Navick with the slightly awkward formality a mid-level corporate scout might exhibit toward a relatively high-ranking military official. "Good to meet you, sir."

Navick regarded him appraisingly, his gaze not harsh but definitely sharp. A tiny twitch of his mouth was the sole sign he gave of any reaction at all. *Teddy bear, my ass.*

"And you, Mr. Roark. Have you known Alex long?"

"Not long, sir. We bumped into one another while scouting the Metis Nebula and, well, found more than we bargained for I'm afraid."

"So I understand." A smile sprung to life on his features as he looked at Alex. It was evident he held great affection for her, regardless of his position or profession. "It must be serious indeed for Alex to willingly grace us here at EASC by her presence."

She began to smile in return, but it faltered away. "You're right, and it is." She glanced over her shoulder. "Lieutenant? Are we allowed to enter now?"

"Um…." The man behind the desk looked down then up again. "Yes, Capt—Ms—Ma'am. And Colonel. And, uh, sir."

Caleb swallowed a laugh and wondered what in the hell he had gotten himself into as he fell in two steps behind them.

The office was well-appointed but spartan and rather sterile. The woman who rounded the desk to greet them wore a dress admiral's uniform, and other than the color of her hair bore almost no resemblance to Alex. She held herself with the stiff, rigid bearing common among high-ranking military officers. Her expression only briefly deviated from the bearing as she faced but did not approach Alex.

"I am sorry for the delay. It was unavoidable, but I know you made efforts to arrive here with due speed and I do appreciate it." Her gaze shifted to fall on him, and deep, dusky hazel eyes penetrated straight into him. He decided—though for reasons he did comprehend—Alex seriously underestimated her mother.

"Mr. Roark, is it?"

"Yes, ma'am. A pleasure to meet you, though I wish it were under better circumstances." He shook her hand warmly but couldn't shake the feeling she had instantly deduced everything about him, and them, and the last week.

"Okay, pleasantries done." With a word Alex somehow dominated the room. "Now about the *aliens* preparing to invade. You've had the report for three days—what are you doing about it?"

Navick had retreated toward the rear of the office; the brief glance he managed told him the man was involved in a private interaction of some sort. It made him nervous having the man at his back, but he didn't dare show it as a simple corporate space scout. Here in this room, he was submissive and in awe and *totally* out of his element. Yessiree.

"General Alamatto has tasked his advisors with reviewing the data to verify its credibility and plausibility and—"

"Oh you have got to be—"

"Alexis, do not start with this. You know I have absolute faith in your abilities and competence. But—"

"My *competence*? I don't—"

"Yes. That was a compliment, in case you didn't notice. I have no doubt as to the accuracy of your report, I truly don't. But mine is not the only opinion which matters."

Damn, this was fascinating. He had surmised Alex's relationship with her mother was complicated at best and knew it was informed by decades of conflict, but...damn.

He was so enthralled by the interchange that for half a second he missed the rigid tension abruptly manifesting in Navick's stance behind and a little to the left of him. When he did sense it he recognized what it meant, even if he didn't know *precisely* what it meant.

He tried to get Alex's attention, but she was fully engaged in antagonizing her mother, who he had already discerned very clearly loved her daughter and just as clearly had no *idea* how to talk to her. He made a mental note to try to find a way to diplomatically point it out to Alex at a more opportune time.

Navick stepped in front of him and produced a military-issue Daemon. He displayed no reaction to the gun pointed at his chest and remained calm as his wrists were grabbed from behind. "Sir, if you will let me explain, you will find I am not your enemy."

Alex finally turned around. Her jaw dropped in considerable surprise to see two MPs handcuffing him and her oldest friend holding a gun on him. Her brow furrowed, eyes searching his for guidance. He gave her a small shrug...plans rarely survived contact with the enemy, after all.

"What the hell is going on?"

"I'm sorry, Alex, but Mr. Roark is not who he represented himself to be. His name is actually Caleb Marano and he's an intelligence operative for the Senecan Federation government."

Her face screwed up at Navick. "I *know* that. We were going to get around to telling you. Why the fuck are you handcuffing him?"

"You know? Alexis, you brought a Senecan operative into *Headquarters*? How *could* you!"

She whipped back to her mother. "Because he's not a threat to—"

"Not a threat? How gullible must you—"

He ignored their yelling to meet Navick's stare directly. "I apologize for the subterfuge, but I am not here to harm the Alliance in any way. I beg you, give me two minutes of your time. I am—"

"I'm gullible? You're the one who fell for this stupid farce of a war. We are trying to save your asses, and everyone else's in the process—"

"You know nothing of the military situat—"

"—here to ask for your *help*."

The man's glare faltered and uncertainty flashed in his eyes, so quickly it was gone almost before it had appeared.

"Richard, get him out of my office *now*."

Navick looked to Alex's mother before returning to him. "Then you shall have to ask the judge for help. You won't find it here." He motioned to the guards. "Take him to the detention facility."

He didn't put up a fight as they manhandled him out the door. He could have fought and very possibly have won—this fight at least—but it didn't seem a good long gamble.

"Richard, what are you doing? Would you listen to me for one goddamn second? He's not—"

The door closed behind him, muting the remainder of Alex's plea. A moment later a pulse flashed into his vision.

I'll come for you as soon as I can

Though knowing what he did about where he presumed he was being taken, it should be impossible for her to do so, he had learned not to underestimate her.

Instead he chose to believe her.

R

"Why did you do that! I *asked* him to come here with me. We want to put a stop to this stupid *khrenovuyu* war and—"

Her mother glared at her with a cold hostility she hadn't seen in…oh, twenty years or so. "Do you have any idea what you have done? By all rights you should be arrested and tried as an accessory—as a traitor. If you were anyone else but my daughter you would be."

She refused to be intimidated; she was too fucking angry to be anyway. "I am not a traitor and neither is he. We are trying to stop you from ruining our best chance at defeating these aliens."

Richard cleared his throat. "Miriam, maybe we ought—"

Her mother's hand slammed down on her desk. "We are at war. I realize you lack a proper concept of what that means, but it most certainly means you do not bring a spy for the enemy *into my office!*"

The woman may be difficult to provoke, but it seemed Alex had located her breaking point. She searched around for a more sympathetic audience. "Richard, how did you know?"

A puzzled expression came over his face. "A copy of his internal Senecan Intelligence Division personnel file arrived in my comms a few minutes ago. Anonymous source."

"Seriously? Isn't that a little odd?" Who knew Caleb was here? His boss Volosk, perhaps? She wasn't sure how much Caleb had revealed to him. And how did anyone know to send the information to Richard? Also, *why?*

He shrugged. "Sure, but does it matter where it came from?"

"Yes it matters, because there are a lot of suspicious things going on around this 'war.'" She pinched the bridge of her nose in a futile attempt to stave off the encroaching headache. "Listen, we were planning to tell you. I wanted to get a few items regarding the aliens covered first is all." Her gaze flitted to one then the other. "I'm sorry we deceived you, but it was necessary to get in the door."

Richard gave her a small smile. Miriam did not, but her glare did soften from somewhere around absolute zero to a mere icy chill. "I believe you thought you were doing the right thing. You're not a professional. You were taken in by a handsome, manipulative man—you always did have a weakness for the roguish ones—and made a mista—"

"Don't you *dare*."

"I'm merely—"

"If you use that condescending tone with me one more time, I swear I will walk out of here right now and you will never see me again."

Cast-iron bitch mode faltered. Miriam's eyes darted to Richard, then the window. Finally she nodded almost imperceptibly. Almost.

Alex smiled thinly, her voice tight under the strain of forcing it to remain even. "Putting aside Caleb's status for a moment, let's get back to the alien army. We can at least do something about *it*, I hope. Do I need to review my report with the Board? With someone else?"

"The science advisors to the Board are still studying the report—" her mother held up a hand to forestall the interruption "—but they should be finished by this evening. I'm certain they will sign off on its veracity, at which point it will be forwarded to the Board members. General Alamatto would like you to present your findings tomorrow afternoon."

"Tomorrow. *Afternoon*."

"Yes. A meeting is scheduled for 1500. Its primary business will be the war of course, but you're tentatively scheduled to present as well."

"You do understand I raced here at practically reckless speed, not getting any sleep working on the damn report, all so I could get this information in front of people who mattered immediately?"

"Yes I understand it. If it were up to me, we would be meeting now. Difficult decisions lie ahead and the sooner we get started on them the better."

"Fine. Tomorrow. What can I do now? Can I talk to these 'advisors'? I imagine they're quite educated and whatnot, but forgive me if I'm skeptical of their sense. Who is—"

"There's nothing you need to do. The matter is well in hand."

She thought about Caleb, locked up overnight in…she had to find out where the MPs took him. "Then if the Board has 'science advisors' and everyone's getting the report, do I need to present at all? I made sure the summary could be understood by laymen, and hell, even bureaucrats. I'm not certain what my presence really adds."

"It transforms a sterile data file into something real. Your passion can convince them when visuals cannot—but not too much passion, please? It will be counterproductive for you to cause a scene. And don't even think about bringing up your wild ideas concerning the war or you are likely to find yourself forcibly removed from the meeting."

"I'll take it under advisement." She tried to pulse Caleb to warn him she might be a little while, but it bounced. She sent a message...which bounced. Terrific.

"Well if there's nothing for me to do, I should get out of your way. I imagine you have a nonsensical, moronic war to run or some such. Richard, walk me out?"

He nodded, though he seemed distracted. "Sure."

"Alexis?"

She looked back at her mother, an eyebrow raised in question.

"I *am* glad you made it back safe."

You have no idea. She left without responding and waited for Richard on the other side of the door.

He was grimacing as the door closed behind him. "Alex, I'm sor—"

"Let's wait until we get outside." He frowned but complied. He probably hadn't been intending on joining her the entire way to her vehicle, but she indicated for him to enter the lift ahead of her. Once it was underway she stepped closer to him, her voice low.

"You're an intelligent, rational, reasonable man. I need you to hear me out with an open mind, okay?" He didn't protest, so she continued. "You know I feel no particular love for Seneca, and why. But we—I—believe they did not intend to assassinate the Trade Minister, and they absolutely did not intend to start a war. Now—" she motioned his interruption silent as the lift came to a stop at the parking lot "—we didn't order the attack on Palluda, did we?"

The flicker in his eyes was all the answer she required. "I didn't think so. Richard, this war is a *setup*. Now maybe it's because someone wants to finish what was started over two decades ago, or maybe it's...maybe it's something worse. Regardless of the reason for it, the result will be to divide and weaken all our forces, leaving us exposed and vulnerable when these aliens attack. We need to see past the trickery and work together."

They reached her skycar and he turned to her. He wore a troubled expression, one she had rarely seen from him. "Do you realize what you're asking? This isn't some little side conflict. This is the real thing. We can't simply hold hands and kiss and make up. And how would we even begin to prove any sort of trickery or deception?"

"That's what we were going to tell you. Caleb's superiors think if they could examine the details of the Trade Minister's assassination they may be able to prove it wasn't committed by the man who's been accused."

"Senecan Intelligence knows as much about the assassination as we do. If they haven't found a way to prove it by now...."

"They don't have his body. They don't have the medical details on how he died."

He rolled his eyes at the heavens and paced in a tight circle. "Alex, you can't expect us to give the Senecans Santiagar's *corpse*."

"And I don't. But your medical people performed an autopsy and analyzed the cybernetics dump, didn't they? It's possible there's information in those findings you wouldn't recognize as important but which might be a clue for them, right?"

He dragged a hand down his face. A heavy sigh escaped beneath it...then he gazed back at her, and she knew she had lost. "I'm sorry, but I *can't*. I may possess a moderate amount of power, but nothing near the power necessary to do what you're suggesting."

Dammit. "Well, can you at least release Caleb? He didn't do anything wrong."

"He gained admittance to Strategic Command Headquarters using a false name and false pretenses. He's an enemy combatant under any definition."

"He did so only at my request—my insistence."

"Which doesn't help him and hurts you. I try to assert that argument and you get arrested, no matter who your mother is."

Dammit. She quickly schooled her expression. If he wasn't going to help, she shouldn't reveal anything further to him. She smiled with as much warmth as she could muster and clasped his hands in hers. "Okay. Thank you for listening. What will they do with him?"

"He's in a holding cell over in the security building for now. A judge will determine his status in a few days, but I imagine he'll be deemed a prisoner of war and transferred to the military prison down in San Francisco."

"I understand. Now I'm afraid I must go home and prepare for this presentation tomorrow. Take care of yourself, will you?"

"Look, I'm not unsympathetic to your position. I wish I could help."

"I know. Just...well, it doesn't matter." She climbed in the car before she gave any more away.

She felt his gaze following her as the car rose and banked away from the lot, but her focus had already shifted inward.

She had a lot of work to do.

42

"It's a good thing you let me know you were on Earth when you did. I was half an hour from catching the transport back to Erisen."

Alex embraced Kennedy warmly then slid into the chair opposite her. The table by the window, high above downtown Seattle, revealed a sea of glittering lights against the night sky, but for once she was almost too distracted to notice. "You didn't have to come all the way up here just for a quick dinner. I wish I had more time."

Kennedy scoffed and poured a glass from the already-opened bottle of wine. "Don't be ridiculous. I hardly ever get to see you as it is." She peered at Alex and frowned. "And you look stressed, so get to drinking."

Alex took a long sip of the wine. "I've had one hell of a week."

"Do tell."

She sighed and relaxed a bit in the chair. "Let's see. I got into a space firefight, blew up the other ship, semi-crashed onto an uninhabitable planet in the middle of nowhere, rescued the pilot, held him prisoner—"

"Ooh, *him*? This sounds exciting."

"Yeah, well. So we repaired my ship and—"

"Wait, 'we'? I thought he was your prisoner?"

"He was. Then he wasn't. Then he sort of...."

Her eyes brightened in delight. "How was he?"

"Ken, I haven't slept with him."

"Why not?"

"Because *I* don't sleep with every handsome stranger who crosses my path."

"So he's handsome?"

She bit her lower lip and took another sip to hide the extent of her grin. "Oh yes. Now would you let me finish my story? It's important."

Kennedy waved a hand in her direction and leaned back as the waiter brought their appetizer.

She waited until the waiter departed before continuing. "So we repaired my ship and went to investigate some strange readings coming from the center of the Metis Nebula—and found an alien army amassing for an invasion."

Her best friend stared at her, flat-faced. "That's not funny. You were never any good at telling jokes, you know this."

"It's not a joke."

Perhaps recognizing the deadly serious expression on Alex's face, a frown grew on her lips. "Aliens? *Truly?*"

"Truly."

"Well, are you sure they're invading? I mean, maybe they're simply dropping by to say 'hi'?"

She couldn't risk displaying an aural where others might see; she sent one of the visuals instead. "What do you think?"

Across the table, Kennedy's eyes widened precipitously in growing horror. The blood drained from her face, blanching her tanned skin pale. "My god...Alex, this...." She swallowed hard. "What are we doing about it?"

"That remains to be seen. The Prime Minister's Science Advisor is 'reviewing' the material. The EASC Board is 'reviewing' the material. I'm shouting at them tomorrow."

"Shit, if they don't take action you should leak this to the media."

"And cause a galactic panic? I'm not sure it's a great idea. The average person can't do anything against this kind of threat. The military is the only one who *can* act."

She frowned again, more deeply than before. "You said they're in the Metis Nebula? The Senecans are much closer than we are. Shouldn't they maybe be warned? I realize apparently we're at war with them again for some reason, but...."

"It's okay. They already know."

"You managed to get this information to the Senecan government? Impressive, even for you."

"Not exactly. My, um...the guy...is Senecan..." her voice trailed off "...Intelligence."

Kennedy's mouth fell open. "Oh my god this is better than one of those intrigue romance novels."

"Ken, it's not a romance novel."

"Mmhmm. So where is he now? Is he here? Can I meet him?"

She cringed and stuffed a bite of escargot in her mouth. "He's in lockup over at EASC Security Detention...."

"You turned him *in*?"

"No, I didn't turn him in. His cover got blown."

"Damn. What are you going to do? Are you going to leave him there?"

"No—well for the moment, yes, because making sure the military gets off their asses and gets ready for these aliens is more important. But that brings me to the actual point of the story. I mean other than warning you there was an impending alien invasion no one knows about."

"Which would be?"

"Is Claire still in San Francisco?"

Kennedy sat back in her chair and crossed her arms over her chest. "What makes you think I know where she is?"

Alex rolled her eyes and leveled a *look* across the table. "*Is Claire still in San Francisco?*"

She blew out a breath through tight lips. "She is."

"Do you know how to get in touch with her?"

"I...do. But not to use her or procure...whatever she might offer. I only, well, it never hurts to keep in touch with former acquaintances and potential future resources. Can I ask why you need to contact her?"

"Because I need a damn good spoofing routine and I don't have time to write one myself."

Kennedy's brow furrowed a moment—then realization dawned. "Oh...I see. He must really be something."

"It's not that. It's my fault he was arrested. I'm the one who asked him to come with me here, and I dragged him right into EASC Headquarters. He may work for *whatever* they are—it sounds absurd to call the Senecans the 'enemy' when there's a real enemy looming in the wings—but he didn't do anything wrong. I can't leave him in a prison cell to rot."

"Because you're a decent person, even if you don't like to admit it. Still…he must really be something."

Alex merely smiled.

43

BORDER OF SENECAN FEDERATION SPACE

The first true battle of the Second Crux War was fought, perhaps not surprisingly, in the space above Desna.

A small Alliance colony in shouting distance of Senecan Federation territory, it had no real economy beyond that necessary to sustain its population in daily life. Founded twenty-seven years earlier, it continued to exist primarily as a silent line in the sand blocking future expansion of the Federation in the direction of Earth and the First Wave worlds.

The 2nd Brigade of the Earth Alliance NE Regional Command intercepted the 3rd Wing of the Senecan Federation Southern Fleet as it traversed the officially designated buffer zone on the edge of Federation Space. Alliance NE Regional Commander Admiral Christopher Rychen deemed their position too close to Desna's system—but it was without a doubt an orchestrated encounter.

Commander Morgan Lekkas' squadron of ten Senecan fighters was the first to depart the 3rd Wing's carrier *SFS Catania* upon being alerted of the approaching force. Their initial directives were to engage and/or deflect any and all attackers, drones and missiles while the frigates moved into combat formation and the other two fighter squadrons took up positions.

The coordinates, speed, bearing, weapons status and physical condition of each of the nine fighters under Morgan's command displayed and updated every eighty milliseconds on one of four whispers projected in her vision. Her team was down two ships lost in the Arcadia offensive. They wouldn't be replaced for another week...but the battle was now.

"*Swarm* on my mark. Two...one...*mark.*"

To the untrained eye, a *swarm* maneuver might resemble chaos far more than any organized strategy. In actuality it represented a highly precise and efficient pattern over any grid of space. Each individual ship's movements appeared random and nearly impossible to predict; together they provided total coverage of the designated area.

The second of her whispers showed all enemy vessels within five hundred megameters. Lacking the deep integration she enjoyed with her squadron, this display only updated every 0.8 seconds.

Three tiny dots flash to life. "Drone launch, N 38.04°z-10.15 E. Flight 3 engage."

Engaged.

Four seconds later—*Down. Down.* A pause. *Down.*

She could see the small explosions on the whisper of course, but it built pride and confidence for pilots to announce their successes, and she encouraged it.

Two larger dots appeared. Alliance frigates; they would represent the forward flank.

A sea of red pinpoints fanned out from the frigates. "Sixteen missiles away. Engage."

Faster than she was capable of speaking, she assigned every fighter a missile based on proximity and trajectory. That left six free missiles—but first things first.

The *swarm* dissolved into precise, directed movements. Her primary attention diverted to her own missile tracking across the translucent screen overlaying her viewport. She banked in a controlled slide to its right until its entire length was centered in the reticle.

Lock. Fire.

"Down."

Five missiles had now been destroyed. She moved to the closest free one.

Track. Drop. Invert. Lock. Fire.

"Down."

Epsilon took out a second missile. Twelve down—and four were through their net.

"Command, four missiles free."

Acknowledged.

The third whisper displayed strategically relevant information from the other two squadron leaders, the captains of the ten frigates (also down two after Arcadia) and the commander of the *Catania*, Commodore Pachis.

2nd squadron (defense) engaging.

Seven seconds later—*All missiles destroyed.*

The attackers likely didn't expect any of the missiles to survive to impact. It was merely an opening volley, designed to occupy and distract. And to some extent, it worked. Three stealth electronic jammer craft had snuck through the outer defensive line and set about scrambling several of the Senecan vessels' targeting ware.

Combat formation active. Begin primary engagement.

"*Harass* on my mark. Two…one…*mark.*"

It was the job of the 1st squadron to engage the frontal force of Alliance fighters and of the 2nd squadron to fly defensive patrol around the carrier and rear frigates. It was the job of Lekkas' squadron to create chaos behind the lines and on the edges, to chase outliers and take advantage of opportunities as the battle spread out across megameters of space.

Though she continued to monitor the status of each of the ships under her command, to a large extent the individual pilots now gained freedom of movement and decision, subject to guidance from the Flight primaries.

She also served as Primary of Flight 1. "Our target is Alliance frigate bearing N 24.51°z18.06 E. Weapons and engines."

Slipping behind enemy lines was not an easy matter. They possessed robust dampener fields, but the fields interfered with targeting and constituted a hindrance while firing. Therefore, her preferred tactic was to activate the field and swing wide out and low in order to pass through the outer Alliance defenses, deactivate the field and use her ship's agility to avoid destruction while making several quick hits, then vanish again.

Her speed, trajectory and ship vitals shone brightly in the fourth whisper. For a moment, beyond it there existed only the blackness of space, lit by the stars outside her cockpit and the faint glow of a sun behind her, as she dropped in near free-fall.

ℛ

The agility and maneuverability Commander Lekkas' squadron would use to their benefit amidst the Alliance fleet was far less of an advantage in head-to-head space combat. With no obstacles to avoid or atmosphere to fight against, the lightweight construction of Senecan fighters was of marginal value against the tougher, hardier Alliance fighters. Even rapid maneuverability couldn't escape plasma weapons which once locked were able to track movement up to 0.6 light speed. The 1st squadron fought hard but quickly suffered heavy losses on the front lines.

The fire of massive plasma cannons on both sides lit the field of battle, at times meeting each other mid-arc in tremendous explosions of light. Though better protected than the fighters, Senecan frigates were still more lightweight and maneuverable than their Alliance counterparts. But the Alliance ships were workhorses and exceedingly difficult to destroy.

Worse, the Alliance had come prepared. Having taken due note of the size of the detachment sent to Arcadia, Admiral Rychen's forces had arrived in strength. In the time it took Senecan vessels to destroy one Alliance frigate, two Senecan ones were disabled or destroyed—and the Alliance enjoyed more to begin with.

For this battle, in this space and under these circumstances, the outcome was inevitable almost before it had begun.

Lekkas did more than most to try to even the odds. Skimming so close beneath the hull of a frigate she was able to clearly see the shimmer of its plasma shield, she accelerated past the stern weapons assembly and pivoted 180°.

Target. Lock. Fire.

The assembly splintered apart in a burst of flame and free plasma. She was already gone, the hint of a smile tugging at her lips. The impulse engine was her next target.

A frigate's impulse engine was too sturdily built to be easily destroyed by small pulse laser weapons—but with concentrated fire it could be disabled. She met her flight members beneath the rear of the ship for a brief, directed, coordinated assault. They had 3.4 seconds before Alliance reserve fighters arrived to annihilate them. In 3.3 seconds the glow of the impulse engine shifted from pale blue to fiery orange in an unstoppable chain reaction which would soon result in a critical overload—and they vanished.

Lekkas and her team disabled the weapons and partially or wholly disabled the engines of an additional three frigates as well as four electronic warfare vessels before Commodore Pachis signaled the retreat. While they likely saved a number of soldiers' lives through their actions, they ultimately didn't change the outcome of the battle.

The 3rd Wing of the Senecan Federation Southern Fleet arrived with ten frigates and left with three. Sixteen of twenty-six fighters survived, but the relatively high survival ratio was due solely to the fact Commander Morgan Lekkas' squadron did not lose a single ship.

44

A heavy, damp fog blanketed the streets as far as the eye could see. Which, given it was 0100 and the previously mentioned fog, wasn't particularly far.

The street lights gave the fog a washed-out champagne glow and created an aura of eerie otherworldliness. This time of year the fog shrouded the Outer Sunset District and Ocean Beach day and night, seeing only the occasional brief clearing after a storm front passed through.

Alex felt the moisture condensing on the fine hairs of her arms. The night air was cold as hell, but she had needed to dress the part. A deep crimson camisole woven with gossamer optic fibers draped to her navel; black leather pants clung low on her hips as she hurried down Taraval. It was even later now, and she still had a *lot* to do.

The club was almost to the beach, and she could hear the surf crashing against the shore. It brought back memories...memories she did not have time to entertain. She pushed them aside and located the unmarked door beneath one of the refabbed Victorian row houses.

The music assaulted her ears as she descended the stairs. Pure synth—no beat and no lyrics, merely a constant wave of complex tonals designed to soothe the mind and body into a state of open relaxation. It was warmer inside at least, though she suspected it would soon feel too humid as a result.

The warehouse space appeared pitch black save for vague shadows of moving bodies and the neon painted sensory address floating near the ceiling. With a sigh she accessed it. She'd never find her way in the dark.

The overlay shimmered to life. Stars materialized beneath her feet and the cool glow of a pale green nebula in the space around her. A triple star system spun in the air above her, comets dancing merrily amongst it in concentric orbits.

She wouldn't spoil everyone's fun, but even a full-sensory overlay didn't come close to matching the real thing.

Men and women danced in the center of the room in slow, languorous, sensual movements to the synth music or occasionally to their own beat. Others slumped against the wall, lost in head trips. Small groups formed circles, each leaning on the other to remain standing while they engaged in group *illusoires* set in what was doubtless fantastical worlds. A few couples pawed at each other in the shadowed corners. A few did more.

Alex. The prodigal daughter returns. You can find me on the balcony.

Her eyes scanned the room until she made out the outline of an overhang high above the rear section of the dance floor. She wound her way through the crowd, most of whom didn't notice her. At the sensation of a hand running along the small of her back and dipping into her pants, however, she did pause to casually knee a strapping young man in the balls then keep moving.

The balcony was nearly as crowded as the floor below—but Claire Zabroi was difficult to miss.

Not because of the cropped, jet black spiked hair or the skin-tight white leather pants and tunic. No, Claire was difficult to miss primarily because of the full-body network of saffron hued glyphs. They didn't swirl or entwine softly like most glyphs did to double as tattoo art. Instead they mimicked the intricate patterns of a circuit board, all straight lines and hard angles. They wound up her neck to run along her jaw and disappear behind her ears, leaving her face the sole visible part of her body untattooed.

She had a woman on one arm and a drink in the other hand, but upon spotting Alex a smile pulled at her lips. She nudged the woman off and motioned to a table in the corner. Alex grabbed a cocktail off a waiter's tray on the way over.

Claire greeted her with a smooth hug. "Alex, babe. It's been far too long. However do you entertain yourself these days?"

"Oh, I manage." She slid into the chair opposite her old...acquaintance. Claire was from a very different time in her life. A time after university, when freed of the rigors of study and serving an externship which was interesting enough but hardly filled the hours, she and Kennedy had found themselves in The City by the Bay while young and single, with money, freedom and few responsibilities.

They had soon met Ethan, then Drake and Alice, and through Alice, Claire. Claire was a hedonist, adrenaline junkie and casual chimeral dealer. But most of all, Claire was a hacker—and not your average hacker.

Though not many people knew it—i.e., she had not thus far been caught—she was responsible for the hacking of TransBank and 'redistribution' of more than six billion credits to seventeen thousand random individuals. She was also behind the hacking and leaking of government documents which brought down the North American Eastern District Governor in 2309, as well as half a dozen less infamous exploits.

Alex may or may not have assisted in any small or large way in all, some or none of those exploits. It was, as she had noted, a different time in her life.

"So what brings you back into the underworld? Your message said it was urgent." Claire grinned; it was a harsh, predatory look on her. "Or are you jonesing? I can drop you some Surf if you want—on the house, for old times' sake."

Alex gave a wry chuckle. "No thanks, I don't indulge anymore. Not often anyway...."

Ethan's penthouse on Rue de Rivoli occupied the entire top floor of the condo tower. The elevator led to a sterile tile and marble foyer and a single door. There was no visible security, no handlers, no lackeys or groupies. She assumed his address must be kept extremely confidential. But though she had never been to this residence, she had always known where to find him.

She pressed the bell and leaned nonchalantly on the wall to wait. Only then did it occur to her the door might be answered by...well, virtually anyone. She hadn't messaged ahead. She hadn't planned or thought any of this through. She was simply here.

But it wasn't anyone who answered. It was him.

He would have accessed a cam of the foyer of course and opened the door already knowing who awaited. He rested on the doorframe and mimicked her pose. His coffee-colored hair was cut shorter than when she had seen him last and barely grazed his shoulders. Chocolate irises sparkled with mischief; that had not changed.

"Alex, love. My birthday isn't until next month, yet here you are."

"Yet here I am." She realized she was biting her lower lip when one of his eyebrows arched and the sparkle in his eyes flared. She didn't stop.

"To what do I owe this smashing surprise?"

Her expression darkened as she stared at him and tried to find a way to respond glibly. 'My lover of two years walked out on me and I don't want to talk about it, think about it or even remember it, I just want to feel' somehow didn't seem a suitable answer, but her brain was not currently operating with enough functionality to craft a lie.

He must have read her mood, because he smiled and crossed the foyer to grasp her hands in his. "Never mind. What matters is you're here." He began backing up, drawing her along with him toward the door and into the penthouse.

She grinned in what she hoped resembled playful seductiveness. "Do you have plans for the weekend?"

Still grasping her hands, he wound her arms around his waist as the door closed behind them. "I do now...." His gaze caressed her face, down her neck to the hollow of her throat, then returned to her eyes. "Miss Solovy, I do believe you're high."

Yes, she most certainly was. "Is that a problem?"

"Bien au contraire, ma chérie."

He was hardly French, but she supposed 'when in Paris'...and true to the stereotype, the words sent a delightful shiver up her spine.

He maneuvered her so her back pressed into the wall and closed the remaining space until his lips hovered a breath above hers. "Stay that way. Stay with me. For the weekend, for however long you have."

She responded by spinning him around, pinning him against the wall and crushing her mouth against his.

Alex forcefully blinked away the memory...damn but it had been a hell of a way to get over a broken heart.

Her voice lowered beneath the din of the crowd. "I need a spoofing routine—military grade, the best you have. Cost is not a concern, but I need it now."

Claire sipped on her drink. "If it were anyone else I'd be tempted to take advantage of your obvious desperation and charge you double for half-assed ware. But once upon a time you had my back, and you never let me down. Also, you know several of my secrets."

She set the glass on the table and eyed Alex a moment. "I do have something which meets your requirements. One of a kind and thus far solely for me. It's not on the market."

"It will be used only once, after which I will wipe it. My word."

Claire's gaze drifted up and across the balcony before settling again on Alex. "I keep it in here—" she tapped her temple with a razor square fingernail, causing a ripple along the glyphs on her forearm "—too valuable to store anywhere else. I can burn you a copy. Twenty-one thousand. And it's worth twice the price."

Alex smacked her lips and took a sip of her drink. It represented a good deal of money, but nothing she couldn't pay. She nodded. "Do it."

"You got it." She reached into a pocket of the utility belt slung over her hips and removed a slim burner interface. She reached behind her head, rested the tiny oval at the nape of her neck and secured the harness above her ears. "Watch my drink for me?" Her eyes glazed over.

Alex scanned the area with careful nonchalance while she waited. The downstairs may be for mindless trips, partying and hookups, but upstairs serious business was being conducted.

The balcony was much larger than it first appeared and sported a number of couches, tables and private alcoves. Certainly, much in the way of alcohol and recreational chimerals were being consumed—but hard tech was also trading hands. Judging from the hints of trunk lines winding along the walls, she expected active hacks were presently ongoing as well—likely some for sport, others for friendly competition, others for thousands of credits...and still others for real stakes.

She noted in her peripheral vision when Claire's vision sharpened. The woman removed the interface from her neck, ejected a tiny reflective crystal disk and pocketed the equipment. Beneath the table she extended her hand, palm open. Alex did the same, placing her hand over Claire's and holding it there as she transferred the funds. She took the disk and slipped it in the tiny pocket in the front of her pants.

"Thank you, Claire. I do appreciate this."

Claire laughed and sank back in the chair. "Fair business trade. You just bought me some fancy new hardware for my lair. Good luck with whatever adventure you're diving into. I'm glad to know you're still in the game."

She started to protest that she wasn't, not really...instead she merely smiled. "Thanks."

"Sure you don't want to stick around awhile? Sandi, Markos and I were thinking of flying the bridge a little later. I seem to remember you enjoy it?"

Alex raised an eyebrow. "*I* seem to remember being the one who taught you how to do it in the first place." Diving off the top of the Golden Gate Bridge using nothing but a tensile double-fiber strand when she was sixteen had gotten her arrested; by twenty-four she had gotten far smarter about it.

"That's right...."

She chuckled lightly and stood. "As tempting as it is, I'm afraid I must go. Urgent doings and all." She leaned over and gave Claire a quick one-armed hug. "Stay frosty. Don't get caught."

"Never."

She took the stairs two at a time and hurried through the crowd to the exit. The damp chill outside was, for the briefest moment, a welcome change from the stifling underground atmosphere. Then it was simply cold and wet.

She rubbed her hands over her arms and hurried up the hill toward the levtram station. She could catch half an hour of sleep on the transport to Seattle. Maybe an hour nap at the loft, but no more. She'd need the rest of the intervening hours to get ready— for the Board meeting, followed by a small jailbreak.

45

Alex finished explaining what the data in the report meant in terms so simple even a non-cyberized five year old could understand it, then gazed down the horrifically gaudy conference table at the collected leadership of Earth Alliance Strategic Command expectantly.

The meeting had started late, on account of she had no idea what. Then she had been kept waiting for an hour while they discussed classified war concerns. Her patience hung by a brittle thread by the time she had finally been shown in...but seeing as the matter was of the utmost importance she refrained from showing it.

Now that it was over, she thought on balance she hadn't done badly at all. Her mother had given her a tiny nod of approval at the end, which from her was high praise indeed.

General Alamatto pretended to study the visuals still displayed above the table—well it was possible he was legitimately studying them, but unlikely—while she fielded nitpicky questions from the others.

No, she didn't believe the ships in the visuals represented the entire force. No, she didn't have any idea how many more there might be. No, she didn't know where the portal originated. No, she didn't possess hard evidence the aliens were using the terahertz signal as a form of communication; that's why she had called it 'speculation.' No, she didn't see their weapons in action, for shockingly she had not taunted the armada into shooting at her.

Perhaps tired of waiting for Alamatto to take the lead, one of the Regional Commanders on holo—the one with the fiery orange hair, O'Connell?—leaned forward. The stance on his stout frame was so assertive he appeared as if he were about to bull rush the table. "Based on Metis' location, these 'aliens' will traverse Federation space long before reaching our territory. We can use this to our advantage. A Seneca under attack from two fronts will be far weaker and easier to defeat."

"Are you fucking *kidding* me?"

O'Connell made a laughable attempt to virtually stare her down. "I will not be talked to in such a manner. I am—"

Her mother *was* staring her down, but she ignored her to meet O'Connell's gaze icily. "Of course. Pardon my manners. Are you fucking kidding me, *sir?*"

The man practically came out of his chair and through the holo, but Alamatto cleared his throat loudly over O'Connell's protestations.

"Ms. Solovy, please. Surely you understand—the goal of war is to defeat the enemy. The General may have put the matter somewhat indelicately, but he raises a valid consideration. If these aliens attack the Federation, it will almost certainly bring a more rapid conclusion to the war and prevent the loss of a great many Alliance soldiers' and citizens' lives."

"Almost certainly—until they get here."

"We will be on our guard, and study them when they attack Senecan worlds—if they attack Senecan worlds. By the time they arrive here we can be ready for them."

"You'll *study* them while they slaughter millions—billions—of innocent people?" She gestured at the images hovering above the conference table. "Do you *see* the size of those ships? They can destroy entire colonies with those monstrosities!"

Alamatto raised an over-trimmed eyebrow. "I must admit I am surprised at your reaction, Ms. Solovy. I would expect you to harbor no love for Seneca, given what happened to your father."

"Do not bring my father into this."

He withered under the force of her glare, shrinking into his chair. "I'm merely saying—"

She laughed darkly. "You know, I don't particularly care for war personally—it did, as you so *delicately* noted, kill my father—but for the most part I don't give a shit what you do in your free time. But this...these aliens aren't going to distinguish between

Alliance, Senecan and Independent. Why should they care? I'm pretty sure we all look the same from space—and even up close. Admirals, Generals, whoever else is here, you ignore this threat and you are signing all of our death warrants."

Alamatto seemed to locate a piece of his backbone and straightened up. "We'll be the judge of that. Thank you, Ms. Solovy, for bringing the matter to our attention. We can take it from here."

"Right." She stood, the picture of calm, and gave the table a final once-over. "Thank you all for the privilege of wasting my time." She didn't wait for the offended expressions and exclamations before walking out.

She was actually surprised when her mother caught up to her at the lift; she'd have thought it too unseemly for her to excuse herself from the meeting so quickly.

"Alexis, wait. You need to understand—"

She whipped around and came *so* close to shoving a pointed finger in her mother's face. "*No.* I understand fine. You work with a bunch of power-drunk, narcissistic *pizdy* with the collective intelligence of one of your teacups."

"Alexis!"

"What? Dad would be disgusted by this. Why aren't you?"

"Your father died fighting Seneca—"

"My father died serving his government and his superior officers—who I'm starting to think were probably no better than those Neanderthals in there. He died fighting a stupid, pointless war which never should have been fought. Don't you dare brandish his death as a totem to justify sanctioning the slaughter of billions."

"That is not fair. I would never debase his memory in such a way." Miriam blinked and took a deep breath. "I fear your petulant little temper-tantrum did far more to hurt rather than help your cause—but it may surprise you to learn I happen to agree with you, at least as to the seriousness of the threat. I will do everything within my power to draw continued attention to it and advise—"

Alex snorted in derision. "You want to do something, Mom? Then goddamn *do* something."

She pivoted and hopped onto the lift as it descended past the floor. After tamping down the urge to hit the closest available hard surface, she checked the time.

Excellent. The Board had wasted her afternoon and now she had precious few hours to prepare.

_ℛ_

Thirty hours later, Caleb still chose to believe her...but the possibility did occur to him that she might not be able to pull it off.

Electronic shielding blocked all communications within the facility. He couldn't send or receive messages or pulses, much less livecomms. The sense of isolation was far greater than it had been in Metis. There diversions had abounded, so to speak. One diversion in particular. Here though....

The trip over had been brief; he had every reason to think he was still on EASC grounds. He sat in a 5x4 cell, bounded on three sides by walls thick with sound-proofing materials. The fourth wall consisted of translucent glass and a small door, allowing any who walked by to see inside while preventing him from seeing out. Not that they needed to stand on the other side of the glass to observe him, for every corner of the ceiling held a surveillance cam.

The cell contained a cot—far less comfortable than the one on Alex's ship—a toilet, a tiny sink and nothing else. Near as he'd determined when they'd brought him in, he was about a third of the way down a long hall of identical cells. He presumed some of the other cells held prisoners, but thanks to the sound-absorbing walls he heard no rumblings in the vicinity.

Other than food delivery through a slot in the glass wall, he hadn't had contact with another person since being dumped unceremoniously in the cell the previous afternoon. No interrogation—pharmaceutically or cybernetically aided or otherwise—and no inquiries as to his mission or intentions. Given they knew his identity, they presumably knew when he had arrived on Earth and assumed whatever his mission was, he'd found little opportunity to pursue it.

The one thing he couldn't figure was how in the bloody hell they knew who he was.

He'd had an ID busted twice in seventeen years, and in neither instance had the culprits uncovered his true identity, just that he'd used a false one. And the Roark ID was strong; it included finger-print and iris overlays courtesy of his cybernetics as well as a well-documented and verifiable personal history, complete with face scan. Granted, security measures would be heightened given the war, but he'd seen no hint of a DNA scan on entry to the premis-es. And he'd made a point not to touch any surfaces once they were inside.

The only possibility he was able to come up with was the ID had been flagged as both false and attached to him by Alliance Intelligence. He hadn't used it in…two years? Conceivably at some point over the period it had been compromised. Unlikely, but conceivable.

He assumed they intended to eventually do something with him. If he were to guess, they would transfer him to wherever they would be keeping the inevitable prisoners of war. He felt certain the Alliance had moved beyond 20th century internment camps to a more refined form of confinement. Nonetheless, he hoped like hell Alex got here before that happened.

As his thoughts drifted back to her yet again, he thudded the back of his head slowly, deliberately against the wall. He hated being dependent on someone else. For his life, safety, finances, freedom—but most of all, for his happiness.

It both pleasantly surprised and unpleasantly disturbed him to find he rather missed her. Part of it was the isolation, the real and virtual silence. But part of it was he genuinely missed her. He'd known her for all of eight, nine days now? And for at least half of the hours of those days she had alternately annoyed, exasperated and infuriated him. The other half, though….

Already he couldn't imagine *not* knowing her.

But he wasn't dependent on her. Not technically. If need be he could break himself out of here. Escaping wouldn't be easy—he'd probably be required to hurt or even kill at least several people who didn't deserve it, which he really tried to avoid doing whenever possible. But if it came down to them or rotting in a cell...it may be an unpleasant choice but it wasn't a difficult one.

He understood quite well how military security facilities operated. Hell, he had even broken *into* one a few years back. He chuckled a little to himself...that was a good time. He'd broken in to break out an insurgent leader on Andromeda so the man would then lead him to the ringleader of a group disrupting commercial shipments out of Elathan. Of course everything had gone sideways five minutes in, as it always seemed to. But it had worked out in the end.

He'd prefer a few upstart insurgents disrupting shipping routes about now. Certainly beat a war with the Alliance—for reasons he continued to be highly suspicious of—being held captive in a secure facility at the literal heart of the enemy's nerve center, and most of all facing the prospect of staggeringly powerful aliens gathering to wreak destruction upon them all.

Well, at least he also had the benefit of a brilliant, resourceful, gorgeous, clever, determined woman on his side. He definitely hadn't had that before.

No, he reassured himself, he wasn't dependent on her. *Technically*. But he was playing a long bet. And even now, thirty-plus hours into his captivity, he remained fairly confident in the rightness of his bet.

So he chose to continue believing her.

46

B *eep*
Beep
Beeeeeeep
Beee—

"For fuck's sake…." Noah groaned and rolled over, squinting one eye open. It wasn't even 0700 yet. He set nanocyanobots working to cleanse his bloodstream of the alcohol and ease the hangover, then stumbled out of the bed and to the kitchen for some water.

Only after he had gulped down half a glass did he run a hand through unkempt hair and activate the holocomm. "What you need, Brian?"

"Boss has got a job for you."

He leaned against the counter and tried to blink away the grogginess. It had been a late night…course, it usually was. "I don't have a boss."

"My boss. Sorry. Tight timetable, but it's a simple fly and drop, and the credits are sweet."

He grimaced. Brian worked for Nguyen, who worked for Kigin, who, though it wasn't common knowledge, worked for the Zelones cartel. He made a point to stay clear of the cartels whenever possible; he knew more than one colleague who had found themselves beholden to a cartel for not merely their livelihood, but their life, before they realized what had happened.

On the other hand, it was a rather tenuous connection. "What's the job?"

"Package drop to Earth, Vancouver. Needs to be there by Saturday night Galactic."

"That's fast. Where's the package?"

"Locker at the spaceport. You say yes and I've got a code for you."

"Ah, hell, Brian. I'm trying to get away from the smuggling gigs. Too much risk for too little reward."

"Well this reward is good."

He did a double-take at the number Brian sent. The reward *was* good. Damn good. He blew out a breath and took another swig of water. His schedule looked light for the next few days...he could squeeze it in.

"Okay. Just this once though. Don't let Nguyen start thinking I work for him."

"Wouldn't dream of it. Sending the code now. Oh and one last thing—boss said not to inspect the package."

"Right...."

⫘

Noah strolled through the spaceport with practiced nonchalance. The usual excess of tourists rich in credits and poor in sense meandered around in search of direction. Merchants and holobabes hocked all manner of maps, temporary cyber-enhancements, pharmaceuticals—mostly amps and boosters that would extend the party—and recreational chimerals.

He rounded the corner and stepped into the long storage room. It was used primarily by those visitors who didn't even intend on acquiring a hotel room for their stay, and for transactions such as this one. So voluminous was the selection of illegal goods in here, anywhere other than Pandora it would get raided by the cops every other day.

The locker in question was located on the second row about halfway down. He pressed his fingertips to the panel and input the code. Inside he found a large pack; it was heavier than he had been expecting, but not so heavy he couldn't carry it.

He hefted the pack over his shoulder and headed for the restrooms. Once ensconced in a stall, he set it on the floor and unlatched it.

Inside lay at least forty kilos of HHNC blocks.

Shit. He dropped his elbows to his knees and groaned into his hands. He knew the job was paying too well. Reason number forty-seven why he was trying to get away from smuggling gigs?

Every so often someone wanted you to smuggle enough damn explosives to bring down a moderate-size skyscraper.

With a heavy sigh he closed the pack up and carried it back to the locker. He stuffed the pack inside, wiped his prints off the door and walked out.

He waited until he was on the street and a fair distance from the spaceport before livecomming Brian.

It took a solid twenty seconds for the response to come. *"Yo, dude. Problem?"*

"Deal's off. Get somebody else to do your dirty work. And do me a favor? Don't come to me with any more jobs for a while."

"What the hell, man?"

"The package is fucking *explosives*. You know I don't traffic in explosives. Nothing comes of them but trouble."

"You weren't supposed to look in the package, man! I told you that!"

"You seriously think I'm going to smuggle a payload through Earth customs in the middle of a damn war without knowing what it is? How stupid do you think I am?"

"Shit, man. Boss is not going to be happy."

"Good thing he's not my boss, then. Adios."

He killed the connection and sank against the façade of whatever building bordered the sidewalk. What the crap was someone planning to do with that much HHNC?

Presumably blow something up, dumbass.

For the briefest second he actually considered notifying the authorities...but it would be asking for the kind of trouble he so did not need.

Not your problem. Leave it behind. Move on.

He headed for the nearest pub. Lunch was still hours away, but he found he wanted a drink something fierce.

47

Caleb sat on the edge of a plain cot, legs swinging leisurely in the air, when the door slid open and she stepped in. At the sight of her his face lit up, his mouth curling up in a quite pleased smirk that sent her stomach straight into flip-flops.

She spun and placed her palm on the panel in the wall by the door; it glowed and pulsed as she fed it new instructions. "I know, it's been a day and a half. Sorry, but I had a lot to do—you have *no* idea—and they've got a field on the building blocking all comms, so I wasn't able to get a message to you."

She felt him approaching and held up a finger. "One sec." The panel shifted to green, and she turned around. "Okay, we—"

—his lips were pressed against hers before she could blink. His left hand was caressing the curve of her neck, while the right grasped her waist in a firm hold. Of their own volition her lips— hell, her entire body—responded enthusiastically. For three-point-two seconds she found herself overwhelmed by visceral sensation and heated desire, while her brain desperately tried to catch up. *Dear god he tasted good. Felt good. Perfect, even. Right.*

She pulled back abruptly, a hand pressing on his chest for added effect. Her eyes were wide in semi-mock indignation. "*What* was that?"

He shrugged, grinning impishly with the rise of his shoulders. "A hello…?"

She did her best to glare at him in annoyance, though she was fairly certain her eyes were telling a different story. She was absolutely certain her pulse was, but didn't think he could *see* it.

"Uh-huh. Hold out your left wrist." He complied, and her thumb hovered above his pulse point to deactivate the prisoner code holo encircling it. "That how they say 'hello' on Seneca?"

"Nope."

She failed to fully stifle the chuckle which bubbled forth as she glanced up at him with a quick roll of her eyes. Then she produced a dark gray cap out of her pack and thrust it toward him. "Put this on. Shouldn't matter, but just in case."

He accepted it without question. "It almost matches yours."

"What can I say, fashion isn't my specialty." She wore a burgundy cap over unbound hair, the better to mask facial features in a stray cam capture. She also wore a black dress overcoat, because it was even colder here than it had been in San Francisco and here she was going to wear a damn coat.

He didn't have a coat of course. He still wore the same clothes, the only clothes, he had worn for as long as she had known him. At least his shirt had long sleeves.

He slipped the cap on over his once again wild shock of curls. "What's the plan?"

"We walk out. Come on, let's go."

"We simply walk out."

"Yup."

He exhaled and smiled gamely. "Okay."

It pleased her more than it should to see he trusted her and didn't argue. She reached into her pack again and removed a small rectangular object. She handed it to him. "Stunner. Just in case. Now let's *go*."

He nodded and followed her out the door and down the hallway. Her voice was low, almost under her breath. "All the surveillance monitors are on a loop for the next hour. I fed in the previous hour's data, and they think they're recording new images. There won't be a record of me arriving or us leaving."

"You hacked Strategic Command military security." It came out not so much a question as a statement of incredulity.

She shrugged as they took a hallway to the right. "I did."

"Seriously."

"*Yes.*" She groaned in feigned annoyance. "I do have a little inside information on the subject. And it still wasn't exactly easy, if it matters. Did you expect me to show up with a commando squad and blood from the guards decorating my face?"

"I...I honestly had no idea how you might accomplish it—only that you would." He reached over and squeezed her hand, sending an ardent flutter up her spine. "What happens when they find me absent?"

"You were released from custody at 0100 on the authority of Staff Commander Willoughby. Until someone shows up to interrogate you—tomorrow at the earliest, maybe never—the people who care won't even know you're gone."

"Nice. And this Willoughby character?"

"He's a complete asshole. Don't worry about—" He pressed her into the wall, into the shadows, and placed a finger to her lips. *Jesus he smelled nice. How could he possibly smell so nice after not having showered for almost two days?* She was having some small difficulty breathing and it wasn't because he was pressed against her too tightly. His eyes flickered in a way which suggested he was enjoying the whisper of her breath along his finger, though she couldn't be sure.

Three seconds later a guard strode down the crossway. He counted down with his fingers; when the last one dropped they stepped out and hurried across.

It was the last hallway. She touched the already-hacked exit panel to open the door and they were quickly on the lift to the parking level.

He rolled his shoulders and sucked in a deep breath of the chill night air. "So...what's the plan? I realize I keep asking. I'm afraid I'm kind of used to being the one in charge of these sorts of capers."

The lift settled to the floor and they headed for her skycar. "We're going to run by my loft. I need to pick up a few things I wasn't able to bring with me earlier, and we've got a few hours. I want to leave during morning shift at the spaceport. I'm familiar with everyone on it and they won't ask any questions. We can figure out where to go once we're off-planet."

An odd expression came across his face as he climbed into the passenger seat. She glanced over curiously. "What?"

"I don't know. I guess I thought you might put me on a transport and wave goodbye. Which would be totally understandable and I wouldn't hold it against you."

He had tasted like cinnamon. Again, how was that even possible? "Look, I'm not saying I won't put you on a transport on some independent world and wave goodbye, but I'll make sure you get out of Alliance space safely. It's the least I can do after I got you arrested and imprisoned and everything."

"Thank you." He sounded, well, genuinely thankful. They lifted off, and she was arcing southward when he pinched the bridge of his nose with a groan.

"Something wrong?"

"New messages pouring in. Apparently the Alliance blew up all our surveillance satellites, and now everyone is running in circles flailing their arms about wailing in despair. Also, so far no word on the aliens from the team they sent to Metis."

"At least there hasn't been any sign of an attack yet."

"Actually, the fact there hasn't been an attack worries me. It means there were probably a hell of a lot more ships still to come through that portal."

Her eyes cut over to him. "Well, fuck."

"Yeah." He rubbed at his jaw. "So what did the Board say?"

"They said they will 'monitor the situation.'" Her mouth worked in agitation; she didn't even bother to hide it.

"And?"

"And nothing. They acknowledged the potential threat but said it was too tenuous to act on for the time being." Her hand slammed on the dash in a burst of frustration. "Idiot mental degenerates. They sit in their soundproof rooms and issue tone-deaf edicts and call themselves controlling the world, and one day they ask you to die for them, and then they keep right on doing what they were doing…."

Her gaze rose to the translucent roof. The moon was enormous tonight, a luminous white glow drowning out the stars. "I just wanted to be left alone to live my life. I don't need this shit."

In her peripheral vision she saw him smile softly. "We don't get to choose what happens to us—but we always get to choose how we react to it."

Also honey. The lingering memory of sugar on the tongue. Damn.
"You can stop being insightful anytime you like, you know."

"What, did I surprise you?"

"You're always surprising me."

A soft breath fell from his lips. She tried to get a look at him out of the corner of her eye. He appeared...speechless. *Huh.*

The seconds ticked by as they flew in silence above the Strait toward downtown. Distracted by competing thoughts, it took her a moment to notice he was regarding her rather sharply. "Yes?"

"What else did the Board say?"

She frowned and looked away. "They said.... *Fine.* They said the aliens would go through Senecan space first, and the distraction would help the war effort."

"And you weren't going to tell me?"

"Why tell you? There's nothing you can do about it, and it's not as though they can helpfully point the aliens in Seneca's direction or anything. It's impotent political blustering."

"I get you have no particular love for my home or its citizens, but surely you don't want them to be wiped out."

"Of course I don't—that's not why I—*dammit*, Caleb." She blew out a sigh through gritted teeth. "So I'm ashamed of those who call themselves my leaders. As if I was proud of them before. I thought...I thought I knew the darkness which could reside in people, I truly did, but I had no idea they had the capacity to be so appallingly ruthless."

"Many people are. Especially those in power, and *especially* those in power in the military. I can't say I'm surprised." He paused. "Then again, I may be a bit jaded."

She arched an eyebrow as she descended toward her building. "Speaking of...Richard knew who you were because your file was leaked to him. Directly."

"What file?"

"Your Senecan Intelligence Division file."

"To an Alliance Naval Intelligence agent? Impossible."

"I'd agree with you, except for the fact it's precisely what happened. Sorry, but it seems you've got a leak or a plant or some such. Who knew you were coming here?"

"Only Volosk. He classified this little 'op' Level V when he approved it, which means no one knew."

"Is it possible he's dirty?"

He laughed. It was the first time she'd heard his laugh in several days; she hadn't realized how much she'd missed it. "Michael Volosk makes your friend Richard look like a flamboyant renegade. No chance."

She circled to the back side of her building and cruised into the parking level a third of the way up. "Well, nothing we can do to solve the mystery for the moment. Let's get upstairs, and you can take a shower."

He followed her to the lift. "Do I need one?"

Not in the slightest. "You were in military confinement for almost two days, what do you think?"

He leaned back against the lift wall. "It's not like I engaged in any strenuous activity, or any activity at all in fact. It was all terribly dull."

When they reached her door she gestured him in ahead of her. "In all seriousness, you can take a shower if you want, it's upstairs to the left. I'm going to—"

"Alex, these are amazing. Did you take them?" He was standing in the middle of the living area, attention not on the view out the windows but on the wall of spacescapes.

She simply nodded.

His expression was unreadable as he glanced briefly at her before returning to the visuals. "They're...really something. You have quite a gift."

"I...thank you." She wrenched her gaze away from watching him and went into the kitchen, dropping her cap and jacket on the dining table. "The laundry port is upstairs, too. If you toss your clothes in it, they'll be ready by the time we need to leave. There should be something in the back of the closet you can throw on."

"Ex-boyfriend's?"

She looked up at him in amusement. "*Yes.*"

His response was a full-throated laugh as he headed up the stairs.

Once he had disappeared, she prepped a brief message to Richard.

> *Sorry.*
>
> *He came here at my request, and I couldn't leave him to rot in confinement. I wouldn't be worthy to be your goddaughter if I did.*
>
> *Okay, that was a cheap attempt at winning your sympathy. I doubt it worked, you're too smart for it. Though you do have a soft underbelly so maybe it at least tweaked your heartstrings a little.*
>
> *He's not a threat to us. You have to trust me on this. And as much as it pains me to say it, the true threat isn't the Senecan Federation either. This war is a lie. I know you haven't the power to end it, but I beg you to do everything you can to expose it for what it is.*
>
> *We need everyone working together to face what IS the true threat: the aliens on the threshold. PLEASE. You know I don't give a shit unless something is real. This is as real as it gets.*
>
> *I'll be in touch when I can.*
>
> *—Alex*

She marked it for time delay and set it to deliver the next afternoon, long after she'd be off-planet and likely after he found himself one prisoner short.

48

Alex glanced up as he came down the stairs, returned her focus to the aural hovering above the counter—then looked up again.

It was odd for a minute, seeing him in Malcolm's clothes. He had a leaner frame, so they hung a bit loosely on him. She had the totally irrational thought *that* was the way they were supposed to fit.

He caught her gaze and shrugged, gesturing to the drawstring linen pants and lightweight unbuttoned shirt. "This was all I could find."

"I never said they would be 'fit for the office' clothes." She didn't comment on the fact the shirt did button. One, she was quite certain he knew and simply delighted in torturing her; two, she found she preferred being tortured by...she blinked. "Get down here and I'll run through what I've got so far. You can let me know if you think we need anything else. As fugitives from the law and all."

He came over to the bar and rested his forearms on it. "Again, thank you. I never intended to turn you into a fugitive."

"Again, not your fault. And it'll be fine. Probably."

"Still, thank you." His hand reached halfway across the bar, then stopped. It reminded her of the night before they discovered the alien army. Then, she had been glad he hesitated. Now she longed for him to cross the remaining space.

"I forgive you. Now about the supplies."

They spent the next several minutes reviewing their requirements and the supply list she had compiled. He leaned on the long side of the bar near the end, her on the short edge near the dinner table; her aural floated in the air between them. It was comfortable and easy and close, and she was using ninety percent of her energy on not being distracted by his clean, soapy scent, by the loose curls of damp hair falling across his forehead, by the way his voice seemed so much huskier and more lilting than normal. It sounded almost musical.

He never should have kissed her, dammit. And now she was royally fucked. Except, not actually.... Well.

Luckily ten percent managed to be enough to get through the list. It mostly consisted of food and new spare parts anyway, seeing as she'd used her previous spare parts repairing her ship after he blew a hole in it and all.

She killed the aural and straightened up. "Okay, I believe we've covered everything. Sorry I didn't have a chance to get you any clothes. I imagine you're sick to death of your one outfit by now. But you can take those, and whatever else is up there."

His head tilted. "Are you sure?"

"Yeah." She smiled. "We'll stop on the way for the extra food, and we should be able to pick up the spare parts at the spaceport." She started walking around the bar, and him, toward the small room tucked under the stairwell. "I'm going to hit the storage and grab some—"

"Alex." Her name on his voice washed over her, sending shivers to dance on her skin. He had turned, followed her path with his body.

His hand rested on her upper arm. Gently. A request.

The surroundings faded to a blur while she, him and the space they inhabited zoomed into hyper-focus, as in a shallow depth-of-field image. And in a blink the last remaining speck of her resistance, tiny though it had been, dissipated away to nothingness.

In one fluid motion she pivoted, closed the distance between them and brought her hand up to wind in his hair. *It was even softer than it looked.*

For one infinite second his eyes met hers. They were open and honest and smoldering with barely restrained desire and so very, *very* blue. His fingertips slid across her shoulder and up the curve of her neck until his knuckles brushed along her cheek.

"Damn you."

His brow furrowed into an endearingly straight line. "For?"

"Everything. Kiss me before I lose my mind—"

—his mouth was on hers—or hers was on his—and it felt as if a dam broke within her, and perhaps within him as well. His lips stole the breath from her lungs; she gasped in his breath to replace it. The hand which had grasped her arm what now seemed hours ago was entwined in her hair, then running over her shoulder, then delicately caressing her jaw.

Her hand that wasn't fisted violently in his hair slinked inside the borrowed shirt. As her fingertips brushed across his ribs he trembled beneath her touch. When he nipped her lower lip in pleasure she grinned and continued on, tickling his skin on the way to the small of his back.

Then everything was tongues and teeth and stolen breaths and arms pulling bodies closer. Her head spun madly from the overload of sheer physical sensation. His skin was a wonder beneath her palm, but she couldn't focus on it for the *spectacular* feel of his lips on hers, the taste of his tongue—

He still tasted like cinnamon and honey, even after the shower. Delicious.

—his hand at her waist tugged the shirt from her pants and immediately dipped beneath it and ran up her spine. She responded by crushing her mouth into his, as though brute force might bring him closer.

Eventually he pulled away a fraction to suck in air and shifted her so her back was to the bar. His body pinned her against it, again with greater strength than she would have imagined. And dear god but it wasn't enough. Her hand slid down to his ass and gripped him tighter against her; his hardness pressed into her, just left of where she urgently wanted it to be.

He moaned into her mouth, a deep, rough tremor of carnal need.

She tore her lips from his and across his jaw to his ear. "Upstairs...." It was little more than a breath.

In an instant he had pulled her from the bar, dropped both hands to her hips and hoisted her up into his arms.

"Your wish is my *very* enthusiastic command." His voice sounded deeper and rougher yet somehow even more musical but definitely not nearly so controlled now.

She gasped in delight and wound her legs around his waist with a slightly wild laugh. Her arms wrapped around his shoulders as he began not-so-carefully carrying her toward the staircase. She occupied herself with his earlobe, his neck, his exquisitely defined jaw, whatever she could reach.

He maneuvered the first few stairs like they were second nature—surprisingly, seeing as he'd traversed them all of twice and her hair spilled over his face—but she must have distracted him too much, because at the midway landing he slammed her against the wall and his mouth against hers. One leg slid to the floor; he maintained a solid grip on the other.

It was her turn to moan as he crashed into her. *God he wasn't wearing any underwear...he would be washing them, of course.* Freed of needing to hang on to him, she shoved the shirt off his shoulders. Her voice escaped into free air as his lips trailed down her neck to the hollow of her throat. "This isn't upstairs...."

He let go of her long enough to shake the sleeve off. This left the shirt hanging on nothing but his other wrist, which still grasped her leg firmly on his hip. His hand returned to snake up her stomach, her own shirt bunching in its wake.

"It's up *some* stairs...." The words vibrated on her collarbone as his tongue teased along it.

She gave a ragged laugh and dragged her other leg free to coax him toward the remaining stairs by nothing more than the threat of physical separation. His shirt fell unnoticed to the landing as hers disappeared over her head.

Support had been woven into her top, and their chests were now skin-on-skin. The sensation of his chest pressed to hers was...was...'pleasant' was clearly too weak a word. A pittance to describe a treasure.

She cursed having to divert a miniscule portion of her attention to feel her way up the stairway backwards. *A few more stairs. Only a few mo*— her legs weakened as his thumb ran over then lingered upon a nipple, and she sank down short of the bedroom landing.

The tiny corner of her brain which managed to continue functioning at a minimal level of rationality noted his hand slid behind her head before it hit the top stair to take the jarring blow for her. Later, she should think about what a shocking act of kindness and sacrifice it was. Yup, lat—

—his mouth was on her left breast and his tongue was swirling around the nipple, suckling it right to the edge of pain while a thumb teased the other, and she thought her eyes probably rolled back in her head.

"Yebat'sya mne...."

His lips ghosted down her chest toward her navel with a throaty chuckle. "It would be my genuine pleasure."

The words fluttered over her skin to send a fierce shiver coursing through her, though his accent now rolled so alluringly thick she could barely understand him at all. She didn't care and oh how she wanted him to keep going.... Her spine arched, begging for him to keep going, but her fingernails scratched up his back and tugged him up to her until his mouth again crushed hers.

He was acting as if he was the one in control, yet happy to indulge her every request. She considered making a mental note for possible future reference, but got horribly distracted by his tongue halfway through.

In a supreme act of will she slid up the final two stairs and shakily stood with him.

Instantly her hands dropped to his waist and yanked the drawstring loose; the pants fell to the floor unaided. She tried to pull his naked form to her, but his hands were in the way, busy sliding her own pants over her hips. Hers were snugger and clingy and she wasted two precious seconds shimmying them and her underwear together to the floor.

Finally there existed nothing between them. For a perfect moment he held her next to him. She could feel every long, taut muscle, his racing heartbeat reverberating beneath his skin. She'd never known his pulse to race. He was *so* warm. It felt sublime and luscious and laced with an unexpected throbbing in her chest.

She looked up—it wasn't far, he wasn't terribly much taller than her—and willingly fell into the ocean of his eyes.

The back of her knees hit the bed. She curled one leg up and sank onto it, bringing him with her as if they were one.

With astonishing gentleness he slipped inside her, and they were.

She wondered if her eyes widened as much as his did, lips a mere centimeter apart, her hands clutching his face and his clutching hers.

"Jesus, you—"

Her mouth smothered his as she scraped a hand down his back and drew him all the way into her. The momentary tenderness melted, burnt away by the scorching passion which flared.

She thought she *must* have been with someone who was more beautifully passionate, more naturally in sync with her every movement and desire, who more perfectly fit within and around and against her, and later she would doubtless recall who it might have been. But damned if she could think of anyone now.

She arched into his grasp to meet his movements...on second thought, it suddenly seemed impossible there ever could have been.

At some point his arms coiled around her and he rose up to rest on his heels as her full weight slid down over him. *Oh my god....*

Her fingers wound fiercely in his hair while the other hand ran along his back as her legs wrapped to envelop him. His hands mirrored hers, until one settled on her hip. It began to smoothly guide her, yet he let her set the pace...and the last remnants of the outside world, of time passing at all, blurred out of existence.

Her lips hovered a whisper apart from his, every so often connecting for a fervent yet somehow gentle kiss, as they exchanged the air necessary to continue living and feeling and experiencing *this*. Gradually the pressure began to intensify within her until she feared she would surely shatter—

—she buried her face into his neck and screamed, every measure of her tightening around him in a tidal wave of ecstasy.

Then she was falling back onto the bed and he was consuming her with a fervency and passion absolutely like nothing she had ever felt. His body was fire on her skin, his breath desperate in her ear, his hands everywhere and—

—she gasped into his shoulder as he carried her with him on his own torrent of ecstasy. His face was tangled in her hair and his arms had encircled her to hold her against him as if she was the only lifeline he possessed, but it was okay because his embrace was warm and wonderful and....

By the time she remembered how to breathe, he was planting feather-light kisses along her cheek, across her jaw and down her neck. Her eyes slowly focused to find him gazing at her, wearing an expression of...unfettered, almost *innocent* pleasure. It was so striking her newly found breath caught in her throat.

After untold moments—hours, days—he rolled them both onto their sides. They lay facing one another, panting slightly but grinning like fools.

She giggled devilishly. "You shouldn't have kissed me in the confinement cell."

"Yes, I quite clearly *should* have."

Her head shook minutely; it was all she was able to manage in his embrace. "No, you shouldn't have. You *should* have kissed me on the ship night before last."

He responded with a winded laugh. "You say that now, but if I had then, I might still be tied up on the ship."

His accent had again faded, she noticed in some disappointment. "You said I wouldn't be able to get you back in the restraints."

"I did, but that was before I knew you. Now, I'm not so sure." He kissed her, long and slow, then sighed in contentment and rolled the rest of the way onto his back. "This is going to be complicated, you know."

She propped up on an elbow and regarded him curiously. "What is? I assumed this was merely a one-time stress reliever, or maybe a 'thank you' for getting you out of confinement."

The corners of his mouth twitched, as if uncertain of which direction to curve. A shadow passed through his eyes as they darted to her then away, darkening them to the color of the ocean depths where no light reached.

She quickly smiled, broadly enough to get his attention. "And the look in your eyes tells me it isn't."

His face scrunched up in disbelief as realization dawned. "I thought *I* was supposed to be the devious one."

"Oh, you are, you are." She placed a soft kiss on his lips; he didn't respond. She pulled back to meet his gaze. "Forgive me for being wary."

A chuckle escaped his throat, but it had a sharp, pained edge to it, reinforced by the shadow lingering in his expression. "You *still* don't trust me."

She coaxed his eyes to meet hers. "I trust you with my life." And she did. She kissed him more deeply, and after a pause this time he did respond.

I just don't know if I trust you with my heart.

It was several relatively blissful minutes later when he sank into the bed and she settled onto her stomach beside him. "So about this 'complicated' part...."

"I'm from Seneca, you're from Earth. We're practically Romeo and Juliet."

"Nah, as I remember it Romeo and Juliet gave a damn what everyone else thought. Hell, we've got more pressing concerns anyway. The galaxy has embroiled itself in an idiotic, pointless war, and any day now a massive alien force is going to show up and crash the party."

She groaned and rolled over to glare at the ceiling. "And even if we get somebody to listen, who says we'll be able to counter them? I have a sneaking suspicion their weapons will be a tad more powerful than ours."

His fingers drew idle circles along her stomach, tickling the damp skin and momentarily drawing her into the rather pleasurable present...but only momentarily. "Maybe if we presented a united front—but no, instead we're busy blowing up the ships and weapons and defenses we'll need to fight the aliens on *each other*."

At the sobering reality they both fell quiet for a while. Finally she took a deep breath and exhaled audibly to break the silence. "So I was thinking. We should go to Pyxis. I know it's a bit far, but it's the closest independent world to Seneca other than Pandora, which I'd really prefer to avoid. You can leave from there and hopefully find a way for your government to end this war, since we failed so impressively here."

He rose up on one arm to stare at her. "Come to Seneca with me. You can explain the Metis data better than I can and help convince them of the severity of the problem. Like you said, two voices *are* better than one."

"Oh, you're not seriously going to use that argument on me now?"

"What? Other considerations aside, it isn't a bad point, and we need every advantage we can get."

She flinched and rolled away. "I don't...I don't think it's a good idea."

"It'll be fine. I promise *you* won't get arrested."

"Yes, because your government is a pillar of right and justice and good."

"Of course not. It just so happens you're not an enemy combatant."

Why couldn't he let it go for the moment? Give her a little time to come to grips with the idea? A few hours earlier she had been defending the Senecans to her mother and the Board. Now she was recoiling at the notion of visiting their damn planet, as though it was somehow a corporeal evil all its own. Which of course it *wasn't*, but....

"I said I didn't think it was a good idea."

He exhaled in obvious frustration. "Come on. *Help me* make them listen."

She refused to meet his gaze this time. *Goddammit.* "I need to take a shower." She started to get up, but he reached out and grabbed ahold of her arm.

"Look, I know you hold no particular love for Seneca or its government. I know you blame them for your father's death. I get that, I do. But I also know you want—"

Stop! Stop acting as if you can stare into my soul so easily! The detached, untethered sensation washed over her once again. She had thought perhaps she might hold onto him as an anchor, but now he was pushing and prodding and behaving as if it were all so simple...she yanked her arm out of his grasp.

"You think a week together and a quick roll in the sack means you *know* me? I realize you're cocky, but please. You don't know the first thing about me."

She shot him a withering glare and stalked off to the bath, lightheaded to the point of dizziness from whiplashing emotions. *No, it wasn't simple at all.*

Caleb banged his head against the bedcovers. In a rush of frustration he grabbed a pillow and threw it angrily across the room; it bounced ineffectually off the wall and tumbled gently to the floor.

With a harsh, bitter breath he squeezed his eyes shut...then climbed off the bed and collected his clothes from the laundry port. He'd steal a skycar from one of the residents and get to the spaceport. He'd use another ID to catch a transport to Pandora or Romane.

Two hours and he'd be gone.

After all, his mission was complete, if a failure in the purest sense of the term. The war had everyone spinning in circles chasing their tails, but he was determined to make Division, the government, the military and whoever else mattered understand they had been fooled. They were wasting precious time and resources on the wrong target, when the true threat loomed hidden on the horizon.

He pulled on his shoes and headed down the stairs. There were things he needed to do, and they did not involve getting entangled with an Alliance Admiral's daughter in the middle of a war and impending alien invasion...even if the peculiar tightness in his chest proclaimed otherwise.

He had done *everything* in his power to get her to trust him; done *everything* her way even when it went against his better instincts. That path had taken him away from where he needed to be, put Senecan citizens at greater risk and gotten him arrested and imprisoned. True, it had also gotten him outstandingly laid— only to be turned on in a fit of spiteful anger he did not deserve.

Dammit she was infuriating! And bullheaded stubborn. Quick to flare in temper. Ridiculously private and emotionally closed- off—

He felt his attention drawn to the wall of spacescapes once more, found himself pausing in front of the panorama.

She had somehow managed to capture in frozen images the sense of wonder and awe one experienced in deep space. The vastness and the beauty. It was as if he was looking into space through her eyes, seeing it as she must see it...and thus glimpsing a mirror into her soul.

—also intriguing, even captivating. Exceedingly talented, capable and independent. Fiercely determined and unafraid. Vulnerable and strong in equal measure. A damn revelation in bed. All in all, kind of remarkable.

His gaze rose to the balcony above. *Never have anything you can't walk away from.* Especially *a woman.*

"Shit."

He grimaced and dragged a hand down his face...and went back upstairs, dropping his clothes in a trail across the floor to the door of the bath.

She stood in the shower, eyes closed and head bowed as the water cascaded over her. Before she realized he was there, he had slipped inside.

Her irises flared in outrage, sparking a pure bright silver. He thought there may have been a glint of tears in them...but it may have just been the falling water.

"What are you *doing?*"

"Invading your privacy. Sorry, I didn't want you to have any more time to get angrier at me."

She shoved him into the glass. "How dare you! Get out—"

He smiled, ignoring her attempts to extricate him from the shower. "Listen, you're right—I don't know you, not really. But I'd very much like to, if you'll allow me."

She stared at him furiously, but at least she stopped trying to shove him out. Her features could be so expressive when the mask fell away. He saw anger, then suspicion, confusion, doubt and perhaps even fear in the shadows crossing her face, in the quirking of her lovely mouth. He wondered what his own eyes were showing her, and whether it was more than he wanted to reveal. Ah well, too late now.

He recognized the softening in her expression before it manifested in the relaxing of her shoulders and dropping of her chin. It took another several seconds for her to roll her eyes in exasperation and step forward to rest her forehead on his.

"You're infuriating—and entirely too clever for your own good. You know this, right?"

He chuckled lightly and reached up to run fingers through her soaking wet hair. "Back at you."

Her face tilted up and supple, moist lips met his. Hesitant, tender, gentle. She tasted of warm spice, like nutmeg in mulled cider. Her skin had felt amazingly smooth earlier; here, softened by the steam of the shower, it was silk beneath his hands.

One arm coiled around her until his palm came to rest at the small of her back. Her body was quite slender; he would have called it delicate but for the long, lithe muscles gracing her frame. It reminded him of a dancer's body, though after watching her spend three days repairing her ship he knew the work which had actually shaped it.

Her hand in his hair tightened, the other grasped his hip and in a flash any hesitancy in her kiss vanished. Urgency was bleeding out of her and into him, and he gathered her fully into his arms as desire battled with and quickly overcame sentiment.

The water flooded over them as he pressed her to the opposite wall. His hand slipped along wet, soapy skin, desperately seeking her toned thigh. He gripped her leg and coaxed it up to his hip...then he was engulfed within her.

She gasped in response but pulled him yet closer and deeper. Demanding, needing all he had to give. As before, she was a force of nature, a whirlwind to which he could do little more than hang on for dear life. The spirit, the *fire* he had first witnessed in the hold of her ship blazed to life in his arms.

Still, he tried to draw it out, to tease her and prolong her pleasure, and his. But she was so damn intoxicating and it was all so overpowering—the deluge of water enveloping them, the steam filling the air, the silk of her skin pressed to his and the incredible, perfect heat within her. The look of wild abandon in her eyes was like staring into a nova at the moment of its explosion.

She clenched around him, her eyes squeezed shut—and he let himself go, following her over the edge into the rapturous abyss.

They very nearly tumbled to the shower floor as they lost control of *everything*...bodies, thought, breath, time and space. He fell deeper into her as his legs threatened to collapse beneath him.

An aeon passed before the world began to regain detail and, eventually, clarity. His lips had found hers, and she grinned into them. "Less than an hour and we've already had our first make-up sex."

He laughed haltingly, still struggling to catch his breath. Reasonably confident in his legs' capability to now marginally support him, he leaned back enough to gaze at her.

"It isn't going to be boring, is it?"

He was leaning against the windows and contemplating the wall of spacescapes—*again*—when she descended the stairs.

Alex frowned to herself. Either he was playing at manipulating her on such a deep and meaningful level as to be reprehensible...or he was like her in such a deep and meaningful way as to be extraordinary. She was a bit shocked to realize how much she wanted to believe it was the latter, and how terrified she was it could be the former.

He turned his attention to her as she reached the landing, smirking in that endearing, annoying, dangerous, boyish way which was so immensely kissable. So when he met her at the bottom of the stairs, she did.

Her arms draped over his shoulders; his encircled her waist. "I have a question."

"Mmhmm?"

"Earlier, your accent...."

He cringed and retreated slightly. "Yeah, I guess I wasn't altogether, um, in control for a while there."

"Is that how you really sound? When you're not on the job?"

"You are *not* a job to me."

Maybe. "You know what I—"

His hands rose to grasp her face as he drew her into an impassioned embrace. The sheer fierceness of the kiss sent her reeling. The world spun in one direction, her head in the other, her heart in a third as his hands, his mouth, his tongue and the press of his body asked everything of her, and offered everything in return.

She was left utterly breathless as he pulled back a trace.

"Tell me you believe me." It was a throaty, desperate whisper against her lips.

"Ya veruyu...."

He smiled softly and at last gave her space to breathe. "Then to answer your question, when I'm home, around my family? Yes. It is."

"You don't need to pretend for me."

"I was concerned you might have negative associations with a Senecan accent."

She shook her head almost imperceptibly. "I like it. And now I'm going to associate it with—" her gaze drifted pointedly up the stairs "—spectacular sex, so...."

He laughed, but his eyes were serious as they seemed to search her face. "Okay." And with a word, his voice regained its full melodic timbre...and his smile shifted indefinably. "'Spectacular,' huh?"

"Don't get cocky—" Her grumble was cut off as his lips met hers yet again. Softer, less urgent than before. Nevertheless, the kiss was rapidly becoming more when she sucked in a deep breath and reluctantly stepped away. "We need to *go* soon."

"Right. Okay."

She went to double-check her pack, then remembered she never had made it to the storage closet. She ducked in, ostensibly to grab a few things. Alone in the shadowy recesses of the room she exhaled slowly, closed her eyes and made a choice.

"I'll go with you to Seneca—on one condition."

She emerged to find him regarding her rather intently. "Lay it on me."

"That you can absolutely and completely guarantee the safety and security of my ship while we're docked there."

His mouth opened to respond, then closed. His eyes dropped away from her. She could only guess at what transpired in his mind as he stared at the floor, hands resting on his hips. When he looked up his expression was distressingly solemn. "Honestly? I'm not sure I can. I mean I think it would be safe, but there's a war on and it's going to be making people crazy."

She ran an agitated hand through her hair in frustration. "*Dammit*, Caleb. I'm trying, but you're not making this easy."

He began pacing behind the couch. "But I can guarantee its safety and security on Romane."

An eyebrow arched in question.

"I know, it's not quite perfect. But it's convenient enough, not too far from here and a quick trip to Seneca. We'll take a transport from there, or we can rent a ship if you want more control. However long we need to be on Seneca, the *Siyane* will be safe on Romane. And when our—" he paused, and his voice dropped in tenor "—or your business on Seneca is concluded it will be waiting on you. I promise you." He frowned a little. "Unless Romane gets blown up by the invading aliens. I can't do a thing about them, and I hope like hell you don't expect me to."

Her gaze roved across the loft...out the windows, where the night sky had barely begun to lighten, and back to the wall in front of her, finally coming to rest on the visual hanging at eye level: she and her dad standing atop Mammoth Mountain. They had hiked it for her thirteenth birthday. He was killed in action two months later.

Caleb was right, it wasn't perfect. But it was a surprisingly decent alternative. Off Earth, on an independent world—which arguably was *better* than Seneca and the safest place to be given the war. Romane enjoyed the solidest reputation of any independent colony, and the location would give them at least some degree of flexibility.

He had leaned against the couch to await her decision. She nodded. "Okay...*okay*. You can tell me why you can guarantee its safety on Romane on the way to the spaceport."

His expression blossomed into a relieved smile. "It's a deal."

She couldn't help but return the smile as she picked up her pack and tossed it over her shoulder.

"Let's go."

PART IV:

ACCELERANDO

"Things fall apart; the centre cannot hold;
Mere anarchy is loosed upon the world,
The blood-dimmed tide is loosed, and everywhere
The ceremony of innocence is drowned."

— *William Butler Yeats*

49

ROMANE

White gold swirled around hammered chrome, weaving again and again until it formed an intricate knot. Red dollops of plasma appeared to emerge from the chrome and glide through the gaps in the knot to orbit it, though it was an illusion. In reality the plasma merely hovered in a deceptive shimmer so as to imply motion.

"In my opinion, this is one of the artist's most powerful pieces. It speaks on multiple levels: how we are prisoners to our own weaknesses, how we inflict far greater damage and pain upon ourselves than anyone else is capable of, how we cannot escape who we are or a prison of our own creation. Some believe it also asserts that emotions themselves—our metaphorical heart—are a flaw dooming us to failure and despair. I myself tend to view it with a bit more optimism."

The woman placed a delicate hand to her mouth. "It's magnificent. I simply must have it."

Mia Requelme smiled with practiced ease. "Certainly. We will want to retain it for the remainder of the exhibit, but I'll be happy to make all the arrangements for you now. If you'll follow me?"

She slipped gracefully amongst the patrons milling in the gallery's exhibit space as the woman trailed behind her. It was a good crowd. Thus far the showcase was a smashing success. A third of the pieces had sold in the first two days, and it would run for another week. Antonio Castile Lesenna created art which was simultaneously garish and elegant, which represented everything or nothing depending on what the observer desired to see. It would soon make him ridiculously wealthy, Mia was quite certain.

She reached the small alcove tucked into the rear corner of the room, activated the screen and turned to her customer. "You can input your information here—"

The priority pulse asserted itself into her vision.
Mia, I need your help.

"Why should I help you?" she snarled.

"Because I can get you out. I'll even get you off-planet, to some-where you can start a new life."

"I already started a new life once. Didn't help."

The man smiled in the dim light of the alley; it made her feel safe, which was something she could not afford to feel. "But I bet you have a list a kilometer long of the mistakes you made and how you would get it right the next time. Help me, and let me help you find your next time."

Mia's eyes narrowed warily. He had intercepted her on a run through The Boulevard, grasping her wrist from behind as she was preparing to palm a set of disks off the adventure illusoire merchant stand. She had thought he was a cop—though there weren't many cops on Pandora—until she whirled around and saw the faded flannel shirt and scruffy beard. Then she had thought he was an undercover cop. His eyes were a cop's eyes—sharp, observant, calculating.

And she had been mostly correct. He *was* a cop, of sorts. Now he wanted her to give him the access codes to Eli's inner compound.

He continued to watch her and she him...but at her prolonged silence, his gaze softened. "I tell you what. Why don't you let me buy you some dinner, and you can think it over while we're eating."

That was low. How did he know she was near to starving? Eli's lieutenant Paul had caught her skimming weeks ago and threatened to rat her out unless she gave him half of everything she made. She'd barely been scraping by before; now she survived on one meal a day and what she managed to steal. It was humiliating.

She scowled and ran a hand through tangled, dirty hair. "Fine. It's your money."

A few minutes later she eyed him over her burrito. "What are you planning to do to Eli's operation?"

The guy—he had said his name was Josh, not as if she believed him—shrugged. "I'm going to explosively dismantle his chimeral production line and bring the cops down on the remains."

"There aren't any cops here."

He laughed. It bore a hint of mystery, as if to imply he knew more about Pandora than she did. "Yes, there are."

"Well, could've fooled me." She took another bite, stuffing her mouth full of rice and beans and olives. She loved olives.

She regarded him a moment. He was quite handsome, with startlingly blue eyes and black hair which fell in soft, lazy curls along his forehead. And he seemed only a few years older than her. She might prefer him without the beard, but she suspected it was temporary anyway. "Why would you help me?"

"Because you're a better person than they are. You're intelligent and quick and you clearly have skills. I can see the potential beneath the grime. Besides, you don't like what you're doing. You don't like being a criminal, and you definitely don't like being beholden to a scumbag like Eli."

"How could you possibly tell all that about me? You just met me."

A corner of his mouth curled up in a smirk. "I've been watching you for a few days and—"

"Impossible. I pay very close attention—I'd realize if I were being followed."

"Yes, you do. But I'm better than you."

She snorted and finished off the burrito.

"As I was saying. I've been watching you, along with several other of Eli's lackeys. I need someone on the inside, and it was simply a matter of deciding who. I chose you. Did I make the wrong choice?"

She finished off the chips next and sank back in her chair. He was right of course. Shockingly, annoyingly so. She had run away from her dad and brother four years ago in search of a better life. But lacking credits, contacts or credentials, she had soon become trapped yet again.

She knew there must be another way, a better way of living. Glimpses of it teased her in the spaceport and on the exanet. She had educated herself over the last few years, far beyond what an official primary education would have taught her. Now an adult, she was able to legally speak and act for herself. She just needed a chance. One real chance.

"How do I know you won't double-cross me?"

He reached in his pocket and pulled out a small translucent film. He laid it on the table but kept two fingers securely atop it.

"Here's a ticket to Romane. Give me the access codes, I give you the ticket and transfer two thousand credits to you. You can leave right away."

Two thousand credits was more than she had earned in six months. Her pulse began to quicken. "How do you know I won't double-cross you and give you the wrong codes?"

His shoulders rose a fraction. "I guess I'll have to trust you. Are you worthy of my trust, Mia?"

She stared at him a moment...and nodded.

Mia motioned Jonathan over to her. "Ma'am, if you'll excuse me a moment. My assistant can walk you through the purchase process. You're in good hands, and thank you again."

She forced herself not to rush down the hall to her private office at the gallery, even pausing to procure a gin-marinated olive off the tray of a passing waiter. The office was one of several located around the city, and as immaculate and refined as each of the others. Like everything in her life now.

The guy had showed up on Romane to check on her four months after she fled Pandora. She repaid the two thousand credits, plus interest—she had made excellent use of the time—then asked him to dinner. That had been twelve years ago.

Once the door closed behind her she sent a livecomm request. "Caleb. What do you need?"

There was a brief pause before the response came. *"Mia, how are you?"*

"I'm splendid, but you don't have to small-talk me. Are you okay? It sounded urgent."

"I'm fine. But I need a favor. Any chance I can borrow a Class I bay at your spaceport?"

"Of course, it's no trouble."

"I'm also going to need the records of its rental and the ship it holds falsified. And once we arrive, I'll need the highest-grade security you can provide for the bay."

"We?"

"I'll explain when we get there—which should be mid-morning tomorrow local. I'm afraid I'm not sure how long we'll be using it."

"It's not a problem, Caleb. You know that. Is there anything else?"

"Yes, but we can talk about it when I see you. Thank you, Mia. I owe you."

She smiled to herself. "No, you don't."

50

Michael regarded the series of financial transactions on the screen with painfully narrowed eyes.

Now that the initial panic of the onset of war had faded a bit, he managed to find an hour here and there to return to the Atlantis investigation. Oh, the politicians were still panicking to be certain, at least when they weren't prematurely gloating about Seneca's inevitable and sure-to-be-swift victory.

There was less panicking over the potential alien invasion, but only because very few people knew about it and most of them weren't the panicking type. The continued silence from the special forces team sent to Metis to investigate worried him, but given the communication difficulties perhaps he was being impatient.

Agent Marano was at last on his way home, and with his prize of a companion no less; when they arrived he would turn his attention more directly to the matter. Until then....

He frowned at the screen. In fairness he had probably been frowning at it for some time now, in which case the frown deepened. As Assistant Trade Director and a *friend* of many corporations, Jaron Nythal maintained a healthy bank account nearly equal to his healthy expenditures. But if one mapped the patterns in his transactions over a long enough period—and it had taken considerable persuasion for him to get a warrant to review the man's accounts for said long enough period—recent unusual activity could be discerned. Barely.

Five deposits, three in the two weeks prior to the Summit and two in the four days following the assassination, totaled almost three hundred percent more than any previous deposit in the last five years. True, they were all for different amounts and from different payers. But it felt like they belonged together.

Two days after being released from questioning Nythal had purchased a fancy townhome in Pinciana. Prior to being pulled, surveillance had reported he toured four downtown condos on the market *after* purchasing the townhome.

As evidence went it was far from sufficient to prove anything, but his gut and years of experience told him the man had been paid off. The question was, for what?

He had studied Nythal's history, and one thing the man excelled at was *access*. Smoothing the way, greasing the wheels. But Candela didn't need help getting access to Minister Santiagar.

So who did?

⋒

Michael was leaning casually against the wall next to Nythal's office when the man arrived for work.

His step stuttered. "Mr....Volosk, is it? I don't recall us having a meeting this morning?"

"Oh, we didn't. A couple of final questions came up. Clean-up stuff really. I thought I'd stop by and we could take care of it quickly."

"Well I—" Jaron glanced down as he opened his door.

"Excellent, it'll only take a few minutes." Michael slid in the door in front of Jaron and settled in one of the chairs opposite the desk. He looked over his shoulder expectantly until the man circled around and sat uneasily across from him.

"So, um, what can I do for you?"

"Enjoying your new townhome?"

"What? I don't—"

"Never mind. I was curious about the different access levels in place at the Summit, and in particular the surrounding safeguards. It seems like the ballroom area where the dinners took place remained fairly open and unrestricted. So tell me about the requirements to get in."

"Your men staffed the security detail. Don't you know?"

"Humor me."

Jaron sniffed and kicked back in his chair. "Well, members of the delegation were granted admission to the area reserved for the

Summit. Some conference rooms required additional special clearance, and the private Alliance meeting rooms were off limits."

"Let's see..." he rubbed at his jaw "...we provided the pre-approved guests, corporate executives and media mainly, special admission codes. They also had to clear security and match the list each time. They were thoroughly investigated before being invited, of course—by your Intelligence Division, I believe."

"Right. Of course." Michael shifted in the chair, appearing to display some chagrin. "Though those 'guests' were recommended and submitted for approval by *your* Trade Division, yes?"

"I believe so, but it wasn't my responsibility so I can't be—"

"You're the Assistant Trade Director. If not your responsibility, then whose? The Director?"

"As a matter of fact, yes, he did make several specific requests and recommendations—"

"So you *were* involved in preparing the guest list, since you know the details."

"Uh...partially, as I have a number of contacts in the community, but...Mr. Volosk, I'm not sure I understand the point of all of this. Chris Candela committed the assassination. It's undisputed at this point, isn't it?"

Volosk tilted his head ever so slightly. "So it would appear."

"There isn't any other possibility, is there?"

He met Nythal's gaze. "No, certainly not. And with the war on, it hardly matters now anyway, does it?" He stood. "Like I said, merely some clean-up questions. If I find I have any more—clean-up questions that is—I'll just swing by for another quick visit."

"I have an extremely busy schedule, so it might be better if you made an appointment next time."

"Sure, sure, I'll try to do so if I can. I have an extremely busy schedule as well—the war and all—so I can't make any guarantees."

Michael smiled coldly. "I'll show myself out. Have a good day, Mr. Nythal."

Jaron waited until the door had closed to punch the chair in frustration. The soft leather-derived material gave with his fist, but it still hurt like a bitch. He shook his hand out while pacing in agitation across an office whose walls now threatened to close in around him.

He forced himself to wait five minutes, then another five, before leaving the office. Once outside he began hurrying down the street, but slowed as he realized he may be under surveillance. It seemed impossible—or rather would have seemed impossible until this morning. Now there lurked a cop in the eyes of every pedestrian.

But he only needed to get outside any possible electronic monitoring; then whatever surveillance he had could go fuck themselves for all the good it would do them.

When he reached the riverfront he stopped to purchase a breakfast gyro. A nice touch, he thought. He wandered over and rested against the railing, for all intents and purposes enjoying the blue-tinged morning light reflecting off the rippling water.

Instead he opened a very private address and sent a very simple message.

We have a problem.

51

"She did *what?*"

"She broke him out of the detention center. I didn't even know until I received a message from her. I checked into it, and the records show him being released last night on a technicality. The surveillance recordings have been doctored, I assume by her." Richard shook his head. "I didn't realize she was capable of such a sophisticated hack."

Miriam laughed, though it carried an almost poignant edge. She sank deeper into her chair and abandoned any pretense of formality. The door was closed, and he was her oldest friend.

"Trust me, she is. I probably don't need to ask, but what was her justification?"

"She again said he wasn't here to spy on us, but rather to help us and request help in return. Also that we needed to get over this war and focus on the real threat."

"She's gone then? I didn't warrant a message."

"Yeah, they're gone—at least there's a transponder record of the *Siyane* using an exit corridor early this morning. I suppose she could have hacked it as well, but it seems more likely they're actually gone."

"Well, that's fantastic." She paused to take a long sip of tea. "If she flies into the middle of this war and gets herself killed, I don't think I...David would never forgive me, were he here."

"It wouldn't be your fault, Miriam. He'd realize that, better than you."

"Maybe." She held the teacup to her lips and breathed in the steam until the bitter pang of loss, still biting after twenty-three years, subsided back into the recesses.

"I don't know. Perhaps I did rush to judgment with respect to her companion."

Richard regarded her with a look of incredulity. "You think?"

She rolled her eyes at the ceiling. "Fine. It is *possible* I overreacted a small amount. She just...she somehow manages to hit all my buttons, every damn time. I get so angry at her and I've no idea how to make her not be angry at me. Sometimes I wish..." her eyes closed "...I wish I could start over. But it's thirty-six years too late, isn't it?"

"You may not be able to go back, but it doesn't mean you can't start over."

"I'm not so certain...and regardless, now is hardly the ideal time for such matters." She ran a hand along her jaw and straightened up in the chair, shocked at the sentimentality she had allowed herself to display.

She busied herself refilling her teacup. "In any event, I've never known her to let sex interfere with her better judgment, so perhaps she is correct about his intentions. Which introduces a whole new set of concerns."

"You think she's sleeping with him?"

A small, arguably devious smile ghosted across her face. "I don't see why she wouldn't be. Do you?"

Richard's mouth opened, closed, then opened again. "Well, he's Senecan...."

"That excuse only works until you discover the person is merely an individual like any other."

His lips pursed together in a show of skepticism, but finally he gave up and chuckled in mild amusement. "Then no, I suppose I don't."

"I didn't think so." She sighed, and the momentary levity evaporated. "Listen, is there any way you can keep her out of trouble over this? Keep her from being implicated?"

It wasn't the first time she had asked such a favor of a colleague, though it was the first time she had asked it of someone so high-ranking, and someone who was a personal friend. But he was a personal friend of Alexis, too, and would want to protect her for his own reasons.

He shrugged. "I don't really need to. There's no evidence of her involvement—or any crime at all—beyond her message to me. Frankly, I'm inclined to simply stay quiet about the situation and let the record stand. He was released due to an administrative screw-up and that's the end of it. In the absence of a trigger it's unlikely the falsified records will be uncovered, and technically he hadn't committed a crime other than providing a false identification, so...."

She nodded. "Makes sense. It's a reasonable plan." She grimaced as a livecomm request appeared in her vision. After a pause she accepted it, but put it on broadcast.

"Admiral Solovy, apologies for disturbing you."

She cocked an annoyed eyebrow at Richard. "Dr. LaRose, what can I do for you?"

"Yes. I was wondering if you might possess another hard copy of your daughter's data I would be able to borrow."

She and Richard both frowned in mild dismay. She knew Alexis had sent her Metis report to the Science Advisor; she had even greased the wheels a bit, albeit to limited avail. Since the EASC Board had a direct line to the Prime Minister she had viewed it as mildly repetitive, but most things in government were. "I'm not sure I understand the problem."

His throat could be heard clearing over the comm. "One of my researchers took the disk home with him last night to study, and he didn't report to work today. It...well it seems he's gone missing, and your daughter's data with him."

"She has a name, Dr. LaRose, and a fair number of master's degrees as well."

"Apologies. Ms. Solovy's data. Admiral, I need another copy if possible."

Miriam frowned again. "You'll need to be more clear, Doctor. Don't you have her report?"

"No...I mean I *have* it, but I require a physical disk to move ahead with it."

"Why?"

"Why? Because I do. Regulation AAS 41767.239.0512c requires all reports be reviewed in physical form to verify their authenticity and—"

"Didn't you verify the authenticity of the physical disk when it arrived?"

"Immediately upon receipt. But I must also retain it in order to advance its contents to the next level to accompany my recommendation."

Miriam was silent a moment. She glanced out the window then at Richard. She muted the comm and laughed; it felt weary. "I must say, sometimes I can almost see where Alexis is coming from."

He tilted his head in agreement, and she scowled as she reactivated the comm. "Doctor, are you certain, given all the material you have reviewed and requirements you have followed, you *still* require a physical disk of the data to proceed?"

"Yes, I'm afraid so. You see the procedures are quite specific and—"

"Fine. Very well. I will send a request to the vault for our hard copy to be checked out. Of course we have our own procedures in place on this end, so it may take several days for you to receive it. In the meantime, I would highly encourage you to act on the information Alexis provided you to the greatest extent you find yourself capable of doing."

52

Alex waved her palm in the direction of the cockpit to check their location. "We should be at Romane in just over an hour."

Caleb came up behind her, one arm encircling her waist and hugging her tight against him while he reached around with the other and set her plate on the table. "Excellent, plenty of time for breakfast."

She laughed and squeezed his hand resting on her abdomen before extricating herself and sitting down. He had snuck upstairs while she showered and cooked panbrioche and roasted potato wedges and sliced up fresh grapefruit. She kept telling him he didn't need to do all the cooking, but he thus far was showing no indication of listening.

He retrieved his own plate from the counter and joined her at the table. She was already enthusiastically digging into what was a delicious breakfast; the panbrioche was so fluffy and tender she would have sworn he had spent the last two hours baking it if she hadn't been curled up in his arms for much of the last two hours.

He sat down, only to stare at his food. After a few seconds he picked up his fork—then set it back on his napkin and looked up at her. "Listen...before we arrive, there's something I need to tell you about Mia."

"She's your lover. I know." She smiled over her fork and slid a potato wedge into her mouth.

"What? No—I mean, not for several years now and—" His face screwed up at her. "*How* did you know?"

She shrugged, a hint of a twinkle in her eye. She did enjoy confounding him, even if the topic was bound to be mildly uncomfortable. "Something in the tone of your voice when you told me about her. It implied a...*familiarity* beyond that of a mere friend. You, um...well, you sounded like men do when they talk about women they've slept with."

"I did? Damn, I'm sorry." He cringed and dragged a hand down his mouth to linger at his jaw. "As I was about to say, it happened several years ago, and it was never serious. We met on a mission over a decade ago. She helped me out, I helped her out, and eventually we became friends. Then a little more. But it was a…I'd drop by when I was in town kind of thing. And after a while we realized we made better friends than lovers."

"Okay."

"I mean it. I wanted you to know, should the past come up—and because I didn't want to hide anything from you."

"Is she going to try to claw my eyes out?"

"*No*. She is not now, nor has she ever been, in love with me. She's far too savvy for anything such as that."

Alex nodded in acknowledgement.

He reached across the table and grasped her hand. "The important thing is, we can trust her completely. She may come off as a bit cold, but it's a defense mechanism. Mia's a good person."

She nodded again. "If you say so."

His eyes narrowed in suspicion. "Because you trust me."

"If you had intended to deceive me, you would have simply promised the ship would be safe on Seneca. There's no reason I can think of for you to go to all this trouble other than my peace of mind."

He sighed, let go of her hand and returned his gaze to his plate. "Right. As long as it's logical."

"What do you want me to say?"

"That you trust me."

Her gazed dropped to her own plate. "I told you, I trust—"

"Did you think I sleep with all the women and half the men on every mission?"

She swallowed a groan. Were they really going to do this? "The possibility had occurred to me."

"Well, I don't."

"Are you saying you never…?"

"No, I'm not. But I don't make a habit of it, and…frankly, I've rarely been in enough of a relationship for it to matter to anyone."

She leapt out of the chair and snatched her plate up to carry it to the sink. "Well I wouldn't want to start cramping your style now—" She cut herself off, wincing at how biting it sounded.

He appeared at her side an instant later. "No. You don't get to do that."

She didn't look at him. "Do what?"

"Project your worst fears about what I could be onto me as though they were somehow *real*."

Was he right? Was that what she was doing? The day before—and night—had been near to magical. Comfortable and romantic and affectionate and most decidedly hot. Despite the alien threat hanging over them, she had slept more soundly and peacefully entwined in his arms than she had in months. Now she was behaving like a drama queen, all bitchy and possessive?

She paused, her plate halfway to the washer rack; she set it in the sink and faced him. "You're right. And I don't care who you slept with, I truly don't. I'm glad you did—I'm getting to reap the considerable benefits of you honing your skills." She tried a little half-grin, but his expression refused to lighten.

"I'm sorry I snapped. You didn't deserve it. I'm merely on edge because of everything going on and, well, because I'm not entirely in control of my situation. I don't like being dependent on you— on anyone. But I'm not...you don't need to explain yourself to me. *Really*."

He reached up to run fingertips along the curve of her face. Damn but his touch still sent shivers up her spine. "What if *I* need to explain myself? I find I don't want you to think ill of me."

She shifted her head and placed a soft kiss on his wrist. "I don't. Promise. Now go get showered. We'll be there soon."

He regarded her for another moment, his expression unreadable, then nodded and headed down the stairs.

She sank against the counter and let her head drop to her chest. What was she doing? Jealousy and possessiveness weren't like her at all. They were both adults, and neither of them was coming into this without baggage.

Yes, she was edgy from not being absolutely and unquestionably in total control of her situation. But that was her problem, not his. If she didn't get her act together she was liable to run him off before whatever this might be between them had even gotten started good.

She took a deep breath and let it out, long and slow. Then she pushed off the counter and went downstairs, dropped her clothes on the floor, joined him in the shower and proceeded to make it very clear just how much she *didn't* think ill of him.

53

"Gold doubloon for your thoughts."

Richard smiled in response to the voice at his ear, relaxing momentarily against the arms at his shoulders. "Tell you what. Buy me lunch and I'll bare my soul."

"It's a deal."

He laughed a little as he turned from the window. "I should warn you, I'm a married man."

Will glanced over his shoulder as they followed the maître-d' to the table. "I'll keep that in mind."

After they had been seated and their glasses filled, Richard exhaled and leaned back in the chair. "Thanks for meeting me for lunch. It's a welcome respite."

Will shrugged while he studied the menu. "Well, since the Demeter project is on hold due to the war I find I have a bit of free time at the moment."

"Have you remodeled our house yet?"

"Not yet, but if I don't have a paying project by next week I'm not making any promises. I've been thinking the wall between the kitchen and the dining area is totally unnecessary."

"Fair enough." He paused. "You know, they're going to have to rebuild the base on Arcadia. Not that I'm eager to have you so far away, but if you're interested I can—"

"No." Will's head shook emphatically. "For one, I never want to trade on your name or position. For another, I would go insane inside of a week from the ridiculous bureaucratic entanglements and regulations and procedures of working for the military. I appreciate the thought, but no."

"Money isn't a concern. You *could* simply take it easy and relax for once. Radical idea, I realize."

The waiter interrupted them to place bread on the table and take their orders. The restaurant was fancy enough to eschew automated ordering for old-fashioned personal service. It was the sort of thing you didn't realize you missed until you encountered it again.

When the waiter had departed Will raised an eyebrow. "With a war on, soldiers dying, you working sixteen-hour days and aliens on the horizon? The guilt would be suffocating."

"Fine, I recognize when I'm fighting a losing battle." His voice trailed off as he studied his salad. He had told Will about Alex's troubling discovery, despite the fact it was classified information, because it's what married couples did—share things which truly mattered.

"So what is on your mind? Other than the obvious."

Richard blew out a breath through pursed lips. "The damned assassination. The Palluda attack. The war. I know, everyone else has moved on, but I've been in this line of work almost forty years now and nothing about any of it makes a lick of sense."

"Okay. Why?"

"Why? Let me count the ways...."

"Sure. Still, I'd be willing to bet there's one thing always jumping to the front of your mind. One niggling incongruity which sets off all the others."

He chuckled. The mind of an engineer at work, using structured failure analysis on every problem. The chuckle faded as he realized Will was, as usual, correct. "Okay. For starters, Candela. The assassin. Putting aside the fact he fits the profile of exactly zero assassins in history, which is another issue altogether, he made no effort to conceal his identity during the attack. Arguably he even flaunted it, leaving his fingerprints and DNA on half a dozen hands and practically mugging for the camera. So then—" he broke off when the waiter appeared with their lunch.

After taking a bite of the fried halibut he continued. "So then why did he work so hard to slip away unnoticed and elude the pursuit, only to commit suicide immediately thereafter?"

Will paused the spoon filled with chili just shy of his mouth. "Because he didn't want to spend the next year in an Alliance prison cell, paraded out every so often in shackles for the media and otherwise awaiting his execution?"

"Admittedly, a good reason. But he could have accomplished the same objective by stopping and pointing a weapon at one of the agents pursuing him, or attacking one. If he intended to die anyway, why was it so important he get away first?"

Will nodded intently; the matter had gained his attention now. "And if he intended to die anyway, why was it so important the world know *he* committed the murder?"

"Exactly." Richard ran a hand along his jaw. "There's something else. Alex showed up at Headquarters the other day with a Senecan intelligence agent."

Will's eyes shot up. An odd shadow passed through them; it was gone after a blink, though his brow had furrowed in surprise. "Are you serious?"

"Quite. We arrested him, she broke him out of detention, they've disappeared off-planet…it's a long story. But the most disconcerting part is, he claimed to be here to ask for our help. He and Alex believe the assassination was not sanctioned by any Senecan authority, nor the Palluda attack by any Alliance one— something I think Miriam is beginning to suspect as well. They insist the entire war is a setup perpetrated by someone else, though God knows who that might be."

"Damn." Will sank deeper in his chair. "Is there any chance they're right?"

"I…have to concede it's not outside the realm of possibility. Given all the questions surrounding these events, perhaps more than possible."

Will delivered a *look* across the table. Firm, almost challenging. "What are you going to do about it?"

"Ha." He swallowed. "Alex asked me for the autopsy reports on Santiagar. She seemed to think if the Senecans were able to examine the details they may be able to prove Candela wasn't the assassin."

"I'm guessing you didn't give them to her."

"I couldn't. It would be a violation of the Military Code and my professional responsibility and arguably treason. A senior

Alliance military officer passing classified files to a Senecan spy? I'd be dishonorably discharged, not to mention probably spend the rest of my life in prison."

"But Richard...what if they're right? Millions of people are going to die in this war, it's inevitable. What if you can prevent that from happening?"

He met Will's gaze and found it animated by a startling intensity. "What are you suggesting I do? Simply hand over the files and hope for the best?"

"Let me do it."

"*What?*"

"Give me the files. I'll send Alex a message—from the company even, something official-sounding related to her loft—and encrypt the files inside it. She's a smart girl, she'll figure it out. Or her spy friend will."

He reached over and grasped Richard's hand in his. "Look. I realize if it all goes off the rails you could still be implicated. But at least it will provide you some protection by putting a layer between you and the Senecans."

"Will, why would you do this? Why get involved?"

"Because I want to believe Alex is right. I want to believe this war is a mistake neither side intended. Call me crazy, but I want peace. I *don't think* the Senecans are bad guys—not en masse. And if there is an opportunity for us to save all those lives, I want to help make it happen."

A heavy breath fell from Richard's lips, until it felt like his lungs, his entire body, had become an empty void. He'd been a lowly major in the First Crux War, responsible for only a handful of soldiers and insulated from the weighty decisions which came with power. Now there was a chance, albeit a slim one, the fate of millions rested in his hands.

His eyes rose to find his husband's staring at him with affection, but also conviction. He nodded. "Give me two hours."

54

They had barely made it back upstairs in time for the approach and landing on Romane, on account of the unexpectedly extended and *amazing* shower.

Mia stepped through the hangar bay door seconds after Alex opened the hatch and they disembarked. He was certain she had been waiting outside and timed her entry appropriately. She wore a flattering yet conservative black pantsuit complemented by a silver top, her long black hair sleek and straight over one shoulder.

It still sometimes amazed him how thoroughly she had transformed herself from a scruffy street rat hacker and thief to a wealthy, respected businesswoman. He had meant it twelve years ago when he told her she showed potential beyond her circumstances, but the extent to which it had turned out to be true surprised even him.

She met them halfway and planted a quick kiss on the cheek. "Caleb, it's been too long." She had retreated before he could respond and was greeting Alex with an impressively genuine smile and extended hand. "Mia Requelme. It's a pleasure to meet you."

Alex accepted the proffered hand somewhat coolly, though he suspected it was no different from how she greeted most strangers. "Alex Solovy. Thank you for indulging us, and on such short notice."

Mia sighed in feigned drama. "I've learned by now with Caleb—it's always short notice. But it's no trouble. Very nice ship you have there. One of a kind, I'd wager."

"I'd like to think so."

"I've seen a lot of expensive ships pass through here. I suspect you are correct." She gestured to several control panels along the wall. "If you'll follow me, you can review our standard procedures and the special services we offer. I understand security is of utmost concern."

"It is."

Mia had clearly already surmised the ship was Alex's baby, the extra measures he'd requested were on her account and when it came to the ship she was the one in charge. The ability to size up a customer and their proclivities in a matter of seconds was no doubt one reason she had done so well for herself.

Satisfied things were on track to proceed relatively smoothly, he looked at Mia as they crossed the spacious bay together. The Class I bays were the largest and best-equipped offered, not merely by her but by anyone on Romane, and every aspect of it shone. "I don't suppose you happened to bring my pack I left here?"

"*Please*. It's in my office."

Alex had dived into the information at the control center, quite intently so. He drew to her side and leaned in close. "The pack contains some personal weapons and tools—I've sort of scattered extras across the galaxy, I'm afraid. Once I grab it, I am going to go buy some clothes, because I'm sure you are beyond ready to see me in anything other than this shirt. It's been a decent shirt, but I'm considering burning it."

She gave him a vague nod in response, her focus still on the details of the hangar bay. He looked over his shoulder. "Mia, after we run by your office can you come back and get Alex set up with what she needs?"

Her expression veered dangerously close to a smirk. "I'd be happy to do so."

He leaned in yet closer, squeezed Alex's hand and placed a delicate kiss at the base of her ear. It was important to him she feel comfortable in the situation, and know he was here for *her* and only her. "I'll be back soon."

Her eyes cut up at him with a distracted glance. "Okay. Have fun."

Mia spun around as soon as the door to her office closed to stare at him in disbelief and perhaps dismay. "Caleb, darling, what have you gotten yourself into?"

He crouched down beside the pack on the floor and unzipped it. He wasn't afraid she had removed anything, but he needed to remind himself of its contents. "I haven't the faintest idea what you're referring to, Mia *darling*."

"Miriam Solovy's daughter? Are you kidding me? I appreciate that you're adventurous, but I didn't think you were insane."

He chuckled darkly while he rummaged through the pack. "How the hell do you know who her *mother* is?"

She glared at him as if insulted. "I'm paid very well to stay current on many details regarding the power players in this little galaxy of ours. And your girlfriend's mother is one of them. You do realize you're at war against the Alliance now, right?"

He shrugged, zipped up the pack and stood. "Your point?"

She stepped forward and grasped his hands in hers. "I have a soft spot for you, Caleb. I always have. I don't want to see you get hurt."

He smiled. "They've already arrested me. What else can they do?"

She didn't. "They can kill you, for one."

"I'm much too good to let that happen. Don't worry. We'll be fine."

"We?" She dropped his hands and took a step back. "Oh my god, you're in love with her."

He exhaled harshly—more harshly than he had intended. "Don't be absurd. I—"

"You are, you're completely in love with her. I can't believe I didn't spot it immediately." She laughed. "I never thought I'd see the day, Caleb Marano in *love*. She really must be something."

"Just stop, okay? You don't know what you're talking about." She definitely did not know what she was talking about. How could she?

She nodded dramatically, eyes wide in mocking. "Of *course*, my mistake. Whatever you say."

"*Mia....*"

"No, I concede the point. You're not in love. Silly of me to even suggest it. Now I'd better get out to the bay lest your girlfriend start suspecting we're in here being bad."

He reached out and grabbed her arm as she turned to go. "Wait. We're renting a ship to take to Seneca, and odds are we'll be there a few days. There's something else I need you to do for me while we're gone. I'll pay you whatever you need for it."

"Caleb, you know I never charge you."

"You haven't heard what it is yet."

$\mathcal{R}$

Mia returned, sans Caleb, after several minutes.

She was rather beautiful, Alex thought. Objectively speaking. Of average height but with exquisite bone structure, her olive skin complimented vaguely Asian features. She carried herself with studied confidence, yet her eyes carried a hint of…Alex wasn't sure. Roughness? Grittiness? Though she gave a flawless impression of it, the woman had not been born into wealth. Of that much Alex was certain.

"How's everything look?"

"Excellent. You have a very sophisticated facility here. I must admit I'm impressed. But can we go over the additional security measures?"

"Absolutely." Mia opened a new display in one of the panels. "A cam monitors the door from the outside, which only I—and now you and Caleb—can access. As you see, this is the sole entrance to the bay except for airborne entry, but while the bay is occupied the force field is one-way. Your handprint here and this door becomes operable solely by you and I."

"And Caleb?"

"Not until he gets back here with his handprint."

"Right. Can it be DNA-coded as well?"

Mia raised an eyebrow but didn't otherwise balk at the request. "It can." Her fingertips manipulated the information on the screen, and a small drawer slid out from beneath the shelf. It held a brushed magnesium encoder.

Alex recognized its purpose and pressed her palm to it. A faint tingle against her index finger indicated the extraction of her DNA signature.

She glanced over at Mia, who was already pulling in the signature and configuring the door security. "So how did you meet Caleb?"

The woman's head tilted away as a guarded expression swept across her face.

"I don't mean to pry. If it's personal—"

"Sorry, gut reaction. My past isn't a topic I make a habit of discussing. But hell, why not. It's certainly been long enough." She added a small smile. "In short, he saved me. I was in the forced employ of the Triene cartel on Pandora, where I had run after I got tired of my father and brother using me as a mule to fence stolen goods—most notably when the last 'customer' got it in his head to relieve me of both the goods and my life."

"I'm sorry."

"It's fine. I stabbed him. I assume he died, but who knows. Unfortunately, I ended up in a situation which was little better. One day Caleb approached me seeking help to get inside the Triene compound. I agreed, and he gave me a ticket off-planet and some credits to get on my feet. He took the whole operation down, then checked up on me a while later. We became friends of a sort."

"Then more than friends."

"Ha...told you, did he?" She rolled her eyes and muttered something Alex couldn't make out under her breath. "Don't worry, it's all far in the past. But he is my friend, and I owe him my life. So...be gentle with him."

"I hardly think Caleb needs anyone to be *gentle* with him."

"You might be surprised." She transitioned the display to a new menu. "Here, we can also add a plasma cage around the docking area." A tap and a field shimmered to life in a box two meters beyond the frame of the ship. "And now I'm linking it to you as well. You can activate and deactivate it from here."

Mia paused, the corners of her mouth twitching. "What about you? How did you meet him?"

Alex cleared her throat awkwardly. "I, uh, shot down his ship and stranded him on a hostile planet...then rescued him from it."

"Nice!" Mia laughed; it was surprisingly rich and sultry. "That explains it."

"Explains what?"

"Why he's so taken with you. Other than the obvious of course."

She felt a bit flustered. Gabbing like teenagers about a guy wasn't an activity she commonly engaged in, or had honestly ever done—at least not with anyone other than Kennedy and even then only after several glasses of wine. "What do you mean?"

Mia leaned against the shelf, crossing her arms over her chest and relaxing her bearing. "There's something you need to under-stand about Caleb. He spends a lot of his time—professionally—

372 | G.S. JENNSEN

manipulating people. Finding their weaknesses and exploiting them. He's quite skilled at it, and it's kind of affected his opinion of people in general. It's not that he doesn't appreciate them—I suspect he's rather fond of humanity as a rule—but it of necessity puts him somewhat apart and above most of them."

She chuckled, seemingly to herself. "Very few individuals truly impress him, and the ones who do are unfailingly strong, independent and resourceful. And should someone actually get the better of him, well he'd be smitten for sure."

"Smitten?"

A mysterious grin grew on Mia's lips, as if she knew a secret and intended on keeping it. Okay, *that* was annoying. "Smitten." She pushed off the shelf and focused back on the display. "Any particular name you want the rental under?"

"I'm sorry?"

"Caleb said you'd be wanting the records doctored. I can choose a name at random, or one of the many corps, but I thought I'd give you the option."

Ever the spy...but he was right. A false name would make the ship more secure, especially should her hijinks at the detention center garner attention. "It's an excellent idea, but I'll let you choose. I'm not much with the spy games."

"Stick with him, and you will be."

"Everything go okay with Mia?"

"Hmm? Yeah, it went fine." She was preoccupied when she glanced up at him, but she had to smile at the new clothes. He wore charcoal casual slacks and a deep navy shirt unbuttoned over a tee of matching hue. The bag in his hand indicated there were more where these came from.

She wouldn't have thought it possible, but the choice of color made his eyes appear an even richer blue. "I like."

He dropped the bag on the floor and joined her on the couch. "Good. Something going on?"

"I'm not sure." She sent the message she had been staring at to an aural. "This came in a few minutes ago."

Ms. Solovy,

With respect to the proposed renovations to your residence, we have attached draft plans based on your specifications. Please review the changes and additions. We hope they meet with your approval.

Regards,

— W. C. Sutton Construction, Inc.

"W. C. Sutton is Will's firm...but I'm not doing any renovations to the loft."

"Who's Will?"

"Richard's husband. Might as well take a look at the plans." The attachment opened to display, as advertised, a blueprint of the layout of her loft. A series of alterations were marked in green. They included the addition of marble flooring to the entrance and dining area, an extension of the kitchen another meter and a half, new windows and an additional closet on the back wall of the elevated sleeping area.

"This is weird. I've never discussed the possibility of working on the loft with him. His expertise is large commercial projects, anyway."

"What's up with the windows? They look odd."

She zoomed in on the specs running along the side of the aural. "It says they're beveled...which is absurd. Who would put in beveled windows? They would totally obscure the view—and the view is the entire point of the windows."

"Well, either your friend Will isn't much of an architect, or...hang on a second. Select the center window."

The remainder of the blueprint blurred into the background as the center window came into focus. It consisted of a pattern of several dozen small beveled squares.

"There." He pointed to one of the squares in the lower left quadrant of the window. Now that she examined it, it did seem to contain a more intricate pattern than the others. She selected it, and the square enlarged to dominate the aural.

The pattern inside consisted of an ornamental capital 'A.'

"That's what I thought. It's a hidden message for you." She looked over quizzically; he shrugged in response. "Spy trick. You should open it."

"Right...." She raised an eyebrow at the image and tapped the 'A.' A dialog opened over it:

What was the title and composer of David Solovy's favorite musical piece?

A wistful smile tugged at her lips as she input the answer:

Capriccio Italien, Op. 45 by Pyotr Ilyich Tchaikovsky

A file popped out of the blueprint to hover in the air.

Autopsy Reports: Mangele Santiagar. September 15, 2322

She laughed in delight and sank against the cushion. "Crafty bastard. I knew I could count on him."

Caleb grasped her face in his hands and drew her in for a long, languorous kiss. He tasted of butter and caramel coffee. *Delicious.*

"You. Are. Wonderful."

"Little bit, yeah." She kissed him again before pulling back. "I talked to him after you were arrested. I told him about our suspicions and the information you were hoping for, but he said there was nothing he could do to help."

"Looks like he had a change of heart—unless this Will guy heard about your conversation and accessed the file himself."

"No. He's a construction project manager, not a spy. Besides, they're very close. This is Richard's doing. Here, let me send the file to you."

He rested his elbows on his knees and took a moment to study it. "The information's quite detailed, so hopefully it includes a key to breaking this whole mess open. But it's got Alliance security written all over it—no way will it pass through the defense net. We'll have to deliver it in person. Which is fine, because we can be in Cavare tonight."

He grinned at her, clearly pleased with the turn of events. "Let's go rent ourselves a ship."

55

Olivia smiled to herself as she toured the newly claimed facility, though she never allowed it to reach her lips. Outwardly she appeared stoically critical and discerning, inspecting every surface and corner for mistakes, flaws or merely a lack of optimization.

She gestured to a series of narrow slits running along the top of the right wall. "Replace those cooling vents. We have access to newer material at half cost. And make certain to get the correct grade for this type of production."

The manufacturing facility had been 'liberated' from the Shào cartel two days earlier, cleaned up overnight and the necessary renovations were now nearly complete. This particular location would increase her supply flow of illegal cybernetic enhancements—vision and reflex enhancers, body state interpreters, sleep deprivation modulators and cyberization overclocks, to name a few—all hyper-concentrated and boosted well beyond safe limits and all carrying a decent risk of blindness, muscular detachment or even catastrophic neural stroke.

It had been a good decision on her part to take what she needed rather than expend the time and effort to build a new plant. The war was heating up in earnest, and they were already seeing a noticeable uptick in demand for the sort of enhancements the plant would fabricate. Everyone wanted to gain an advantage in the rising chaos generated by the war; she was happy to supply them with the necessary tools to do so in whatever manner they saw fit.

She took a last look around the long rectangular chamber. Workers busily installed equipment on the primary production floor. Crates filled with components lined the walls, in many cases stacked almost to the ceiling. Enforcers guarded every door, inside and out; more stood watch in a hundred meter perimeter. Shào wasn't some street gang, and she didn't expect they would take the seizure of their property particularly well. There would be repercussions, but nothing her people couldn't handle.

"I've seen enough. Carry on. Contact me if you encounter any last-minute difficulties." She nodded to Gesson and headed for the lift to the roof, entourage in tow.

The muggy blue haze of a New Babel morning greeted her as she strode across the roof to her transport. She had a dinner date with the CEO of a pharmaceutical corporation, one who had displayed a degree of moral *flexibility* when it came to his business endeavors.

For the right price, she was confident he could be convinced to provide her the ingredients she required. Once combined with other ingredients from other pharmaceutical companies, legitimate and otherwise, the result would be a new variety of high-potency chimerals for the market, available exclusively through the Zelones cartel.

In the midst of the war, when death and destruction abounded, people inevitably sought a way to escape from it all. Yet another avenue of opportunity opening up thanks to the predictable incompetence and reactionary behavior of politicians.

That and a few well-placed missiles.

The colonized worlds which called themselves civilization represented a powder keg lying dormant for far too long. Apply the right amount of pressure and it would erupt into chaos. She could *feel* the galaxy beginning to convulse.

The transport rose above the industrial area and banked toward the spaceport. The pharmaceutical executive didn't dare risk being seen on New Babel, *of course*, so she was doing him the tremendous favor of traveling to Atlantis for the dinner. A one-time concession—but one time was generally all that was required.

An incoming message captured her attention as she was about to begin reviewing new cost analyses. On opening it her expression darkened to a scowl.

Ms. Montegreu,

Target refused the Vancouver job. He also discovered the contents of the parcel.

— Kigin

She instantly pulsed Kigin.

Is he dead yet?

Um, no, ma'am. I thought I should check with you for instructions.

My instructions are for him to be dead. Now.

Yes, ma'am. I'll take care of it.

She sighed and pinched her nose in annoyance. This was why plans existed, and why they should not be deviated from unless there was no other viable option. She succeeded in this business in part because she maintained plans for her plans, short and long-term strategies for numerous scenarios and multilayered schemes to be executed over years, even decades. Indulging ad-hoc modifications to meticulously crafted plans was a recipe for disaster which had brought down more than one otherwise brilliant leader.

She should not have done it.

The thought of informing Marcus his little 'opportunity' was a no-go crossed her mind for less than a millisecond before being dismissed. He insisted on QEC only, paranoid beyond reason about secrecy, and she did not remotely have the time to return to the office now.

And besides, she had made him no promises. She'd said she would make an effort to accommodate his last-minute special request, and so she did. Perhaps she might let him know when they next talked. But he had pushed the limits of their business arrangement in making the request, and she wasn't inclined to reward bad behavior.

She would, however, clean up the mess which had resulted though it was an inconvenience—because she, at least as much as he, held a vested interest in their arrangement continuing forward with great success.

56

Caleb started over to the small stairwell of the rental ship to tell Alex to dress warmly, as Cavare was quite cool at night—then froze when she ascended the stairs.

She was wearing a deep violet turtleneck made of a silky, shimmery material; when the light hit it hints of indigo and crimson rippled across the fabric. It was paired with sleek, form-fitting black pants and wedge-heeled black boots. Her hair was loosely pulled back to cascade over and behind her shoulders in waves. She had allowed a few strands to escape and frame her cheekbones. It was simple, functional and ordinary attire. It was *spectacular*.

She paused at the top of the stairs. One hand lingered on the railing. "What? Did I forget something?"

"You're beautiful." His voice came out soft and almost reverential. He had told her so the night before as well, while she had straddled him, naked in the starlight shining through the viewport above her bed. It was no less true now.

She blinked. "I...thank you. I didn't bring a lot of non-work clothes. Maybe I should have picked up a few things with you on Romane...."

He smiled and crossed the space to her, wrapping one arm around her waist while the other hand drew along her jaw. "You look beautiful in those, too, by the way. In case I haven't told you."

She appeared utterly flummoxed, which he didn't understand. He was certain he wasn't the first man to tell her she was beautiful. No computer algorithm would produce her features as the ideal example of beauty—they were too dramatic, too unique—but make no mistake. She *was* beautiful.

Finally she relaxed into him, her lips meeting his with a whisper. "You thinking flattery will get you in my pants?"

"That's the plan."

A beep in the cockpit signaled their initial approach to Seneca, and he reluctantly disentangled from her and went to the cockpit. It was a little odd him being in charge of the flying, and he knew she found it disorienting. But for the moment at least, this was his show.

"Wait—" he glanced over his shoulder at her, startled at the outburst "—are they going to let me through? Should I have, I don't know, procured myself a fake ID or something?"

"You've been cleared."

"What do you mean?"

"I mean you've been cleared. It's taken care of."

"Under my own name."

"Under your own name." He grasped her hand as she draped her arms along the headrest of the cockpit chair. "It'll be fine. Promise."

SENECA
CAVARE, INTELLIGENCE DIVISION HEADQUARTERS

They were meeting in a conference room on the first floor of Division Headquarters, for several reasons. This way Caleb wouldn't be running into a number of people who might be curious about where he had been and what he may have been up to. Also, Volosk wasn't exactly comfortable giving Alex a red carpet tour of Division's inner sanctum. From an outside perspective Caleb could understand the concern, so he didn't argue the matter.

He input the security code, which changed every twenty hours, and his own personal ID scan at the outer door and motioned for her to enter ahead of him. Two hallways and another door, then a final door and they reached the small conference room.

Volosk had been notified of their arrival and was waiting on them. He stood and shook Caleb's hand. "Agent Marano, glad to see you made it back in one piece."

"As am I, sir."

Volosk's gaze shifted to the left. "Ms. Solovy, I presume." He extended a hand in a more formal manner. "Michael Volosk, Director of Special Operations."

She graciously accepted the proffered greeting. "It's a pleasure to meet you."

He gestured to the table and they took up seats opposite him. Caleb clasped his hands on the table and leaned forward. "I'm sending you a file I think you will find most useful."

Volosk raised an eyebrow, but his expression transformed once he received the file. His eyes unfocused for a solid ten seconds before his attention returned to them. He smiled in what looked like relief but was definitely appreciation.

"You have my sincere gratitude—both of you. As soon as we're done here I'll start analyzing this information. Perhaps...well, let's not get our hopes up too high, but perhaps we can do something about the current state of affairs. For now, though, we should talk about Metis."

Alex caught Caleb's gaze briefly, then reached in her pocket and removed a small crystal disk. The pause was almost imperceptible before she slid the disk across the table. "A hard copy of all the raw data we collected."

He accepted it with the deference it deserved. "Thank you." His head tilted in contemplation. "Alliance leadership also has this information, I take it?"

"They do."

"If I may ask, is there anything you're comfortable telling me in regard to their response?"

"Chush' sobach'ya...." She cleared her throat. "Pardon me. They said they will monitor the situation."

He smiled, though it came off a bit cold. "They're hoping the aliens will attack us first so they can take advantage of the opportunity."

This pause was noticeable. "Something to that effect."

"And how do you feel about their response, Ms. Solovy?"

She met his stare evenly, without flinching. "I'm here, aren't I?"

He dipped his chin to concede the point. "Fair enough. I meant no offense."

Caleb squeezed her hand under the table. "What's the word from the GOI platoon we sent to investigate? Did they find the alien ships?"

Volosk's lips pursed. "We've had no word from them since they entered Metis four days ago. As communications are not possible inside the Nebula, it's too early to draw any conclusions. They may simply still be investigating."

"I imagine they had instructions to deploy drones back out with updates?"

The man's expression was admirably neutral. "They did."

Shit. He *told* them it was too risky to send an entire platoon in, he didn't care if they were stealth special forces. "I see. Hopefully you'll hear from them soon."

"I hope so as well." The uneasy silence lingered only a breath longer than what was comfortable. "So I've reviewed your report, but if you don't mind I'd like to go over a few details." His eyes roved over each of them; they each shrugged in acceptance.

"Your spectral analysis of the ships' composition—it returned no matches, correct?"

"Correct." She nodded, intrinsically slipping into expert mode. "Chemically, the closest equivalent is lonsdaleite diamond, but this metal is far darker in color than lonsdaleite and isn't appreciably close to a match. Whatever the metal is, it appeared quite dense and strong. Unfortunately, the sole other fact we've determined with any certainty is that the ring is constructed of a similar but not identical material."

"Okay. So we're looking at previously undiscovered elements then. And regarding the electromagnetic waves, you suggested the terahertz signals might be a form of communication. Can I ask what your thinking is?"

"Again, it's merely speculation, but a couple of things. For one, the signal was hyper-precise—focused and compressed, with no detectable bleed. This means it wasn't an emission byproduct of their technology and was clearly being used for *some* purpose. Also, Metis doesn't have significant background terahertz radiation—but in the portal region the terahertz waves were pervasive. And lastly, because we don't use it for communications. It might not occur to us to eavesdrop on the band."

"Hmm." He nodded deliberately. "Not bad as reasons go." He was quiet a moment before shifting his attention to Caleb. "Where do you think the portal originates?"

It would be the question for him. There were no hard, objective facts or data to rely upon—pretty much no information whatsoever in fact. Nothing but instinct and observation skills born of experience, and a dash of inborn talent.

"Another dimension."

"Are you serious?" The eyebrow transformed from appreciation to skepticism.

"It may very well lead to the other side of the Milky Way or just as likely to another galaxy. But here's the thing—and I'd never have thought of it if Alex hadn't raised the idea of a dimensional portal as a conceivable possibility—the portal had to be built. And as impressive as those superdreadnoughts are, they are miniscule compared to the portal. Building it must have been a tremendous undertaking for even highly advanced aliens."

He straightened his posture, caught up in the argument. "So why send the workers and machinery and materials to build the portal across the galaxy or universe via conventional means—why spend all the time and effort—to build a shortcut? How much more time would it have taken to simply send the ships instead?"

He sensed Alex regarding him curiously. He hadn't actually had the opportunity to share his theory with her. There had been escapes to execute and sex and planning and organization and sex and meals to cook and...*well*. He grinned at her with a corner of his mouth.

Volosk, however, was frowning. "I can imagine plenty of explanations. The personnel and fuel involved, to name one."

"Absolutely. I concede the point. But I think it's safe to assume these aliens possess the capability to travel at least as rapidly as we can. So say they're from the other side of the galaxy. At most it's forty or so Galactic days' travel, in no way a trip worthy of building an expensive magic portal instead. If on the other hand we're talking another galaxy, the trip is nearly half a year at a minimum and in all likelihood far longer, in which case why expend the time and manpower to send the builders but not the fighters?"

He leaned in and dropped his elbows on the table. "And what fighters? Granted, there *could* be soldiers, organic beings of some sort, inside the dreadnoughts or the tentacle ships—hell, they probably *are*. But we saw zero evidence of them." He lifted a hand in preemptive protest. "Before you say it, I agree you wouldn't see us from the outside of our fleet either. Still, there was a feeling, an impression the ships evoked...like nothing was present that lived and breathed."

He shrugged, consciously dialing down the fervor. "Either they travel very slow and thus need the portal, which contradicts their otherwise obviously advanced technology, or they travel very fast, which obviates the need for the portal at all. Unless it was the only way."

Volosk was silent for a long time. Finally he nodded. "Decent assertions—except for one point. If the portal is the only way, how did its builders get here?"

Caleb bit his lower lip. "I'm no expert on hidden dimensions, but...I'm not certain they would need to."

A ponderous silence again lingered for a moment, until Volosk chuckled wryly. "Well, for now we should focus on how to defend against them. More esoteric musings can wait for the victory party."

He straightened up in his chair, as if he had convinced himself of the rightness of his conclusion. "I'm trying to arrange a meeting with Delavasi and the Defense Director for later tonight, though their schedules are unsurprisingly rather full. If the two of you can remain available for the next several hours, I'd appreciate it. I'll let you know as soon as I hear anything definitive."

He stood and leveled a keen gaze at Caleb. "Until then I must get back to the details of managing an..." he managed not to glance at Alex "...unfortunate war. Agent Marano, until further notice your sole mission is the investigation of these aliens and matters related thereto."

"Of course. Any special instructions?"

"In the brief time I've worked with you, I have come to realize one thing. Of all our agents, you are the last person who needs micromanaging. Act as you see fit—but do try to avoid blowing up any more Division starships if at all possible."

"I'll do my best, sir. Though in fairness, the last one was *her* fault."

57

The basement command center of Earth Alliance Headquarters remained a flurry of activity on this, the sixth day of the Second Crux War.

Aides ensured the secure files were loaded and all necessary information available, the refreshment table was fully stocked and the EM shielding field was in place and active. The noise amplified off the reinforced walls to create a din above which it was difficult to carry on a normal conversation.

The Chief of Staff's arrival in the bunker served as the aides' cue to depart the immediate area surrounding the situation room. They filed past the woman and dispersed—some upstairs to their offices, others to stations elsewhere in the command center to monitor war developments.

Marcus Aguirre exited the lift alongside Prime Minister Brennon. They continued their conversation as they walked down the long hallway. "Yes, sir, I believe under the regulations you definitely have the authority to appropriate the necessary—" Upon reaching the situation room he cut himself off. "But we can discuss it in the meeting." He stepped to the side and allowed Brennon to enter the room ahead of him.

The Assembly Speaker and Chairman of the Armed Forces Committee had already arrived, along with the Defense Minister. Marcus went over to the hutch in the rear of the room and poured himself a glass of water before taking his seat a third of the way down the conference table. He presented himself as reviewing materials for the meeting while he discreetly observed the others through the translucent screen.

Speaker Barrera was a long-time acquaintance and political ally. They had met for dinner two nights earlier; it was a timely reaffirmation of their alliance and a subtle reminder to the Speaker of favors Marcus had granted him in the past. It could be argued the Speaker owed Marcus for his position, but he never spoke of it aloud. He didn't need to. Such was the way of the political game. Besides, the debt would come due soon enough.

The Armed Forces Chairman was a sharp one. Retired military, he had earned several medals of valor for his service during the First Crux War. He held his current position for those accomplishments, not on account of any political skills. So though he deserved keeping an eye on, realistically he should be out of his league in the coming maneuvers.

Defense Minister Mori spoke quietly with the Chief of Staff across the table. Mori was weak, a bureaucrat when he had been in the military and even more of one in the government. Any military influence he had was far overshadowed by EASC. But he was an unabashed Senecan opponent; as such, his intense dislike of the enemy may prove useful. The Chief of Staff, on the other hand, was shrewd and highly intelligent, and loyal to Brennon to a fault. She had been at the man's side for over twenty years, since his early political campaigns.

He glanced up as the Foreign Minister walked in, followed by—

Well this was a complication.

Mori slid his chair back and rose to salute. "Admiral Solovy, it's a pleasure to see you again. I take it General Alamatto is otherwise engaged today?"

Miriam Solovy nodded politely. "Yes, he spent the afternoon on the Orbital meeting with the Regional Commanders. He's returning now, but would be unable to arrive here in time. He sends his regrets."

Alamatto was supposed to be *here*, and thus out of danger. He could control Alamatto. *Solovy* was supposed to be in Vancouver, sitting in her office at EASC Headquarters like a good girl.

His face maintained a perfect mask while he tamped down his annoyance and considered his options. It didn't take long, because for the moment he had none. He couldn't call off the operation now if he wanted to—and he didn't want to, as to do so would cause far more complications than it solved. He considered trying to waylay Alamatto and delay his arrival in Vancouver...but he personally didn't have a viable way to make it happen, and those who might were not currently available.

It would be a setback, but a minor one. The primary objective and several secondary ones would still be achieved. And Solovy would soon find herself facing her own difficulties in any event. He did need to factor her continued presence into matters and formulate countermeasures, but it would have to wait.

Brennon signaled for the meeting to begin with a glance around the table. "Thank you for coming, everyone. The purpose of this meeting is to review the state of affairs one week into hostilities and discuss our strategy going forward."

His smile beamed across the table as though the room were populated by constituents. "First, the good news. Admiral Solovy?"

Solovy spared a small nod for Brennon. "Thank you, Prime Minister. As you are all likely aware, four days ago we destroyed fifteen major Senecan hyperspectral scanners, significantly crippling their ability to track our military movements and buildups. With heightened defense measures now in place we don't expect them to be able to replace the lost surveillance capabilities in the foreseeable future.

"Also, I'm pleased to report Admiral Rychen's forces engaged the Senecan detachment responsible for the attack on Arcadia and achieved a decisive victory near Desna. It was the first head-to-head battle of this conflict and represents a clear win for the Alliance."

"Excellent news, Admiral. Minister Mori?"

The Defense Minister frowned; it was an unpleasant expression on his thin lips and pinched chin. "Unfortunately, it isn't all good news. Five hours ago a Senecan strike force destroyed the production facilities of Surno Materials on Aquila. Surno was our largest supplier of the metamaterials used in the construction of Alliance starships.

"Now while this isn't an immediate emergency, it is inevitable we will suffer losses in the war and will need to replace ships. I've recommended that we invoke Regulation ERS 26608.577.2034g and appropriate fifty percent of the production output from the five next largest manufacturers of the relevant metamaterials."

Marcus cleared his throat. "I've advised the Prime Minister he does have the authority to do so under said Regulation. There is, however, public perception to consider as well. We don't want the government to appear too heavy-handed this early into the conflict."

Mori shrugged. "What are our other options?"

Solovy shifted her posture in an indefinable way which somehow increased her presence at the table. "We can approach the suppliers as customers and negotiate new contracts."

"Ha!" Mori snorted. "Wartime is not the place for capitalism. We require the materials. That should be the end of discussion. Surely you recognize this, Admiral?"

"*Surely.*"

"Yes, well." Brennon nodded. "I will make a decision later today. Admiral, do our military forces have any further pressing requirements?"

"Many, sir, but we are addressing them."

Brennon smiled a little. "Of course you are. Now we should probably move—"

"Sir, if I may, there is one additional matter we should discuss."

If Brennon was taken aback by the interruption, he gave no sign of it. "Certainly, Admiral."

Solovy looked around at the others. "Forgive me if I'm stating the obvious, as I don't often have the opportunity to attend these meetings, but the information I'm about to share cannot leave this room."

Marcus had a deep suspicion as to the nature of the information and swiftly made an effort to deflect it. "Admiral, if this information is so sensitive perhaps it would be better if it were handled offline, with a smaller group?"

Her gaze snapped to him, and he felt a faint shiver run up his spine. "Mr. Attorney General, is this not the Select Military Advisory Council? Is this not the most secure location in Alliance space? I was under the impression there *was* no 'smaller group' with which to consult."

"It is all of those things. Nevertheless, it might be more—"

Brennon's hand extended out on the table. "She's correct, Marcus. We are all trustworthy here. Let her speak."

Son of a *bitch*.

"Thank you, sir. The visuals I'm going to show you were taken inside the Metis Nebula just over one week ago."

58

SENECA
CAVARE

"We have a couple of hours before Volosk will be able to pull off a meeting." Caleb grabbed Alex's hand and tugged her into the parking lot. "You impressed me right and proper on Earth. Give me a chance to impress you."

Her eyes slid away with a grin. "Okay. Where are we going?"

"It's a surprise."

She followed him to the bike, giggling under her breath as she draped the wrap on her neck and activated the helmet, threw a leg over the bike and grasped him tightly around the waist. It was every teenage girl's wild, rebellious fantasy: speeding off on a sleek, sexy bike holding onto her sexy renegade. She would never admit to it being one of *her* fantasies, but...it didn't suck.

The air carried quite a chill whipping past as they sped through a rather impressive downtown area. She snuggled closer against him.

Everything looked as though it had been built in the last two years; it all still carried the gleam of *newness*. And the city was large, far larger than she had been led to believe. The streets bustled with foot, vehicle and air traffic and all the hallmarks of a vibrant, lively culture. It didn't come close to comparing to the Atlantic Met, nor half a dozen other metropolitan areas on Earth. But it did have a freshness and vivacity to it she hadn't expected.

It was a few short minutes before he slowed and veered into another parking lot, to her mild disappointment. Then she saw the reflection of Seneca's enormous moon in the river across the street and grinned yet again. She climbed off the bike and wandered to the water's edge while he secured it.

He sidled up behind her, his arms encircling her waist as his chin rested on her shoulder. "Pretty, isn't it?"

She drew in a deep breath and savored the feel of him pressed against her, of his arms wrapped around her. She could get used to this, and quickly. "Very."

"Come on." He grasped her hand and again tugged her along.

"This wasn't what you brought me to see?"

"Uh, no."

They entered an outdoor market and entertainment area. Mellow synth strains, the hum of the crowd and pleasant aromas from several restaurants and grill stands filled the air, but he continued to lead her on past all the tempting diversions.

The crowd began to thin and they veered back toward the river. In the distance she saw several tall, glittering arches. Beneath the arches the water gained a faint glimmer.

They approached a simple kiosk. He manipulated the display a moment and gestured toward the water.

A small personal craft had appeared out of nowhere alongside the ledge. It had a very minimal structure, flat save for sides which bowed up maybe a meter high and containing only two cushioned couch-like seats.

"After you."

She raised an eyebrow at him but stepped in and sat down. He joined her, and the craft glided forward.

"Are you driving?"

"I could, but no, it's automated for the moment."

"Where does it go?"

"The lake."

She waited, but no more information was forthcoming, so she shifted to check out the view of downtown. The lights from the many skyscrapers reflected in warping patterns along the river, though the reflection of the moon continued to dominate. "It really is a beautiful city, Caleb."

"It is. You should probably turn around now."

"Hmm?" She twisted again in the seat. They were now passing under the first arch. It was a mammoth sculpture of bronze, copper and brushed graphite, wound through by golden optic fibers. It towered nearly a quarter kilometer above them at its peak. Already the next arch was in sight, and beyond three more arches a brilliantly lit structure rose out of the water.

She realized the river was now widening rapidly, and also had begun to...glow. Faintly at first, yet brighter with every meter. She looked over at Caleb curiously. "Bioluminescence?"

He had kicked back in his seat, his legs stretched out along the floor and ankles crossed leisurely. His hands were clasped behind his head. "Of a sort. You ready?"

She laughed incredulously. "For *what*?"

His eyes twinkled in amusement, revealing an infinite recursion of facets cut into their sapphire hue. She only tore away from them when a field shimmered into existence, extending up from the edges of the craft high enough so they were able to stand within it.

Then the craft began to submerge.

"What...?" Her voice drifted off, stunned into silence.

Fully submerged beneath the surface and still moving forward, they became enveloped by an incredible white-blue luminescence. The closest comparison was phosphorescent algae, but she discerned no trace of even miniscule particles. The water simply *glowed*, more intensely than any nebula.

The material composing the craft turned out to be a transparent glass material. She stood, and was surrounded in every direction by the radiant splendor. The field was all but invisible, giving the impression she could reach out and immerse fingertips in the water. Colorful fish sporting metallic scales and tiny eyes periodically swam past them. One tried to swim into the craft and collided with the field, causing a slight ripple across it as the fish jerked back in surprise.

"Caleb...." She turned to find him watching her, a delighted smile on his face and a look in his eyes that sent a wicked flutter through her chest.

She plopped in his lap and wound her arms around his neck. "*Okay*. Congratulations, you've impressed me."

"Good," he whispered against her lips. "And we're not even done yet."

"No?"

"Nope." He motioned in the direction ahead of them and she somewhat reluctantly pulled away to see.

What she presumed was the large structure she had seen from the surface extended deep beneath the lake as well. As they approached, it became obvious it continued down at least thirty levels. Hundreds if not thousands of people milled about on the other side of the glass. Restaurants, several dance clubs and numerous shops could be made out as their craft circled and docked.

The field surrounding the craft vanished, and they were inside. She stepped out behind him.

This was clearly a high-class entertainment hub. The patrons tended to be well-dressed in expensive attire, though there was the occasional throng of slacker teens among the crowd. The noise level was considerable due to the enclosed environment, but not so loud she was unable to hear him beside her. As they strolled along the curving path, the floor-to-ceiling glass revealed the luminescent waters unmarred. It was actually so bright there was almost no lighting inside.

"Do you want to get some dinner?"

Her eyes cut over to him. "Why, yes I do."

He laughed and guided her toward the outside of the wide walkway. A moment later they stepped on a lift cut into the glass wall. It sped upward, swooshing past water rushing in the opposite direction. The lift broke through the surface and continued up another forty levels or so.

Then they were in the open air. A cool breeze from the lake far below drifted over them, yet the space felt warmed in some artificial manner.

The roof consisted entirely of a restaurant, complete with white tablecloths and optic candles. Though it seemed full to capacity, they were nevertheless shown to a table bordering the outer edge. Nothing blocked their view of the glowing lake below or the cityscape in the distance. The moon above them appeared close enough to reach up and touch.

She spent a good thirty seconds looking at the sights, peering down the sheer cliff of glass and twisting about in her seat, so much so she was surprised when a bottle of wine arrived at the table.

She settled back in the chair and eyed him suspiciously but playfully as he poured her a glass. "Okay, how did you get this table?"

His lips curled up in a sly smirk. "It's possible I went to primary with the restaurant manager."

"Well." She regarded him over the rim of her glass. When she spoke, her voice came out uncharacteristically soft. "I'm sorry we tried to destroy this place."

"Alex, that isn't what this is about—I mean, yes, I hoped you might realize we're not the enemy, but—"

"I know. And I'm...I'm sorry I wanted us to destroy this place."

His smile was exceptionally gentle. "Apology accepted."

She glanced around again briefly before returning to his gaze, to find it had never left her. "So what *is* this about then? I feel like I'm being wooed, but I think we're a little beyond that stage."

"Are you complaining?"

"Nooo."

"I'm glad." He reached across the table and took her hand in his. "I know you're out of your comfort zone. I recognize it isn't easy for you to follow someone else's lead. And I just want you to know I appreciate it, and maybe convince you it doesn't always have to be so bad."

She squeezed his hand. "There's certainly nothing bad about all this...in fact, I'd say it's pretty damn wonderful."

59

Richard strode brusquely toward the Archives building. The late afternoon sun at his back almost hinted at warmth in the moments before it would drop below the horizon.

Much as Miriam had expressed the previous day, he found himself ruing the…extensiveness…of Alliance regulations. The assassination investigation having been closed on account of the war and the obvious-to-everyone perpetrator, all the files pertaining to it—thankfully except for the medical files due to a few test results still outstanding—had been moved to Archives and personal copies ordered scrubbed. Because that was how things were done.

Thus his trek across the EASC campus over to the Archives to review the files there. He would not be allowed to check them out and take them to his office. Because that was how things were done.

Alex's insistence that the assassination, the entire war, was a setup had troubled him even prior to his lunch with Will. Seeing as he'd now arguably committed treason against the Alliance on a bet she might be correct, it seemed a good idea to look deeper into the matter on his end as well. If he—

The blast of heat hit his back before the sky brightened, which was odd—nearly as odd as his brain insisting on noticing such details above far more dramatic ones.

Maybe he was simply too close for the difference in speed to be noticeable.

Yes, that must be it.

He spun around at the same instant as he was thrown tumbling through the air by an invisible force.

He caught the briefest glimpse of the towering, white-hot ball of flame pluming into the sky just as the sun began to set beneath the water and he—

When he regained consciousness—slowly, groggily—the flames clawed at the heavens, but they were increasingly obscured by the thick smoke which now roiled across the broad courtyard toward him.

He scrambled backward on his hands and heels to escape the approaching smoke, which was of course a ludicrous thing to do. The smoke surged over him in a massive wave, choking his lungs and stealing the breath from them.

Shouts and screams cut through the haze in the air and in his mind, closer than the roar of the flames and screeching metal reverberating from everywhere and nowhere.

Feet pounded against the stone of the courtyard. People running. Panicked.

It occurred to him he had been almost to the Archives.

If he could get inside then perhaps he could breathe. Perhaps he could live.

He crawled to his feet...and realized the smoke was far too dense to determine in which direction the Archives was located.

The lack of oxygen spread foggy tendrils into his brain, mucking up the works and colliding with spots of yawning blackness from what must be a concussion.…

He somehow managed to call up a map overlay on a whisper.

That way.

He half-ran, half-stumbled twenty meters and fell through a door and into merciful darkness.

※

Hands reached down and helped him up.

He coughed smoke out of his lungs. His vision began to clear. Breath by breath his mind sharpened the fog away.

His head hurt like the devil and he suspected he'd fractured his right shoulder. But he was able to think again, and thus allow the soldier within to push aside the terror and take control.

Smoke obscured everything beyond the glass doors. A quick glance around indicated those in the lobby appeared largely unhurt, so he rushed to the lift and headed for the top floor.

The Archives building stood only thirty-five stories, but it should be tall enough to get above the worst of the smoke. When the lift slowed to a stop he hurried to the windows, ignoring the sharp jolts of pain shooting along his shoulder and neck.

The once-towering Headquarters building was fully consumed in flames and crumbling in on itself. One corner of the foundation was completely blown out, causing the structure to list and gradually sink into the gap. Midway up and again near the two-thirds point where the flames burnt strongest, entire sections of the frame were missing, sending the higher floors canting back the other way.

The destroyed building had acquired a ragged, zigzagged appearance. It reminded him of a child's haphazardly constructed tower of blocks right before it collapsed.

He used his ocular implant to capture several visuals, because the tower in front of him would also soon collapse, and he may be one of the few people seeing this particular vantage.

As the adrenaline continued to dissipate he studied the scene with a more critical eye. Based on his experience, it looked as though high-powered explosive charges had detonated at the base in the front left corner as well as at strategic points throughout the building.

No way did explosives get past security into the building—which meant the bombs must have been assembled inside.

They had traitors in their midst.

A renewed war. Aliens on the approach. Now insurrection from within. Had Alex and her Senecan companion been more horrifically right than even they imagined?

The sirens of emergency vehicles rose above the rumble as craft began circling overhead. There was certainly plenty of water available to douse the fire…but there was also a *lot* of fire.

God, how many people had been in the building? Five thousand? Six? Many would still be alive and trapped. Rescue personnel were already dropping beneath aircraft and attaching themselves to the burning, dangerously crumbling walls.

The pulse leapt into his vision, startling him out his reverie.

Richard! Are you there? Are you okay?

Miriam. Yes, I'm fine. I was over at the Archives. Are you still in Washington?

On the way back. What's the situation? There's been an attack on HQ?

Oh, Miriam...I'm afraid it's far worse than a simple attack.

What do you mean?

Headquarters is gone.

There was a weighty pause.

I'll be there soon.

When the connection ended he dragged a hand down his face; it came away coated in soot and blood.

Miriam possessed inside information, but the news would be hitting the exanet any second now, if it hadn't already. He took a deep breath and pulsed Will.

60

They strolled along the promenade, Alex's hand wrapped snugly in his. Dinner had been delicious and romantic, and the return trip beneath the lake's surface doubly so. Caleb wanted nothing more than to whisk her away to his apartment and spend several hours ravaging every single centimeter of her lovely body. But alas, there was still work to be done. *Later, however....*

"Do you think we—" He broke off mid-sentence, frowning at the abrupt, unnatural movement of people toward one of the nearby exanet news broadcast screens. They instinctively joined the crowd, though he was also pulling up his own customized news feed.

The large screen showed an aerial view of an island in late evening light. An uneasy sensation rippled through his skin; the location looked uncomfortably familiar, though it was difficult to be certain due to the remainder of the scene.

A towering pillar of copper and crimson flames roiled to engulf a high-rise and lick at the sky. Dense clouds of smoke billowed out from the structure to flow over the island. Scattered strewn debris and huge chunks fallen from the edifice decorated gaps in the smoke. At least a dozen emergency craft circled in the air above, many dangling rescue responders beneath.

"This footage is from Earth Alliance Strategic Command in Vancouver, where fourteen minutes ago a series of massive explosions rocked the building which houses—"

"Alex, you—" She thrust a palm into his chest, holding him at bay. Her gaze was unfocused, her stance rigid. He watched her instead of the footage.

It was a full ten seconds before she exhaled and focused on him, her features losing a mere fraction of their tautness. "She's safe. She was traveling from Washington. Richard's safe, too, though he had a much closer call."

She ran a hand down her face as her attention was drawn inexorably to the screen. "Caleb...."

"I know." Had his government done this? In war everything constituted fair game, but it nevertheless struck him as incredibly dirty tactics. A hell of a lot of noncombatants worked in that building. On the other hand, wiping out a good portion of Alliance military leadership in one fell swoop would definitely knock them on their heels, sowing confusion and perhaps chaos. Arguably a brilliant tactic...but still dirty.

He grasped her shoulder. "Let's get to some place quieter where we can find out what's going on."

She nodded in agreement, but her eyes were clouded and troubled. He honestly couldn't blame her.

The crowd thinned then vanished as they wound their way to the end of the riverwalk, up the stairs and across the street to the parking lot. It was dark and maybe a third full.

The hairs on the back of his neck stood on end. It was too dark. Some of the lighting had gone out—which was impossible unless it had been deliberately eliminated.

A shadow moved in the corner of his vision.

Another deep in the recesses of the lot.

All his senses sharpened into hyper-focus as nanobot-aided adrenaline flooded his veins and fueled his limbs to enhanced speeds.

"Get down!" He shoved her behind one of the skycars the same instant a laser streaked between them from the left.

She landed on her hands and knees next to the car door. He crouched beside her but kept his focus outward as infrared augmentation activated in his ocular implant. Not wanting to risk a sound, he pulsed her. *Stay here.*

He drew his kinetic blade out of its sheath and flicked it on as a heat signature grew at the front edge of the vehicle. He crawled forward, staying low and against the frame.

When a foot appeared at the rim, he grabbed it and yanked to send the attacker sprawling to the ground. In one fluid move he landed on top of the man, knocked the Daemon from his hand and slid the blade in beneath his ribcage and up into his heart.

As soon as he felt it pierce the heart he pulled it out, picked up the Daemon and sprinted to the next nearest vehicle.

The shadow he had seen in the rear of the lot moved closer. This one was cloaked, but in infrared he saw the faintest shimmer to indicate the outline of a person. He rose and aimed over the top of the roof.

One shot, center mass. The outline collapsed.

He immediately scanned the vicinity for more targets. Nothing...nothing...*there*. A heat signature slinked along the wall on the other side of the lot.

Toward Alex.

He flung the Daemon against a vehicle three rows over and ducked to sprint back. The racket succeeded in momentarily distracting the attacker, who paused to glance in the direction of the sound.

By the time the man resumed advancing Caleb had reached him. He grappled him from behind and with a fierce wrench snapped his neck.

He dropped the body and kneeled beside her. "Are you okay?"

She nodded weakly, staring at him in the darkness with wide eyes and dilated pupils. A knot of dread began pooling in his chest. He didn't—

"Behind you!" It came out as a cracked whisper of a shout.

He spun as he stood, right leg swinging up with the motion.

His heel smashed into a wrist and jarred a Daemon out of the attacker's grip as it fired. The laser stream skidded off the hood of the skycar, cutting the front in two and burning across the wall of the neighboring building.

His opponent delivered a left hook to his jaw. His head jerked, but the overload of adrenaline meant he didn't notice the jolt of pain. He kneed the attacker in the stomach while he shifted his grip on the blade, then plunged it into the man's gut.

The attacker stuttered in surprise, but the angle had been too low and he wouldn't be dead for a while yet. Running on his own adrenaline, the man clawed at Caleb's face in search of an eye socket in which to jam a thumb.

He pulled the man into a bear hug, shoved the blade in deeper and forced it upward, slicing him open a centimeter at a time.

When the man finally sagged lifelessly in his grasp, he tossed the body to the side.

"We need to leave, *now*. Let's get to the bike."

Getting no response, he turned to Alex. Even in the dim light he could see all the color had drained from her face. She clung to the frame of the vehicle as she haltingly climbed to her feet. Her gaze roamed around wildly, looking at anything except him.

In an adrenaline-fueled combat state everything was knocked off-kilter. Time moved rapidly and slowly all at once. Light and shadow gained contrast, and the world appeared as an over-processed image, full of sharp edges and too-crisp colors. Movement leapt out as jagged gashes against a frozen frame.

He struggled past all this to see what she saw.

Three dead bodies lay within four meters. Blood pouring from two of the bodies pooled to join together and creep inexorably toward them.

Intestines spilled forth out of one; the flickering illumination from the riverwalk created the illusion of slimy tentacles slithering forward in the treacherous shadows.

The third corpse's head was twisted at an impossible angle upon the ground, eyes open to stare blankly at her and into the void.

He stood before her coated in repulsive bodily fluids. He felt the warm stickiness of blood streaked along one cheek, across his chin, dribbling down his neck.

Without a doubt, it was an utterly horrific panorama of violence and death. A tableau of nightmares.

And as he watched her recoil from the gruesome scene—and him—his heart plummeted then left him entirely. The moment he had always dreaded, worked to ensure never came to pass while trying his damnedest to pretend it never would, met him full on in her shell-shocked eyes and blanched face.

It occurred to him that perhaps Mia had been right after all. Which only made it so, so much worse.

He swallowed the lump in his throat. "We *have* to get away from here, and quickly. It's not safe. Will you come with me?"

Having reached a standing position, she gave a semblance of a nod.

Taking it as assent, he headed for the bike several rows further in...and realized there had been no jagged gash in his peripheral vision. She had made no move to follow him. His chin dropped and his eyes squeezed shut so tightly halos flared in the blackness.

He forced them open to gaze at her.

"*Please.*"

"Right...." She shook her head roughly and gingerly pushed off the vehicle, skittering to the side of the encroaching pools of blood to trail behind him at a distance.

When they reached the bike he had to remind her to put on the helmet wrap. Her hands rested warily midway around his waist; he felt them trembling through the cloth of his overshirt.

He wanted to scream and rage. He wanted to hit something and kill a few more people. He wanted to grab her and shake her and beg her with every ounce of his soul to not react like this...

...but he knew it was already far too late. And the rest of his body and brain were still in combat mode and he had to get them to safety.

"Alex, you need to hold on tighter, okay?" His voice sounded hollow and strained, like a too-taught string on an antique violin.

But she complied. He pulled out of the lot and onto the street.

They'd go back to Division, where security was high, then...well, he didn't know what then. He didn't know if she'd consent to go anywhere with him after this. If not, he could...he could send an escort to accompany her to the spaceport and she would be able to leave. Go to Romane, and from there, Earth.

He tried to focus on the road. The artificial lighting had returned to normal; in his distorted vision the added light gave the surroundings a washed out, achromatic sheen.

It was what it was. It was done and there was nothing in the universe which could change it. He accepted the deadening of his heart and began prepping the stoic mask he would desperately need in the coming hours.

He sent Volosk a message to let him know they were on their way and under assault.

> Message unable to be delivered. Recipient is not connected to exanet infrastructure. Message will be queued until it can be delivered.

Fucking bloody *fuck*.

And just like that everything became considerably more complicated. If they weren't the only ones being targeted....

But for the moment, a single thing mattered: staying alive. *Her staying alive.*

He broadcast a local Division alert and slowed as they neared HQ. The information relayed to him indicated Volosk's last recorded action was to leave the office to run an errand.

He swung to the rear and came to a stop alongside the building across from the entrance.

Alex stumbled off the bike, sending another dagger into his soul.

It didn't matter.

He kept his voice low. "Stay here a minute. I need to make sure the way is clear." She nodded mutely and backed into the wall. The void in his chest swelled to a yawning chasm at the sight of her looking at him in such a manner, shrinking away from him.

It didn't *matter*.

He peered around the corner, blade at the ready. He saw no movement nor anything out of the ordinary—save for the lump on the ground near the reserved area where the subdivision directors parked.

He knew what awaited him as he approached from the shadows.

Michael Volosk lay on his back in a pool of blood, one arm fractured at the elbow and the other wrenched behind his head. He had fought his attacker, if to no avail.

His throat had been sliced clean through from ear to ear by a gamma knife. His eyes stared blankly into the void, no different in death than the assailant's at the park.

Caleb blew out a harsh breath, his hand coming up to abuse his jaw. Volosk was an honorable, decent man. He had a wife and two young children and a spotless record. *What reason did they have to kill* him?

He spun around at the echo of footsteps, arm cocked and blade raised. But it was her. His arm dropped to his side.

She approached with caution, her focus locked on the body of the man she had met mere hours earlier—until it darted jerkily up to him.

God, she looked *so* scared.

He would give the wealth of nations to be able to convince her she never need be afraid of him. But he had no such wealth to give.

"He can't have been dead long or someone would have found him. The attackers might still be nearby." He glanced at the Division building, at the door fifteen meters across the lot. "I think we should get out of here, to the ship. It isn't safe, even here. If they got to him this close to Headquarters, they could have gotten inside."

He gazed at her imploringly. "Will you do that? Will you go with me to the spaceport at least? From there you can...whatever you want. But I need to get you to safety."

She blinked. "Of course...." She took a step, faltered and sank against the wall grasping clumsily at her right side.

"What is it? Are you hurt?"

"Yeah...I...I got nicked back there at the park...it's fine though...cybernetics will take care of it...."

Then her legs buckled beneath her.

He had already been moving and reached her a split-second before she hit the ground. One hand slid under her head, much as it had in another, far, *far* better circumstance.

He eased her down. "Alex? Alex, talk to me."

Nothing. She had lost consciousness.

He carefully shifted her arm out of the way. Her sweater was soaked through with blood. It blended into the deep purple of the material, which was why he hadn't seen it until now.

A frantic breath fell from his lips. "Oh, baby, no...."

Time screeched to a halt while he *oh-so-gently* rolled her onto her side. The back of the sweater was soaked in blood as well.

He lifted the sweater up to reveal entry and exit wounds. They lay in a direct trajectory, above her hip. The laser had traveled straight through and at a location which in all probability missed any vital organs.

Okay.

He willed what combat mode still remained to the forefront. Time resumed its skewed rapid slow progression forward.

There was a med kit inside, but there may also be assassins inside—or worse, traitors from within. If they were being hunted a hospital represented a death trap, and his apartment was doubtless being watched.

The rental ship had a Grade III med kit on board. If her cybernetics and genetic enhancements were as advanced as he was certain they must be, it would be enough.

If he got her to it soon.

The bike was clearly out. *Something he could walk away from.*

He stood, walked six meters and broke into the nearest vehicle. He rummaged through the compartment; as expected, there was a gym bag. Division employees loved their workouts, if solely for the stress relief they provided.

He tore it open and removed a t-shirt, climbed out and rushed back to her. With a rip of the seam the shirt became a long strip of cloth which he wound around her abdomen and secured over both wounds to staunch the bleeding.

He gathered her up in his arms.

Though he had endeavored to smother any emotions beneath an iron façade, a cry found its way to the surface when she sagged bonelessly against him.

He choked it off in his throat as he positioned her in the passenger seat and secured the harness over her. Then he bolted to the driver's side, scrambled in and hacked the controls.

The instant the engine fired he lifted into the air and accelerated toward the spaceport at reckless speed.

61

Kennedy exited the lift at the top floor of IS Design's offices, heels *clack-clacking* on the marble floor as she strode across the wide foyer. The deep green business suit she wore was cut rather conservatively, though at least it complimented her eyes, and her hair was uncharacteristically pulled up in a dress knot—a few minor concessions to the stodgy formality of a Board of Directors meeting.

The secretary smiled as she approached. "You're expected, Ms. Rossi. You can go right on in."

"Thank you, Nance. Oh, before I forget, congratulations on your daughter being accepted to MIT. I know you must be proud."

The woman beamed. "Very much so, though I will miss her. Thank you again for the personal recommendation. I'm sure it helped quite a lot."

Her grin held a hint of teasing. "*I'm* sure it had far more to do with her accomplishments, but I'm glad if I helped out a tiny bit."

She gave Nance a wink and continued into the boardroom. The four men and three women were engaged in a heated discussion over new efficiency measures, so she quietly took a seat along the wall.

It was several minutes until the conversation quieted down and the chairman motioned to her. "Ms. Rossi, thank you for coming."

She stood and approached the empty end of the table. "My pleasure. I'm glad to have the opportunity to—"

"A situation has arisen regarding a materials supplier which we'd like you to turn your attention toward."

What? She was here to present the final specs on the EM reverse shield. "I'm sorry, sir, I'm not clear on—"

"You're aware the Surno Materials facility on Aquila was destroyed by the Senecans yesterday?"

"Yes, sir. Most unfortunate. I know they were a major supplier of ours."

"Not merely of ours. They were also a significant supplier of metamaterials to the Alliance military. Now the Alliance is busily soaking up the remaining available supply from other manufacturers."

He glanced a little nervously around the table. "Of course this company has a long history and tradition of supporting the Alliance, and we stand fully behind the war effort. But the fact remains we will also need supplies if we expect to deliver on existing orders, not to mention future ones."

She couldn't help but frown. "Without a doubt. But while Surno was a reliable supplier, there are numerous metamaterial manufacturers on Alliance worlds and friendly independent ones."

"Yes, and they are all now being courted heavily by our competitors and every other provider of space-worthy end products."

"Ah, well, I can see the difficulty. However, as Director of the Design and Prototyping Division, I'm not certain how I might be able to help."

One of the directors, Amanda Vashi, clasped her hands on the table. "We recognize it isn't your normal area of focus. But your, shall we say, 'social' talents and networking connections are well known and respected, by this Board and the community at large. Combined with the stature of your family, we believe you would make an excellent ambassador for the company and a shrewd negotiator."

She suppressed a laugh; that had to be the most polite way of saying 'you're very attractive, can work a cocktail party like nobody's business and excel at fooling powerful men into believing you're flirting with them' she had ever heard. "I'm flattered, Ms. Vashi, but there are a number of important projects ongoing in DPD right now which I would hate to neglect."

The chairman smiled in his usual annoying, condescending manner. "Certainly there are, but I'm sure they will survive a couple of days without your direct guidance. We want you to go to Messium and persuade the president of Palaimo Metallurgy to supply us a minimum of sixty percent of our metamaterial requirements for the next year—for reasonable and fair compensation, naturally."

Her weight shifted to her back foot and she crossed her arms over her stomach, deciding she could stand to lose a bit of deference. "Can't those negotiations be conducted over holo? I really don't see the need for a personal visit."

"Palaimo's president is something of a prima donna, I'm afraid. And he is, as I noted earlier, being wooed by other companies as well. We believe a personal touch and a touch of extra attention will be required to make the deal happen."

She pursed her lips together to swallow annoyance. She didn't particularly want to trek all the way out to Messium to kiss some self-important corporate executive's ass. But she didn't see how it was particularly up to her either. With a silent sigh she nodded and gave the chairman a brilliant if somewhat plastic smile.

"Then I am happy to assist the company in any way I can. I'll make the arrangements today." She looked around at the directors. "If there's nothing else, I'd like to give my presentation now."

"Absolutely, Ms. Rossi. Please, continue."

"Thank you." She sent the presentation to the large screen above the table. "As you may recall from my earlier visit, the proposed EM reverse shield is intended—"

Nance burst into the room. The woman's eyes were wide, and she appeared out of breath though she couldn't have run more than a few meters.

"Turn on the news feed! Alliance Strategic Command has been destroyed!"

62

The 2nd Regiment of the 4th Brigade of the Earth Alliance NW Regional Command patrolled the Fionava-Balta-Orellan corridor, as had been its duty for more than a decade. Periodic superluminal traversals ended randomly to avoid predictable patterns and were interspersed with lengthy periods of impulse propulsion. Of course this being the Earth Alliance military, 'randomly' actually meant one of seven predetermined sequences.

Lieutenant Colonel Malcolm Jenner paced in front of the CO chair as the seconds counted down to the shift from superluminal to normal impulse propulsion. They would be at full ready when the transition occurred, as always, but particularly so after the EASC bombing hours earlier had put the entire fleet on Level IV alert status.

He had been the commanding officer of the *EAS Juno* for all of twenty-three days, and ready state still made him apprehensive. It wasn't like commanding ground forces, where you could hear and smell and sense the situation you were heading into—where even as a commander you had a weapon in your hand and at least the illusion of control over your own fate.

Here, standing on the deck of a starship in the void of space, he could request information and give orders but do little else to affect his fate or that of his men. It was one reason he disliked space, but only the latest one.

He had tried to comprehend the appeal, to grasp the wonder and amazement others felt toward the stars. For Alex, he had tried. But he had failed.

It wasn't as if he was a luddite; he embraced humanity's continued advancement as much as anyone. He simply preferred the sensation of soil beneath his feet and wind in his hair, of fresh, non-recycled air which carried on it the scent and taste of *life*.

He preferred what was solid and real, where if you could see it you could touch it, feel its texture between the tips of your fingers. As far as he knew, no one had ever touched a star.

Not even her.

Yet here he was, commander of a starship for twenty-three days and flying into the middle of a war.

He had been happy serving as the operations officer for the 3rd BC Brigade in Vancouver. It was a good posting, with plenty of responsibility and solid officers under him. But if he wanted to make full colonel in the next decade—or possibly ever—a flight command tour was all but a necessity. And he did want to make colonel, almost as much as Veronica wanted him to.

It was only because she believed in him and thought he was capable of greater things that she pushed him so. He knew this in his heart.

So he had left behind his beautiful new wife of two months, his honorable if slightly staid job and his charming house in the North Vancouver foothills for a half-year space tour. Seventeen days in he had found himself in a war. Alex would be laughing her ass off if she could see him now....

"Flight Lieutenant Billoughy, prepare to idle the sLume drive at 14:35:00. Helmsman Xao, is the Orellan asteroid belt survey loaded into the navigation system?"

"Yes, sir."

"Very good. Impulse in two...one...*mark.*"

In the large viewport dominating the bow of the bridge, stars crystalized into focus. Though nearly 3.4 AU away, the sanguine light from the system's red giant sun cast an eerie hue over the scene. Two of the other four frigates in the formation materialized in the port and starboard peripherals as well as on the tactical map to his left.

"All systems—"

An explosion off their port viewport blew a hole in the side of the *EAS Somerset* 2.3 seconds after it emerged from superluminal. The shockwave shuddered across the bridge, causing him to grab for the arm of his chair while he implemented Level V alert status. Alarms rang through the deck, but he filtered the increased noise to the background.

He quickly sat down so as not to stumble around the bridge like some ground-pounder. Miniature versions of the tactical and sector maps leapt onto small screens beside him. He watched in dismay as the *EAS Caroline* ventured forth to their starboard, never seeing the 'asteroid' beneath it which detonated and blew out its impulse engine.

Lt. Colonel Jenner: Command, the asteroid field is mined. I repeat, the asteroid field is mined.

The field had been mapped to a three-meter level of accuracy so ships were able to avoid collisions. Now it appeared mines had been disguised to resemble asteroids to the casual observer—'asteroids' which would not be on the map.

"Science, I need active visual scans. Update navigation on new obstacles as they are found. Tactical, deploy drones in sets of four spaced one hundred fifty meters apart. Billoughy, keep our course at least two hundred meters rear of the drones. Systems, divert non-critical power to plasma shield—"

The tactical map flared red as a dozen Senecan fighters dropped out of superluminal into the middle of the asteroid field and spread to engage. Based on the speed they were approaching, they did possess detailed mappings of the mines' locations as well as the asteroids themselves.

The *Caroline* made for easy pickings with its impulse engine disabled. It took under eight seconds for the small ships to destroy its sLume drive and blow a hole through its shields and into the port stern hull.

The comm screen to his right shouted in bold letters when their own fighters launched from the carrier accompanying them, the *EAS Sao Paulo*. The surrounding space lit up in arcing laser streams and small explosions as numerous asteroids fell victim to the crossfire.

For a breath he paused to acknowledge the scene depicted in the viewport. *So this is what space warfare truly looked like. Admittedly, it was beautiful.*

"Weapons, you get a clear shot on one of those fighters, you take it. Billoughy, increase minimum distance to drones to four hundred meters and prepare for evasive maneuvers." A bright plume flared ahead; he thought it might be a drone catching a mine, but a glance at tactical confirmed it was a fighter. *One of ours.*

He stared at the screen, briefly transfixed as a Senecan fighter drew its opponent into a mine, diverting at the last instant and leaving the Alliance ship to disintegrate.

"*Jesus...Science, get the updated scans out to the other ships.*"

Lt. Colonel Jenner: Recommend all capable vessels initiate active visual scans to update navigation maps. Our optimal range does not encompass entire battle sector.

Rear Admiral Tarone (Sao Paulo*): Michigan, Hirami, assume defensive positions off* Sao Paulo *flanks.* Juno, *get your ass back here on the double and assume point.*

The carrier, having been lucky enough to arrive at a location absent of any mines, had little choice at the moment but to hold its position. Given its size and relative lack of maneuverability, it faced certain damage and probable crippling if it attempted to navigate the asteroid field. Requesting protection was understandable.

Nonetheless, Malcolm bristled at the order. It left their fighters with effectively no support and created a giant stationary target for the enemy.

"Billoughy, reverse course and adopt a position 0.8 kilometers N 5.00° E of the *Sao Paulo.*"

"Sir?"

"You heard me. Those are our orders."

"Yes, sir."

"Tactical, continue deploying drones to replace those destroyed." By this point the drones were doing a decent job of clearing a path forward in about a 60° arc. Maybe the fighters would be able to use it to their advantage...he looked back at the screens. Shit, they only had four still flying to the Senecans' nine?

This was a bloodbath.

Even without the mines the battlefield favored the opponents' superior maneuverability—undoubtedly one reason it had been chosen. The Senecans clearly had identified their ostensibly 'random' routes and knew they would eventually traverse the asteroid field.

He sent a private pulse to Tarone.

Admiral, we've lost two-thirds of our fighters and a third of our frigates. Perhaps we should consider retreating.

Run from a few tiny fighters? Ridiculous.

...Yes, sir.

With the dwindling number of Alliance fighters to offer resistance, several of the enemy vessels began advancing on their position.

"Weapons, be ready to lock on to the first ship to come in range."

"Yes, sir." Seven seconds later a pulse beam leapt out of the well of the *Juno.*

It was virtually impossible to escape a pulse beam once it had locked on, and the ship did not. But it did execute a hairpin turn to drop behind a real asteroid an instant before the beam reached it. The asteroid exploded into hundreds of shards, some of which surely caused damage to the fighter—yet it emerged from the debris to resume advancing.

Dammit.

But perhaps the Admiral was correct. There was no way nine Senecan fighters could survive against the weaponry of three Alliance frigates and a carrier long enough to do any real damage.

The error in his thinking became apparent when five fighters converged toward the *Hirami* off the *Sao Paulo's* port flank, dancing and weaving almost too rapidly for the eye to follow. Frigates wielded only two plasma weapons.

The comm screen lit up again.

Lt. Colonel T'soki (Hirami): *Request weapons support from* Sao Paulo.

Rear Admiral Tarone (Sao Paulo): *Negative, cannot fire from this position without hitting* Hirami.

"Weapons, any chance we can target one of the fighters without catching the *Hirami?*"

"Possibly, sir. Searching for a target in right quadrant...locked."

Lt. Colonel Jenner: Hirami, *we've got one of them for you.*

Lt. Colonel T'soki (Hirami): *Much appreciated.*

"Weapons, if you can take any more out, do so."

But it wasn't enough. Three of the fighters were destroyed, but by the time the *Hirami* was able to retarget, the remaining two were on top of them. They dropped in a deep arc beneath the *Hirami* and targeted the impulse engine. It would require a lot of firepower for so few fighters to take out the engine though; maybe he could take them out before they succeeded.

"Weapons...."

"Trying, sir."

Then the Senecan vessels did the unthinkable. They accelerated and suicided into the impulse drive.

The blast ricocheted through the *Hirami's* hull, ripping it to shreds in seconds.

He couldn't hear the metal tearing apart, nor the screams of the crew. Nonetheless it was a horrific sight, witnessing the destruction of 74,000 tonnes of starship and as many as a hundred lives. He vaguely noted the Senecan pilots had ejected just prior to impact; not quite so suicidal after all.

Still, he had to remind himself, the enemy was down to a mere three ships. Even if those ships had eliminated two more Alliance fighters while the others had engaged the *Hirami*.

"Weapons, target remaining fight—"

The tactical map flashed an angry red as two Senecan cruisers and six frigates materialized on the map.

Lt. Colonel Jenner: Admiral, we must retreat.

*Lt. Colonel Pniewski (*Michigan*): What about rescuing survivors?*

Another Alliance fighter vanished from the map.

Lt. Colonel Jenner: The Senecans will pick them up. They'll be POWs, but they'll be alive. Admiral? Do we have a retreat order?

A long pause.

*Rear Admiral Tarone (*Sao Paulo*): Retreat. Rendezvous Fionava.*

"Billoughy, engage the sLume drive immediately. Fionava heading."

It took approximately 7.2 seconds for a frigate-sized sLume drive to power up and engage. The sole intact Alliance fighter sped into the *Sao Paulo's* bay with five seconds to spare.

Malcolm kept an eye on tactical while the drive powered up. He—

*Lt. Colonel Jenner: *Michigan*, watch your starboard!*

The remaining Senecan fighters had cloaked in, revealing themselves less than a second before their weapons fired into the sLume drive. The developing warp bubble cavorted wildly then detonated in a massive sphere of exotic particles, vaporizing the *Michigan* as it expanded at an alarming rate—

"Flight?"

"Drive active...now!"

The glare of the explosion blurred to nothingness as they accelerated away at hundreds of times the speed of light. He sank into the chair, stunned, as the adrenaline abandoned him in waves.

The formation had been all but wiped out, none but the *Sao Paulo*, the *Juno* and a single fighter surviving to retreat.

It would take nearly six hours to reach Northwestern Regional Command on Fionava. But when they arrived, Malcolm was damn straight departing the ship and finding himself some fresh air to breathe.

63

The first thing Alex was aware of was the chill of gel medwraps melded to her abdomen and back. Next came the dull but not insignificant pain.

Her eyelids fluttered open.

A wave of disorientation washed over her—the cushions beneath her felt wrong, the walls looked wrong, the lights...then she remembered. Not her ship. A rental.

Caleb sat cross-legged on the floor, back to the wall, hands fisted at his chin, eyes downcast. He must have caught the telltale signs of movement in his peripheral vision because his eyes shot up to her. They shone brightly, but their color had paled to that of heavenly blue morning glories blooming with the dawn.

"Hey, you're awake."

She blinked and frowned. Her brain felt like muddled mush. Had they been outside the Intelligence Division building? Everything since they left the riverwalk was a blur. "How did we get here? We were...I don't know."

"You passed out—you'd been shot. I took a skycar to get us to the ship, then treated your wounds. How do you feel? Can I get you...something...?"

He quickly stood but didn't approach her. He didn't seem to know what to do with himself, and even in her addled state she noticed the light fading from his eyes. It was as if he were disappearing away from her down a long tunnel—which was ridiculous, because he still stood *right there*.

"Water, maybe?" She steadied both palms on the couch cushion and gingerly sat up, letting her legs trail to the floor. *Ow*. Yes, she most certainly had been shot. Vague memories began to bubble up, all jumbled and fragmented. It had been the first volley, as they dove behind the vehicle a millisecond too late. She tried to arrange the memories in a sequential order, but after the laser sliced into her the rest was chaos through a smudged lens.

Her hands clutched the cushion in a death grip to keep her upright until he showed up at her side, outstretched arm holding a glass of water. She hesitantly released one hand and reached up. Still upright. *Excellent.*

Once she took the glass he started pacing. The cabin in the rented ship was small, and it made her a bit dizzy to watch him constantly turning. "Are we on our way to Romane?"

"Yeah. I didn't think anywhere on Seneca was safe under the circumstances."

She sipped on the water and struggled to get her bearings and force her brain into some semblance of proper function. After a few more sips it occurred to her that he wasn't looking at her...and had yet to touch her. A troubling sensation stirred in her gut, right next to the gunshot wound.

He continued pacing. And turning. "We'll be there mid-morning. You can get back to your ship and head home. They can protect you there. I'll try to find out what the hell's going on. Maybe I can discover who's behind these attacks, who put the hit on us and Volosk and why...."

She swallowed, her throat unaccountably dry though doused with water. "You're leaving?"

His voice had a strange flat, detached quality she had never heard before; it matched his flat, blank expression as he nodded. "I'm sure you'll want to be getting back to Earth, and I should go after these guys. It's fine."

She stared at him not looking at her. "*What's* fine?"

"Me leaving. I'm sorry you got hurt, I...I didn't want that. And I understand, so—"

"At least one of us does." She heard the sharp acrimony in her tone, though he didn't appear to. "Unless...."

The blur of the evening's events raced in crocked circles in her head—his now odd, dispassionate manner, what Mia had said about what impressed him, his own admission of why he had chosen his line of work—and the ache in her gut leapt into her chest and flared to drown any pain from her wounds.

"Sure. Okay. I get it." An incredulous breath forced its way past her lips. She was so angry at herself. She had actually allowed herself to begin to…believe. How *stupid* must she be!

His brow contorted, as if uncertain what direction to adopt. "Listen, I know you're probably disgusted with me right now. I mean there's still blood on my clothes, even if some of it is yours. But—"

She laughed harshly. *Owww*. "I'm seriously considering being disgusted—why *is* there still blood on your clothes?"

For the briefest moment the blank mask he wore faltered, and emotion flooded his features. He looked stricken—as though he had learned the universe was to be annihilated in the next hour, or his mother or perhaps his favorite pet had died. Seeing as none of those were particularly likely, damned if she could figure out why he might look this way.

She instructed her eVi to have her cybernetics ease up on the wound healing for the time being and send a bit more oxygen and, if need be, adrenaline to her brain. It suddenly seemed quite important she be able to think clearly.

"I didn't want to leave you alone while you were unconscious. But you're okay so…" he moved toward the small stairwell which led to the sleeping area "…so I'll go change now. I'll bring you up a shirt."

She hadn't bothered to notice her sweater was gone and she wore only a bra. Whatever. Sheer anger and disbelief had now risen to drown both the ache in her chest and the ache from her wounds. She would *not* show weakness.

"We're not finished here."

It took him two seconds to turn around. Seconds which stretched into an eternity. The mask was back in place, while the tenor of his voice carried less inflection than a rudimentary VI. "Okay. Say what you need to."

"Gladly. Yes, I am disgusted with you for wanting to ditch me the second I'm the smallest burden to you. I knew you had a strong survival instinct and all, but I didn't think you were—"

His eyebrows drew into fierce streaks of discontentment. "I'm not—I didn't mean—"

"No, it is, as you say, '*fine.*' You go ahead and do whatever the *fuck* you want to do. Don't give it a second thought." She forgot she bore a small injury, wrenched around to stand and storm off to the cockpit—because it's what she would have done on her ship—and doubled over as a sharp jolt of pain lanced into her side.

As she sank down onto the couch he materialized at her side. "Are you okay? You should—"

"Don't *touch* me," she growled through gritted teeth.

He backed away, eyes wide with what closely resembled anguish. "I'm sorry...I only wanted...I'll leave you alone."

He again moved toward the stairs, his murmur little more than a whisper. "You may not believe me, but I would *never* hurt you."

"You're leaving aren't you," she grumbled under her breath, and immediately cringed. She should not have said that aloud. *Dammit.* The pain was wreaking havoc on her brain-to-mouth regulator.

"That's what you want, isn't it?"

Shit, he had heard her. She closed her eyes and dropped her head against the cushion. "It is now."

There was no response; she assumed he had grown bored with the verbal sparring and gone downstairs. She sank further into the cushions, all the energy seeping out of her. She was tired, she was in pain and she was—

"I'm not certain I understand."

She winced at the realization he hadn't left after all and squinted one eye in the direction of the stairwell. He stood with one foot on the landing, the other hovering above the first step. "You don't understand what?"

"You said 'it is now,' as if it wasn't before. And earlier you seemed to imply leaving was somehow my choice."

She groaned and sat up enough to glare at him. "Do not try to play mind games with me, Caleb. I am not in the mood, and I will not let you pin this on me, *vrubilsya?* You want to leave, I get it—so just *go,* but don't try to turn it into something else to ease your guilty conscience."

The expression of pained patience flitted across his face, but it was as if he hadn't the strength to maintain it. His gaze roved around the cabin, and when it again found her his eyes had gone harsh. Sapphire chiseled into brittle edges. His jaw could have been carved of stone, and his formerly deadened voice now bled bitterness.

"*No*. I won't let *you* turn this into something else. If you can't take what I am so be it, but the simple truth is my actions saved your life. I am not the enemy and I won't allow you to paint me as one."

God, she wished he would end this torture and leave her alone to curl up in a ball.... Now he was deliberately taking advantage of her less than optimal state to confuse her and render her unable to fight back. It was dirty fighting and it wasn't fair.

"I'm perfectly well aware you saved my life, so thank you for doing that at least before you discarded me to run off on your next adventure. I'm so sorry it will take a few hours until you can rid yourself of me. But I don't intend to spend those hours propping up your ego, so you—"

His mouth twitched furiously. "My *ego*? What the bloody hell are you talking about? Alex, what do you think is happening here?"

"What do I *think*? I *think* you're a selfish narcissist who only goes along for the ride until it begins to interfere with your good time. I *think* you're an even better liar than I gave you credit for and I fell for it even though I goddamn *knew* better! I *think* you should—"

"*Stop*, please, for one second." He dragged a hand raggedly through his hair. "No. After the attack you were distant and wary and shell-shocked. I killed those men and I know it was brutal and violent and ruthless—"

"Is killing people ever not those things?"

"Well it isn't always so bloody, but...." His voice trailed off as he stared at her for the first time since right after she had awoken, and she swore beneath the surface anger she saw raw pain tarnishing his beautiful eyes. *Damn he's good at this. Even now, he makes me want to believe him.*

He frowned...no, it wasn't a frown. It was something else. "Are you...." He stopped, drew in a deep breath, let it out and began again. "Are you telling me you aren't horrified by what I did back there? By the violence of it, the brutality? You're not...you're not afraid I might hurt you, or simply appalled I'm a killer?"

"What? Why would I be?"

"Because it's happened before. Because good people often are. Because I *am* a killer. And the way you looked at me, the way you—"

"I had been *shot*. I was a little distracted. Then a little weak, then a little dizzy, then, well...."

He blinked and shook his head as if trying to clear cobwebs from it. "Which you neglected to tell me."

In the recesses of her mind, her memories had been gradually solidifying and assembling themselves into a proper order. She tried to focus in on them. "I admit I wasn't thinking overly clearly, but...I thought I'd be okay. I didn't want to slow you down."

"Oh, Alex, I would do anything...." He swallowed and met her gaze once more, an odd glint in his countenance. Like a dying man catching sight of an oasis yet afraid it was a mirage. He spoke slowly. Deliberately. "You weren't planning to kick me out of your life as soon as we landed?"

"Planning when? When I woke up after being shot, of course not. As of a few minutes ago? Hell yes."

He looked confused, hopeful, terrified, all at once; he really did. At this point she was feeling rather confused herself...she checked to make sure her eVi had executed her instructions, though she recognized it commanded diminished resources.

He started pacing again, this time in considerable agitation. His movements were uncontrolled in a manner she had never seen.

Then words began tumbling over one another as they spilled forth. "I thought—I thought you were. I thought you wanted nothing else to do with me upon seeing the bloody reality of what I can be, and do, when I need to. I thought you were in horrified shock—and you were, only maybe it was from being shot and not because of what you saw and—"

The blur of the evening's events raced around in her head again, this time with greater clarity and colored by his perspective. She recalled things he had hinted at over the past days, topics he had been reluctant to talk about. What *else* Mia had said about him—

—and in a rush it all made sense, in a crazy way that wasn't.

Silly, hardened, sensitive man. Her head swam from a deluge of relief and whiplashing emotions. Dammit, he was always *doing* that to her. But she felt the strangest desire to…protect him.

"You are *such* a dumb ass."

His face scrunched up in greater confusion, but the pacing screeched to a halt. "Excuse me?"

"You're a *dumb ass.* You honestly believe such an incredible display of badass heroics would scare away someone like me? Frankly, I'm offended. Did you take me for some delicate flower who faints at the sight of a drop of blood?"

He laughed; it had a wild, reckless timbre. "No, I would never—"

"Come here." She didn't quite trust her body to stand just yet. He was going to have to come to her. Perhaps in more ways than one.

He blinked. She watched his throat working. Finally he crossed the cabin to the space in front of the couch and crouched on the balls of his feet. He seemed to search her face but didn't stop to meet her gaze directly. *Hesitant. Cautious. Guarded.*

She reached up with her good arm and wound her hand tenderly into his hair, letting it curl softly around her fingers. He sucked in a breath as his eyes closed and his lips fought to tug upward.

"Caleb." His eyes reopened at the sound of her voice. The ocean within them roiled like a hurricane, and her heart decided to go careening off the walls which held it in place.

"I've always known what you are. *Who* you are may have been in question…." She struggled to find the right words. "I come from a family of soldiers. I understand the necessity for violence. If you hadn't acted as you did, we would probably both be dead. And I, for one, prefer being alive."

She smiled weakly. "I won't deny it was a bit jarring for a second or two, seeing you like that. But…."

Her hand drew down along his jaw to his chin, and she urged it up so he was unable to turn aside. "I knew what I was getting into. And I am *not* afraid of you." *At least, not in that way.* "Now if this routine is something you concocted as cover for you wanting to leave—"

"*No.*" He fell to his knees before her; his hands grasped her shoulders and his forehead dropped to rest against hers. "I don't want to go."

Her breath lodged in her throat. The emotion bleeding out of his words crashed through her with more intensity than she could possibly absorb. Her chest burned hot as it nonetheless insisted on *trying.*

Her throat eked out a trembling whisper. "Then *stay.*"

He nodded silently against her. They didn't move for untold seconds, struggling to pick up the pieces and put themselves back together, to regain some control over the inner tumult.

Finally he pulled away a sliver. His eyes rose to meet hers as a hand rose to cup her cheek.

"You are a most remarkable woman, Alex Solovy."

64

ROMANE

"Are you ready to get to work, Meno?"

I am looking forward to this endeavor, Mia. I expect to learn new things.

"I'm not sure we'll learn anything more worthwhile than the name of Miss Solovy's first pet or her favorite author."

Yet that will nevertheless be something new.

"Ha. Fair enough."

Mia stood at the top of the ramp in the hangar bay, the fingertips of her right hand pressed to the embedded panel of the *Siyane's* external hatch. The contact pad of the remote interface rested snugly against the base of her neck. Her eyes were closed—but she was not blind.

Instead she saw what Meno 'saw': a seemingly infinite three-dimensional grid of pulsing, spinning translucent orbs. The orbs grouped together in formations ranging from tiny to massive and complex. Threadlike filaments connected the groupings, and always there existed structure and order, sharp lines and hard right angles.

The grid overflowed with color. The entire spectrum was represented in the spinning orbs, every and each color all at once. When viewed in the corner of her eye, an orb appeared a prismatic swirl. If she turned her focus to one, however, it transformed to pure white light.

The orbs, of course, signified the qubits composing the *Siyane's* security control system. Much as Schrödinger's cat, until observed a qubit held all possible quantum superpositions of 0 and 1. When she observed one, the prism resolved to white; when Meno 'observed' one, he measured its true state.

As such, her presence here was largely superfluous other than to guide Meno to the appropriate access points—and to make certain it didn't rewrite the *Siyane's* weapons, propulsion and life support systems to be more efficient while he was in there.

Besides, she liked the view.

"Begin recording." She needed to image the security controls because when she finished it had to be put back as she found it, leaving no trace she had been there. She didn't want to cause trouble for Caleb, even if she was a little worried about him. The odds of this new relationship of his working out well in the end were only slightly north of nil...but he never had been the cautious sort.

Recording initiated.

"Excellent. Overlay Alexis Solovy's fingerprints."

Overlay successful. Security is requesting secondary encryption key. Analyzing.

Meno had named 'himself' at her suggestion. At the time it was devouring ancient philosophical texts and had taken the name from the Plato Socratic dialogue on virtue, knowledge and belief. It continued to burn spare cycles contemplating the notion of inborn knowledge and whether, lacking a soul, it nonetheless possessed such knowledge.

Secondary encryption key: Д085401H129914C. Would you like to know my hypothesis on the meaning of this key?

She smiled to herself. Artificials were tightly regulated, monitored, circumscribed, feared and often reviled, and with good reason. Perhaps excepting the last one, anyway. They possessed incredible processing ability—but computers ran many facets of society. Those CUs were also powerful, capable of zettaFLOP calculations and zeptosecond accuracy. Yet no one feared them, because they were dumb. They did not think; they simply calculated. Oh, a well-designed VI could create a convincing impression of thought and even personality, but it was still executing defined programming.

Synthetic neural nets, on the other hand, were designed for that exact purpose: to *think*. To learn. To adapt. To improve.

Their greatest feature was also their most dangerous one: curiosity. Mia delighted in Meno's childlike inquisitiveness and thirst for knowledge. But though it wasn't registered, she otherwise obeyed all the prescribed safety precautions. Because it was like a child—a hyper-savant child wielding unfathomable power and no perspective, no wisdom born of hard lessons and experience and no sense of boundaries which might keep it in check.

So while she supplied Meno with endless zettabytes of information—history, art, literature, science, data on the very universe itself—she provided it no connections to the exanet or the local Romane infrastructure network. In fact, its hardware did not include any external networking capability, save for the single point-to-point node which allowed her to remotely interface with it. While interfacing, the only outside information it received came through her personal cybernetics. Hence the fingertips on the panel.

"Maybe later. Are there any other authorized entrants?"
Kennedy Rossi and Charles Blalock.
"Is the secondary encryption key the same for them as well?"
It is.
"Terrific. Register Caleb Marano as an authorized entrant and input his fingerprints. I'll let him know the key when he returns. Then mask the authorization."

Caleb hadn't specified precisely why he needed access to Alex's ship. Most likely there wasn't any precise reason at all; he would merely be preparing for multiple possibilities. She did have a good idea why he didn't simply ask for access. The possessiveness—and protectiveness—Alex exhibited regarding her ship had been blindingly obvious within thirty seconds of meeting her.

Mr. Marano now enjoys authorized access, should he provide the ship his fingerprints and the key.
"Thank you, Meno. Open the hatch, would you? We're going to need to get him usage of the flight systems, too."

PANDORA
INDEPENDENT COLONY

"What? Dude, I can't hear you."
Noah leaned in closer to Dylan, to no avail. Between the strobing prism beams dancing across the sky and the synchronous musical and visual performance, he could hardly hear himself think, much less hear anyone else speak. Then again, the point of the circus wasn't to think, but rather to experience. To feel. To get wasted.

I said do you want another drink? I'm heading to the bar.
A beer, man—but a good one.

He leaned against the railing and drew in a deep breath, enjoying the warm night air and the smoothness of the sensory deluge.

Yet his thoughts inevitably drifted. He had caught the news of the destruction of the Surno facility on Aquila. His father must be so pissed. It wasn't his sole interest by far; Surno accounted for maybe ten percent of his holdings at most. But it would definitely sting.

When he realized what he was doing he groaned and dropped his head back to stare at the art painting the night sky. *Don't even think about getting involved, Noah. Not your problem—not the business, not the war. Just keep the party going.*

He accepted the beer from Dylan with a wry smile and greedily turned it up.

At that moment Ella lurched out of the crowd and fell into him. He held the bottle out to the side with one hand to avoid sloshing it all over him and grasped onto her with the other. "Hey baby, careful there."

She gazed up at him, eyes unfocused and blurry. "Noah, hi…. Whatcha doin?"

He chuckled. "Not what you are, apparently." He steadied her and tried to position her on the railing next to him, but she draped her arms clumsily around his shoulders. "You're hot, you know that righ…?"

Ella was pretty enough. But she was unstable when sober, which was an increasingly rare occurrence, and nuts when she was high. And if there was one rule he lived by on this mad planet, it was *never stick your dick in crazy.*

He eased her off him. "Yeah, baby, I know that."

"You wanna—" She reached for him again, missed and tumbled to the floor.

He squeezed his eyes shut, muttered a curse under his breath and crouched to pick her up. Sometimes having a conscience goddamn *sucked.* "Come on, Ella, I'm taking you home."

"Don't wanna—"

"Yes, you do." He rolled his eyes at Dylan and began guiding her through the reveling crowd to the lift. It wasn't terribly late; if he got her tucked into bed reasonably quickly, perhaps he'd return.

The lift circled the building as it descended, and she swayed unsteadily against him. He willed patience. She didn't...'live' was a strong word. She wasn't staying far from the club.

The lift settled to the street level and he maneuvered her in the proper direction. They walked slowly down the street, then veered onto a narrower thruway. The entrance to the residences where she stayed was located about a hundred meters farther on the left.

"Oops!" Ella tripped and stumbled forward.

Noah leaned over to try to save her from sprawling upon the ground—

—the brilliant white stream of a laser pulse sliced centimeters above his head.

"Ella, get down!"

"Wha—?"

He grabbed her arm and dragged her along the thruway, trying to stay low and near the wall. They came to a door, and he shoved her into the alcove. He slammed on the door but it appeared hard-locked. "Dammit! Okay, I need you to stay here, stay hidden. I'm going to—"

"But I wan—" She pulled away from him and staggered into the thruway.

"Ella, get back here!" He reached for her at the same instant the laser sliced through her neck and she crumbled lifelessly to the ground.

"Motherfu—" The shot had come from close range. He yanked the small kinetic blade he carried from the narrow pocket in his pants and lunged toward the shadow he saw moving against darker shadows.

He plowed into a body and they both crashed to the ground, each grappling for an advantage. He swung blindly in the dark and connected with bone, at least if the loud *crack* was any indication. Before he could do further damage a knee came up and rammed him in the nuts, sending a wave of nausea up his chest into his throat. He fought it back and stabbed wildly while struggling to hold the flailing gun away from his body.

Abruptly his knife met pliant, sluggish resistance. When the man's grip on him fell away, he decided the knife had found the man's gut. He wrenched the gun out of the attacker's hand, climbed to his feet and pointed it at the attacker's head.

"Who do you work for?"

The man writhed on the ground, clutching at his stomach in the darkness. "Fuck you. They'll send more. You won't last the day."

"I'll take that bet." He pulled the trigger.

─────

It took twenty seconds of banging on the door for Brian to open it. Music wafted from the living room, punctuated by high-pitched laughter.

"You need somethi—?"

Noah grabbed his shirt by the collar. "Why is somebody trying to kill me?"

"What? Hey, let go! I don't know!"

"Is it because of the explosives job? They were for the Vancouver bombing that just happened, weren't they?"

"I told you, I don't know! Give me a break, man…."

He tightened his grip instead. "Why did you offer the job to me? Did Nguyen tell you to?"

"No, man. Calm down, okay?"

"I am *not* going to calm down. I got shot at and an innocent girl is dead!"

Brian's eyes widened into saucers. "*Shit.* Look, the request came from higher. They didn't tell me how much higher."

"Why?"

"I don't *know.*"

His grip clenched to the point it began choking off Brian's air.

"Okay, okay…." Noah loosened his hold a miniscule amount, and Brian gasped in a breath. "I did overhear one thing—I got no idea what it means though."

"*What.*"

"Something about you needing to do the job cause you'd worked with some guy named Marano."

"*Caleb?* What the hell does Caleb have to do with this?"

"I got no idea! That's all I heard, I swear. I didn't know they would try to take you out, man, I *swear.*"

"Fuck." He let go of the shirt and shoved Brian into the apartment. "Don't come looking for me, you understand?"

He spun and stormed down the hallway, pausing once to punch the wall in frustration. He had no choice. He was going to have to bail, and bail *now.*

ℛ

Noah scanned the travel schedule from the relative safety of a group of tourists. It was the middle of the night, but there were always tourists at the spaceport. He wore a cap he'd bought on the way pulled low over his face.

He'd sent Caleb a brief message a few minutes earlier. *Watch your back. Something screwy is up.* He'd expand on it later, if he was still alive.

He couldn't go where they would expect him to. Aquila was out, as was New Babel and Atlantis. Hell, if it was Zelones after him all the independent worlds were out. Even Romane, tempting though it was.

No, he needed to go somewhere random. Somewhere which also offered him some cover and the opportunity to make a few credits until things settled down.

He scanned the list again.

Messium. Boring as shit and home to more military than he'd like, but it boasted a healthy population to hide in and a robust tech industry to service. And he was technically an Alliance citizen.

With a sigh he slid away from the crowd and headed for the boarding platform. So much for the party....

65

SPACE, NORTH-CENTRAL QUADRANT
SENECAN FEDERATION SPACE

Alex watched him sleep.

She lay against him, her injured side facing up and unhindered. His arms were wrapped gently around her in slumber. Despite his best efforts otherwise he had dozed off, albeit only after going to prodigious lengths to ensure she was comfortable in the bed and not in pain and had everything she needed. It had been overprotective and unnecessary and rather adorable.

She had insisted on getting downstairs under her own power, much to his frustration. 'Bullheaded stubborn,' he had called her; she hadn't disputed the point. Her wounds still ached, but she felt as if she had her bearings again. By morning she should be functional. Not one hundred percent by a long shot...but functional.

He must be beyond exhausted. She knew enough about military-grade cybernetics enhancements to recognize both what they empowered the body to do and the toll they inflicted in the aftermath. Human physiology was being pushed to its very limits. Thus far it was keeping up, but barely.

She probably should be asleep as well...even if three hours of unconsciousness really *should* count.

Instead she watched him sleep. She allowed her gaze to trace the line of his jaw, the curves of his exquisite and talented lips and the angular path of his nose.

Her brow furrowed up a little. Something about the set of his mouth, the relaxed muscles in his cheeks and neck, the way...

...then she realized. This was how he looked when it was the two of them—when they were talking or working or not doing much of anything and the mood was easy and comfortable. He appeared more serene and peaceful in slumber of course, but it was unquestionably the same aspect.

He truly *wasn't manipulating her.*

Endorphins flooded through her body; it was all she could do not to laugh out loud.

Though she had allowed him into her bed, had shared secrets with him, risked arrest and even her ship for him...a part of her had still assumed he was deceiving her. Whether for some purpose or because it was his nature and he didn't know any other way to be, when he had no further need of her a switch would flip in his eyes and he would be gone.

His words and especially his actions told her over and over again he was genuine, yet she couldn't bring herself to foreclose the possibility the persona he showed to her only represented another face of the chameleon—a chameleon he readily admitted existed.

A mere hour ago she had thought her fears confirmed, thought the day a part of her had assumed would come had done so earlier than expected. Then, when he had fallen to his knees before her, raw and exposed, every sense she possessed had screamed at her to give in and believe the truth of him.

But now...why now? Was it simply that now she was ready to trust and searching for a reason to do so?

In the end it didn't matter, for it was already done.

She leaned in and kissed him lightly then settled on the pillow to watch him wake. She shouldn't have done it; he needed the rest...but she needed him.

He stirred and shifted. After a few seconds he blinked a couple of times to reveal blurry, unfocused irises; warmth flooded them even before they grew clearer. "Hi...."

Her perception hadn't deceived her: the set of his mouth, the line of his jaw, the impression his visage conveyed remained unaltered, enhanced solely by the addition of dazzling irises. She matched his smile. "Hi."

"I fell asleep?"

"Just for a little while."

He reached up to stroke her cheek. "You should sleep."

"I did, remember? Most of the evening I believe."

"I'm not certain that counts."

"Well...." Her smile broadened. "I'll sleep in a bit."

His eyes narrowed. "What?"

She tried her best to look innocent. "Nothing."

He drew her closer against him. "It's not nothing...but since you're smiling, I'll just go with it."

She responded by kissing the corner of his mouth and snuggling into the crook of his arm.

They lay there in silence for several minutes, and in truth she might have begun to drift off when he shifted beneath her. She blinked awake and covered any drowsiness by dancing fingertips along the curly hair trailing down his abdomen to his navel.

He raised an eyebrow at her. "Since we're hanging out here *not* sleeping, mind if I ask you something random?"

"Hmm? Sure." She propped her chin on his chest to be able to catch his gaze.

"The name of your ship. I've run it through every Russian dialect and half a dozen other languages and encyclopedia compendiums, but no matches. And I was...wondering."

She laughed and scooted up onto one elbow. "It wouldn't match anything."

One side of her mouth curled up of its own volition. "So the story goes—I was three years old, far too young to remember it with any clarity—my dad and I were stargazing in the backyard one night. I babbled away, asking dozens of wacky questions only a child could think of about the stars and ships and what space was like. He was humoring me, like he always did.

"And I uttered some nonsensical proclamation like, 'One day I'm gonna be a star.' And he...he hugged me and said, '*Na den' vy siyat' s snova siyaniye chem vse svetilo v nebesnyy nebesa*,' which roughly means, 'One day you will shine with more radiance than every star in the celestial heavens.'"

He chuckled. "Quite a mouthful for a little girl."

"I know, right? He had a definite flair for the dramatic. I understood '*na den' vy*,' common words and all, but I'd never heard the rest before and didn't yet have a full eVi with a translator. I looked up at him, my face scrunched up in a child's perplexity, and tried to repeat it. But I stumbled over the 'vs' and 'sv' phonetics, since English doesn't often use them. I garbled out 'siya...ssn...niye...v nebe...ne...,' stopped, went back and tried again and still totally mangled it.

"Finally I stared at him in desperation and whispered, 'siya-...ne-...?' then waited for him to fill in the rest. He laughed, hugged me tighter and said, 'Siyane is perfect, sweetheart. My little star shining brightly.'"

She swallowed away the lump in her throat. "And it sort of became his pet name for me. He didn't use it a lot, but whenever he was acting particularly affectionate or melodramatic he'd whip it out for added impact."

She shrugged in his arms. "So I guess the best way to put it is...the name represents an affirmation that I'm trying to live up to his belief in what I could be."

He pulled her yet closer, careful not to press on her wounds, and kissed the top of her head. She wished she was able to see his expression, but he held her securely against him.

"I'd wager if he were here, he'd say you're doing a hell of a lot more than trying."

"In fact..." his embrace loosened "...that's what it is, isn't it?"

"What's what?"

"What you do."

She regarded him curiously. "I have no idea what you're talking about."

"How you find things others cannot. How you somehow knew the TLF wave wasn't coming from the pulsar, and discovered its origin point. How you stared into space and saw where to find a tiny, cold, silent star buried deep within nebular clouds."

She bit her lower lip, her gaze drifting away from him. After a moment she rested her head on his chest. "It's not magic or anything. It's simply...the universe has rules. Even the exceptions obey the rules. Though so immensely complex it appears to most like chaos, in truth the universe is ordered and structured and perfect.

"More than that, I *understand* the structure. It makes sense to me. I look out into the void and I see the interconnections and relationships—the gravitational pull of a supergiant subtly tugging at a stellar system kiloparsecs away, the excess glow along the edges of ionized gas as it collides with an H I region, the *absence* which marks a dark star or a gray hole."

His hand wound leisurely through her hair, reassuring her she wasn't crazy, encouraging her to continue. "And since I understand the way things must be, when something seems out of place, wrong or merely odd...I can recognize the reality of it. The hidden object or event or force which brings space back into alignment with the rules of the universe."

She lifted her head to crinkle her nose up at him. "But I don't get what any of this has to do with the name of my ship."

He brushed a strand of hair out of her eyes. "When we were at the center of Metis and you were looking for the pulsar's companion, you stared out the viewport and whispered, 'Come on you little star, shine for me.'"

"No, I didn't."

"*Yes*, you did."

"I don't.... Well, I suppose it does kind of feel as though that's what happens, but.... Even if it's true, the stars do the shining. Not me."

He drew her up his body until his lips met hers. They were soft and gentle, like the ocean breeze on a rare warm Pacifica summer afternoon. She'd never imagined a man capable of such violence, of such intensity, could also be capable of the extraordinary tenderness he showed toward her.

He pulled back a fraction to meet her eyes and gaze into her soul. "Are you sure?"

66

Miriam did all her staring in disbelieving horror at the unimaginable landscape of destruction from the transport as it circled twice overhead.

She had seen destruction before. During the First Crux War she had witnessed firsthand the aftermath of more than one battle. But that war had never come close to reaching Earth. To reaching *home*. This, though…she had spent the last fourteen years of her life working in the building which now lay crumbled in smoldering ruins.

By the time she stepped off the transport she was instructing on-scene EASC staff who were ambulatory to meet in the primary conference room in Administration in twenty minutes and generating a queue for the intervening minutes.

She used the limited moments to review the updated list of deceased and missing and set up a routine to customize the condolence notifications. Next she tracked down the head of emergency response and received a personal status report, implemented additional security measures beyond the hastily erected checkpoints, and lastly located Richard and give him a quick, and private, hug.

Now she stood at the front of the conference room and regarded the gathered staff members. Many were covered in dust and debris and several still bore streaks of blood.

She gave the room a genuinely sympathetic smile, an expression most had never seen from her. "I won't take much of your time. I recognize you have a great many things you want and need to do. I imagine for some of you this includes helping in the rescue efforts—but we have emergency responders from the entire Cascades region on-scene, so I ask you to let them do their jobs and instead focus on helping to restore order.

"For those of you who had offices in the Headquarters building, we will be taking over the 14th–20th floors of the Logistics building for the immediate future. This means most of you will have to double-up. It's a necessary and hopefully temporary situation. Submit your request to this address—" she sent the new account to the staff "—and you will receive a space assignment."

She paused, pursing her lips for a breath. "Take what time you need to recover your files and anything else you're able to salvage, but unfortunately there is still a war going on—and make no mistake, our adversary will be all too happy to take advantage of our distraction in the aftermath of the attack. Therefore, I must ask you to return to your regular duties as soon as you are capable of doing so. We have doubtlessly lost a number of good people and good friends today, but we cannot allow this to make us weak. It's what the enemy wants. Instead, let it make us stronger.

"Things are bound to be a bit chaotic for the next few days. Route any problems or special requests to the 'issues' queue at the same address. Also, please monitor the news updates at the address. Important information, changes and new procedures will be posted there."

She nodded sharply. "That's everything for now. Let's get to work."

As they began to disperse she grabbed her bottle of water and quickly exited. She did not have the time to entertain questions or desperate inquiries regarding loved ones. The fatalities list was available for everyone to examine and she possessed no further information. Many of them would require comfort and that above all was something she could not provide.

In front of an audience she managed to perform well enough; one-on-one, gazing into broken eyes, however…. In the long run comfort was a hollow, shallow lie, and she simply couldn't find the will to pretend otherwise.

She headed down the hall toward her next meeting, with the military police commander. It would be followed by meetings with the admin managerial staff, the transport supervisors, preliminary planning with the maintenance and construction chief, another update from the head of emergency response, and the first of what was certain to be numerous press conferences.

She wouldn't be seeing a bed for quite some time.

ℛ

Some five hours later she snuck away for a moment of respite in the small gardens between Administration and Logistics. The thermos of coffee warmed her hands and the optic fibers embedded in the pavement lit the path beneath her feet against the late night darkness, though the glare from the enormous floodlights placed by the rescue crews added a sallow glow to the sky.

The death toll already stood at upwards of two thousand and was likely to double by the morning. While rescue efforts continued, the simple fact was the detonations had been scorching and violent. The few who survived the initial blasts had found themselves with no way down or out before the fire or the pervasive smoke reached them.

Even five thousand dead represented a mere blip on the scale of historic disasters. But these were the best, the most dedicated and patriotic of humanity. They were also the people essential to managing the bureaucratic intricacies of fighting a war. An indelicate and unfortunate reality.

Thousands upon thousands of troops needed to be moved around, assigned in a strategic yet orderly fashion and supplied with millions of munitions and foodstuffs and bunks. Important assets needed to be protected while blind spots minimized. Every person and resource needed to be utilized in an efficient and optimized manner.

War was a complicated affair when spread across the galaxy; it always had been. This she knew all too well.

"Director of Logistics for the entire North American Region? Miri, that's wonderful."

The moonlight shone through the window to transform his beautiful eyes to liquid silver as he grinned at her. She lay facing him in the bed, snuggled up so close their noses almost touched. "Maybe."

"With a war on it will be an enormous responsibility and even more work...."

She frowned. "You don't think I can do it?"

"Naoborot dushen'ka, I think you will be spectacular at it. If I possessed your brilliant mind I might get to stay on Earth in a prestigious job, too."

"Don't even start with that, David. They're not giving you command of a cruiser because of your looks—" his mouth turned down in a playful pout "—they could, of course, but it would make for a poor war strategy."

She kissed the pout away then rolled onto her back to stare at the ceiling. "I'm not sure I'm going to accept. I don't want to send you out into the middle of the war while I get to remain comfortable and cozy in our home. I should be fighting as well."

He propped up on an elbow to catch and hold her gaze. "You will be. If you don't do this job correctly, the whole damn operation falls apart. And besides...it would give me so much peace of mind while I'm out there to know you're safe."

"But David—"

"Hush. I realize I'm being overprotective—I don't care. And you'll be here for Alex, which will make me very, very happy. She needs you."

"Perhaps, but she wants you."

"Miri...."

"I know, I know...I'm glad you're her favorite, honestly. You're my favorite, too, so it shows good judgment on her part."

She exhaled quietly. "Okay. If you're so certain it's the right choice, I'll take the position." She shifted to face him once more and run a hand through his hair. "But you better come back to me, you understand?"

He smiled against her lips. "I will. I promise."

He had not kept his promise. But David had been right in at least one respect—she had excelled at the job. Now she oversaw logistics for the entirety of the Alliance military, and it wasn't her sole responsibility.

But she had just lost a significant percentage of the people who made it happen. She'd give it another full day, then start a recruitment search, keeping the hiring standards as strict as possible but—

Startled, she spun at the sound of approaching footsteps. Richard hurried along the path toward her. Figures...he'd be the only one to know where to find her, after all.

"Richard, you look terrible. You really should get some rest, or at least take a shower. I'm assuming you have let a medic take a look at you."

"Later." He reached her and came to a stop, at which point she saw the expression on his face.

"Is something wrong? What happened?"

"We may have a problem. I think you need to see this."

67

LONDON, EARTH ALLIANCE ASSEMBLY

Every Alliance news feed and most of the Senecan and independent feeds carried the open session of the Earth Alliance Assembly live. Some fourteen billion people stopped what they were doing to watch, likely sensing an event of import was on the horizon.

The Assembly met in the historic Palace of Westminster. It had been gutted nearly two centuries earlier, its foundation restructured to prevent it from sinking into the Thames then redesigned from the ground up to house a single congressional body and support the essentials of the modern world.

What once had been the Central Hall now formed the core of the Assembly Chamber, an enormous fan-shaped auditorium modeled after the old U.S. Congress—the justification being semicircle seating provided closer vantage points for a greater number of people than the rectangular arrangement of the former British Parliament. Homage had been paid to the original styling in numerous ways, however, from dark oak beams adorning the ceiling to brass accents gilding the doorways and classic fresco paintings decorating the walls.

The Majority Leader of the Assembly, Charles Gagnon, took the podium as the Secretary gaveled the session to order. In other circumstances it might have been the Speaker at the podium, but in the current situation such an act would have appeared unseemly and transparently self-serving.

Gagnon's gaze moved with deliberate attention across the cavernous chamber. "Ladies and Gentlemen, Senators and honored guests. I come before you now in this dark moment for the Alliance to raise a matter I never wished were required.

"A few short hours ago we experienced a horrific loss in the terroristic bombing of Strategic Command Headquarters. The enemy struck at the very heart of our leadership structure, killing not only the Chairman of Strategic Command and three of its Board members but over 4,500 of our brave fighting men and women. Men and women who had committed their lives to keeping the Alliance and its citizens safe and secure.

"While emergency responders were still pulling the dead and injured out of the rubble, ships from Northwestern Regional Command were ambushed by Senecan forces while on patrol, the victims of cowardly mining of an asteroid field. They suffered devastating losses which could have been—should have been—avoided."

He paused to sigh with dramatic flair. "The grim but undeniable fact is, Alliance governance now lies in chaos—within the military and within the administration. These latest events confirm something many of us had already begun to recognize. Prime Minister Brennon is not prepared to lead us in a time of war."

A low rumble rippled through the chamber; he waited for it to subside before continuing.

"An ill-advised Trade Summit led to the tragic assassination of Mangele Santiagar. Anemic defenses on one of our most important Alliance worlds led to the *annihilation* of the Forward Naval Base on Arcadia. An inexcusable security lapse allowed high-powered explosives to be smuggled into EASC Headquarters, resulting in the death of thousands and the destruction of Strategic Command.

"This morning, the Prime Minister issued an executive order appropriating significant production outlays from a number of large Alliance-friendly corporations. Though it pales in comparison to so much loss of life, this move suggests he views this war fundamentally as an opportunity for a power grab rather than the grave threat it is.

"In these events and more, the Prime Minister has proven himself utterly incapable of responding to the realities of war. Nor can he provide the leadership necessary to drive us to victory over the rebels calling themselves a 'federation.'"

He nodded, as if he had only now convinced himself of the necessity of his action. "Therefore, I find I have no choice but to call for a vote of no confidence in Prime Minister Brennon and his administration. Let us adopt new leadership while there is still time to ensure the Alliance remains strong and unbowed. Mr. Secretary, I submit Special Assembly Resolution SGR 2322-3174 for an official vote."

The thin young man in black formal attire nodded and loaded the resolution into the Assembly voting system.

Perhaps cognizant the galaxy was watching, the vote went swiftly for 510 politicians. Four minutes later the vote tally flashed on the oversized screen floating high above the chamber. A low cheer erupted in the chamber, the dissonant contrast of boos echoing beneath it.

> SGR 2322-3174:
> For: 267
> Against: 243

Within seconds the Majority Leader had returned to the podium. "Thank you all for following reason and logic in performing your solemn duties. Per Constitutional mandate, until the next election the Prime Ministership shall pass to Speaker of the Assembly Luis Barrera, a man I have known for many years and in whom I can confidently entrust the safety of the Alliance. Speaker?"

Barrera appeared out of nowhere beside Gagnon at the podium. They exchanged a firm yet collegial handshake; then Barrera stood alone.

"Citizens of the Earth Alliance, of all free space, in service of the future of this great Alliance I humbly accept the position of Prime Minister. Under my leadership and the guidance of a new administration, we will not allow terrorists and insurgents and rebels to threaten our way of life, our freedoms or our safety. We will take the fight to them, we will show them no quarter and we *will* emerge victorious."

In an archway along the left wall of the chamber, offstage and off-camera, Marcus Aguirre smiled.

68

SPACE, NORTH-CENTRAL QUADRANT
BORDER OF SENECAN FEDERATION SPACE

Alex rested her elbows on her knees and a palm at her chin. She felt far, *far* better this morning. Better than she had expected. Of course, she'd never been shot before so she didn't exactly have anything to compare it to. She doubted she'd be running a marathon or hiking mountains today, but only a very observant person would notice she was injured at all.

"So what are we going to do once we get to Romane? I mean if we're truly being hunted, I damn sure want to find out why."

She felt his hands rest on her shoulders from behind. He began kneading the muscles up to the curve of her neck. "At this point we have to assume we *are* being hunted. I can't get a handle on why, though. A number of people are aware of the alien threat now and—"

She frowned and twisted around, ignoring the dull twinge in her side. "You think this is about the aliens and not the war? Why—"

In an instant his expression morphed from thoughtfulness and affection to...horror? Cold hardness and perhaps even fury.

He backed away from the couch in an explosion of movement. "What in the bloody *hell* is—*Jesus!*"

"What's wrong?"

His hand ran violently down his face. "Turn on the news feed...."

"What is—" Her message indicator began flashing angrily, along with an unfamiliar yellow alert. She waved the news feed on as she opened it.

> *Earth Alliance Military Police Order:*
>> *You are requested to report to Military Headquarters in San Francisco for questioning regard—*

On the embedded screen, front and center, floated an image of Caleb.

"Caleb Andreas Marano, an agent with the Senecan Federation Division of Intelligence, has been named as the prime suspect in the horrific bombing of EASC Headquarters in Vancouver, Earth yesterday. He should be considered armed and extremely dangerous, so approach with caution."

Her focus started to shift to him, but froze mid-motion when the image on the screen transitioned—to one of her.

"Mr. Marano was last seen in the company of Alexis Mallory Solovy. Ms. Solovy is the estranged daughter of EASC Director of Operations Admiral Miriam Solovy and the deceased Commander David Solovy, a well-known hero of the First Crux War. Ms. Solovy is being sought for questioning, but is not currently considered a suspect in the bombing itself."

"'Estranged'? Thanks, Mom...."

Her eVi continued to blink and beep as an avalanche of messages rolled in; she silenced the entire interface to concentrate on him.

He paced in even greater agitation than the previous night, his eyes dark and ominous. She found herself reminded of her very first impression of him: *dangerous*.

"Caleb, what the hell is happening here?"

His jaw had clenched into a razor-sharp edge. "Apparently since they failed to kill me, they decided to frame me for mass murder instead."

He sank against the wall and brought his hands up to seize his jaw in a death grip. "Goddammit! This is fucked up beyond all reason."

"I'm sorry. This is my fault. I shouldn't have forced you to go to Earth." She stood to go over to him.

His hands fell away from his jaw. "No." He met her halfway and grasped both sides of her face. "It was worth it, no matter what happens. And you didn't force me—I chose to go."

A smile pulled at her lips, but refused to materialize. "Is it possible EASC is blaming you solely because they have evidence you were there? To put a face on the enemy?"

"Maybe…." He resumed pacing, though it had gained a more methodical, deliberate quality. "The thing is, the information I saw—before I was locked out of Division's network, as it appears I now *am*—indicated we had no idea who ordered the bombing. I'm not at all convinced Seneca is responsible."

"Who else would do it? Terrorists, taking advantage of the war as an opportunity to sow chaos?"

"Conceivably. Still, that scenario doesn't jibe with the hit on us or Volosk."

"You think they're related to the bombing?"

He came to an abrupt stop. "They are now."

With a deep breath he visibly *willed* himself in control. More of the barely restrained rage seeped away. "Okay. We already suspected someone or a group was manipulating events to trigger the war. The bombing could easily be part of it. Any reluctance on the part of the Alliance will evaporate if they believe Seneca attacked their military leadership. And killing me would obviously prevent me from proving I didn't do it. In which case I'm only a pawn, a convenient patsy."

"Why kill me though?"

"Same reason." He gave her a smile, yet his expression was *so* troubled. "You know I didn't do it." The smile faded into concentration. "But why kill Volosk? It's impossible his murder is unrelated."

She found she had joined him in pacing, worrying at her lower lip while they crisscrossed the cabin. *There was something ticking at the back of her mind….*

She grabbed his shoulder as they passed one another, her eyes lighting up. "You know what you and I, Volosk and EASC Headquarters have in common? The Metis report—" and darkening again "—but others have it, too. Dr. LaRose, for one."

"Well, what's his status?"

She queried the exanet and scanned the results. "No mention of an attack…hold on." The scan had also picked up an unread message in her eVi…so she was a little behind in reading her messages. She *had* been shot.

"I have a request from him for another hard copy of the data. It seems one of his researchers took the disk home—and never returned."

"To work?"

"To anywhere."

A frown grew across his face, tugging his mouth downward. "Okay, that's...suspicious."

The frown deepened into a full grimace. "But still, you were right before—a lot of people have seen the information. Director Delavasi, analysts and scientists on both sides, the rest of the EASC Board, probably our Director of Defense and Field Marshal. The secret's out. And they didn't try to kill LaRose—the report is simply missing."

He shook his head. "I'm not convinced it isn't about the war. If there is a conspiracy, the conspirators would absolutely want to eliminate us before we exposed it. And Volosk had the assassination autopsy reports...is that what got him killed?" He pinched the bridge of his nose in frustration. "Is he dead because I pulled him into this mess?"

"He's dead because they're bad guys. And while they haven't tried to kill LaRose, what if they killed his researcher?"

He nodded. "Right, the report. I wonder—"

She was pacing rapidly now, any ache from her wounds forgotten and fire now animating her irises. "Not the *report*. The hard copy of the raw data. Others saw the report, but I only made four copies of the raw data: for us, EASC, LaRose and Volosk."

Her gaze shot up to meet his. "We missed something."

"What do you mean?"

"There's something else in the data I captured. Something important."

He stared at her, slowly letting out a weighty breath. "Do you realize what you're saying?"

"That the aliens are already among us, or at least have agents working on their behalf? Yes, I do."

"Just making sure."

"Do you disagree?"

He shrugged gamely. "No...I don't believe I do. Because you know what? Last night wasn't the first time on this mission someone's tried to kill me. With everything that's happened I had almost forgotten about it, but three merc ships attacked me on the way to Metis. That's why I opened fire on you in the first place—I thought you were one of them."

She groaned. "And *that's* what the job was about…."

"What job?"

"Right before I left for Metis, I was offered an absurd amount of money to go to work for the government overseeing the Alliance's deep space exploration program. The Minister for Extra-Solar Development practically fell on his knees begging me to accept the post, and accept it immediately. I don't see how anyone knew where I was headed, but it has to be related. Dammit, I knew something was up with that." With a sigh she flopped down on the couch and opened an aural.

He resumed a more leisurely pacing, and after a moment gave a wry laugh. "Are we actually saying there is both a conspiracy to foment war *and* a conspiracy to conceal the nature of the aliens? Stretches the limits of credulity a little far."

His eyes rolled at the ceiling. "Unless it's all one conspiracy—they instigate a war to soften us up ahead of the invasion and ensure we're so busy killing each other we'll be unable to mount an effective response. Nope, *that's* crazy. Right?"

She glanced up distractedly. "Hell if I know. You're the spy." She had begun scrolling through the data files, looking for the answer. The *reason*.

And with a blink it leapt out at her. In retrospect, it was blindingly obvious and she was a *svoloch* for missing it. "I found it."

"Seriously?"

"Perhaps not all of it, but I found one rather important detail we missed. It's the TLF wave. I pegged the terahertz as communications in part due to the way it permeated, spreading out across the area as if to blanket the ships. The TLF though…."

She met his gaze. "It's coming from the portal. More specifically, from the inside of the portal. See, here? The furthest the wave can be traced back to is the center of the portal, at which point it's mid-waveform."

"*Damn.* But is it enough to kill over?"

"For one thing, I'm not sure it's necessarily a high threshold—see Exhibit A, the fleet of superdreadnoughts. For another, if it draws attention to the portal itself—and to whatever is on the other side of it—then to them it very well could be. Remember, nothing in the universe emits waves at so low a frequency. So the question becomes, what does?"

She fixated on the aural as her fingertips drummed a staccato étude on her thigh. "There's one way to find out."

"You want to go back to Metis? It'll be risky."

"Not *that* risky. I'll need a new dampener field module though. Ken can probably bring one to Romane and—"

"Ken? Another 'good friend' of yours?"

She returned his smirk in full. "Ken is a *she* and yes, albeit not in the way you're implying."

He chuckled, but she saw the strain still pulling at the corners of his eyes and the edges of his mouth. "Okay. This is a good plan. I'm in."

Her voice dropped to a tentative whisper. "I'm glad…but I'm not certain you grasp the full extent of the 'plan.'"

An eyebrow rose. "And it would be?"

"We'll see what we find when we get to Metis, but…I expect to find answers we will need to go through the portal."

"*Through* the portal. Alex, I may be crazy, but you are *insane*."

She grinned hopefully. "Is that a problem?"

He closed the distance between them and draped his arms over her shoulders. "No. In fact, it might be one reason I—" an odd light flickered across his eyes "—think you're kind of amazing."

A tingle of dizzying pleasure raced down her spine to her toes. She kissed him softly. Languidly. For a moment the fact people were trying to kill them and they were now wanted fugitives didn't matter so much.

She sank deeper into his arms, letting him envelop her. "Maybe the key to clearing your name is on the other side of the portal."

He nodded against her lips. "Maybe the key to defeating those aliens is on the other side of the portal."

"Yeah, that too."

ℛ

> Richard. Mom.
>
> > You need to understand Caleb did not do this. Irrespective of any moral, philosophical or political considerations, he was with me every second he wasn't under military guard. It is a physical impossibility for him to have played any role whatsoever.
> >
> > Something else is going on here. Something far more sinister than a mere civil war or even a mere alien invasion. I plan to find out what it is.
> >
> > In the meantime, Richard, it would be awesome if you could clear his name (and mine). Someone deliberately framed him. If I know you, it should really rankle you. It also means this war truly IS a lie.
> >
> > Mom, do try to prevent the aliens from destroying Earth, and as many other worlds as is feasible, until we can return with answers.
>
> — Alex

She sat cross-legged on the floor with her back against the couch. While Caleb reached out to whoever he could in search of any information—answers were too much to hope for—she cleared out the deluge of messages. Most of them she deleted without reply; many without reading. Not all of them, though.

> Alex,
>
> > Love, have you gone and gotten yourself mixed up in this sodding war? Daft idea, if you ask me—which of course you never have. Protect that lovely ass of yours and try not to die, please? The world would be a darker place without you in it.
>
> — Ethan

She smiled to herself—as much at memories of a simpler time as at the message itself—and sent a quick reply.

> > I'll do what I can to not die. I make no promises regarding the state of my ass, however.
> >
> > And...thank you.
>
> — Alex

When the backlog had finally been obliterated she sent a livecomm request.

"Ken, you got a second?"

"*I'm just going to go ahead and assume this little unpleasantness is a small misunderstanding, or a frame job, or simply the fog of war. Are you okay?*"

"Yeah, but it's worse than you know. I need a favor."

"*Always.*"

"I need you to bring a new dampener field module to Romane."

"*What's wrong with your current one?*"

"I blew it out running from the aliens. I didn't tell you at dinner the other night?"

"*No, you neglected to mention it. I told you to watch the power spikes.*"

"I know, I know. I panicked. In fairness, I had good reason."

"*True enough. When do you need it by?*"

"As soon as you can get it there. Yesterday should be fine."

"*Right. I was leaving for Messium in the morning, but I can leave tonight and swing by Romane first.*"

"We'll be at the Exia Spaceport, Bay D-24. You're the best."

"*I really am. I'll get to meet him now, won't I?*"

"Yes...."

69

Mia paced around the open space of the gallery office, prepping for the day ahead. Her movements were unhurried; in truth it was more of a stroll than a pace.

She liked to come in early, when the gallery and the neighborhood outside were quiet and peaceful. Here, unhurried by the daily frenzy which inevitably came with the dawn, she could consider what she must do, what she needed to do and what she hoped to do, and plan accordingly. On good days there was plenty of time for the last category. On bad ones, unexpected ones and surprising ones...well, she just rolled with it.

This day included a tour group from a local elementary in the morning, gallery open hours interrupted by a lunch meeting at a business owners' industry association, and the continuation of Ledesma's exhibit from mid-afternoon until late in the evening. A busy day to be sure. But she enjoyed the exhibit, so not a bad one.

She was reviewing the discussion topic for the lunch meeting when her eVi flashed a custom alert. She had a number of flagged items for which her eVi maintained a constant passive filter; if one of them showed up in any major news feed, she was notified.

Seven alerts cascaded in before she finished reading the initial one. She sank against her desk with a long sigh. "Oh, Caleb darling, you truly have gotten yourself into a mess this time...."

A hand rose to her chin. Her gaze drifted to the windows on the far wall, where the first rays of light from one of Romane's two suns began to peek over the horizon. After a moment she pivoted and walked out of the office, pulsing Jonathan as she strode through the empty exhibit room.

> *Can you cover the tour group for me this morning?*
> *Uh, sure...how much trouble can twenty nine year-olds be?*

I'm not going to respond to that question except to say 'thank you.'

Once the doors to the gallery had closed behind her she sent Caleb a message, presuming he was far too occupied to answer a pulse at the moment.

Caleb,

I'll have the items you—both of you—will need ready by the time you arrive.

— Mia

She paused briefly on the sidewalk to consider her options, then headed to the parking lot. She'd go home first, to her very private and very secure office. From there she could hack the entry records and create an ID, which were the most important components. Then if there was time, she'd go shopping.

So this would be an unexpected day then.

***

This time Mia was standing at the airlock when it opened. In noted contrast to their prior arrival, she wore jeans, boots and a red cowled sweater. After all, this was no longer about formality and proper impressions; it was about survival.

She waved them back toward the rental ship and followed them in. "We need to take care of a few things before you return to your ship."

She dropped a large bag on the table and started handing out gear. "Fashionable—but not too fashionable—hat, sunglasses and jacket for each of you." Caleb accepted the items with a nod. Alex looked a little perplexed and vaguely suspicious, but after a hesitant pause took the gear.

Next to come out of the bag was several small containers. "Drops to change eye color. They last around two days. Hair dye as well." She glanced at Alex. "I'd still recommend pulling your hair up, and maybe curl it or something when you go out."

Alex frowned at her—frowned more, anyway. "Are you certain? I thought it would be better to wear it down and obscure my face."

Mia regarded her curiously, then shifted her attention to Caleb. He was leaning against the wall in an attempt at appearing relaxed. It was a good attempt; she wasn't fooled. "She honestly has no idea, does she?"

A corner of his mouth tweaked up as his head shook. "No, she doesn't." His focus drew over to Alex and...*oh god, he really is in love with her.*

"Um, hello? Standing right here?"

She gave a dry laugh. "Alex, how you've never realized this in your however-many years of existence is beyond me, but you are a rather uncommon-looking woman—especially with that hair of yours. Not in a bad way, mind you. But your image is being spammed across the galaxy right now, and people are most definitely going to remember it. So try to keep that in mind when you show your face in public, okay?"

She didn't give Alex a chance to respond. "Now I took the liberty of setting up a comprehensive false identity for you. Load it into your cybernetics and it will pass a mid-level scan, change your fingerprints, the whole works. The name's Zoe Galanis. I hope it works for you. Caleb, you have many of those. Pick one."

"Already done. Riley Knight, mechanical engineer for Atmospheric Solutions."

Alex studied the details on the ID. "How did you manage to get your hands on this so quickly?"

Mia shrugged. "I set it up myself."

Alex's eyes shot over to her. It was possible this time they showed a glint of appreciation. "Impressive."

"Well I did pick up a few useful skills during my indentured servitude. The serial number and registration for the *Siyane* were doctored when you arrived, and as soon as the news broke I back-masked the corridor records. You'll want to load the doctored information into the ship before departing."

She checked the bag to confirm it was now empty, then turned to them, a sigh on her lips. "Listen guys, even given all this, you should try to lie low. Your faces are everywhere, and with the war heating up the Romane government is having kittens trying to make sure it doesn't piss either side off. Independent or not, they will extradite you in a heartbeat if you're caught."

Alex nodded distractedly while she continued to study the ID. Caleb smiled. "You're a lifesaver, Mia. We owe you."

Were you able to take care of the other matter?

Your girlfriend has some ridiculously tight security on her ship—but yes, it's done. Secondary encryption key is Д085401H129914C.

Makes sense...an anagram of the dates of her father's birth and death with his initials.

Yeah, Meno said the same thing.

Meno?

My Artificial.

Mia....

Don't lecture me.

Fine, I trust you're being careful. Listen, thank you. I mean it. And know—it's only in case I need it to save us both.

You never have to explain yourself to me, Caleb. Are you okay?

No. I'm pissed.

Then they had better watch out.

She shook her head. "No, I still owe you—but I think I might see 'even' on the horizon."

He chuckled...and she suddenly realized how tired he looked. "Fair enough. We'll be here for another day, day and a half. We need to make a couple of upgrades and stock up on supplies."

Mia's eyes narrowed. "Stock up for...what, exactly?"

70

Marcus reviewed colony reports while the workers moved his furniture into the new office. He wore a perfect mask of grave concern as befitted the situation, but beneath it he was feeling quite pleased.

The Foreign Minister merited both a larger, better-appointed office and a suite filled by aides to go with it. The view was different; instead of the gardens, his office now looked out on the Potomac. It painted a congenial scene, but he didn't intend on getting attached to it.

Barrera had come to him the night before the Assembly 'no confidence' vote to bring him up to speed on developments and to provisionally offer him the post of Foreign Minister.

Barrera had emphasized the severity and gravity of the circumstances and reiterated what everyone in settled space already knew: the post was, for all intents and purposes, the most powerful one outside of the Prime Ministership itself. He had expressed confidence Marcus was up to the task of serving as the Alliance's ambassador to the galaxy.

He had reminded Marcus that while in cases of removal of a Prime Minister by the Assembly *for cause*, the position passed to the Speaker, this was not the case in the event of a Prime Minister's death or unforeseen inability to perform his duties. In those instances the administration otherwise continued unchanged, and the line of succession passed through the Foreign Minister's office before any others.

He had asked if Marcus was willing to bear such a solemn responsibility.

Marcus had carefully and thoughtfully considered the question, then answered in the affirmative.

Barrera actually believed it was all his idea.

Marcus switched from the colony reports to personnel matters and walked over to one of the windows to give the movers more room. Most of the existing bureaucracy would remain, since it consisted of career civil servants capable enough at their jobs and generally not beholden to any party or faction.

Nevertheless, there were a number of appointments for him to make—an opportunity to put sympathetic and loyal personnel in place. Then there were additional postings which he did not bear responsibility for filling, but with respect to which his opinion had been requested.

He scanned the list...and a smile grew on his lips as for a second he forgot the need to publicly maintain a troubled demeanor.

See, Marcus? If you are patient, solutions to difficulties will often present themselves—almost as if the winds of fate act on your behalf.

It seemed a vacancy had opened at the position of EASC Chairman, on account of General Alamatto's tragic death in the bombing. It was the Prime Minister's appointment to make, but his recommendation—along with the Defense Minister's, for the pittance it was worth—carried significant weight.

He may not be able to eliminate Miriam Solovy right away, but perhaps he could render her irrelevant until the scandal of her daughter's involvement in the bombing ultimately forced her to resign. And the best part was, he didn't have to do anything more than submit a name. He was certain the man he named would take care of the rest on his own initiative.

He pulled the draft report containing his recommendations back up and added an entry to the bottom of the list.

Earth Alliance Strategic Command Chairman: Southwestern Regional Commander General Liam O'Connell

When the movers had at last departed, he sank into the plush, natural leather chair. Behind the privacy of a closed door his lips rose in a smile which reached his eyes in a bright sparkle and his posture in the rise of both shoulders.

As with all plans, not everything had proceeded as envisioned. Solovy's daughter and the Senecan spy remained on the loose for the moment. Though as fugitives they were actually easier to incriminate for the bombing than his initial plan, due to Olivia's failure to deliver the final element of an airtight frame there existed a miniscule but nonzero chance the two might eventually be exonerated. Not that he expected either of them to live long enough for it to matter. Miriam Solovy lived and Alamatto did not. A high-ranking Senecan Intelligence official had been killed—necessarily so, but when it occurred on the same night a string of bodies littered downtown Cavare it risked attracting unwanted attention.

A series of loose threads lay scattered around their corner of the galaxy, any one of which if tugged on sufficiently hard would unravel the entire operation. But so long as events continued on their current trajectory they would soon move beyond the point where anyone could alter their path. The inertial force of a galaxy-spanning plan in motion would soon become far too powerful to be diverted.

He only had a minute to relax, so the boxes cluttering the office were going to have to stay packed for now. Following a quick meeting with Barrera to receive instructions and guidance as to the new administration's official stance on numerous issues, he was headed to the Orbital to meet the governors of the First Wave worlds. The meeting would be followed by visits to Romane, Sagan and several other notable independent worlds in the hopes of persuading them to express public support for the Alliance in the war.

Such support would be the first step in coaxing them under the political and military umbrella of the Alliance, but one step at a time. He should—

We require your attention.

Jesús Cristo! He scrambled to make sure the security shielding remained active from the office's previous occupant, then took a deep breath and straightened up in his chair. The alien couldn't see him—at least, he didn't think it could—but it helped set the proper frame of mind and demeanor.

"Certainly. I have news as well. Matters are proceeding according to plan, and I have achieved a position from where I will be able to exert far greater control over events."

Your plan is now irrelevant. We warned you escalation may become unavoidable, and so it has.

"I request you exercise restraint for a short while longer. The war is approaching criticality and will soon overwhelm all other concerns. I promise you, everyone will forget the Metis Nebula even exists, much less the fantastical ramblings of two wanted fugitives."

Knowledge of our existence has expanded beyond our or your capability to contain it. Already others have ventured near, seeking answers. We are left with only one option.

For a brief moment his polite, respectful composure cracked in frustration. He was trying to save the human race, dammit— he simply needed a little more time. "Pray tell, what option might that be?"

Annihilation.

71

ROMANE
INDEPENDENT COLONY

Alex gave Kennedy a quick hug at the hangar bay door. "Thank you so much for coming."

"Of course. But what's going on?"

"We'll talk about it in a few. Come on inside. Caleb's heading out, but he wants to meet you."

"Does he now? And what have you told him about me?"

"That you're a spoiled, over-entitled daddy's little rich girl."

"You didn— "

"I'm *kidding*. Not much I'm afraid. We've been a bit busy."

"With what you're doing that you're not telling me."

"Right." She motioned Kennedy ahead of her into the ship.

Caleb was leaning casually against the data center, an easy smile lighting his features. He pushed off the table and met them halfway, his hand extended. "Caleb Marano. It's a genuine pleasure, Ms. Rossi."

She was as always the picture of grace and accepted his hand in style. "The pleasure's all mine—and please, call me Kennedy. I understand you and Alex have had quite the two weeks."

"It's been...well, I'm very glad we met."

A wicked grin fought valiantly to pull her lips ever further up. "Indeed."

"And now, I will let you two get to work."

Alex had paused at the edge of the couch to enjoy their introduction. Caleb came over to run his hands gently along her arms while pressing his mouth equally as gently to hers. She rested her hands on his hips and, when the kiss finally ended, whispered against his lips. "Watch your back, will you?"

"Always. I'll only be gone a few hours. Promise."

As soon as he had left Kennedy spun around, eyes wide as saucers. "Oh, girl—"

"Let's go downstairs. You can help me get the module installed."

"And you can tell me how you managed to win the romance lottery while cavorting in uninhabited deep space...Alex, are you okay?"

She glanced over her shoulder from the second step. "Sure, why?"

"You're...limping. Stepping gingerly. I don't know, not barreling through the ship as per usual."

"Oh, yeah." She rolled her eyes at the ceiling. "I got shot."

"You're serious."

"I told you it was worse than you knew."

They reached the hatch to the engineering well, and she gingerly climbed down the ladder. "Which is why we're heading back."

Kennedy skipped the last two rungs and landed on the floor. "Back where? Not to Metis—not to the alien ships?"

"Yep. Though there's no reason to assume the ships are still there. Regardless, we need answers and Metis is where they are."

"You're insane."

She laughed a little and removed one of the panels protecting the core engineering systems. "That's what Caleb said. But no one else is going to do it. I don't trust anyone else to do it anyway. Someone, perhaps the aliens themselves—don't look at me like that—doesn't want the portal investigated. So it's exactly what we intend to do."

"Wait. You're not planning to go *through* the portal, are you?"

"Um..." her nose scrunched up "...probably."

"Dear god, you really are insane." Alex motioned for the module, and she handed it over. "You know, you ought to think about...." Her voice trailed off as she peered at the floor. "What happened to your hull?"

Kennedy's attention had been drawn to the wide streaks of almost luminous silver winding along the center of the hold. It matched neither the onyx of her hull material nor the muted bronze of the salvaged material from his ship.

"Caleb ripped it open with a pulse laser—to clarify, this was before we were sleeping together—and we had to patch it using scrap from his ship."

"Which you blew up," she mumbled, bending down so close to the floor she was all but lying on it.

"Right."

"What was his ship made of?"

"Amodiamond. The discoloration is on the seams where we melded the two materials together. It started changing color once it cooled. Some kind of chemical reaction I assume. Do you think it's weakening the structural integrity?"

"No, quite the opposite." She reached behind her and pulled a small scanner out of her bag, then ran it above a segment of the discoloration. "Integrity is definitely solid. Stronger, even. The materials have fully bonded together and...." She glanced up at Alex. "Is it okay if I take a piece back with me to analyze? Just a sliver."

"Sure, but why?"

"Because I think you've made something new." A metamat blade materialized out of Kennedy's bag; she carefully shaved off a thin three-centimeter long strip. She placed it in a gel pouch and dropped everything back in her bag. At Alex's raised eyebrow, she chuckled and hugged her knees to her chest. "Ship designer, remember? Exotic metals turn me on."

"Everything turns you on."

"Hey, that's low. True, but low—especially when your sex life is far more interesting than mine at the moment." Her voice lost most of its teasing tenor. "I can't help but notice you're using 'we' and 'us' a lot."

"I know." Alex shrugged. "What do you want me to say? I like him."

"Clearly. And I am the *last* person to dissuade you from running off on a crazy romantic adventure, but this is serious business. He's accused of terrorism and murder and you're already being sought for questioning."

"He's being framed. Someone tried to kill us, and did kill his boss. Besides, I could give a fuck about political posturing."

"Believe me, I know—though I'm not certain I'd call the military police 'political posturing.' Regardless, I wouldn't be your best and most marvelous friend in the galaxy if I didn't point out there might be a few negative consequences from all..." she gazed upward and twirled her hand in the air "...*this*."

"Well, as for the frame, Richard's on it. It'll get sorted out."

"And your mother?"

Alex closed her eyes and dropped her head against the wall. "What about my mother?"

"You being implicated in the bombing is going to complicate her job, particularly since she—thank goodness—wasn't there when the bombs went off."

"I can't care about that right now, I don't have the bandwidth. My mother can take care of herself. She excels at it. And if she needs to disown me in order to keep her power, so be it."

"Alex—"

"Don't, Ken. We've had this conversation dozens of times. Nothing has changed."

"There's another war. An impending alien invasion. Your life is in danger."

"*Granted.* Look, I actually mean it. She needs to concentrate on this war—not the Senecan war but the war to come. If she has any sense—and she does, as much as I hate to admit it—she won't let me interfere. It's too important."

"Have you told her any of this?"

"Well, I think so. I mean, I told her to *do* something. I thought I was pretty clear."

"Oh, Alex, your communication skills are legendary for a reason...."

"*Whatever.* Okay, we're good. The conduits and infrastructure were still in place so I only had to replace the main box. I'll run some diagnostics, but I don't want to hold you up." She grinned. "Thank you. Thank you, thank you, *thank* you. Now you're off to...Messium, was it? Dare I ask why?"

Kennedy groaned and glared at the low ceiling. "The Board's pimping me out for materials."

"Are you kidding?"

"Well not literally. Oh, I hope nobody expects it's going to come to anything so extreme. No, we require metamats to build ships—big surprise—and our primary supplier got blown up by your Pleasure Model's military."

"Ken!"

"Fine, *fine*...your dark, dangerous, subversively sexy intelligence agent's military. Anyway, I've been dispatched to woo a potential new supplier."

"Woo how?"

"With my name and my dazzling smile, apparently."

Caleb returned to the spaceport feeling reinvigorated. He knew it probably showed, but he couldn't help it. While out he had received a message from his sister...he read it again as he entered the hangar bay.

> *Hey big brother,*
>
> *I'm sure you have a lot going on and a lot on your mind right now, so I won't bother you with a livecomm. I merely wanted to say I am certain you had nothing to do with the bombing. I know what you do—what you really do. I've always known. I understand you were trying to protect me by keeping it a secret, but I will never not be here for you.*
>
> *I know your soul. And I believe in you.*
> *— Isabela*

In the space of two days, the two people he cared for most in the world—wow, the unexpected realization of *that* truth jarred him for a second—had both willingly accepted him, darkness and all. He'd spent so much time and effort over the years shutting himself off from others emotionally, erecting walls around his heart strong enough to repel any inquisitive soul...when maybe he simply should have had a little faith.

Then again, Isabela wasn't just anyone. She was his *sister*— intelligent, strong, loving and understanding, but not foolish. And Alex...well, she wasn't just anyone either. To say the least.

He had told her she was insane for wanting to go through the portal—and she was. But if she hadn't suggested it he likely would have, because in truth he viewed it as the only strategy worth a damn.

It was one of the most fundamental lessons in his line of work, if one many never managed to learn: when you find yourself under siege, outnumbered and out of options—attack. Don't play defense; the enemy's superior numbers or position will whittle you down until you have nothing left. Don't run away; the enemy will only shoot you in the back. Once you're backed into a corner, you've already lost.

While you're still strong, still have weapons and will and time, do what the enemy least expects—attack. Turn into the punch, grab ahold of the gun, leap into the arena. Take control of your own fate. If you're quick, good and lucky, you just might survive and be out the other side before the enemy realized what had happened.

Thus far in his life, when it truly mattered, he had been all three. Now, though….

Now the enemy was maddeningly elusive. Hidden in the shadows and presumably spread across numerous worlds. There was no target he could locate to attack in settled space—and one very clear one at the edge of it. Every instinct he'd relied upon for almost twenty years to survive seemingly impossible situations told him the real enemy, the ultimate enemy, lay on the other side of that portal.

Alex intended to go through the portal to search for answers. He intended to go through the portal to *win*.

He stepped in the *Siyane* and found her at the data center, the Metis data spread in front of her yet again. He set his bag on the couch. "Kennedy leave already?"

"Yeah. The new module installed no problem, and she needed to head out. I've set diagnostic tests running, but everything checks out so far."

"Well at least you were able to—" In his peripheral vision he sensed an…incongruity. Something was different. His gaze shifted toward the cockpit.

To the right of the pilot's chair sat *another* chair. A bit more minimalistic in design than hers, it fit snugly but completely within the margins of the cockpit space.

He approached the cockpit curiously. "Alex, what is this?"

She briefly diverted her attention from the data to glance over, an uncertain smile tugging at her lips. "I got you a chair."

"You...you got me a chair." It was less a question and more a statement of incredulity.

"It's only so I don't always have to be looking over my shoulder to talk to you. It's not safe, honestly. And I'm sure you must get tired of leaning against the wall."

His hand ran along the top of the headrest; the chair glided smoothly beneath it. His gaze returned to her, a vaguely stunned expression on his face. "Alex...."

Her eyes slid away from him and her voice turned formal tinged with a hint of awkwardness. "It's magnetically grounded, so it's not like I tore up the floor or anything, and we can move it if we need to. It's just practical."

But it wasn't just practical. It was touching and kind and an exceptional gesture on her part. Giving him a place on her *ship*, even if only a simple chair—hell, *especially* a simple chair—was tantamount to giving him a place in her life. A real place, in the form of a chair.

He crossed the cabin and wound his arms around her, pulling her away from the data and into him. "Of course it is...." His lips met hers. "*Thank* you."

No, she wasn't just 'anyone' at all.

72

VANCOUVER, EASC HEADQUARTERS

Miriam paced in tightly coiled agitation around the temporary office space. With a frown she nudged the temporary hutch flush to the wall.

Nothing had been salvageable from her office. Not the antique bookcase and certainly not the antique books, of which there remained none in existence to replace them with. Not the leaded glass tumblers that had been a wedding present to her and David and not the heirloom china tea set that had belonged to his grandmother.

She picked up the teacup—part of the set she had brought from home—off the temporary desk and took a long sip, then set it back down. Too hard; it wobbled unsteadily. Unless the desk was uneven....

She looked over at Richard. He leaned against the wall, quietly watching her flutter about. "I don't care how angry Alexis may have been after the Board meeting. There is no way she was involved in the bombing."

"Absolutely not. It's an absurd idea. She's not a killer."

"No, she's not. But this Marano character?"

"Oh, he definitely *is* a killer. His file says he took out two dozen criminal insurgents and blew up an entire hangar bay two months ago, and it's merely his latest exploit. Conveniently enough he has something of a history of using explosives to get a job done. But he's not a terrorist. He infiltrates and eliminates dangerous criminal groups in the service of his government. His record indicates no deviation into more questionable activities."

She crouched and adjusted the rug beneath the desk. Perhaps it was the source of the unevenness. "We're at war. Maybe he didn't consider it terrorism?"

"From the Senecan perspective, arguably it wasn't. But regardless, Alex swore he was never out of her sight except while he was in custody. Miriam...."

Recognizing the tone in his voice, she stood up and met his gaze.

"In the end it comes down to one very simple matter: either you believe her or you don't."

She sighed and let her eyes drift to the window. Logistics was all of twenty stories tall; outside were only other buildings. "I believe her."

A smile sprung to life on his face, possibly in relief. "So do I." The smile didn't linger as his hand came to his jaw. "Which means we have a different problem. She said he was framed, and she's right. The evidence was doctored to implicate him, and by extension, her. By whom? And even more importantly, why?"

"Between the nonsensical Summit assassination, the Palluda attack nobody ordered and now this? Something is severely wrong with this entire situation. The explosives used on the upper levels had to be assembled inside Headquarters. Marano may not have done it, but someone did. They both claim the war has been manufactured by *someone*, and I'm beginning to suspect they're right about that, too."

She crossed the temporary space and placed a hand on his shoulder. "Luckily, conspiracies and subterfuge happen to be your area of expertise. Richard, get to the bottom of this. And most of all, do whatever you need to in order to clear her name. Please." She patted his shoulder and returned to the temporary desk, her voice dropping in volume and perhaps in confidence. "I wish I knew where she's gone."

"You never know where she goes."

"This is different." Her gaze drifted once again to the windows, but the view had not improved. She took a deep breath and squared her shoulders. "Nevertheless, there's nothing I can do about it for the moment. And now it seems I have to find a way to win a war."

"There's no way Seneca can stand up to our military strength in the long run."

"It's not *that* war which has me concerned…at least, not only that war."

"Well, one thing at—"

The priority pulse forced itself into her vision.

Acting Chairman O'Connell requests your presence in his office in five minutes.

Her lips smacked in annoyance. "It appears I am being summoned to kiss the feet of the new Chairman."

"He doesn't waste any time, does he? He's been here all of, what, half an hour?"

"Less than." Another sigh found its way past her lips. "You know, Alamatto was a weak leader, but I'm afraid O'Connell is going to get everyone killed. You're correct—Seneca can't stand up against our military strength. But if he's in charge, they just might outsmart us."

⨤

She stood formally in the doorway while O'Connell discussed something with an aide. After twenty seconds she decided he was deliberately dragging it out in an attempt to make her uncomfortable. *Silly, petty man.*

After another thirty seconds he finally dismissed the aide and glanced at her. "Ah, Miriam."

"Yes, Liam? You wanted to speak with me?"

He scowled and bowed up his stance in an apparent attempt to intimidate her with his towering, burly build. *Also, slow to learn.* "You're as insubordinate as your daughter. I believe you meant 'General.'"

"And I *believe* you meant 'Admiral.' You may be head of the Board for now, but you are not my superior officer. In public I will grant you the respect of your position. In private I will grant you the respect you have earned. Thus far you haven't earned any."

His eyes narrowed in blatant hostility. "You arrogant *bitch.* Your lax security allowed those explosives to be planted. Your daughter gave that fucking Senecan cocksucker inside access and caused the deaths of thousands. You aren't worthy of your position or your rank." He paused, as if to see the effect of his intimidation. She refused to flinch.

With a blink he continued. "I may not possess the authority to fire you, but I plan to do everything in my power to ensure you soon find yourself out on your ass. No rank, no title, no power."

The corners of her mouth curled up in a cold, malicious smile. "We'll see, won't we?" She turned to go, not waiting or wanting to be excused. When she reached the door she paused to look back at him.

"Oh, and Liam? Thank you for the warning."

73

Seraphina breathed in the cool morning air, drawing it deep into her lungs as her diaphragm expanded. *And hold...hold.* With a slow, steady exhale she opened her eyes.

She floated a meter above the water, suspended by the resistance of the magnetic field generated by Gaiae's waters against the fibers woven into her stockings. Indigenous fish danced in the waters beneath her, their iridescent scales reflecting brilliantly in the dawn light. They were poisonous to humans, but it was no matter; neither she nor any of the other residents would have stooped so low as to impinge upon Gaiae's precious ecosystem.

The glowing pastels of the nearby fauna lingered in her vision when she closed her eyes and inhaled once more. Her ocular implant was enhanced to expand the spectrum of her sight beyond visible light into the ultraviolet range. The effect was spiritual in its beauty, but the odd hues tended to leave halos in their wake.

And hold...hold.

She opened her eyes to a shadow.

It broke her meditation, and she suppressed a frown as she twisted around—careful to engage her core—and looked up.

The shadow slithered across the landscape until it reached the water's edge. Her frown deepened. Gaiae had no moons; there could be no eclipse.

What appeared next was of a nightmare. An impossibility. An evil blackness—harsh, bleak, cold metal surely made of the void itself.

It continued to grow in the sky, and soon veins of blood slashed the blackness like the war paint of ancient primitives.

Even as the breadth and length of the blooded darkness grew ever greater, another materialized alongside it. Then another.

Soon a dozen phantasms—devils of Hades come to life—blanketed the sky, blotting out the sun and turning morning to dusk.

Seraphina stood to balance unsteadily atop the magnetic resistance. What horror might this be? She only rarely accessed the so-called 'exanet,' but she did not believe even the most powerful governments possessed ships such as these.

Gaiae was a peaceful planet. Its residents strived ever to be in harmony with all living creatures, with the land and the air and the stars. What sin against nature could possibly have brought such devils down upon them?

Then the bellies of the beasts wrent apart, and all legions spewed forth. Creatures born of the bowels of Tartarus, their arms counted greater than those of Mahākālī and writhed madly around blazing crimson eyes—a cyclopean blood-gorged eye for each creature in the legion army.

Their multitudes descended from the sky, and at last she screamed.

74

They approached Metis as quietly and furtively as the *Siyane* permitted. Their route was circuitous, winding around the Nebula until their trajectory was nearly opposite of before.

All her instincts screamed at her to hurry, to get there faster and to generally *get on with it*. Yet along about the time her fingers stretched out to hover above the controls, Caleb's hand found its way to her shoulder or the curve of her jaw. She wouldn't have expected him to be the calm one...though if she pondered it she had to concede he had often been the patient one.

When the golden-blue wisps of Metis' outer bands at last surrounded them, she initiated the sLume drive a final time. One final run for the core at maximum speed, as swift as any human could travel across the stars.

They would drop out of superluminal 0.1 AU from the portal's location but still within the thickest of the towering pillars of gas and dust. The instant the sLume drive idled the dampener field would kick in. She had paid a princely sum for a barely legal power allocation optimizer, and now the dampener field could operate at full strength without them being forced to freeze.

Still the trip took hours upon hours. As many hours as it had taken when they had previously made the journey, in fact. Unlike the prior journey, however, this night they spent together.

They passed the hours as couples facing the unknown yet temporarily powerless to influence their fate do: they made love as if it were the first time, murmured secrets to one another in the darkness, slept for a bit, and made love as if it were the last time.

Then there was no space left to travel and their fate returned to their hands.

They returned to the cockpit as the sLume drive idled and the scene beyond the viewport sharpened into clarity. The ship hovered in luminous, dense fog; as it did not actually travel forward under separate propulsion while inside the superluminal bubble, on exiting it the ship was already at rest.

Instantly she was a flurry of activity, confirming the dampener field had engaged, beginning scans for threats or any movement whatsoever in the area and attuning the spectrum analyzer across all bands.

The flare from the pulsar leapt to life on the spectrum display. The gamma beam pulsed in a regular, rapid spin. She filtered it out—and immediately frowned. "It's gone."

"Everything?"

Her head shook minutely. "The gamma radiation, the local one whose source we weren't able to pinpoint. The terahertz radiation, too."

He leaned closer to stare at the spectrum display with her. "But not the TLF."

"But not the TLF." She blew out a long, slow breath. "Okay. Nothing to do but find out why." She started the impulse engine.

The nebular clouds soon began to thin, then abruptly evaporate as before. Yet in stark and rather disturbing contrast to before, the clouds evaporated to reveal only the void.

The ships were gone. *And so was the portal.*

Neither of them spoke. They simply regarded the empty blackness in stunned disbelief. She had prepared herself for a number of scenarios. None of those scenarios involved the portal being *gone.*

Because that was impossible.

He dropped his elbows to his knees with a heavy sigh. "So, new plan then."

"No. The portal is there."

His attention shifted from the viewport to her. His voice held calm conviction—and trust, she thought. "Okay. Why?"

"The same reason we're here."

"The TLF signal is still being generated from somewhere."

"Correct. Now the question is...." With her left hand she strafed until the ship was positioned exactly perpendicular to the direction the wave propagated. She focused the spectrum analyzer sensors in on a point in space and took two snapshots. Then she threw both measurements to a waveform screen.

A wondrous breath fell from her lips as she sank into the chair. She was looking at a phase shift across the portal.

When measured given the precise point where the portal had floated as the origin, the TLF wave exhibited a 4.65° phase difference in each direction. On its own it didn't tell her anything about the nature or breadth of the realm within the portal, as any number of cycles could have occurred inside—but it did tell her there existed a realm within the portal.

Caleb's eyes narrowed at the screen for a moment before he shook his head and chuckled wryly. "And space falls back into alignment with the rules of the universe. The portal *is* there."

"Told you." She gave him a teasing if weighty smirk. "Now we just need to trigger it."

"Which you've already determined how to do."

The smirk softened to a smile. "Harmonics."

He glanced at the row of screens and back to her. "The gamma radiation was a harmonic of the TLF, wasn't it?"

"It was, though the frequency disparity was tremendous. I think the gamma frequency was an activation code. It kept the portal open while our alien friends traversed it and shut off once they no longer needed it. But I can mimic it."

His gaze met hers, and the look in his eyes sent her stomach into somersaults and a delightful tingle rushing along her skin. She wanted nothing more in the world than to wind her fingers in his hair and pull him close and ask him if he might tell her what the look in his eyes meant.

Instead she swallowed and focused on the HUD. Her fingertips danced on a holographic panel to her left as she built the gamma wave. Once it was prepped she maneuvered the ship so it lined up directly on the invisible point which represented the center of the former portal.

"Here goes nothing...." She sucked in a deep breath and turned on the signal.

From nothingness burst forth a perfect circle of obsidian metal. Luminescent pale gold plasma filled the ring as it expanded in diameter. In two seconds it had attained its previous size and a halo of roiling clouds had billowed over its edges.

"Well that's not something you see every day." She nodded mutely in agreement.

After the explosion of energy which had propelled the ring outward vanished, a stilled silence seemed to engulf the landscape. The vertical pool of plasma undulated as peacefully as the surface of a pond on a quiet spring dawn. Even the churning clouds appeared to settle into a soothing rhythm. Other than the portal itself, there was no evidence of technology, of an alien force or any force at all.

The TLF wave continued to pulse—steady, deliberate and strong, as though it were the very heartbeat of the universe—from the exact center of the ring.

Like the dulcet tones of a siren it called to her, singing a promise of answers beneath the tranquil waters. Waters which happened to be composed of an unknown breed of plasma and 'lapped' vertically while suspended within a ring of unknown material and origin in the void of space.

Caleb's presence beside her during the trip had been a comfort and a wonderful indulgence. But now it wasn't close enough, for him or her. He pushed out of his chair to kneel in front of her and draw her into a slow, languorous kiss.

He drew back a mere centimeter, his voice a whisper upon her lips. "You realize we could die, simply by going through."

She closed the centimeter to claim another kiss, lingering an eternal second beyond when it might have ended. She breathed in...breathed *him* in. "I do. But if we don't go, maybe everyone dies. And even if I don't particularly *like* most of everyone, I find I don't want that on my conscience."

He nodded against her. "Nor do I. So we go together—but only if you're sure."

She smiled—a tiny little smile—and bravely rolled her eyes as she straightened up and settled into the chair. "I'm sure. It'll be an adventure. New sights, new wonders, new discoveries. It's what I live for. You too, right?"

"Absolutely." He returned to his chair, kicked his feet up on the dash and crossed his ankles. "Lead on. Show me this supposed 'adventure.'"

"You got it."

His hand reached over and wrapped around hers as she gunned the impulse engine to full power and accelerated into the portal.

SUBSCRIBE TO
GSJENNSEN.COM

Receive updates on AURORA RISING, new book announcements and more

They were falling into a black hole.

People referred to regions of space where the distance between stars stretched to kiloparsecs as 'the void.' But even the void retained a murmur of light, the pale glint of distant stars and infinite galaxies.

This darkness was boundless and unbroken.

Dizziness clawed at the corners of Alex's vision, brought on by the absence of a fixed point, of any spatial reference whatsoever to lock on to as a lodestar.

In a fit of what could be mistaken for panic she cut propulsion and sought the rearcam visual—golden plasma rippled placidly inside the massive ring sustaining it. She let out the breath she hadn't realized she had been holding, and the dizziness receded upon the knowledge they were not after all *in* a black hole.

The hand wrapped over hers squeezed with reassuring strength. She looked over to find Caleb wearing an air of easy confidence, complete with sparkling sapphire irises.

"Not dead."

She knew the aura he projected was for her benefit, to give her comfort. And it worked. Her pulse began to slow and the pounding receded from her ears. A laugh bubbled forth, only to morph into a mild protest halfway through. "Not dead. Excellent point. But what *is* this place?"

She returned the squeeze, then let go of his hand and directed her attention to the HUD as readings began coming in. Sensor sweeps were picking up no transmissions save the TLF wave, which continued unabated for as far as her instruments reached. Analysis of the surroundings measured...absolutely normal.

"The immediate area has the same fundamental characteristics as our galaxy. Based on these readings, the laws of physics purport to be alive and well and functioning correctly. The impulse engine is able to operate within parameters. If the portal is a brane intersection..."

she glanced over with a frown "...the dimensions of this place are identical to ours. So why a portal?"

She checked the visual overlay. "We are definitely not anywhere in the Milky Way, though. It'll take the system time to analyze all the possibilities, assuming it *can* with no locus...but I don't believe we're anywhere in mapped space."

"Maybe the portal merely sent us a long way." He shrugged. "Maybe even 'the other side of the universe' long way?"

"Well the other side of the universe is a damn boring place. There's nothing here."

"But there *was* something here. There were ships here, a lot of them, and they had an origin point."

She pinched the bridge of her nose in a futile attempt to ease the dull throbbing behind her forehead and rested her elbows on her knees.

This wasn't what she had expected.

She hadn't known *what* to expect. Perhaps a fresh armada of alien superdreadnoughts eager to return them to the stardust whence they came? Or more preferably, a dazzling civilization of exotic space stations, Dyson rings and planets subsumed beneath cities? She had idly entertained the notion of a mind-exploding dimensional shift to a gestalt of reality she hadn't the acumen to comprehend.

But she hadn't expected *this*.

She stared at the varied screens intended to display a plethora of information. One by one they updated. *Nothing.* Nothing save the portal and the *Siyane.* Yet somewhere beyond this barren expanse lie the aliens who dispatched an armada through the Metis Nebula.

"I think...I think we follow the TLF wave for now. It's still being generated by something farther in. We can use the portal as a heading reference so we don't go in circles. I'll keep scanning on wide-band, and eventually that 'something' will show up. It has to."

Hearing no agreement, or any response at all, she toed the chair around to face Caleb. He was staring out the viewport, shoulders taut and eyes narrowed in a suggestion of unease. "What's wrong?"

He blinked and straightened up in his chair. "Sorry. That sounds fine." A corner of his mouth tweaked up in a hint of a smirk. "I wouldn't dream of arguing with you on the best way to navigate uncharted space. This is your show. But I was wondering…the portal had vanished until we reactivated it, which means they never expected anyone to come through it. So why are they hiding?"

"Maybe they're not hiding. Maybe they're simply…farther. Let's find out." She reengaged propulsion and accelerated until they attained a steady eighty-five percent cruising speed. No reason to overtax the impulse engine on the off chance the laws of physics weren't *exactly* the same here.

In the pervasive darkness there was no visual perception of movement, and only the subtle *purr* of the engine argued otherwise. It was rather disconcerting, so she sought solace in watching the portal in the rearcam. For the time being the sight of it shrinking in the distance did at least convey a sense of motion.

Then it vanished, and the void truly was absolute.

"Fuck!" She killed the thrusters entirely before confirming the gamma wave was still transmitting. It took considerable effort to resist the powerful urge to whirl the ship around and bolt for where the portal had been—to flee this suffocating *emptiness*.

Instead she slumped in her chair, arms flopping weakly to drape over the armrests. Her instruments would have been able to keep a lock on the portal long after it had passed from visual sight. But now….

"Must be a distance limit on the signal to keep it open. *Dammit.*"

Caleb had stood to pace behind the cockpit. In the wake of their discovery of the alien armada she had quickly deduced he did his best thinking while roving. Had it been only weeks ago? It felt like a lifetime had transpired since they had uncovered the terrifying secret at the heart of Metis and the universe had turned upside down.

"Can we use the TLF as a guidance mechanism? A sort of beacon?"

"So long as we don't lose track of which way is forward and which is back. The key is going to be..." she swiveled to the dash, magnified one of the HUD screens and began entering commands "...I'm setting the navigation system to record our relative movements. It will create a mapping of our path, in essence. If all else fails, we can retrace our steps."

"Will it work?"

"It'll work." Instructions completed, she sank back to stare out into the yawning abyss once more.

It was a bleak panorama. Forbidding. Oppressive. She yearned for stars to light the way, to shepherd and inspire her—but there were none.

In lieu of stars she reached behind her, somehow knowing his hand would instantly be in hers, warm and comforting. Solid. *Real*.

On finding what she sought, she sucked in a deep breath and continued on.

ℛ

They had been flying for nearly two hours when the first blips emerged on the long-range scanner.

Bored to tears and craving reassurance life remained possible in this desolate wasteland, she was curled up in Caleb's lap when the alert sounded. In *her* chair in his lap, on account of it being larger and more comfy and all.

She leapt up and magnified the USAR data while motioning him out of the chair impatiently.

"What do we have?"

"Looks like—" More blips materialized on the scanner. Then more...and it occurred to her she didn't technically *have* a plan for this particular scenario. "We found them."

She yanked the ship sixty degrees starboard and pushed the impulse engine to its limit. The inertial dampeners prevented them from being thrown to the floor, but she quickly engaged the safety harness in her chair, as did he.

"Let's see if..." what was now a veritable sea of increasingly larger red dots shifted on the screen "...hell. They can track us. Worse, they *are* tracking us."

He huffed a wry groan. "Their dimension, their rules. Can you outrun them?"

She checked the numbers beneath the display tracking the vessels to see how rapidly they were approaching. "No."

"Can you beat them back to the portal?"

She swerved one more time to make certain, and watched in dismay as they tracked her movement yet again. "Not a chance. They'll be on us in minutes."

"What can I do to help?"

"You can *shut up* and let me think." She magnified the longest-range scans of the region. She wanted to FTL. At superluminal speeds she'd outrun them, or at least they wouldn't—surely couldn't—be able to track her. But she had no sense of how large or small this *space* may be or what might even happen if she initiated a warp bubble.

"Right."

The tightness in his voice and harsh smack of his lips jarred her. She softened her own tone. "Sorry. Just...hang on."

In the corner of her eye she noted the muscles in his jaw twitching. "Okay."

The last time she had been in a firefight she had been shooting at *him*. In a less stressful circumstance she would have chuckled at the irony, but there was no time. The first of the blips came in range of the visual scanner.

It was one of the insectile tentacled vessels from the alien armada.

"We're being chased by an army of squid. And goddamn are they fast squid."

Her gaze raced across every display, every sensor, every reading...but perceiving no answers, it fell to the oblivion outside the viewport. They couldn't run; the ships were almost upon them.

They certainly couldn't fend off what now constituted a solid one hundred pursuers.

She thought Caleb might have said her name, but it was background radiation accompanying the hum in her ears and the symphony in her head—a song of quantum mechanics and trajectory calculations and astroscience physics and *where to go, where to go, where to....*

With a long sweep of her hand the entire HUD vanished. At the end of the gesture her wrist flicked and the lights in the cabin shut off. The inside of the ship was now as featureless as the landscape outside it.

She engaged the autopilot, unfastened her harness, stood and stepped up to the viewport. Her eyes closed.

Moya milaya, do not be afraid of the dark, for there is always light within it struggling to shine through. Be fearless, and you will see it.

She reopened her eyes, and the world outside was no longer cast in charred ebony. More of a dull charcoal now really, except...there. An *absence* within the emptiness. Hollow. An echo of the space around it.

She fell back in the chair, re-latching the harness with one hand while disengaging the autopilot with the other and pulling the ship up in a long arc before veering another twelve degrees starboard. Once the harness was engaged she reactivated the HUD and the lights.

"What do you see?"

Anyone other than him would have quizzed her when she shut everything off...or questioned her sanity. But he had recognized she needed the silence.

"Somewhere darker than black."

A few adjustments and she coaxed another two percent out of the impulse engine, but their pursuers were still gaining on them. It was going to be *close*.

What was going to be close? She was flying headlong into another black hole, and she couldn't fathom what waited inside it.

It hardly mattered now. She had no other option.

The lead row of vessels fired, scarlet-hued lasers bursting out from flaming crimson cores. The writhing arms ignited, lengthening to amplify the beams and direct them to their target.

In the instant before the beams impacted she flung the *Siyane* into a full spin, praying the rapid revolutions might cause the beams to lose tracking, or simply cause them to miss.

Her stomach joined the *Siyane* in its spins as the inertial dampeners failed miserably to compensate for the speed of the revolutions. In the cabin 'up' and 'down' lost meaning.

"Jesus, Alex...."

A growl escaped through gritted teeth. "Just...hang...on...."

It took every iota of her concentration to keep the nose of the ship pointed toward what was a perfect eclipse of infinite blackness, a void in the purest sense of the word. The walls blurred away, along with everything else in her peripheral vision. She kept her focus directly ahead, for if her attention drifted a millimeter off-center she would be lost.

The ship shuddered in her grasp as a laser beam grazed off the lower hull. She ignored it to stay locked on the chasm racing toward her; yet as it consumed the viewport terror bubbled up into her throat. *Dad, I don't think—*

—they breached the edge and plunged in—

—and were inexplicably careening through an atmosphere. Shadow became brilliant sulfur as light flared to life around them.

Utterly unprepared for *light*, of all things, she was temporarily blinded. She fought to pull out of the roll she had created while blinking furiously and begging her ocular implant to give her *something* before the atmospheric forces tore her beloved ship to pieces and them with it. "I can't *see.*"

"I can—in infrared at least. Let me help you."

Then he was beside her. One of his arms wound tightly around the armrest; the other curled over hers on the controls. She willed her grip relaxed and let her hand respond to his guiding touch.

It took a few seconds, but the spinning diminished to wild gyrations, then to mere turbulence. Down and up returned to their proper positions, and the bright halos overwhelming her vision began to fade.

"I...I'm okay. Mostly. Enough."

He collapsed to the floor next to her chair. "Good job, baby."

His voice sounded terribly weak, trembling from the effort of speaking. She didn't understand how he had managed to get to her side, much less remain there without a harness, *much less* stay focused ahead and be her eyes. She wanted to wrap her arms around him and cradle him against her, but she still needed both hands.

The atmosphere did show signs of thinning, though. With a deep, calming breath she transitioned to the pulse detonation engine for planetary flight and allowed her fingers to sink into his hair.

A moment later the haze coating the sky evaporated away.

"When you can, you're going to want to look up...."

He steadied himself by resting one palm on her thigh and the other on the armrest, and rose to his knees. "I'll be damned."

"Possibly. But not today, I think."

They flew high above savanna grassland. The sky was the deep cornflower blue of a sunny late afternoon on Earth...*exactly* the color of a sunny late afternoon on Earth.

Only there was no sun. Whatever was lighting this planet, it wasn't a star.

VERTIGO: AURORA RISING BOOK TWO
AVAILABLE NOW
HTTP://WWW.GSJENNSEN.COM/VERTIGO

Author's Note

Thank you so much for reading *STARSHINE*.

If you enjoyed this book, would you consider telling others about it? Reviews are the lifeblood of an author's success. They help to influence potential readers and shape a book's reputation, and just a few words go a long way. Share the books on social media or in your favorite forums, or simply tell your friends about them. You have my sincere thanks.

A complete list of my books and where to find them (including *Vertigo* and *Transcendence*, Books Two and Three of the *Aurora Rising* trilogy) can be found at www.gsjennsen.com/books.

Visit www.gsjennsen.com to explore concept art and other media and get the inside scoop on *Aurora Rising* and the sequel trilogies, *Aurora Renegades* and *Aurora Resonant*. Subscribe to the website to stay up-to-date on all the latest news and be the first to know about special announcements and new book releases.

You can always email me at gs@gsjennsen.com with questions or comments, or find me on a variety of social media platforms:

Twitter: @GSJennsen
Facebook: facebook.com/gsjennsen.author
Goodreads: goodreads.com/gs_jennsen
Google+: plus.google.com/+GSJennsen
Instagram: instagram.com/gsjennsen

I look forward to hearing from you, and I hope you continue to enjoy the world of *AURORA RISING*.

*

Find G. S. Jennsen's books on Amazon:
http://amazon.com/author/gsjennsen

ABOUT THE AUTHOR

When she was two years old, G. S. Jennsen informed her parents that she would be learning to read now. When she was four, she brought the dinner-table conversation to a screeching halt by inquiring as to what they knew about the nature of infinity. The rest is history. A long, convoluted history that wound across the United States and back again—and back again—through a shocking variety of windowless libraries, windowless corporate boardrooms and windowless engineering labs.

She has been a corporate attorney, software developer, freelance editor and is now a full-time author. She lives in Colorado with her husband and their two furry, four-legged children. There are many windows in her home, half of which look out on the Rocky Mountains.

Her first novel, *Starshine*, was published in March 2014 by Hypernova Publishing.

24111493R00301

Printed in Great Britain
by Amazon